PRAISE FOR THE AUTHOR

"Richard Phillips has led such a life that he absolutely nails the science aspect of this new sci-fi classic [*Immune* (Book Two of The Rho Agenda)] and yet also gets the action and the political aspects exactly right as well. Speaking as an old sci-fi writer myself, I know how hard it is to do what Phillips has done . . . I've read *Immune* to its brilliant and completely satisfying end—but only because this new writer is so skillful and this storyline is so inventive and moving that I don't want to miss a chapter of it . . . as good as any science fiction being written today."

—Orson Scott Card

THE
KASARI
NEXUS

THE RHO AGENDA ASSIMILATION

● ○ ○

BOOK ONE

Also by Richard Phillips

The Rho Agenda

The Second Ship

Immune

Wormhole

The Rho Agenda Inception

Once Dead

Dead Wrong

Dead Shift

THE KASARI NEXUS

THE RHO AGENDA ASSIMILATION

● ○ ○

BOOK ONE

RICHARD PHILLIPS

Published by 47North, Seattle
www.apub.com

Amazon, the Amazon logo, and 47North are trademarks of Amazon.com, Inc., or its affiliates.

ISBN-13: 9781503933538
ISBN-10: 1503933539

Cover design by Shasti O'Leary-Soudant/SOS CREATIVE LLC

Printed in the United States of America

I dedicate this novel to my lovely wife, Carol, who has been my best friend and companion for thirty-four years.

:CHARACTER LIST

Jennifer Smythe (19) – Sister of Mark Smythe, she is one of four young people who have been altered by the technology of an alien race called the Altreians.

Mark Smythe (26) – Husband of Heather Smythe and brother of Jennifer Smythe, he is one of four young people who have been altered by the technology of an alien race called the Altreians.

Heather McFarland Smythe (26) – Wife of Mark Smythe, she is one of four young people who have been altered by the technology of an alien race called the Altreians.

Robert (Robby) Brice Gregory (8) – Young son of Jack Gregory and Janet Price, he is one of four young people who have been altered by the technology of an alien race called the Altreians. He is named after Jack's long-dead brother.

Jack "The Ripper" Gregory (37) – An ex-CIA assassin who revived from his deathbed in a Calcutta clinic, sharing his mind with an alien rider known as Khal Teth, a.k.a. Anchanchu. Husband of Janet Price, he is Robby's father.

Janet Alexandra Price (35) – An ex-NSA operative, she is Jack Gregory's wife and Robby's mother.

Khal Teth, a.k.a. Anchanchu (immortal) – A former member of the Altreian High Council, Khal Teth was found guilty of an attempted assassination of the High Council Overlord. His body confined in a chrysalis cylinder, his memory was wiped and his mind cast out into a multidimensional void. Millennia ago, he discovered the ability to link with a human mind at the moment of their death and return them to life, thereafter becoming a rider, able to experience his host's thoughts and emotions. He only chooses hosts with a special destiny—among them, Alexander, Caligula, Attila, and now, Jack Gregory.

Raul Rodriguez (19) – A young man who was experimented on by Dr. Donald Stephenson, the deceased head of the Los Alamos National Laboratory's top-secret Rho Project. The experiments turned him into a legless, one-eyed cyborg who can interface directly with the alien starship known as the Rho Ship.

Dr. Donald R. Stephenson (deceased) – The Nobel Prize–winning scientist and head of the Los Alamos National Laboratory's Rho Project who successfully reverse engineered advanced alien technologies from the crashed starship known as the Rho Ship. He led an effort to build a wormhole gateway to link Earth with the Kasari Collective, the alien empire that sent the Rho Ship to Earth. He was killed in the nuclear blast that destroyed the Stephenson Gateway.

Alexandr Prokorov (61) – The ex-head of the Russian FSB, he is the minister of the Federation Security Service (FSS) for the United Federation of Nation States (UFNS), an alliance of Earth's four superpowers. He and the UFNS as a whole desires to rebuild the Stephenson Gateway that will connect Earth to the powerful alien empire known as the Kasari Collective.

Daniil Alkaev (40) – The top FSS assassin, he reports directly to Alexandr Prokorov.

Galina Anikin (32) – An FSS assassin and partner of Daniil Alkaev, she is slender, wiry, and lethal.

General Dgarra (middle age) – A seven-foot-tall, powerfully built, brown-skinned humanoid on the planet Scion. Like all Koranthians, he has a bony unibrow ridge that turns upward at the outside of each eye and extends over the top of his hairless skull. He commands the Koranthian Empire's northern front in its battle against Scion's other inhabitants, the winged humanoids known as the Eadric, and their Kasari allies. He is also the nephew of Emperor Goltat and first in line for the Koranthian throne.

Senator Freddy Hagerman (55) – The United States senator from Virginia and past winner of two Pulitzer Prizes for investigative reporting about the Rho Project, he is the founder of a movement that seeks to stop the UFNS from rebuilding the Stephenson Gateway.

Dr. Eileen Wu, a.k.a. Hex (26) – The NSA's top computer scientist and former Caltech prodigy.

Jamal Glover (30) – Former top NSA hacker, he is a handsome black man with a penchant for 1920s-style clothing. He currently designs proprietary high-speed trading software for the Maximum Capital Appreciation Fund.

Dr. Denise Jennings (69) – Former NSA computer scientist and designer of the NSA's data-mining artificial intelligence known as Big John.

President Ted Benton (62) – President of the United States, he was instrumental in securing the necessary votes in the U.S. Senate to approve the treaty that made the U.S. one of four member nations in the United Federation of Nation States (UFNS), alongside the European Union, the New Soviet Union, and the East Asian People's Alliance.

Levi Elias (63) – The NSA's top analyst.

Dr. Hanz Jorgen (60) – The current head of Los Alamos National Laboratory's Rho Project, having replaced the deceased Dr. Stephenson.

Yachay (55) – A member of the Quechua tribe and descendant of the Incas, she has worked for Jack Gregory for years and is Robby Gregory's nanny.

Eos – An artificial intelligence designed by the Altreians, Eos was accidently downloaded into Robby's brain when he was a baby. It now shares Robby's mind.

Gil McFarland (58) – Heather's dad is a former chief technician at the Los Alamos National Laboratory. He is tall and likes to wear a floppy old fly-fishing hat.

Anna McFarland (56) – Heather's mother is a nice-looking, motherly woman with graying brown hair.

Fred Smythe (58) – Mark and Jennifer's dad is also a former technician at the Los Alamos National Laboratory. He is a gray-haired, blocky former college football player.

Linda Smythe (56) – Mark and Jennifer's mother is a tall, slender woman with short gray hair.

Group Commander Shalegha (indeterminate age) – The four-armed, two-legged member of the Kasari Collective commands the Kasari forces on Scion.

Admiral Connie Mosby – The first black female director of the NSA, she is a very smart and aggressive military officer.

Minister Tsao – Head of the Ministry of State Security for the East Asian People's Alliance.

Jim "Tall Bear" Pino – The six-foot-six Navajo ex-cop was the first president of the Native People's Alliance (NPA), an organization that has united the native peoples of North, Central, and South America into a nation within nations. He now serves on the NPA council in La Paz, Bolivia.

Mary Beth Riles (70) – Wife of the deceased NSA director, Admiral Jonathan Riles, for whom Jack Gregory, Janet Price, Jamal Glover, and Dr. Denise Jennings once worked. Gray haired and somber, she lives in an old house in Annapolis, Maryland.

Dr. Stan Franklin (45) – The Rho Project scientist in charge of studying the Altreian starship known as the Second Ship or the Bandelier Ship.

Major Kamkin (37) – Commander of a Spetsnaz commando unit.

General Magtal (middle age) – A typical Koranthian warrior, the seven-foot-tall general is General Dgarra's chief rival and is second in line for the Koranthian throne, behind Dgarra.

Chief Engineer Broghdon – The big Koranthian is General Dgarra's chief weapons designer and engineer.

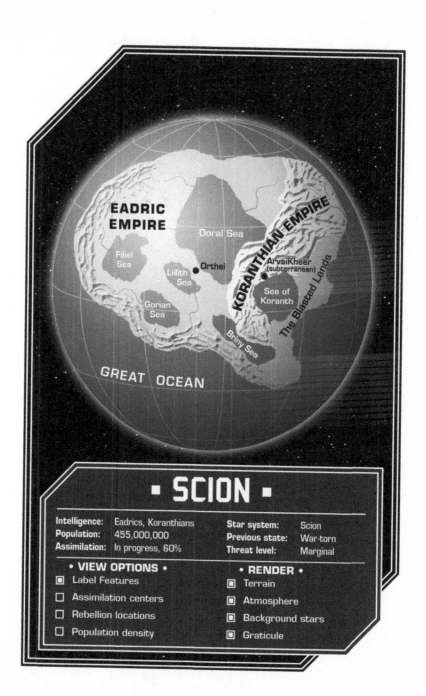

EADRIC EMPIRE

Doral Sea

Filial Sea

Lillith Sea

Orthei

KORANTHIAN EMPIRE

ArvaiKheer (subterranean)

Sea of Koranth

The Blasted Lands

Gorian Sea

Briny Sea

GREAT OCEAN

▪ SCION ▪

Intelligence:	Eadrics, Koranthians	Star system:	Scion
Population:	455,000,000	Previous state:	War-torn
Assimilation:	In progress, 60%	Threat level:	Marginal

▪ VIEW OPTIONS ▪
- ☑ Label Features
- ☐ Assimilation centers
- ☐ Rebellion locations
- ☐ Population density

▪ RENDER ▪
- ☑ Terrain
- ☑ Atmosphere
- ☑ Background stars
- ☑ Graticule

:CHAPTER 1

"My God!" Raul gasped. "You've killed us both!"

Jennifer Smythe turned her back on the legless apparition who had once been a handsome young man. As she adjusted the alien headband over her temples, its translucent length shifted colors, almost disappearing into her short, spiked blonde hair. Feeling the Altreian headband pour its power into her mind, a barely audible whisper slipped from her lips.

"I know."

● ○ ○

Inside the Bandelier Cave, a dozen miles southwest of Los Alamos, New Mexico, a coffee mug slipped from Dr. Hanz Jorgen's fingers and shattered on the stone floor, spewing its hot wetness up his pants leg. As a brilliant white glow replaced the alien starship's normal soft magenta, he didn't even notice.

Hanz didn't know how he knew, but he did. Something powerful had just grabbed control of the Altreian starship's computer, drawing every cycle of its immense processing power. He could practically hear the alien circuits groan under the terrible demand being placed upon the system. Staring at the starship, he wondered what could tax it so intensely. Then, as a shudder traversed his body, Hanz decided he didn't really want to know.

● ○ ○

They were as good as dead. Raul felt the awful knowledge rip at his brain. No living thing could survive the awful g-forces of reentry from an unanchored wormhole transit. But somehow this Altreian-altered mutant had tricked him into activating the Kasari world ship's wormhole engines. An unstoppable sequence had been initiated that would soon complete the gravitational wave packet meant to fold space-time and thrust the world ship through it. And when the Rho Ship emerged on the far side, its two quasi-human passengers would be little more than organic splatter in the ship's forward compartment.

Thrusting aside the panic that had immobilized him, Raul called upon his connection to the Rho Ship's neural net and initiated a desperate query, one final attempt to stop what was happening. The nanocrystals embedded in his human brain delivered the perfect connection that wedded his mind to the Rho Ship. Unfortunately, the answer that formed in his consciousness left him shaking. *Not good!*

Once again he felt Jennifer's thoughts touch his, a caress that left him with a sense of calm determination accompanied by a vision. *How the hell was she doing that?* But before he could attempt to eject her from his head, the vision resolved into a plan. Not a great plan, but one that might have the barest theoretical chance of saving their lives.

Raul focused the Rho Ship's neural net on the proposed workaround, trying to ignore his mental countdown. Only a few seconds remained until the gravitational wave packet stabilized, but on the timescale at which the starship's neural net operated, that would be enough. It had to be.

His mind one with the massive neural net, Raul felt the solution lock in, marveling at its simplicity. In all the millennia that the Kasari Collective had been sending out these robotic world ships to find new civilizations and instruct them on how to build a wormhole gateway, the aliens had never managed to solve the central problem. They could send the ships across the galaxy in an instant, but because the far end wasn't anchored at a gateway, they couldn't send living passengers.

So instead of performing one space-time fold between here and there, the solution Jennifer had proposed involved breaking the entire trip into a series of much smaller folds, sort of like a Chinese fan. If everything went right, the series of space-time coordinates would produce a jitter in the gravity distortion drive, resulting in a sequence of minor wormhole steps that should be individually survivable.

Wrapping himself in the ship's internal stasis field, Raul glanced at Jennifer, tempted to leave her to be thrown about. But the terror at the idea of being the lone survivor of a trip to a random point in the galaxy ended the thought before it fully formed. With a flick of his mind, the stasis field tightly cradled her body, locking it in place.

Then the universe came apart around them.

● ○ ○

Standing inside the Kasari starship that rested within the Los Alamos National Laboratory's Rho Division, Jennifer felt its wormhole engines ramp to full power. In seconds, a gravitational wave packet would thrust this ship through the resulting wormhole to an unknown destination, hopefully somewhere in this galaxy. Raul had used the Rho Ship to interfere with Jennifer, Mark, and Heather's efforts to destroy the Stephenson Gateway, thus forcing her to take drastic action.

The sudden vision of what the wormhole would do to the surrounding high-bay and the scientists who were on duty left her sick to her stomach and almost made her lose focus. But if she was to have any chance of surviving this, she couldn't allow her concentration to lapse.

The connection through her headset to the Altreian starship that rested inside the Bandelier Cave, a dozen miles southwest of the Rho laboratory, had provided her with the solution she'd mentally transferred to Raul. But that didn't mean it would work.

When the force field draped her body, it startled her so badly that she almost succumbed to a panic attack at her inability to move even a finger. But then she understood. Raul had caused the Rho Ship to generate the field that immobilized both their bodies and suspended them inside this compartment. Not a bad idea considering what she feared was about to happen. And then it did.

The first of many thousands of mini-steps was instantaneous. It was a sudden unintelligible shift in perspective as the cells in her body tried to tear themselves apart. Pain exploded in her mind and she lost sight in her left eye. Only the extensive neural augmentation she'd received when she'd first tried on the headset allowed her to restrict the blood flow to the ruptured vessels.

Then it happened again. And again. And again. The transitions happened so quickly that she barely retained consciousness and then wished that she hadn't. She experienced an endless battering that left her blinded and gasping as overstressed bones cracked and splintered within her body. Jennifer felt a scream crawl to her lips and bubble out in a bloody froth that spread along the invisible force field encasing her.

Despite the best efforts of her augmented mind and musculature, she was dying. A part of her begged for death to release her from the agony, but Jennifer refused to let death take her without a fight, although she knew this was a fight she wasn't going to win.

● ○ ○

Despite the amazing regenerative powers his nanite-infused blood granted him, Raul felt as if he were being hammered into pieces. Although each individual wormhole transit was instantaneous, the unanchored step into a new piece of space-time generated g-forces that the human body couldn't handle. And the pauses between those steps unleashed an unending sea of agony. But as he glanced across at the bloody mess that was Jennifer Smythe, he had a hard time feeling sorry for himself. She was still alive but, given that she lacked the nanites that worked to repair his wounds, he really didn't know how.

When the series of transitions came to an abrupt end, Raul endured several seconds of dread that the wormhole transits would begin anew. The knowledge that he had made it, that his nanites would be able to fully heal his injuries, sent a wave of relief that brought bloody tears to his eyes. Another look at Jennifer Smythe's suspended body swept that warm feeling away in a fresh wave of terror.

Manipulating the stasis field, Raul lowered her body gently to the alien compartment's gray floor, where her blood pooled around her. The neural net told him many things, all bad. Jennifer wasn't breathing and her heart had stopped beating. Worse, she had taken so much damage that chest compressions were out of the question. But she still had brain function.

Suspended by the stasis field, Raul floated to her side, gasping from the pain even this gentle movement caused. Forcing himself to concentrate, Raul visualized a thin tube tapping a large vein in his left arm and connecting to a similar vein in Jennifer's. The stasis field complied, funneling his nanite-infused blood into her body.

He could tell immediately that it wasn't going to be enough to save her. The damage was so widespread that by the time the nanites spread throughout her form, she would be dead. And then Raul would be alone, trapped on this lonely robot ship in the vastness of uncharted space with no idea of how to get home, even if Earth still existed.

A new idea formed in his mind, one that just might kill him, but his desperation left him no choice. Raul changed his visualization and hundreds of the virtual transfusion tubes sprouted from his body to Jennifer's, delivering his blood to all parts of her body simultaneously. And as it did, Raul felt himself weaken. Missing legs, he just didn't have the blood capacity of a normal person.

As he felt his vision narrow and his consciousness fade, Raul terminated the flow and let himself settle to the alien floor beside her. His fingers touched her right wrist and he held his breath. Nothing.

Damn it!

Then he felt it, the faintest of pulses beneath the bruised skin of her forearm. Raul took her hand gently in his, felt the broken bones of her fingers shift beneath her skin, and withdrew his hand in horror.

Dear God!

Raul caught himself as a new horror filled his mind. God had nothing to do with any of this. The light of religious belief he'd always held to so tightly had finally been snuffed out, and along with it, any relief that prayer might have brought.

Weak from blood loss, Raul rested his head on the cool gray floor, closed his eyes, and wept.

●　○　○

Lying on her back, Jennifer blinked her eyes as her red-limned vision swam back into the light. Everywhere she looked, things were a very blurry red, no doubt a consequence of the ruptured blood vessels in her eyes. Christ. It was a miracle that she could see at all. She rode a tidal wave of pain but, for the first time, its intensity seemed to lessen. Perhaps her nerves had merely passed their pain saturation threshold. But no. The fact that her sight had returned meant that she was getting better.

She raised her hands to gently rub her face and then froze. *What the hell?* She'd felt the bones in her hands and arms break under the stresses produced by the wormhole transitions. But now, as she held up her hands, she could see that they were whole and functional. Despite the fact that they still hurt like hell, they were healing. And apparently, so was the rest of her body.

A sudden panic seized her. There was only one thing she knew of that could produce this type of healing. The Rho Project nanites. And there was only one way they could have gotten into her system.

Lying on her back, she tried to raise her head, but a fresh wave of agony made her suck in a breath and threw her into a paroxysm of coughing. It took all of her augmented neural control to avoid a bout of the dry heaves.

Jennifer longed to scream but couldn't have managed it even if she'd dared try. Only a weak gasp escaped her lips.

Raul! What had that crazy son of a bitch done to her? Why couldn't he have just let her die?

Jennifer saw Raul's legless form float through the air toward her, raising a question in her mind. If the Rho starship was in the void of empty space, why wasn't she also floating instead of lying on the floor?

He came to a stop an arm's length above the spot where she lay, his artificial right eye extending on a short, metallic stalk from its socket and moving independently of his human eye. The top and back of Raul's skull had been replaced by a translucent material through which his brain was vaguely visible.

This being the first time she'd had the opportunity to study him, Jennifer found his cyborg appearance so fascinating that it momentarily distracted her from her pain. As consciousness gradually slipped from her grasp, a new idea assaulted her. Was that what he had in mind for her? But even as she mulled it, the horror of that thought failed to keep her awake.

● ○ ○

Floating above the jumble of gray alien conduits that filled almost half of the Rho Ship's forward compartment, Raul approached the large empty space where Jennifer Smythe lay, his body propelled by his control of the stasis field. Technically, the field was controlled by the Rho Ship's neural net, but his mind was so thoroughly integrated into the net that it was a distinction without a difference.

After having awakened briefly three hours ago, Jennifer had slipped back into unconsciousness. Considering the extent of the injuries that her blood-transfused nanites were working to repair, it was probably for the best.

Other than his terror of being alone, he wasn't sure why he cared. It all went back to his junior year at Los Alamos High School, when the madness had begun.

Raul had been diagnosed with terminal brain cancer, the reason his father, Dr. Ernesto Rodriguez, had secretly injected his son with Rho Project nanites even though the serum had only undergone animal testing. The treatment had worked, but his dad hadn't revealed what he'd done, letting Raul believe that his supernatural healing powers were a miracle, a gift straight from God Almighty.

He had gone back to school and fallen in love with Jennifer's best friend, Heather McFarland. And despite his dislike of her brother Mark, Raul had thought Jennifer quite nice.

He paused to study her, not only in the human-visible spectrum, but in the ultraviolet and infrared too. There was little doubt that she would recover. Raul just wished he could say the same thing for the Rho Ship.

On the positive side, the gravity distortion engines were still functioning, as evidenced by the one g that held Jennifer and the various supplies down. Of course, Raul could have achieved the same effect with his ability to manipulate the stasis field generator. But why bother when the vessel's gravity distortion drives determined the direction and magnitude of its acceleration vector? Inside, a different gravitational manipulation gave you a consistent floor-ceiling reference and allowed you to stand and move about irrespective of what was happening to the ship as a whole, although even that bit of gravitational wizardry couldn't provide enough inertial damping for a survivable wormhole transition.

The distortion drives were operational . . . fabulous. Unfortunately, all sensor systems were off-line, so they were flying blind. And from his examination of the data provided by his neural net, that was the least of their problems.

Decades ago, the Rho Ship had battled its Altreian counterpart in the skies over the American Southwest, with both ships ultimately crashing to Earth. But as badly as the Rho Ship's control systems had been damaged in the fight, it was Dr. Donald Stephenson who had almost destroyed it. The scientist had abused its gravity distortion engines to generate an anomaly inside the Large Hadron Collider in Switzerland, an extinction threat that had forced world governments to build the Stephenson Gateway to transport the nascent black hole into deep space.

Raul had spent a year gradually restoring the systems that enabled the robot ship to repair itself, although he'd made those repairs while it rested safely inside Los Alamos National Laboratory's Rho Division, not lost somewhere in the void of space.

The thought of Dr. Stephenson brought a low growl from Raul's throat. The head of the Rho Project had surgically altered Raul, removing his legs and replacing his right eye, all in an attempt to build a cyborg interface to the Rho Ship's neural net. The procedure had worked, but at the cost of Raul's humanity, transforming him from a vital nineteen-year-old man into a neo-Frankenstein monster. The horror he'd seen in Jennifer's eyes when she'd looked at him brought that truth thundering home.

Raul shook off the self-pity accompanying his thoughts of Dr. Stephenson. After all, Stephenson had merely been a tool of the

Kasari Collective, the alien empire that had built this robotic world ship and sent it to Earth, packed with technologies designed to seduce humanity into building the wormhole gate. Almost every horrible thing that had happened to Raul—the loss of his family and sacrifice of his form—could be traced directly back to the Kasari.

As he watched, Jennifer stirred and groaned. She opened her eyes and met his gaze with a new clarity.

"Is there any water?" she rasped.

Her question made Raul realize just how thirsty he was. Hungry too. The nanites worked hard to fix anything that was wrong with your body, but they also heightened hunger and thirst.

"Lie still. I'll bring some."

Jennifer ignored his advice and struggled to her knees, her head drooping from the effort. Raul floated to the stack of supplies Dr. Stephenson had stashed in the compartment more than a year ago, shocked at how few of the cases of ready-to-eat meals and five-gallon water bottles remained. But then Raul hadn't planned on leaving Earth so suddenly.

Thank you, Jennifer Smythe!

He filled a plastic glass, drank greedily, refilled it, and returned to Jennifer, who was now seated with her back against the stasis field generator. When she took the glass from his outstretched hand, she sniffed it warily and then took a small sip.

Raul felt the heat rise to his cheeks. "What? You think I poisoned it?"

Jennifer glared back at him. "Crossed my mind."

"I just saved your ass!"

She started to respond, shrugged instead and took a deep drink, pausing to see if the water was going to stay down. It did and she finished the remainder. When her gaze again met Raul's, he realized her eyes were brown, just as he remembered from high school. But back then her hair had been brown too.

"Your eyes."

"What about them?" she asked.

"When you stepped into the ship they were blue."

"Ever hear of colored contact lenses?"

The muscles in Raul's jaw tightened. "What's with the attitude? If anyone's got a right to be pissed, it's me."

Jennifer struggled to her feet, standing so that she faced him. "Really?"

"You damn near killed us both!"

"Bullshit!" Jennifer jabbed a finger at him. "You caused this."

For a second, Raul was tempted to fling her across the room with the stasis field. But she was partially right, though Dr. Stephenson was the chief cause of the disasters that had led to this. He and the Kasari Collective.

Years ago, shortly after the first test of the atomic bomb, humanity had attracted the attention of the two biggest players in the galaxy, the Kasari Collective and the Altreians. They had each sent a starship to Earth with very different agendas.

The Kasari were engaged in the most aggressive expansion of its recorded history, assimilating the populations of world after world, leaving the Altreians scrambling to stop that advance. Both alien empires had extremely advanced but vastly different technologies.

The Kasari had mastered the manipulation of gravity and thus could create wormholes through which they could send unmanned starships. No living being could survive the g-forces involved with exiting a wormhole that was not anchored at both ends by a gateway. The Kasari sent these world ships to populated planets that had acquired sufficient technology to be of interest. Those world ships landed and offered the local population technologies that could extend lifetimes and solve clean energy problems, along with a host of other scientific breakthroughs. Once they had sampled those goodies, few civilizations could resist the final enticement . . . to build a wormhole gate that would form a doorway to connect the populace with their alien benefactors.

The genius of the Kasari scheme was that it allowed them to assimilate whole populations into the collective without the massive cost of huge wars. The military principle of economy of force was thus applied on a massive scale. There were, of course, clashes with parts of the population, but these usually could be put down by providing advisors and equipment to the pro-Kasari elements of the targeted world. And that efficiency allowed the Kasari to expand on multiple worlds simultaneously without having to gather a large force to conquer one world at a time. Willing recruits were far more valuable to the collective than those recruited by force.

As for the Altreians, they employed a technology that allowed them to shift their starships into subspace, where faster-than-light travel was possible. More importantly, the process allowed them to send starships with living crews to distant worlds. The feat was impressive, but the Altreians had no chance of scaling to the extent that the Kasari Collective could manage through their approach. So the Altreians tried to detect when a Kasari world ship was sent forth so that they could launch a starship of their own, hopefully intercepting the enemy vessel before it could reach its target population.

In the late 1940s, the Kasari craft in which Raul and Jennifer Smythe now found themselves had been intercepted on its way to Earth by an Altreian starship. The two ships had shot each other down over the American Southwest. Only the Kasari vessel had been found. The U.S. government had spirited it away to Los Alamos National Laboratory, where a top-secret effort known as the Rho Project was tasked with reverse engineering the damaged ship's technology.

Over the decades that followed, the project's legendary lead scientist, Dr. Donald R. Stephenson, had been wildly successful. Unfortunately, along with the ship and its technologies, he'd resurrected its Kasari agenda.

Jennifer's voice pulled Raul from his reverie.

"Earth! Did it survive? Is it still out there?"

Raul felt his gut clench as he looked into her terrified eyes.

"I don't know."

● ○ ○

Jennifer struggled against her rising panic. "What do you mean you don't know?"

Five feet away, Raul shook his head.

"The ship's sensors are off-line. I have no idea where in the universe we are and, until we get them working, we can't figure it out." Raul's human eye locked with hers as a sad look settled on his face. "Even if we get them working, we're almost certainly too far away to check on Earth."

The realization stunned her. The Rho Ship's gravity distortion engines had created a wormhole and thrust them through. In all likelihood this ship was now many light-years away from Earth. Even if they could see Earth, the light they would be seeing had been traveling across space for all those years that it took to get here. They would be looking back into Earth's past and glean nothing about the planet's present.

A new idea gave her sudden hope. She was still wearing the Altreian headband. It communicated with the crashed Altreian starship in the Bandelier Cave through subspace, and the speed of waves through subspace was far greater than the speed of light.

So why wasn't she feeling the familiar connection to the Bandelier Ship?

It had been three years since she, her twin brother Mark, and Heather McFarland had first stumbled upon that crashed ship in the steep canyon country near Los Alamos, New Mexico. They'd discovered the alien headbands on the damaged craft and foolishly tried them on. She could still feel the pain of that first experience. Each of them had been left altered, with their neural connections and physiological abilities enhanced in different ways, even after they removed the headbands. Once a headset had attuned to an individual mind, it would never link to another for as long as that person lived.

The trio had been rewired with eidetic memories, enhanced senses, fine control of their neuromusculature system, and some ability to communicate telepathically with each other. But even though the iridescent headsets had looked identical, they were each programmed for one of four different crew positions on the Altreian craft.

Mark had been altered for the security officer role, his muscle coordination and strength augmented beyond any of the others, along with his ability to learn languages and mimic voices. Heather had chosen the commander's headset, gifting her with savant mathematical abilities that included instantaneous calculation of the odds of upcoming events.

Jennifer had chosen the communications officer headset, gifting her with strong empathic and telepathic abilities.

The fourth headset was designated for the crew's political officer, the one assigned to keep an eye on the rest of the crew and make sure they were complying with the will of the Altreian High Council. Jennifer didn't know its full capabilities and didn't really care to. Truth be known, that headset scared the hell out of her. The amazing enhancements imparted by the other headsets had ensnared the three of them in the Altreian agenda, destroying their once-comfortable lives.

But whenever they put the headbands on, no matter where they were, they could interact directly with the Altreian starship's computer, and that was an awesome experience.

Now she wasn't feeling that connection. Perhaps the Altreian headset's subspace communications capability was range limited. Right now, Jennifer really, really hoped that was it.

● ○ ○

For the last hour, Jennifer had felt herself getting stronger as the amazing nano-machines healed her body. Despite her knowledge that her mentors, Jack Gregory and Janet Price, had been the recipients of Dr. Stephenson's nanite infusions, she couldn't shake her revulsion at the thought of thousands of tiny machines derived from Kasari technology crawling around in her bloodstream.

After consuming two MREs and a quart of water, she'd let Raul bring her up to speed on their situation.

The Rho Ship's matter disrupter, the device that transformed any kind of matter to energy, was fully functional. Having studied the theory behind the disrupter that Dr. Stephenson had built at the Large Hadron Collider site, she understood how it worked.

She and Raul had power, working gravity distortion engines, food, water, and a portable camp toilet. So much for the good news.

"None of the onboard sensors are working?" Jennifer asked.

"We're flying completely blind out here."

"And life support is failing too?"

"No, there's nothing wrong with the life support system," said Raul. "It's just not running."

Normally, Jennifer would have used her computer skills to help identify and fix these problems, but since Raul was the only interface to the Rho Ship's neural net, she was stuck asking frustrating questions. His answers weren't improving her mood.

"Why not?"

"This ship's only designed to carry living passengers for sub-light journeys. Since nobody can survive an unanchored wormhole transit, the life support systems automatically shut down whenever the wormhole drives engage. They don't come on again until the ship takes on new passengers."

"But it has passengers."

"And if its sensors were operating, the ship would probably detect that."

Jennifer felt her teeth grind and forced her jaw to relax. "Seems like a pretty important problem. What the hell are you doing to fix it?"

Raul scowled at her. "That's just it. I can't fix it."

"You're not even trying!"

"Bullshit. The sensor systems are located in the aft, along with the gravity distortion engines and the weapons systems. Normally I would use the stasis field or the nano-material controls to make repairs throughout the ship. But without the worm-fiber sensors I can't see a damn thing back there."

"Then float your ass back there and fix it!"

Jennifer watched as Raul floated toward her, invading her personal space. "I can only connect with the neural net in the forward compartment. Without that, I won't be able to control the stasis field or the nano-materials. I'd just be crawling around on the floor, even more worthless than you."

Jennifer took a deep breath and pulled forward the perfect memory of how she felt during deep meditation, feeling her alpha waves smooth out as she centered. This bickering was only using up more of their precious oxygen, getting them nowhere closer to a solution. If they were going to survive, she needed Raul's help. And whether he recognized it or not, he needed hers. It was time for her to step up and take control.

"What if I could be your eyes?"

Raul looked surprised at her sudden change in tone and she subtly reached into his mind, amplifying the warm feeling but not so much that he would notice her influence.

"You want me to let you back inside my head?"

Jennifer almost smiled at Raul's naïveté, thinking that he could block her if she chose to force her way in. Yet that approach wasn't likely to lead to a cooperative working environment for the longer term, assuming they survived long enough for that to be a possibility.

"Unless you can think of a better plan."

Raul hesitated, his robotic eye elongating to scan the wall behind him, reminding her of a sea snake wriggling out of a coral hole. Jennifer imagined that the move enhanced his interaction with the massive computation systems behind the wall.

After several seconds, he shrugged. "I guess it's worth a try."

"Are you sure the rest of the ship has air?" she asked.

"Unless there was a hull breach, it should still have the air that was trapped inside when the outer hatch closed."

"So you're just going to open the door and hope for the best?"

"I'll seal the entrance with the stasis field before opening the door."

Jennifer followed Raul's human eye, looking toward a spot on the rear wall of the compartment where she could just make out the vague outline of a door.

With all that had happened, she'd barely taken notice of the alien equipment that crowded the back half of this forward compartment. There was nothing beautiful about the ship. Everything was gray, shaped for efficiency and utility, not aesthetics, functionality trumping beauty at every twist and turn. The Kasari had made no attempt to group equipment in any way that made its functionality apparent, instead positioning everything so that the translucent tubes and bundles of conduits that connected the various apparatuses optimized efficiency. Very narrow walkways led through, around, and over an assortment of machines and instruments, all built to be operated by the Rho Ship's neural net and manipulated by the nimble fingers of the stasis field.

Floating over the equipment, Raul beat her to the closed door, its outlines barely visible in the cool, gray light. "You ready?" he asked.

"As ready as I'm going to be."

Behind Raul, the nano-particles that made up the door melted away into the surrounding walls. Although she knew the opening was draped by the invisible cloak of the stasis field, Jennifer still found herself holding her breath. Then she heard a slight hiss as Raul opened a tiny hole in the field. It wasn't a significant air leak, just a slight variance in the relative air pressures between the rest of the ship and the sealed-off forward compartment.

Jennifer stepped forward until her outstretched fingers touched the repulsive barrier, located the tiny hole, and sniffed. Air was definitely entering the forward cabin instead of leaving it and, as judged by her enhanced senses, it smelled just fine. Two positive signs. During the time the air replenishment system had been off-line, the CO_2 levels in the forward compartment had been rising as oxygen levels decreased. Allowing outside air to mix in would buy them a considerable amount of additional time to try to make repairs before the atmosphere became toxic.

"You can drop the stasis field," she said. "The air's good."

Raul complied and Jennifer felt a gentle breeze as the air pressure equalized.

"I guess it's time to try your mind trick again," Raul said.

Jennifer noticed a tightness in his face and knew he was recalling the mental force she'd brought to bear when she'd forced her way into his head a few hours earlier. That psionic talent to enter another person's mind to share thoughts and feelings was another of her Altreian alterations, perhaps the most powerful of them all. Her power had simpler beginnings, starting as an empathic ability to feel and alter the feelings of others. Then had come the occasional flashes of mental communication between Mark, Heather, and herself while they weren't wearing the Altreian headsets.

Still, it had taken the psychopathic Colombian assassin known as El Chupacabra to show her just how little of her abilities she was using. She hadn't gained full control of her power until she, Mark, and Heather had been imprisoned in the secret NSA supermax facility known as the Ice House.

The thought of her twin brother and best friend brought a sudden tightness to her throat, but she pushed the feeling aside. Now was not the time for grief.

Although Raul didn't like submitting to this experiment, he would have to remain in the forward compartment, seeing into other parts of the ship through her eyes as he manipulated the stasis field and nano-materials to fix the damaged systems.

Jennifer inhaled deeply, exhaled slowly, and centered. For better or worse, the time had come to test her limits.

● ○ ○

Raul felt Jennifer step across the boundary to his mind like a cool breeze. Although he knew it was just her manipulation of his feelings, it still felt wonderful.

"I need you to show me the ship's layout."

Raul watched her in fascination. Her thoughts sounded exactly as if she'd spoken to him but her lips hadn't moved.

He tried thinking a response. "Can't you access the neural net through me?"

"You still have free will. I can delve into your thoughts and emotions, but I can't make you do something you don't want to."

A sudden coldness brought gooseflesh alive on his arms. "How deep can you dig into my head?"

Again, Raul felt a sense of warm reassurance as she answered. "Until you learn to put up some mental blocks, I can go as deep as I want."

The horror returned, only to ramp down to mild concern as Jennifer continued. "You'll know exactly what I'm accessing in your mind whenever I do it. But I promise not to poke around too deeply inside your head, at least until we get this ship fixed. Then, if you play nice, I'll teach you how to set up those blocks."

Despite the reassuring feelings, Raul didn't trust her, although right now that didn't matter.

Accessing the neural net, he pulled up a detailed 3-D diagram of the ship and felt Jennifer's mind absorb it. Interesting. Through their mental linkage he could actually sense what she was feeling as he focused on it. Right now he sensed amusement at his amateurish exploration of that linkage. *Shit.* She was laughing at him.

Raul rotated the diagram around the x-axis and then around the y and finally around the z, observing it from multiple angles. The cigar-shaped ship was designed with a single deck, divided into thirds. The forward compartment housed the vessel's neural net, along with control interfaces to the engines, sensors, weapons, and maintenance/environmental systems. The middle third of the ship was a honeycomb of compartments, most of which were nano-particle adaptable living quarters, automatically configured for whatever species occupied them. A narrow hallway circled this hexagonal collection of inner rooms. The external hatch and ramp were located in the exact center of the ship on the starboard side.

Raul thought of the rear third as the engineering bay, home to the gravity distortion engines and guts of the other systems controlled from the forward command bay. The rest of the ship's systems, as well as the connections between them and the controlling neural net residing below the main deck, were accessible via narrow crawlways. If the interior gravity system failed, all the passages would become float-ways.

"Okay," she thought, "that's enough to get me started."

Raul watched as Jennifer turned and walked out the door into the warren of middle compartments. As she disappeared around the corner, a wave of dizziness assaulted him. A disorienting vision filled his head. He found himself seeing through her eyes, amazed at the clarity of it. She paused before a closed doorway that had no apparent means of being opened.

"Well?" Her irritation was readily apparent in the thought. "Are you going to make me wait all day?"

Catching her meaning, Raul visualized the operating instructions, watching as she traced the intricate command on a panel and entered one of the passenger compartments. Then she paused. A single platform bed stood in the center of the room, with facilities arrayed along the port wall that appeared to be configured for humanoid use, something Raul's neural net immediately confirmed. Not surprising since the ship's last detected occupants were human.

Jennifer stepped back out into the hallway and continued along the starboard side, past the compartment that housed the exterior hatch and the instrumentation that the Rho Project scientists had used to study this ship. With each step closer to the engineering bay that held the key to their survival, Raul felt his tension rise. They were about to find answers to some very weighty questions.

He just hoped those answers weren't all bad.

● ○ ○

Jennifer remembered her excitement when she, Mark, and Heather had first climbed aboard the crashed Altreian starship they had come to call the Second Ship or, subsequently, the Bandelier Ship, its smooth flowing lines and abundant colors so wondrous they had taken her breath away. But this ugly monstrosity filled her with a cold dread, as if it were a ghost ship that had been drained of all life and beauty. Without viewports to let her see the stars, the inner honeycomb structure left her with the feeling that, at any moment, a nano-particle wall would dissolve to unleash one of the Kasari horrors they had battled for control of the Stephenson Gate. Her skin crawled.

When she rounded another of the outer hallway's hexagonal turns, Raul's voice spoke in her mind.

"Stop. This is the place."

Again she traced the symbols and the wall on her left melted away, revealing a room filled with hulking machinery that towered from floor to ceiling, all dimly illuminated with the same shadowless gray light as the rest of the ship. *Lovely.*

Just inside the engineering bay, Jennifer stopped to listen. The room pulsed with a deep thrumming sound, a slow heartbeat that made it feel alive. She stood in the dull light, breathing hard and dripping sweat despite the chill that clawed its way into her bones.

Only one thing required her attention, but she found herself having difficulty focusing. The strain of maintaining her mental link with Raul was starting to take a toll on her. The ceiling was fifteen feet above her head and as she looked around and through the strangely shaped machinery, draped with thick, translucent conduits, she felt as if she stood in the narrow confines of a lava tube. A wave of claustrophobia assailed her, but she shoved it aside with an angry thought. *Christ! What the hell is wrong with me?*

"Take the passage on the right," said Raul's mental voice.

Jennifer slipped between bulbous columns of machinery and Raul's thoughts tagged them with their shipboard functions. The huge matter disrupter occupied the centermost portion of the room, containing a belly chamber that could open to ingest external items. The conduits that draped its exterior ran to the gravity distortion engines or disappeared into the floor or walls, carrying power to the ship's other systems.

When a portion of the floor panel dissolved away two steps in front of her, Jennifer halted.

Raul's next thought confirmed her fears. "The sensor system's primary power coupler is below deck. You'll need to go down there."

A tight crawl space. Wonderful!

The thought that Raul might be playing games, guiding her forward along the most difficult route possible, occurred to her, but a deeper glimpse into his mind dispelled that notion. This was the only way to get to the likely cause of their sensor problems.

Swallowing hard, Jennifer climbed down into the tight space, knelt, and then slithered forward, crawling around, between, and over the tightly packed conduits and hard-edged equipment.

Although the light down here was much dimmer than it was above deck, it was more than sufficient for her neurally augmented vision. As she looked around for the easiest spots to squeeze through, she almost wished she couldn't see what was coming or what lay behind. If she hadn't seen the large gorilla-spider pursue Heather in the Atlas Cavern electrical cage, contorting its body through tight places, she would have had trouble believing that large species could traverse this part of the ship.

Then again, robot ships should be able to repair themselves. And this one probably would have if she hadn't forced its engines beyond their design limits.

Raul's mental voice pulled her out of her thoughts. "There it is, on top of the crawl space six feet ahead."

"I see it."

"Get me a better view."

Jennifer crawled to the indicated spot, lay down, and rolled onto her back. The nature of the machinery that surrounded her had changed. Directly above her a rectangular gray access panel shifted as the nano-material flowed aside to reveal the workings within.

She felt Raul's query to the neural net return an answer in the form of a three-dimensional wireframe diagram that seemed to float before her eyes. The image expanded, twisting to exactly match the orientation of the equipment she was looking at, then moved so that the wireframe draped the equipment, changing colors so that red indicated the problem areas. Unfortunately, she now found herself looking at a lot of red. Several of the lines that should have matched the arrangement of equipment weren't even close, pieces having been torn from their moorings or snapped off completely.

"Shit!" The panic in Raul's thoughts hammered her.

"How long?" Jennifer asked.

"What?"

"How long will it take to fix it?"

The neural net performed the required calculations and the answer formed in Raul's mind.

Jennifer froze. "Sixty-three hours?"

"That's the estimate," Raul said.

"And how long until the CO_2 level gets toxic?"

"No problem there. This ship holds a little over 108,000 cubic feet of air, which should keep us alive for at least a hundred days."

A wave of despair engulfed Jennifer. There was no chance she could lie here and work for six straight hours, much less sixty. Even if she could force her mind to maintain the link, her physical demands would require periodic breaks. With that factored in, this repair job would take a minimum of four days. Lying on her back for that long in this claustrophobic space wasn't something she looked forward to.

If only Heather were here, her savant mind might be able to arrive at a better solution. But Heather wasn't here, so Jennifer would have to come up with some ideas of her own, even though her mind was already tiring from the effort of maintaining her mental link with Raul.

Okay, Jen, she told herself, *just relax and breathe.*

Her mother had always reminded her of how you eat an elephant—one bite at a time. Jennifer repressed the memory before it could deepen her depression. Over the next four days she was in for a hell of a lot of chewing.

● ○ ○

The breakthrough came on the eighth hour of day three. As Raul felt Jennifer's mind near the point where she could no longer maintain their mental link, the first of the sensor systems came back online, this one an electro-optical array on the Rho Ship's outer hull. The sensors delivered video imagery across the wavelength spectrum, from deep IR all the way into far ultraviolet.

With the delivery of that imagery into his mind, he could feel Jennifer sigh in delight at the shared view of the beautiful, star-filled space that surrounded them. Raul felt it too, that feeling described by inmates upon their release when they stepped out through the prison gates and inhaled that first breath of freedom. Marvelous.

"Where are we?" Jennifer asked, awe lacing her voice.

Raul manipulated the view, searching for a known point of reference. They were in the Milky Way, but where exactly, he couldn't tell. Definitely not in one of the outer spiral arms, and he had no idea in which of those distant arms Earth resided.

It was odd. He would have thought that the Rho Ship's data banks would contain detailed star maps of the galaxy, but they didn't, at least not in any of the areas Raul could access. That thought worried him. Was it possible that he was still being denied access to key portions of those data banks, even with his enhanced connection to the neural net?

Of course, it was also possible that the Kasari intentionally omitted uploading their robotic world ships with information that could be used against them should a ship be captured by an advanced species such as the Altreians.

"Somewhere in the middle of the Milky Way," Raul responded. "Beyond that, no idea."

He felt her probe his mind to see if he was lying. It pissed him off, but before he could respond he felt her mental connection die. *Crap!* She had hung up on him.

● ○ ○

The shock of what she'd seen in Raul's mind hit her in the head like a sledgehammer, instantly severing her mental link. That brief glimpse of the relative positions of known stars within the galaxy had brought her mind to an inescapable conclusion, the certainty of it curling her into a fetal ball.

She shuddered. Whispered sobs of denial escaped her lips. "No . . . no . . . no . . ."

Travel through a wormhole was supposed to be instantaneous. But she'd thrown the gravity distortion engines out of their normal mode of operation, and that had produced a time dilation. During what had been only a couple of horrible minutes for her, several years had passed back on Earth.

As badly as she missed Mark, Heather, and her parents, the consequences of that time dilation tore at her spirit, robbing her of one more connection to her former life.

Jennifer and Mark Smythe were no longer twins.

:CHAPTER 2

United States senator Freddy Hagerman leaned back in a soft leather swivel chair, his artificial left leg propped up on a footstool as he watched the crime of the century unfold on the television centered on his mahogany-paneled wall. He rolled his lucky marble in the fingers of his right hand. The marble had been in the box of Admiral Riles's notes that Mrs. Riles had given Freddy, the notes that had nailed down his second Pulitzer. He could damn sure use some of that luck now.

The very reason he'd quit investigative reporting and gone into politics was to try to stop the lunacy for which the president was about to officially sign up the country. Had it been only seven years since Dr. Stephenson had tried to flush the world down the toilet by welcoming an alien species through his wormhole gate? Seven years of wars had since ravaged large swaths of Central and Eastern Europe, the Middle East, Africa, and Southeast Asia, along with South and Central America. Old conflicts were fanned into flames by the Rho Project's release of "beneficial" alien technologies that promised to improve and extend the lives of everyone. What a sad joke!

But that wasn't what was about to destroy all that Jack Gregory, Heather McFarland, and the Smythe twins had managed to save. No. Revisionist history would accomplish that.

Freddy watched the revisionist-in-chief, President Ted Benton, sit his stately, patrician ass down at the circular treaty-signing table, his perfectly coiffed gray hair unusually long for a president. He was accompanied by a host of international dignitaries representing the New Soviet Union, the East Asian People's Alliance, the European Union, and the United States. Broad smiles all around, especially for the cameras. The sight of those false smiles got under Freddy's skin.

The fact that this agreement was being signed in the Peace Palace, the home of the International Court of Justice, commonly called the World Court, didn't improve Freddy's attitude toward it.

As impotent and corrupt as the old United Nations had been, Freddy almost missed it. A new alliance between three of the world's four superpowers—the New Soviet Union, the East Asian People's Alliance, and the European Union—had replaced the UN with an entity meant to usher in what had once been referred to as a new world order. Many believed that the EU had been pressured into joining the alliance after the New Soviet Union had reabsorbed the Baltic states and threatened greater European expansion.

Headquartered in The Hague and known as the United Federation of Nation States, or UFNS, this was no assemblage of every half-ass country on the planet. The group was a true federation with authority over its member nations. Disputes were arbitrated by the International Court of Justice, whose dictates were enforced by the Federation Security Service.

On this side of the Atlantic, more than two years after the United States Congress granted statehood to nine of the ten Canadian provinces, Freddy was still getting used to the idea of fifty-nine states. Only Quebec had refused to petition for statehood, electing instead to become its own sovereign country.

The desire to join together for common defense and the fact that we shared a common language and border had greased the path to union. But fear had been the driving factor. That and the economic advantages associated with paying for only one military. The same common defense argument had now driven the majority of Americans to conclude that membership in the UFNS was the next desirable step.

The multi-continent religious wars had been the primary impetus for this bonding. Freddy included sectarians among the warring parties, some of whom sought conquest, while others fought to save their way of life. World War IV had been deemed too politically incorrect to be the name of this ongoing collection of conflicts, but, in Freddy's mind, that was exactly what it had become.

Almost a year into his second term in office, President Benton finally had what he had long desired, a two-thirds majority in the 118-member United States Senate that had pledged to ratify the treaty he was about to sign. And once the U.S. ratified it, the UFNS would have all four superpowers on board. Other nation states might petition to join the UFNS, but good luck with that. The big boys' club didn't need strap hangers.

In a few minutes, at midnight Central European Time, the symbolic start of a new day, the president would sign the UFNS treaty. Then at noon tomorrow, on the seventh anniversary of the nuclear explosion that had put an end to Dr. Stephenson and his wormhole gateway, President Benton would journey to the site of the new Stephenson Center for Interspecies Reconciliation in order to participate in its ribbon-cutting ceremony.

Freddy snorted in disgust. Benton was on a roll during this European trip: ceding U.S. federal authority to the UFNS as the new day began and honoring that crazy bastard Stephenson at midday.

Happy Thanksgiving!

The camera zoomed in on the man engaged in smiling conversation with President Benton, an elegantly dressed, bald Russian looking trim and fit for his sixty-one years, his shark's eyes glittering in the flash of the cameras. Nanites did that for you. Alexandr Prokorov, ex-KGB operative, ex-head of the FSB, was now the UFNS minister of federation security, or, as Freddy thought of it, KGB 2.0. The sight of that man seated at the right hand of the president of the United States felt like a bad omen.

Freddy continued to watch as the president signed the treaty, but he switched the television off before the dignitaries could parade before the microphone to welcome the United States as a full member of the UFNS. There was, after all, a limit to what he could stomach.

With a glance at his watch, an old-school Swiss mechanical timepiece, he sighed and stood. It was getting late and he would just have time to get home to his two-story Watergate East apartment, eat dinner, and get ready for tonight's fund-raising gala in his honor. Lord knew that if he wanted to be able to continue heightening public awareness of the dangerous direction the world government was taking, he would need every dime he could collect. And the event would give him a chance to see some old friends.

The walk from his Senate office to his car took five minutes. His new artificial leg was much more comfortable and responsive than his previous leg, and if he would have allowed his doctor to inject him with the latest version of nanites rolled out from Los Alamos National Laboratory's Rho Division, he wouldn't be experiencing any discomfort from the old wound. But discomfort and pain were important parts of the human condition, and Freddy damn sure didn't want to live for another five hundred years. He was scared to think about what would happen during the next five.

When he stepped out of the elevator into the topmost level of the Hart Senate Office Building's underground parking garage, his car and two bodyguards were waiting for him. These driverless vehicles still amazed him, and not in a positive way. No matter how much they improved public safety and traffic flow, to be denied control of one's own driving felt like one more freedom lost.

In cities like D.C., there was no reason to even own a car. Whenever you needed to go somewhere, the nearest available driverless vehicle of the type you wanted simply came to you, dropped you off at your desired destination, and then marked its network status as AVAILABLE. The U.S. Senate had its own private fleet of armored cars that would even notify you if you left something inside when you got out. These vehicles looked no different than typical luxury models from an assortment of manufacturers. It made sense from a security perspective—the government didn't want the cars screaming *U.S. SENATE VEHICLE*. The armored bodies were barely heavier than stock models thanks to carbon fiber–bonded titanium and bulletproof glass.

Freddy climbed into the backseat while his two bodyguards slid into the front. Since the car had no steering wheel or pedals, all his people had to focus on was their guarding duties. Freddy just had to tell the car his desired destination, kick back, and enjoy the ride. Weren't robo-chauffeurs grand? He doubted all the ex-drivers thought so. Then again, they weren't the only ones who had lost their jobs to this brave new world of super-technology.

There were still a few military pilots left, but only until the older military equipment could be phased out or converted. Pilotless planes, trains, ships, and automobiles. Every day it seemed that new categories of jobs were wiped out. One day pilots were gone, the next, cabbies.

And that wasn't even counting the economic devastation from the reverse-engineered alien technologies that continued to be derived from Dr. Stephenson's work on the Rho Project. Why would you need a doctor when you could inject nano-machines that read your DNA and kept you fixed up?

Between that and the advances in robotics and automation, the number of unemployed had skyrocketed, but so had productivity. In order to avoid revolt, all of the first-world countries, including the

United States, had been forced to adopt new laws guaranteeing a "fair" distribution of the proceeds of that productivity to the population. It had worked, after a fashion, if you called countries filled with idle and bored people success.

The third world was a complete goddamn mess.

Freddy shook his head to clear it of the depressing thoughts. He'd known for a long time now that he was on the wrong side of a losing fight. But that didn't mean he wouldn't go down swinging.

When he stepped out of the car, flanked by his security detail, the chill of the November night's breeze made him wish he'd worn a heavier jacket. But the sky was clear and, despite the bright glow of the city lights, he could see Jupiter and a few stars. Nice night for a party.

Yes. It was about time to get all tuxed up.

● ○ ○

Heather's slender fingers slid along the back of Mark's neck, her delicate touch sending shivers of pleasure down his spine. His own hand responded, fingertips barely touching the naked hollow of her back, lingering there, nerves so alert that it seemed each contact produced tiny sparks from her skin to his. He felt her ear touch his, the scent of her bare throat filling his nostrils.

She moved against his six-foot-three-inch body in perfect rhythm, the feel of her breasts against his chest robbing him of any lingering self-control. Heather's skin shone with sweat in the dim light and her breath came in small pants of exertion, barely audible above Mark's heart. Her right leg encircled him and her body swayed. As Mark's body writhed within her limbs, Heather's back arched until only his right arm kept her from falling. Then, in a thunderous, climactic crescendo, the tango ended.

As Mark lifted Heather back to her feet, the applause from the crowd that filled the Marriott Marquis Ballroom was accompanied by exclamations that, in a less-cultured crowd, would have qualified as catcalls. With his arm still encircling Heather's waist, they both smiled and gave a slight bow of acknowledgment before Mark signaled the orchestra to continue with the music.

Ignoring the people who moved out onto the dance floor, Mark straightened his tuxedo and then took an extra moment to appreciate his wife, stunning in her black evening gown, split down the right leg from hip to ankle. He took Heather's outstretched hand and walked with her to the spot where Senator Freddy Hagerman waited, the crowd parting before them as if they were royalty. And, in a way, they were.

When the senator smiled and stepped forward, Heather hugged him warmly, planting a kiss on his cheek before stepping back to let the two men shake hands. Despite his artificial leg, Freddy looked good in his black tux, his dark-rimmed glasses and trimmed beard adding a certain gravitas to his appearance. Quite a change from his old investigative reporting days.

Mark gripped Freddy's hand and smiled. "Good to see you, my friend."

"Speaking of looking good, I thought you two were going to set the ballroom on fire. Half the crowd left to get a room. Steamed up my glasses, that's for damn sure."

Heather laughed and Mark found his eyes drawn to her again. At twenty-six, she looked sexy as hell, projecting an aura of confidence and power. Then again, she was the CEO and cofounder of the world's fastest-growing technology company.

"Thank you for hosting this fund-raiser," Freddy continued. "If the president was in town, he'd be green with envy."

The mention of President Benton darkened Mark's mood. "I don't think any of us are on his Facebook friends list."

"Did you watch his little ceremony in the Netherlands?"

Heather's eyes narrowed slightly. "As much as we could stomach. But let's not talk about him. Tonight's all about helping you and your Safe Earth movement."

She took Freddy's arm and led him toward a nearby group of people. "Let me introduce you to some deep-pocket donors."

As Mark turned to follow Heather and Freddy, he saw an elegantly dressed Jack Gregory moving leisurely through the crowd, Janet Price on his arm. Damn, they were good. Any casual observer would be hard pressed to recognize that they headed up Mark and Heather's security detail. While others scanned the crowd, Jack and Janet's effortless mingling allowed them to make an individual, up-close assessment of hundreds of guests.

It had been three years since Mark and Heather had lured Jack out of South America and talked him into taking over as the head of security for their Austin-based Combinatorics Technology Corporation, also known as CTC. Yet the seven-figure annual salary hadn't closed the deal. The clincher had been their offer to help Jack and Janet with their young son, Robby, and his unusual developmental needs, something for which Mark and Heather were uniquely qualified.

Thinking about security, Mark amplified his senses to the point where he could listen in on conversations anywhere in the room. His perception of the room itself had changed. The thick, wavy, gold and black lines that threaded their way through the maroon and tan carpeting took on a garish quality, whereas only moments before the decor seemed elegant. The fourteen-foot-high ceiling, with its grid of dark brown rectangles framing hundreds of can lights, was so expansive that Mark felt like he was inside a monstrous ice-cream sandwich, waiting for a giant to take a bite out.

He shook off the worried thought, painted on his pleasant party face, and walked to the spot where Heather stood in animated conversation with Freddy and two titans of industry. Mark was confident that if any danger arose, Jack would detect it. In the meantime the tech giant would focus on radiating positive energy.

After all, if they were going to help Freddy build a movement that had any hope of stopping President Benton's agenda, they had money to raise . . . and lots of it.

● ○ ○

What the Netherlanders called a late November chill would have felt like a warm spring morning in Moscow. Alexandr Prokorov strolled through Het Plein, the peaceful square in The Hague's city center, pausing to enjoy the statue of William the Silent bathed in the peach-colored glow of sunrise. It was just after 8:00 A.M. and the encrypted call he'd just received had left the minister of federation security with a warm feeling to match the view. The last of the pieces in this grand game were finally falling into place.

Alexandr's meeting with the four top UFNS military officials, one from each member nation, wasn't scheduled until 9:30 A.M., so he had leisure time before heading to the towering new Federation Security Service headquarters, three blocks to the east. That was good. Despite his ever-present security detail, this square held a small measure of the tranquility of his family dacha on the outskirts of Volgograd. It was an excellent spot to clear his head for strategic thought.

But today's strategic thinking had nothing to do with welcoming the United States secretary of defense to the UFNS military chain of command structure. The true objective was to follow up on the United States treaty signing and ensure that nothing unfortunate happened to derail its expected U.S. Senate ratification. In that regard he would soon be taking the first steps to marginalize the growing Safe Earth movement that Senator Freddy Hagerman had spawned in the U.S. and that had now spread its tentacles to a number of countries around the world.

If A Safe Earth's major backers, the young tech billionaires, Heather and Mark Smythe, were left to their own devices, the nascent movement would take root and spread until it became an incurable cancer. Alexandr would not allow that to happen.

But any attack on the Smythes or their financial empire wouldn't be easy. Not with Jack "The Ripper" Gregory heading up their extensive security operation. Alexandr had spent a considerable amount of time going through The Ripper's dossier, and even though he discounted some of the more outlandish acts attributed to the ex-CIA assassin, he had to admit that the man was remarkable. Even someone such as Daniil Alkaev would be hard pressed to take him out.

Nevertheless, there were other ways to strip the Smythes of their protection. Careful planning and deft manipulation, two of Alexandr Prokorov's specialties, were in order. His lips curled into a tight smile as he turned back toward his headquarters. He would soon make the opening gambit in an epic match.

Epic . . . but not lengthy.

● ○ ○

President Benton stepped away from the microphones, accepted the large ceremonial scissors, and cut the red ribbon. Loud applause from the gathered crowd echoed through the streets of New Geneva. He was surprised to find his hands were sweating despite the cool breeze that swept in off Lake Geneva. Then again, this building was the symbol of a dream he and others had worked so hard to bring to fruition.

As he looked out over this crowd, the image of Martin Luther King Jr. delivering his famous *I Have a Dream* speech before tens of thousands on the National Mall played out in President Benton's mind. Dr. Stephenson's dream was every bit as important as Dr. King's—not just that all races could live together in harmony, but that all species of intelligent beings could do so, no matter their planet of origin. It was what this grand new building, the Stephenson Center for Interspecies Reconciliation, symbolized.

The great Dr. Donald Stephenson had devoted his life, not only to reverse engineering beneficial alien technologies that could eliminate pollution and disease, but to welcoming the species that had made these miracles possible. Leave it to President Benton's militaristic predecessor to screw up first contact, big-time, by provoking the aliens as they came through the gateway and then by nuking Stephenson's gateway, killing the great doctor and many of the world's finest scientists, along with tens of thousands of EU citizens, due to the blast effects and fallout.

It had taken time but, at last, the United States public had come to embrace what he and others had been proclaiming ever since that horrible day. The American people had elected him president with a mandate to fix this mess. The cleanup and rebuilding of Geneva had been a healing first step, one that this center symbolized. But it would take a strong, centralized world government to finish the task by rebuilding the Stephenson Gateway and carefully establishing communications with the aliens in order to explain what had gone wrong. Only then could our little planet become a productive member of a much larger galactic community. Only then could we receive the guidance of those who had already solved the problems plaguing humankind.

President Benton stood tall and inhaled deeply, feeling the crisp air fill his lungs. Yesterday, the United States had joined the UFNS, the final superpower to enter this new union. Now nothing could stand in the way of human enlightenment.

A new day had indeed come.

CTC's corporate jet was less than an hour out of Austin and Heather was tired. Political schmoozing often seemed to suck the life out of her as surely as if the entire room was filled with vampires. But it had been for a good cause, a critically important one. She knew from firsthand experience what the lead elements of a Kasari invasion force looked like. She had the emotional scars to prove it and so did Mark. While their physical scars had healed, the loss of Jennifer continued to tear at both of their souls. She'd be damned if she'd allow naïve, politically correct revisionism to turn what happened seven years ago at the Stephenson Gateway on its head . . . damned if she'd let the UFNS rebuild that portal.

She glanced out the window, watching as the first hints of sunrise painted the distant Austin skyline with its peachy glow. This wasn't the life she and Mark had dreamed of when they'd bought their New Zealand farm. For two years, they'd been happy there. But Heather's steadily worsening visions had forced them to leave that idyllic existence to embark on this dangerous new road.

Now all their hard work and planning was coming to a head. Freddy Hagerman had spearheaded the creation of A Safe Earth, a movement meant to be a roadblock on the UFNS highway to madness.

Unfortunately, according to the polls, President Benton's supporters were winning the argument, constantly repeating a mantra of talking points that focused on a central question: Why had the Kasari starship provided us such wonderful technologies if they didn't have humanity's best interests at heart? Along with advanced cold fusion, we now had nanites that could cure disease and extend human lifespans, tech to convert matter to energy, and plans for building a wormhole gateway that could be a portal to the stars. Such thinking ignored the fact that the Rho Ship and the Bandelier Ship had shot each other out of the sky back in the '40s. So much for the peaceful alien theory.

Heather's mind automatically calculated their odds of success, but she gritted her teeth and forced her thoughts back to the positive. Long ago Mark had told her that it wasn't how the odds were stacked against them that was important. As long as the odds weren't zero, they still had a fighting chance.

She turned to look at Mark, who leaned back in the leather couch beside her, his eyes closed in meditation. A perfect memory formed in her mind: the boyish look of excitement on his laughing face as he had given her a hand up into the wondrous Altreian starship after they had stumbled upon its crash site near Bandelier National Monument. She had felt that same thrill, and though Jennifer hadn't admitted it, Heather had known that Jen had felt it too.

The Altreian starship had altered them for better and for worse. And it had destroyed their comfortable little lives.

Refocusing on her husband, she compared the man Mark had become to the high school boy she'd known back then. In the last few years he'd grown taller and his body had filled out magnificently. At six foot three, two hundred and ten pounds, his neurally augmented strength and reflexes were off the charts. So were many of his other abilities. Lying here beside her, he looked so good that she found herself longing to run her fingers through his wavy brown hair.

After they'd put a stop to Dr. Stephenson's attempt to bring the Kasari through the Stephenson Gateway, they'd changed their names and moved to a rural farm in New Zealand to find peace together. That first year of marriage had been wonderful. The physical toil of farm work and isolation had cleansed their souls. Too bad that time couldn't have lasted. World events had inevitably dragged them back into the fray.

Glancing up, she caught Janet's knowing smile from the opposite side of the aircraft. Not only did Heather have an audience but the jet was now on final approach to Austin Executive Airport.

Ah well. Fingers through Mark's hair would have to wait a little longer.

Jack Gregory stepped off the bottom step onto the tarmac, nodded to Jim Richards, the leader of the security detail that had come to meet them, and then ushered Mark and Heather into the back of an armored sedan. Janet slid in on the passenger side. Jack climbed into the driver's seat. Touching the console, he entered the command that enabled the manual-drive feature, then grabbed the joystick that rose from the center console.

"Damn, I miss steering wheels and pedals!"

Janet's laugh eased his irritation. Even the stick's placement bugged him. If it was on his left he could reach over and place a hand on Janet's thigh instead of just thinking about it. Since their duties had kept the two of them on different schedules for the last three days, he'd been thinking about those legs a lot.

He eased the stick forward and the powerful car responded, maneuvering onto Aviation Drive before turning southwest onto Cameron Road. Ten minutes later, after a brief stop at the perimeter security gate, the car entered the Combinatorics Technology Industrial Park, wound through the wooded green space that separated the manufacturing buildings, and parked beneath the entrance to the headquarters dome. Per security protocol, Jack and Janet were the first to exit the vehicle, which could, if necessary, be verbally commanded by the backseat occupants to speed away.

The Combinatorics corporate headquarters was unlike any other. Built of transparent titanium, one of the many patented materials manufactured on campus, the building glittered in the sunlight like a jewel. The four-story dome reminded Jack of a huge flying saucer, rising only ninety feet above the ground at its peak. Divided into four floors, the topmost was Mark and Heather's penthouse. The third floor provided living quarters for Jack, Janet, and Robby, with a separate apartment for Robby's Quechua nanny, Yachay. Corporate offices filled the second level, while the security lobby, meeting rooms, gym, and cafeteria occupied the ground floor.

Belowground, things went from interesting to amazing. Tunneled into the stone three hundred feet below their headquarters, the Smythes had constructed a computing center, training facilities, and a warren of automated research laboratories. There they invented materials and equipment derived from a combination of Altreian and Kasari technologies, with modifications envisioned only by Heather's savant mind.

Powered by twin cold-fusion reactors and manned by custom-built industrial robots, the only links to external networks were through untraceable subspace receiver-transmitters, or SRTs. But all of the sensitive research, most of which had not been released, was isolated on a supercomputer in New Zealand. Access to the lower level was limited to a core group of six. That underground world was where they worked with Robby.

Janet's voice brought him out of his reverie.

"Where will you start the security inspection?"

"I want to tour the perimeter fencing, then work our way through each of the facilities and end up back here."

"I'm going to stop in and check on Robby first. I'll meet you at the main gate."

Jack nodded and watched her walk into the security lobby before climbing back into the car. The thought of what Robby would face if anyone found out about the things he could do scared Jack. And Robby's growing rebellion against the restrictions that prevented him from going out and experiencing the real world, from mingling with other kids, would soon make keeping his secret all the more difficult.

Hell. Jack couldn't blame Robby for pushing back. Jack and Janet continually argued about the restrictions imposed upon their son. Despite Robby's rigorous training regimen and extreme talents, she was adamant that he was still a kid and lacked the wisdom and experience to keep himself safe. When Jack had pointed out it was tough to get that experience in a padded cell, he'd been in Janet's doghouse for two weeks.

Maybe she was right. When one public slipup could bring Robby to the wrong people's attention, the right approach might be the cautious one. Regardless, it raised a much darker question.

How much longer could they hope to constrain the gifted child who had inherited so many of his father's traits?

● ○ ○

Janet Price strode into the elegant security lobby that formed the entrance to the CTC headquarters, her thoughts so focused on Robby that she paid no attention to the glorious sunrise visible through the building's transparent titanium walls. The weight of the Glock holstered at the small of her back was so familiar that she noticed it no more than the six-inch needle that pinned up her dark hair. Her black jumpsuit and leather jacket highlighted her athletic body, but it was the urgency of her long stride and her serious expression that attracted the attention of the security guards as she approached their station.

"George," Janet said, directing her attention to the supervisor. "I'll be up in my quarters for the next few minutes if anyone needs me."

"Yes, ma'am."

Bypassing the desk, Janet walked to the elevator lobby and pressed the up-arrow call button.

At eight years old, Robby no longer required a traditional nanny, but Yachay was anything but traditional. The indigenous woman who had helped bring him from Janet's womb into this world was a fierce combination of godmother and bodyguard. She was the only one besides Jack, Mark, and Heather who Janet trusted with her son's dangerous secrets, and those secrets were many.

The memory of the Bolivian night that had altered Robby sent a shudder through Janet before she could shove it back into the recesses of her mind.

She'd stepped onto the veranda, little Robby slung against her left hip, taking in the scene at a glance. Inside the open case on the low table, the lone alien headband picked up the flickering light from the hurricane lamp. Mark, Jen, and Heather leaned back in their chairs, their own headsets firmly seated over their temples, eyes staring sightlessly into the night. Jack sat in another chair, his alert posture reminding Janet of a Ranger taking point.

Setting Robby in his child swing, Janet gave the handle a couple of turns and started its gentle back-and-forth motion before settling into the chair beside Jack.

"How long have they been at it?"

"About twenty minutes."

"Any sign of trouble?"

"Mark seems to be under some stress."

Janet focused her attention on Mark's face. The powerful line of his jaw stood out prominently . . . not clenched, but very tight. She'd seen that look before on a trained operative resisting torture.

"How much longer are you going to give them?"

Jack shrugged. "Maybe ten minutes. Depends on Mark."

Based on the concern she heard in Jack's voice, she knew Mark was closer to the precipice than he would have liked. Darkly fascinated, Janet leaned forward, determined to aid Jack in the last few minutes of his vigil. An extra pair of trained eyes watching for a sign that Mark was about to break couldn't hurt.

Robby dropped his pacifier and stretched his arm out for something even more interesting. Somehow, as he swung back and forth in his rocker, his grasping baby fingers had snagged the glittering alien headset from the open case and, as he mouthed it, its twin beads had slid up onto his temples.

Janet spun, horrified by the sound of Robby's scream. She froze, her mind momentarily refusing to accept the sight of the glistening headband attached across the front of her baby's face.

Recovering, she lunged toward Robby, hands outstretched to snatch the hateful thing from her baby's head. Just before she reached him, she felt herself snatched back into powerful arms. Struggling, she tried to kick herself free, only to find herself bound more tightly, her blows absorbed by her lover.

Jack's voice wormed its way into her brain. "Janet, stop! We can't remove the band. Not before the link is finished."

"It's killing him!"

"No, but we might. If we remove the band before it finishes the link, it might kill Robby or leave him brain damaged."

Janet stopped struggling, sinking to her knees in Jack's arms, sobs bubbling to her lips from the darkness deep within her soul. She looked at her baby's face, contorted in agony.

She struggled to speak. "But it's changing him."

Jack pressed his forehead to hers. "Yes. Probably in the same way it changed Mark, Jennifer, and Heather. They turned out all right."

"He's only a baby."

Then she breathed out the thought they both dreaded. "And it's the Rag Man headset. El Chupacabra's headset."

"Trust me. This'll be different."

For the first time since she'd known him, as Jack held her quivering body against his, Janet didn't believe him.

Snapping herself out of the hated memory, Janet's thoughts turned to the alterations the Altreian headset had made to her son. It had given him many of the same abilities exhibited by Mark and Heather—an eidetic memory, an enhanced neural system, and unnatural control of his body. Although he was only eight, he looked like an athletic thirteen-year-old, yet another attribute that forced Janet and Jack to keep him isolated.

When Robby was very young, Janet had noticed his ongoing conversations with an imaginary friend, sometimes aloud and sometimes only in his head. When these continued through the years, Janet's concern for her child's mental health had risen to the point of desperation. Thus she had leaped at the chance to take Heather and Mark up on their offer to bring Robby to CTC, where the two could assist with his education and training. More than that, Janet knew that Heather's savant mind offered the best chance to understand and help her son.

At this hour of the morning, Robby would be eating breakfast and then preparing for the training rigors of another day. Like Mark and Heather, he had no need for sleep, but nighttime gave him what he valued most: privacy for meditation and communion with the Altreian artificial intelligence that had downloaded itself into Robby's brain.

When Janet stepped out of the elevator on the third floor, she walked directly to their apartment. The wide terrazzo-tiled entryway was decorated in a Mediterranean style with a warm, welcoming feel in conflict with Janet's darkening mood. She needed to shed that mood before she carried it into Robby's presence. Pausing just outside the apartment, she applied a smile that would have made her grandfather proud, opened the door, and stepped in.

The great room opened up just beyond the foyer, separated from the open kitchen by an eight-foot-long granite counter. Yachay stood at the counter, the Quechua woman's weathered face as hard as her body. Ageless and impervious. Sitting at the kitchen table, Robby looked up as Janet approached, his brown eyes meeting hers.

"Good morning," she said, leaning down to kiss his cheek.

"And a fine morning to be good on," Robby replied with a grin. It was one of his games, stealing the words from his favorite books to form a response.

She sat down across from him, wishing that he would continue eating the fluffy scrambled eggs and bacon on his plate before they grew cold.

"Good news. You get a break from your studies today. You can read, play computer games, or do whatever you want."

"How about letting me go around with you?"

"Not today. Your dad and I are conducting a security inspection."

"Mom! You don't have to hide me here all the time. I can help."

Janet saw the resentment in his eyes. She shook her head. "No. Your dad and I need to focus on our jobs without worrying about your safety. Your time is coming, just not yet."

"Why not?"

Janet felt her temples pulse. She loved Robby so much that she'd sacrificed much of what she loved to do in order to keep him safe. This rebellious phase might be normal, but it was pissing her off.

"Please, just do as I ask."

"How am I ever going to learn if I'm always stuck inside?"

"This discussion is over."

For a moment it looked like Robby would push his luck, but he slid his chair back, stood up, and left the table, walking directly to his room and slamming the door behind him. Janet stared after him for a moment, then took a deep breath and turned to Yachay. Her countenance gave no clue as to whether she approved of the way Janet had handled Robby's behavior or not.

"Please take Robby down to the training level as soon as you get the dishes put away."

"Yes, Miss Janet."

Janet nodded, then turned and strode back to the elevator. By the time she reached the security lobby, she had almost recovered her composure.

● ○ ○

Robby heard the door slam behind him before he realized that he had slammed it. *Uh-oh.* For a moment, he stood frozen in place, certain that his mom would storm into his room at any second. When it didn't happen, he breathed an audible sigh of relief.

Walking to his unmade bed, he kicked off his sneakers and sprawled atop it, staring up at a brilliant Hawaiian sky. Picking up the remote control from his nightstand, he pressed a button and the outer wall and high ceiling darkened until they were almost opaque. The inside walls and ceilings had been coated with a special electronic ink that was capable of displaying pictures, videos, text, or colors with configurable transparency.

His aunt Heather had made the supercool improvements to an existing technology. He knew she wasn't really his aunt, but that's what she'd asked him to call her, so it had stuck.

To think that he'd started this morning in such a great mood, looking forward to his mom and dad getting home. And then, instead of telling her he loved her, he'd opened his big fat mouth and stuck his foot inside, all the way up to his ankle. Before he knew what had happened, he was mad, his mom was mad, and poof . . . all the good feelings had disappeared.

Now he lay here in bed, feeling hungry and miserable, but too dang stubborn to walk out and apologize.

"Do you want my advice?" The feminine voice in his head didn't improve his mood.

"Not really."

She had been with him for as long as he could remember. Although she had originally referred to herself as the Other, Robby had never liked that name. He liked Eos, the Greek goddess of the dawn. A new day was dawning. He and Eos were a part of it.

When Robby was much younger, he'd thought of her as an invisible friend. Only after his family had moved here had he learned that she was an artificial intelligence. Eos had once existed inside the alien computers aboard the Bandelier starship that Uncle Mark and Aunt Heather had found. Robby figured that if the alien headset hadn't altered him similarly to the way his aunt and uncle had been altered, it would be awfully crowded inside his head right now. Aside from neural enhancements that gave him an eidetic memory, heightened senses, and tremendous muscular control and coordination, he had yet to develop the psychic abilities that let Mark and Heather communicate via thought at times. But just in the last few months, he'd begun to show a slowly growing telekinetic ability that let him nudge very light objects.

Eos had her own special magic that, through their linked minds, allowed her to take control of any computer or automated device, as long as he could see it. Robby let her use his weak telekinesis to manipulate the electrons within the device's circuits. He let her flow from him into the machine. Not all of her essence flowed through the link. Just enough. A ghostly arm reaching inside a tiny computer brain.

Robby knew Eos scared people who knew about her, even Heather, who was her own kind of crazy-smart. And he knew he had to be careful about using his inner deity lest others learn to fear what she could do, what the two of them could do. People feared their gods if they knew those gods walked among them. And compared to the abilities of everyday humans, he, Mark, and Heather might as well be gods.

He didn't think of his mom and dad as gods. They were more like mighty demigods who had been sent down from Olympus to wage battle for humanity.

Robby stretched and climbed back out of bed, his good mood gradually returning. This was almost like living on Olympus, waiting on Zeus's permission to go down to Earth and mingle with the humans. He knew one thing for certain: he wasn't willing to wait very much longer.

:CHAPTER 3

Raul felt the ship's worm-fiber generator come back online and mentally sent Jennifer a high five, although she scoffed at the gesture. He didn't care. Being able to generate those tiny space-time pinholes between here and there gave him the ability to remotely view other parts of the ship or the worlds outside of it. But unlike the wormhole drive, the worm-fiber range was limited to a few million miles. In this case, it meant that he wouldn't have to use Jennifer's eyes to make the remainder of the repairs.

"Thank God!" Her tired thought was filled with relief.

Her vision winked out in his head, but he reestablished his view of the below-deck crawl space, initiating a dozen worm-fiber pinholes manipulated by his neural net to create a 3-D view of the damaged equipment.

"What's that smell?" The alarm in Jennifer's mental voice startled Raul.

Then he smelled it too, a sour ammonia smell that burned his nostrils and eyes. His neural net provided an instantaneous answer.

"Shit!" Raul gasped and then wished he hadn't as he pulled more of the noxious gas into his lungs.

The ship had detected passengers and restarted its life support system in its default mode, which would have been fine for the Kasari with their advanced nano-bots that were capable of making any atmosphere breathable. But that wasn't true of the relatively primitive nanites that Dr. Stephenson had created via reverse engineering, nanites that now populated the bloodstream of Raul and Jennifer.

Even with their heightened resistance, the poisonous atmosphere would eventually kill them. Raul didn't want to think about the agony that would accompany that kind of slow death.

"What the hell?" The outrage in Jennifer's broadcast thought was palpable. "Do something!"

Her words snapped him out of the terror that had frozen him. With the repairs to the primary controller incomplete, his only choice was to command a life support system shutdown, so that's what he did. The problem was that the shutdown wouldn't get rid of the noxious gas that had already poisoned the ship's nitrogen-oxygen atmosphere.

Raul didn't know how long he could hold his breath, but he didn't think it would be long enough to complete the necessary repairs.

Jennifer strode through the open door into the forward third of the ship, her angry eyes matching the wave of emotion that buffeted his mind. Clearly she'd gone deeper into his head, picking up thoughts he hadn't meant for her to listen in on.

Holding her breath, she didn't speak. Her thoughts slammed him. "How long will it take to fix?"

Again the neural net supplied a less than satisfactory answer. "Thirteen minutes for the custom atmosphere controls, ten to recalibrate for the nitrogen-oxygen mix, and another eighteen to flush the bad air and replace it with the good."

Raul was surprised when she didn't hurl an angry response at him. Instead, Jennifer Smythe stopped two strides in front of him and softened her thoughts. "How long would it take to produce pure oxygen?"

Interesting thought. Raul was starting to see where she was going with this. Pure oxygen would also kill them, but much more slowly. Resisting the growing urge to breathe, he placed the query.

"Seven minutes for minimal repairs and another fourteen to raise the oxygen levels to make the air breathable."

"How long to make one of the living compartments survivable?"

The answer formed in his head, giving a glimmer of hope. "Eight minutes, but it'll be marginal."

"Fine. Program the neural net to handle that and then have it continue making primary controller repairs until it can flood the ship with Earth's atmosphere. In the meantime, we'll try to survive in the smaller space."

"I'll lose my connection to the neural net. We won't know when it's finished."

Jennifer placed a reassuring thought in his mind. It did little to damp down his need to fill his lungs with air, even if it was bad air. But he did as instructed and then let her lead him to the door, where she placed her arm around his waist. As they passed through the portal, he felt his link with the neural net die along with his ability to control the stasis field that supported him.

What happened next surprised him. Instead of lowering him to the floor, Jennifer's grip tightened, supporting him as easily as if he were a small child, carrying him into the hexagonal room on the far side of the hallway. Setting him down on the alien rest-pallet that vaguely resembled a bed, she walked back to the portal, her fingers perfectly tracing the symbol that closed the door.

Christ. He had to keep reminding himself that, even after he'd watched Heather, Mark, and Jennifer battle the Kasari who had come through the Stephenson wormhole gate, he knew next to nothing about the extent to which the Altreian starship had altered them. She seemed to be handling the lack of oxygen better than he was. If her lungs were screaming like his, she damn sure wasn't showing it.

Raul gasped involuntarily and the resultant fit of coughing sent him into a panic spiral that pulled another lungful of agony down his throat. A hoarse scream boiled from his lips and he rolled onto his back, his body convulsing.

Then she was there, sitting beside him, her confident mind sliding into his, bringing with it a wonderful sense of calm that extinguished his panic as if it had never existed. He exhaled the poisonous gas and this time he didn't inhale. The need was still there, as was the pain that speared his chest, but now that he'd stopped harming himself the nanites were keeping him alive.

But for how long? Without his connection to the neural net, it was a question for which he had no answer.

●　○　○

Jennifer was scared, but she masked it from her thoughts. Right now, Raul needed her strength in order to survive, and if he died, since she couldn't operate this ship, her death would soon follow. She was almost glad that Heather wasn't here to recite the odds of that happening.

With her lungs screaming to inhale, it was taking all of Jennifer's concentration to keep soothing thoughts flowing to Raul while she maintained a mental countdown. Three more minutes for the repairs that would allow the Rho Ship to begin flooding their compartment with O_2, replacing one toxic gas with a lethal concentration of a breathable one.

One could recover from oxygen toxicity if handled early enough. The problem was that euphoria and loss of concentration were among the early symptoms, not great if you were trying to solve difficult problems. A new thought occurred to her. If she'd told Raul to have the neural net lower the cabin pressure, the oxygen toxicity would have been manageable.

Christ! Another damn mistake.

As her countdown progressed, the urge to inhale became greater along with a light-headed feeling that threatened to break her mental link with Raul. Just as that link began to falter, she felt the first change in the atmosphere. The stinging in her eyes began to subside. She dared a small sniff. Definitely better, but there was still an ammonia smell, so she decided to hold her breath a bit longer.

Raul's body went into a spasm. He pulled in a great lungful of air and then exhaled in a mighty fit of coughing. He rolled onto his side, gasped several times, and relaxed into a series of panting breaths, each of which seemed to grow easier.

Jennifer allowed herself a sipping breath that tasted and felt wonderful. Her next breath was a full one that evoked its own coughing fit. But now she understood. It wasn't the new air that was the problem. Her lungs were merely clearing themselves of the remnants of the noxious fumes she'd breathed in several minutes ago.

"That was fun," Raul said as he scooted himself back to lean against the wall.

Coming from Raul, the wry comment was so unexpected that it amplified the relief she felt at breathing again, pulling from her lips a snicker that became laughter, doubling her over onto her knees. Wiping her eyes, she looked up to see a broad grin spread across Raul's face. It struck Jennifer that beneath that horrifying, cyborg exterior lurked the person who had so entranced Heather back in their high school days.

Then again, it might just be the oxygen high.

● ○ ○

By the time Jennifer informed him that the ship should have completed the atmospheric conversion outside of this chamber, Raul felt so light-headed and dizzy he didn't care. But she was persistent, so he opened his eyes and nodded.

"Okay, I'm up."

"That's good, because I was getting ready to open the door and drag your ass back into the command bay."

"Try it and I'll wrap you up in the stasis field and hang you in a corner."

"Not if I break that weak little mind of yours first," she said.

"Good luck flying the ship after that."

Jennifer frowned, and then gave a reluctant grin that was half grimace.

"Guess we'd better call a truce then."

"Looks like."

As Raul watched her stare back at him, the thought of just how good she looked surprised him. At five foot six, her body was slender yet powerful and her short blonde hair framed a face that looked elfish. Having long since discarded the white lab coat that she'd worn when she first stepped through the portal into this ship, the hand-washed remnants of her bloodstained jeans and vintage T-shirt emphasized a very sexy body. If it hadn't been for how bad they both smelled, it might have been a major turn-on. Her rags certainly had more appeal than his stained pullover shirt or the cutoff, folded-over blue jeans that looked like a glorified diaper.

Shit, he thought. *The oxygen toxicity is making me delirious.*

"You ready?" she asked, her fingers reaching for the almost invisible door controls.

"Go ahead."

When the nano-particles dissolved into the wall, there was no whoosh of pressure equalization, but he found himself holding his breath. Then Jennifer put her arms around him and effortlessly lifted him from the bed. *Christ.* He could get used to this. Maybe he'd have to arrange a stasis field malfunction in order to find out.

As Raul began to inhale, the air in the hall proved breathable and so did the command bay . . . better than breathable. Raul had little doubt that this was a mixture of 21 percent oxygen, 78 percent nitrogen, and 1 percent other. Damn close to Earth normal . . . minus the argon, water vapor, and smog.

Unfortunately, coming off the pure oxygen high left him with a skull-cracking headache. *Freakin' fabulous.* As great as his nanites were at fixing injuries, they didn't seem to care a lot about his comfort. A glance at Jennifer's bloodshot eyes told him she wasn't doing much better.

Still, it felt good to reestablish his connection with the Rho Ship's neural net, feeling as if he'd shifted from a groggy stupor to hyperalert. A sense of raw power came with the return of his control over the stasis field. Raul lifted himself up toward the ceiling, experiencing the Rho Ship as if it were a living extension of his body, the damaged systems producing a sensation akin to physical pain.

"Are you having fun up there?" Jennifer asked, her voice weary.

Raul looked down at Jennifer's location in the central open area, fifteen feet below. She looked beyond exhausted. He immediately realized just how much of the load she had been carrying over the last five days, maintaining her mental connection with him as they fought to repair the ship and survive. Now she had let that mental link slip away.

"Just getting a feel for the ship's status. We've done well, all things considered."

"But?"

"Tell you what . . . get some rest while I run a complete diagnostic. I'll bring you up to speed when you wake up."

She blinked slowly and when her eyes opened again, it was with great reluctance. Although she rarely needed sleep, these last few days had taken a severe toll on her.

"Maybe I will take a short nap."

With that, Jennifer sat down on the smooth gray floor, rolled on her side, and fell asleep. Raul watched her breathing steady and then gently lifted her with the stasis field, molding it to cradle her body.

Leaving her floating on a bed of air, he turned his attention to the task at hand.

● ○ ○

Jennifer felt like she'd just closed her eyes when Raul roused her, but her mind told her that she'd slept for more than six hours. When she lifted her head from the pillow, a thin line of drool dangled from the corner of her mouth. *Lovely.*

That's when she realized she was floating in midair. As she sat up, she discovered that her invisible bed had edges, just like a real one. Five feet in front of her, Raul studied her, concern painted on his face. He had done this for her. The sweetness of the gesture moved her to the verge of tears, something she hid while sliding off the air mattress to stand up.

"Thank you for that," she managed.

"I wouldn't have awakened you, but there's something you need to see."

The way he said it brought Jennifer back to her senses, replacing her thankfulness with worry.

"What's happened?"

"We're approaching a planet."

Now she felt a great need to see what Raul saw. Jennifer's mind linked with his and the neural net–supplied vision pulled a startled gasp from her lips.

"My God!"

She had expected to see some ringed gas giant or a cold and barren world, but the planet that loomed before her was a beautiful jewel of blue, green, and white. As she watched, Raul zoomed in. Unlike Earth, the oceans covered less than half the planet's surface and the land was dotted by a number of lakes and a half dozen inland seas.

But it was the night portion of this world that deeply startled her. Scattered patches of light indicated cityscapes, lots of them, some larger than any city on Earth.

A new concern flashed into Jennifer's mind. "How close are we?"

"We're thirty million miles out."

The ship's camera zoomed out and the world dwindled until it was merely a bright point of light orbiting an orange star. Anticipating her next query, Raul displayed a diagram showing that the planet was the fourth from the sun, just one of eighteen planetary bodies that composed this star's solar system. The object of their study was tagged with a name. Scion.

She refocused on Raul's face. "Don't you think it would have been a good idea to discuss it with me before you steered us toward an inhabited planet?"

Raul shrugged. "I didn't have anything to do with it. This ship has several planetary systems loaded into its database, one of which belongs to our sun. This is another. From what I've been able to learn, when you initiated the unplanned wormhole jump from Earth, the ship picked a destination from another of the systems in its database."

Jennifer swallowed hard. That answer made sense but it certainly didn't alleviate her growing anxiety. She knew damned well why Earth was in the Rho Ship's database. Their home was a target planet for the Kasari Collective, one to which this world ship had been dispatched as a precursor to invasion. The fact that the Rho Ship had now brought them here couldn't be good.

"Why haven't you stopped our movement, at least until we get a chance to think this through and make a plan?"

"That's the problem. The destination is locked in and I can't override it. Even if I could, we're low on food and water. We could get water from other planets or asteroids in this system, but the only place to restock our food is where we're headed."

"From what you just showed me, that civilization must be at least as advanced as Earth's. Odds are they'll detect us before we enter orbit."

"I don't think so. The ship has activated a local gravity distortion field that's deflecting electromagnetic radiation. For now we're invisible to radar and to electro-optical devices."

"For now?"

A web of worry lines creased Raul's forehead. "The ship is low on energy. We can feed some trash into the small matter disrupter in this compartment but if we don't capture some significant material for the primary disrupter to convert to energy, we won't even be able to land. And since I can't steer the ship, we can't divert to the nearest asteroid field to refuel."

"Shit!"

"Yeah."

Jennifer felt her lips tighten into a thin line. She forced herself to think. Computers were her thing, an ability tremendously augmented by her initial headset connection to the Altreian starship. But her hacking ability was useless without an interface to the neural net, and unless she figured out a way around that problem, they would soon find themselves aboard a dead vessel.

Then, despite all their struggles up to this point, she and Raul would follow the ship into the dark.

:CHAPTER 4

With Mark at her side, Heather entered the dungeon, what Mark called the underground complex where they spawned the technological miracles that might yet save Earth. But this wasn't the birthing chamber of those miracles . . . that was in New Zealand. Heather had to admit that, despite the technology layered throughout this facility, it had the ghostly feel of a post-apocalyptic missile silo.

The facility had started as a long north-south tunnel through rock, bored out by robotic mining machines controlled from the surface. The original borehole had been drilled straight down from within the massive building they called Shipping Facility One. A model of efficiency, CTC had built additional manufacturing facilities from the stone extracted during the construction of the underground complex.

Once the tunnel had been extended beneath the construction site for the corporate headquarters dome, a second elevator shaft had been bored out, the one that had just transported Mark and Heather down to the research complex. Upon the completion of the north-south tunnel, the work had shifted to digging out chambers on either side of the central tunnel.

The underground facilities were completed and brought to full operational capacity in two years and three months. Money was no problem, flowing like water from U.S. military contracts and the licensing of CTC patents to other corporations. Profit was supplemented by the sale of materials manufactured in the surface facilities on the Combinatorics campus.

Everything that Combinatorics did was strictly legal. Heather confined her illegal activities to the web of shell corporations they had initially created eight years ago under Jack and Janet's tutelage while they'd been at Jack's Bolivian hacienda. During their time in New Zealand, Mark and Heather had extended that web into an impenetrable network of seemingly unrelated companies with no traceable connections back to them.

Two years in New Zealand had laid the groundwork for the creation of CTC. And during the last five years, the monstrous cash flow generated by CTC had enabled Mark and Heather to fund the secret facility in New Zealand.

She shifted her attention to the long hall stretching out before her, its metallic walls lit from above by the soft glow of ceiling panels. She paused at the third door on the left, waiting as sensors scanned her face, eyes, and body. Then the door slid into its wall slot, allowing her and Mark to step inside the command center.

One of the smaller rooms in the complex, the command center was an exact replica of the Second Ship's command deck that included four gently curved couches, one for each wearer of the four alien headsets. Each couch seemed to have been extruded from the translucent material that composed the floor, curved walls, and ceiling, rising in a single pedestal that flowed outward and up to form a chair that molded itself to your body as you sat down.

Although Robby was still too young to assume his place here, the incredible rate at which he was advancing meant that wouldn't be true for much longer. As for Jennifer's command couch, it would forever remain empty in tribute to their missing member.

As always, Mark slid onto the leftmost chair while Heather sank into the one on the right. Heather touched a control pad on her right armrest and a panel opened to reveal two glittering, translucent headbands. U shaped, each had small beads on both ends. She reached inside the compartment, ignoring the alien headband that would provide a subspace connection to the computers on the Altreian starship, instead selecting its doppelganger, this one of her own design. Beside her, Mark did the same.

A sudden memory surfaced of that moment when she and Mark had tried to use the Altreian headsets while they attempted to destroy the Stephenson Gateway, but the headsets had gone dead. They had later discovered that the loss of a link had been caused by Jennifer drawing on all of the Second Ship's computing power, just before the Rho Ship, with Jen and Raul on board, had been thrust through a wormhole of its own creation. Jennifer's Altreian headset had gone through that wormhole with her. Heather and Mark had been unable to contact her once their own headsets came back online, confirming their worst fears. Jennifer was dead.

Heather shook her head, drawing a questioning glance from Mark that she ignored.

She slipped the headset on, letting the beaded ends settle onto her temples. The room melted away, replaced by lifelike imagery of a distant place supplied via a subspace link. The computer that supplied this link was located inside an abandoned gold mine in the mountains northwest of the small town of Murchison, New Zealand.

She felt Mark's link activate and smiled. It was time.

With a thought, the imagery dissolved away, leaving them staring at two men and two women seated in a small office-workshop. The sight filled her with a joy that Mark's mental link echoed.

"Hi, Mom and Dad," she said, knowing that their parents were now seeing the projection of her and Mark on a large flat-panel display as their voices played through speakers.

Mark chimed in with greetings to his parents, then the conversation turned to family chitchat. It was a biweekly ritual that kept them close, despite the distance that now separated them. Today's call was unusual in that the seventeen-hour time difference meant that their parents had stayed up past midnight. Normally, Mark and Heather would have waited for a more convenient calling time, but the business that would follow this call couldn't wait.

In their late fifties, all four of their parents looked well. Heather's dad, Gil McFarland, had added some weight to his tall, once lanky frame, as had her mother, Anna. Linda Smythe was as slender as ever, but it was hard to tell whether Fred's blocky form had expanded or not. The last few years had added a healthy dose of gray to their hair, but the move to the remote New Zealand mining property had done the parents good, an amazing circumstance considering that they had given up their old lives to adopt new identities.

When the family conversation ended, the two dads remained on the line after Anna and Linda left the room. Gil and Fred had spent years as two of the most important technicians at Los Alamos National Laboratory before they had retired, dropped out, and moved to New Zealand. Since that time, Heather and Mark had made extensive use of their expertise. The automated machinery that Heather had designed was incredible, but skilled people were still needed to pick up and transport shipments to the secret facility, to get the robots and computers up and running, and to fix unanticipated crap that went wrong every so often. Today, she and Mark would again be needing those skills.

The last five years of research and plain old hard work had finally led up to this inflection point. In the coming hours, if everything went right, they would bring the rest of the New Zealand mining complex to life.

And then things would get very interesting indeed.

●　○　○

As the conference call with Heather and Mark ended, Gil McFarland stood up, stretched, and looked at Fred Smythe, who had also risen from his chair.

"Looks like we've got a long night ahead of us."

Fred grinned. "Won't be the first time."

Grabbing his old fishing hat from the hook and setting it on its normal perch atop his curly, salt-and-pepper hair, Gil opened the door and stepped out of the steel building into the cool New Zealand summer night. Anna had taken one of the two cars and driven herself and Linda down to the clearing where their two houses sat side by side.

Since Mark and Heather's Tasman Mining Corporation owned this mine and a hundred and ten thousand acres of the surrounding wilderness, the nearest neighbors were eight miles to the southeast, near the small town of Murchison. But the dirt road that wound its way down to the highway made that distance seem twice as long.

Beauty, peace, and quiet . . . the two couples had it. And the mountain stream fishing was out of this world. Linda was the only one who suffered from a bit of withdrawal, missing her beloved Santa Fe flea markets. With that in mind, Anna made sure to accompany her on periodic weekend outings to Christchurch. The South Island's largest city had a population of more than three hundred thousand people. Hell, it was almost as big as Albuquerque.

Turning his attention back to the task at hand, Gil followed Fred past the large steel warehouse and toward the old mine entrance, twin LED flashlights lighting their way. The night seemed unusually quiet, missing the usual insect or night-bird sounds. The crunch of their work boots on the gravel road was the only sound to break the stillness.

At the point where the road ended in dense woods, Gil switched off his flashlight, put it in his pocket, and turned to look up at the Southern Cross, brilliant in the moonless star-filled sky, actions that Fred mimicked. For several moments, the beauty of the sky held them transfixed. Then, still gazing at the stars, Gil stepped backward through the cloak.

Day or night, the experience was awe inspiring. Although he couldn't feel the projected alien hologram, the way it altered reality always left him with gooseflesh. Looking at the road from outside the cloaking field, onlookers would believe that it dead-ended into thick brush and trees. But when you stepped through the holographic projection and looked out, the outside world dimmed as if seen through a gossamer curtain. The same alien technology was at work here that had concealed the alien craft Mark, Heather, and Jennifer had stumbled upon ten years ago.

Gil didn't bother to switch on his flashlight. There was no need. Instead, he followed Fred toward the brightly lit mine entrance that was invisible from the other side of the cloak.

The first time he'd been here, the mine entrance had been completely overgrown with vines that covered the boards and safety warnings that had sealed it for decades. Initial shipments from CTC had consisted of two robots, a Dumpster-sized cold-fusion power station, the cloaking device, an advanced 3-D printer, several racks of blade servers, and the SRTs that provided the secure communications links to the Austin laboratory. But over four years, CTC robots had widened the tunnels, braced them with hardened steel beams, and then walled the area off with titanium.

Gil had to hand it to his daughter. Her robotic designs were an amazing advancement, but they didn't require full-blown artificial intelligence to function. The robots merely learned to do what they were shown and then memorized that task. It was an old idea, but the real breakthrough was in the virtual reality headsets through which Mark or Heather could establish a subspace link to one of their robots from anywhere. Robots thus became extensions of their own bodies.

Sequenced tasks became activities, and once those activities were saved, the robot could transfer that knowledge to the blade servers or to other robots. The robots learned to do anything that Mark and Heather did, including building more robots. And they only required parts printed on site.

Sensors recognized the two men approaching and the metal door whisked open, giving Gil and Fred access to the labyrinth beyond. Moving from the forest environment into the subterranean, titanium-walled world always jarred Gil's senses. Despite the extensive ductwork that circulated the HEPA-filtered air, he thought it carried a slightly oily, metallic smell, very similar to his machine shop.

The tunnel didn't go straight into the hillside but followed winding, branching paths that the original miners had dug through the mountain as they attempted to follow the veins of golden ore. Many of those branches had been hollowed out to form large chambers to house a cold-fusion generator, a computer center, manufacturing facilities, clean rooms, a laboratory, bath and shower spaces, a medical clinic, an armory, and more.

When Gil walked past one of the custom boring machines working in a side passage, a sensor array mounted on one of the four armlike appendages twisted toward him, the sudden movement making him jump.

"Shit!"

Fred's laugh didn't help. Never a big fan of underground spaces, Gil had worked through that issue on this project, but he knew why he was jumpy tonight. Just outside the door, Gil paused, took a deep breath to steady his nerves, and followed Fred inside. Tonight they would fire up the device that deeply concerned him. Ten feet from the tractor-trailer–sized machine, Gil halted alongside Fred and two quasi-humanoid–looking robots.

Even though he knew that Mark and Heather would be using them to bring this system online, he and Fred had insisted on being present. If one of the robots experienced a problem at the wrong time, it wouldn't hurt to have the two dads there to step in. Besides, there was no use hiding out at their houses. If this machine went haywire, everything for miles around would be instantly atomized.

With one more deep breath, Gil looked at Fred.

"You ready for this?"

The grin on Fred's stout face failed to mask his underlying tension. "Ready as I'll ever be."

Gil turned to face the robots, wondering which was Heather and which was Mark. A weird thought on a weird night.

"All right, guys," he said to the robots. "It's your show. Let's get this over with."

● ○ ○

The avatar projection was something Heather would have thought she'd be used to by now. Logically she knew that her real body sat in one of the command couches in a chamber three hundred feet below CTC headquarters, but that made little difference. Right now all her sensory input was being provided by the robot.

The visual experience alone was startling. With a thought she could alter the primary visual range from visible light into infrared or ultraviolet spectrums. The robot's light detection and ranging LIDAR provided enhanced depth perception and her mind provided a heads-up display with exact measurements. Combined with tactile sensors and microphones, this metal body sure felt real. But unlike traditional virtual-reality experiences, she didn't need to move her real body to maneuver the robot. She merely needed to visualize what she wanted to do and the robot responded appropriately.

Heather turned to look at the identical robot that stood beside her, its seven-foot-tall body gleaming in the glow cast by rows of LED lights mounted on the ceiling. Although these particular robots were roughly humanoid in shape, their heads consisted of horizontal metal mounts for the sensors.

"You ready?" she asked Mark. Her voice sounded louder than she'd intended so she reduced the speaker volume.

His robot body manipulated its fingers in a maneuver that made Heather think it was trying to crack its knuckles. It was funny. Even in these virtual bodies, old habits died hard.

"You bet."

She turned to look at her dad and Fred Smythe, both men looking small from this perspective.

"We'll stay out of the way unless we're needed," Gil said.

"Fine."

Heather knew their presence was unnecessary, but she'd lost that argument. Both robots being there already provided safety redundancy. The only manual tasks that needed to be performed were simple—connect the thick power cable to its wall socket and then lift the breaker switch into the closed position to bring the machine to life. Once the boot-up process was completed, Heather would shift her mental connection from her robot to the matter disrupter-synthesizer.

The MDS was merely a scaled-up version of what they had designed and successfully tested in the underground laboratory in Austin. Mark had wanted to call it Deus Ex Machina, but Heather had rejected that out of hand. Still, she appreciated his wit. Without Mark's unabashedly positive outlook, she would have descended into darkness long ago.

At its core, the MDS was based upon the Kasari technology that Dr. Donald Stephenson had used to design the matter ingester that had powered the stasis field generators and the wormhole gateway in

Switzerland. Stephenson had revolutionized physics by reworking the old ether theory. It wasn't that space-time was filled with a substance through which light waves traveled; space-time was a substance made up of quantum-sized grains.

Stephenson had postulated that certain rare combinations of frequencies could form harmonic standing-wave packets within the ether, those chords resulting in all the various types of matter. The practical applications were obvious. With an understanding of the set of frequencies that made up each specific type of matter, it was a relatively simple process to add a set of canceling frequencies to form an anti-packet that would cancel out the original. Thus both sets of energy would be released in a matter/antimatter reaction.

A perfect anti-packet wasn't even necessary. If a sufficient subset of canceling frequencies were added, the harmonic chord of the stable packet would be disrupted to the point that the particle would tear itself apart, again releasing excess energy as it moved down to a set of simpler stable chords or particles. This process was composed of a few discrete steps: analyze the target matter to determine its frequency set, add a sufficient subset of canceling frequencies, harvest the released energy, and repeat.

Heather stepped aside and watched Mark lift the end of the thick power cable and connect it to the wall socket. Then he placed a metallic hand on the breaker switch handle, ready to lift it into the closed position at her signal.

"Do it."

Mark lifted the handle into place and Heather saw the MDS status panel light up as it initiated its boot sequence. But the vision that suddenly formed in her mind startled her. One second everything was fine and then it wasn't. She had just started to yell at Mark to pull the breaker when a sudden flash terminated her subspace link with the robot, leaving behind a sensory overload that felt like a lance through her brain. She was momentarily blinded.

On his command couch, Mark gasped. "Shit! What just happened?"

Ignoring his question, Heather tried to establish a direct link to the MDS despite knowing the probabilities that told her it wasn't going to happen. A power glitch had activated circuits that caused the MDS to start the matter conversion process while it was still in the boot-up sequence, which should have been impossible. And both she and Mark had lost their robotic links at the same time, meaning only one thing: the malfunctioning MDS had generated a local electromagnetic pulse that had fried both robots' circuits.

Now there was no way to remotely shut the MDS down until the boot-up sequence completed, something that would take another forty-two seconds. When she met Mark's eyes she could see that he understood.

They didn't have another forty-two seconds.

● ○ ○

"Shit!" Mark gasped as he turned to look at Heather. "What just happened?"

But her eyes had gone milky white as she delved deep into one of her savant visions. The strain on her face told him all he needed to know. Whatever it was, she wasn't finding a quick solution. Her words soon confirmed it.

"Some kind of EMP just fried everything in the MDS chamber."

"Won't that shut down the disrupter?" Mark asked.

"The disrupter and its power cable are shielded. The robots weren't."

"Neither were our dads."

"They don't have pacemakers, so if we can get this stopped, they should be okay."

"What about bringing in other robots?"

Heather's voice went cold. "It'll be over before we can get them in there."

"It won't hurt to try."

Mark turned his attention back to his headset, issuing the mental command that shifted his subspace link to one of the robots working in the warehouse. The sensory link stabilized through a moment of haze and then Mark was running, having tossed aside the large crate that the robot had been carrying. Without slowing down he hit the door, blasting it off its metal hinges and sending it cartwheeling along the floodlit gravel path ahead of him. As he entered the cloaking field, he heard Heather's robot racing to join him.

He wasn't surprised to see that the mine's titanium outer door was closed. But when it opened on its own, he skidded to a halt. *What the hell?* He'd expected to have to stop and shift his connection to the door's controls to give the open command. But when Heather passed him and raced into the mine he understood. She'd managed a dual connection without breaking concentration on her primary link, another new trick that his wife had just pulled from her savant hat.

But as his metal body raced after her, Mark knew that this time even her wizardry wouldn't be enough to save their dads.

● ○ ○

One second Gil was watching RoboMark push the circuit breaker handle into place and the next the ceiling lights spit sparks and went out. The dim screen on the matter disrupter still glowed with the words *SYSTEM BOOT IN PROGRESS . . . PLEASE WAIT.*

"What the hell . . . ?" Fred asked the question in Gil's mind.

Unable to see anything except the dimly glowing panel, Gil yelled, "Mark! Pull the breaker!"

When Mark didn't answer, Gil lunged forward, racing through the darkness toward the spot where the breaker switch was mounted to the wall. Before he reached it he ran directly into the big Mark robot, the impact sending him sprawling on the floor.

"Aaaahh. Goddamn it!"

Fred moved past Gil as he climbed to his knees, his eyes adjusting to the near darkness so that he could see his friend grab the breaker switch that was still held in the robot's grasp.

"Shit! The robot's holding it closed!" Fred yelled as he threw his whole body into the effort.

The switch didn't budge and Gil scrambled to help him. Behind him the MDS made a sound that he was pretty sure it wasn't supposed to make.

"Not the switch," Gil screamed. "The robot! Help me push it over."

Fred released the breaker switch and ducked into a football lineman stance, driving his thick shoulder into the big robot's chest as Gil threw his weight into the entity as well.

"Mooove, you metal bastard!"

For seconds that seemed like an eternity, the thing refused to budge. But when the robot finally toppled, both he and Fred came down on top of it. A quick glance upward brought a gasp of relief from Gil's lips. The lights on the MDS panel had winked out, leaving the room in total darkness. Even better, the only sounds he heard were his and Fred's panting breaths.

"Did I ever tell you how much I hate robots?" Fred's disembodied voice asked.

Gil harrumphed. "You kidding me? You're the one who loves robots."

"Yeah. That was yesterday."

"You got your flashlight?"

"Must have fallen out of my pocket during the tussle. Yours?"

Gil shook his head, knowing full well that Fred couldn't see him. "Not working."

"Funny how the MDS didn't fry its own circuits."

"Must have been its shielding."

"Makes sense," said Fred, his voice scornful. "The only part of the damn system that worked almost killed us."

Gil climbed back to his feet, feeling a twinge in his left shoulder from where he'd landed on top of the robot.

"I think I've had enough fun for tonight," he panted, hearing Fred rise beside him. "What do you say we get the hell out of here?"

"Sounds good. I've got a cold six-pack down at the house that's calling our names."

"We'll need to call Mark and Heather to let them know we're okay."

Gil started moving carefully through the dark in the direction of the door. Behind him, Fred's response brought a relieved grin to his face.

"I say we crack open a couple of brewskies before we make that call. Won't hurt them to sweat for a few more minutes before they find out their old dads aren't so stupid after all."

● ○ ○

As Heather raced through the opening into the rebuilt mine, the robo-sensors filled her head with information. The traction pads on her metal feet hammered the floor, producing a thunderous sound that echoed down the titanium-walled corridor. When she turned into the tunnel that veered off to her right, what she saw brought her to a sliding stop that ripped grooves in the concrete floor and almost caused Mark to crash into her from behind.

Ten feet ahead, her dad and Fred Smythe walked down the hall directly toward her.

"Coming to save the day?" Gil asked as he passed them without stopping.

"Too late," said Fred. "We already did."

"You two can clean up the mess."

Heather stood rooted in place, trying to process the mixture of relief and confusion that flooded her. The two men disappeared around the corner, lost in conversation about the cold beers awaiting them in Fred's fridge.

:CHAPTER 5

It had taken four hours of frantic work, but with Jennifer placing the design specifications into Raul's mind, he'd managed to build a rudimentary terminal with an interface to the Rho Ship's neural net. She felt a touch of awe at the capabilities of the nano-materials to form themselves into whatever Raul instructed them to create. Advanced 3-D printing on steroids. Mistakes and setbacks arose, but eventually they got the thing working.

Jennifer was confident that she could recreate the subspace receiver-transmitters that she, Heather, and Mark had designed based on Altreian technology. If she and Raul built the transmitters into an Altreian-style headset, they should both be able to mentally communicate with the ship's neural net. Even better, they should be able to link up from great distances. But those grandiose plans would take time that, right now, they just didn't have.

With Raul watching, she slid into the seat that faced the terminal. It was definitely old school, a simple keyboard and a monitor that was only capable of displaying monochrome text. That's what a time crunch did—made you take shortcuts that involved scrapping everything except basic functionality, leaving her sitting in front of something that belonged in a museum instead of a starship.

"Wow," Raul said as he floated up behind her. "Impressive design."

"Yeah? You built it."

His laugh carried a genuine ring. Jennifer was surprised that she liked the sound of it. Not looking at Raul helped her forget the horrifying transformation that Dr. Stephenson had inflicted on him.

"You still sure it wouldn't be faster for you to get inside my head and let me do whatever you need done?"

Jennifer snorted. "By the time I show you what I want and then watch you stumble around trying to pass those instructions to the neural net, then analyze the results you get back, I'll go crazy. Besides, I type faster than I can talk . . . even mentally."

Seeing Raul shake his head, Jennifer turned her attention back to her workstation. Her initial interactions consisted of a series of queries and responses as she slowly felt her way around the system. As her familiarity with the data structure and programming interface grew, so did her speed. Each advance opened a new level of understanding, a process that resulted in an exponential increase in her capacity for interaction with the neural net.

In her mind, the keyboard and monitor disappeared as surely as the words did when she read an engrossing book. Instead, she strode through worlds of data that formed pictures in her mind. At this point she wasn't trying to do anything fancy, just exploring. She recalled how Jack Gregory had directed them to explore the Second Ship's data banks through their Altreian headsets. That journey had turned very nasty, almost getting Mark killed when they attempted to bypass the ship's security protocols and drawing an attack from that starship's resident artificial intelligence. The memory sent shivers up her spine.

Although she had not detected any evidence that this ship's neural net contained an AI of its own, she had no desire to repeat the experience by acting prematurely here. But events would soon force her to attempt to override the ship's preprogrammed instructions. She only hoped that, when that moment came, she had acquired adequate understanding.

● ○ ○

As Raul watched Jennifer work, his attitude evolved from skepticism to appreciation and to slack-jawed wonder. If he hadn't been observing her actions through the neural net as well as with his eyes, he was sure that he couldn't have kept up with the words and symbols that flashed across the simple monitor. She flitted through his neural net, a hummingbird among honeysuckle blossoms, sampling this and that with unnatural control.

For someone's fingers to move that fast and accurately was quite simply impossible. At least it should have been. He had no doubt that Jennifer Smythe was every bit the freak that he was, albeit one with demonstrably different abilities and vastly superior packaging.

Turning his attention from what she was doing, Raul focused on the ship's dwindling energy supply, which moved him to drop their latest refuse bags into the small matter disrupter. He considered scrounging up the remaining pieces of the Rho Project instruments that had been left on board and battered into scrap during the wormhole transit, but that amount of matter wouldn't compensate for the energy the Rho Ship was expending to maintain the gravity distortion field that cloaked them.

In the moments immediately prior to their sudden departure from Earth, the ship's stasis field generators had gobbled up a large portion of the Rho Project high-bay where the ship had rested, along with some scientists, a big chunk of cement foundation, and the ground beneath. Those items had then been transferred directly into the primary matter disrupter to fuel their jump. Under normal circumstances, assuming you could call any wormhole transit normal, there would have been plenty of reserves left after the trip. But Jennifer's survival work-around had burned through almost all of it.

As the hours passed and the ship's energy reserves sank deeper and deeper into the red, Raul changed his mind and directed the stasis field to gather up all the scrap metal, feeding it into the command bay matter disrupter. It helped, but not by much. If Jennifer didn't manage to bypass the security protocols that continued to prevent Raul from overriding the ship's mission plan, they'd have to start feeding nano-materials into the ingester. The depletion of that precious resource would leave them unable to build devices or make necessary repairs.

An hour after the Rho Ship slipped into an elliptical orbit around Scion, Jennifer let out a whoop that would have made Raul jump if he still had legs.

"Got it!" When she turned to him, her smile was radiant. Jesus, she was beautiful. "You should now have complete administrative control of all systems."

And as she said it Raul felt his mental control of the ship expand. Engines, weapons systems, shielding, sensors . . . even protected portions of the ship's database that he'd had no idea existed filled his head. Damn. He'd never realized how blind he'd been before this moment.

"You're a goddess!" he said and, at least for the present, he meant it.

Jennifer's laugh held the relief that flooded through him. Yet he also detected an undercurrent of worry.

"Do we have enough energy to make it to the nearest asteroid?" she asked.

Raul pulled up all the sensor data, feeling a lump rising in his throat as he did.

"Not without dropping our gravitational cloak. Even then it'll be damn tight."

"Crap!" Jennifer paused. "What about space junk or dead satellites? Do you see any of those?"

Raul checked. "These people have a bunch of satellites in different orbits. As for space junk, I don't detect anything."

"What about the moons? Can we reach one of them?"

"We can get there, but we won't have enough power left to land. No use asking if we can land on the planet."

With every idea that failed them, Raul felt his desperation increase. They might just have to drop the cloaking field after all.

Jennifer rose from her workstation and began pacing slowly across the open portion of the command bay. Suddenly she stopped and turned back toward him.

"Fine. We'll just have to ingest one of their functioning satellites . . . preferably a big, unmanned one."

"They'll damn sure detect that."

"It can't be helped. Hopefully they'll think it was hit by some space junk."

"I just told you, they don't have space junk."

He saw Jennifer throw up her hands in frustration. "A meteor then. Whatever."

Raul nodded, turned his attention back to the sensors, and began a much more detailed set of scans focused closer in to Scion, prioritizing potential targets by their mass and ease of access. When he identified a wonderful target not far inside their own orbit, he felt a grin spread across his face.

Just as he was about to adjust their course, his attention was drawn to a sensor scan of the planet's surface.

An anomalous reading radiating from just outside one of Scion's largest cities pulled a groan from his lips.

"Oh no!"

He felt Jennifer slide into his mind and felt her recoil in horror. The signature of the anomaly was unmistakably familiar.

There, on the planet's surface, was an active Kasari gateway.

:CHAPTER 6

As if her insides had frozen solid, Jennifer struggled to breathe. *Goddamn it!* Had she and Raul survived only to have the Rho Ship return them to one of the Kasari home worlds? Tears fell from her eyes and she wiped at them angrily with the backs of her hands. Was the rest of her life destined to be one hopeless, unending suck?

"You okay?"

Raul's thought brought her head up to see the pain and worry in his face. *Shit!* She'd been so shocked she'd forgotten to drop her mental link with him. He knew exactly what she'd been thinking and feeling. But she saw in his mind emotions that matched her own in their bitter intensity. If anything, he felt even more lost and alone than she did. For a moment, she felt the urge to hug him, to share some small bit of human comfort.

Jennifer blinked and dropped her mental link. Jack and Janet hadn't trained her to give in to weakness when the situation called for strength. She flashed back to what Jack had told the three of them on that Bolivian morning, replaying the scene in perfect detail.

"No victory is certain. No situation is hopeless. When you find yourselves in a hopeless situation, change the rules."

"You mean cheat," Mark said.

Jack grinned. "Like the devil himself."

The memory of that cocky grin, of the power that radiated from Jack "The Ripper" Gregory, stiffened her spine. Taking a deep breath, Jennifer forced a semblance of that grin onto her own lips. The result was miraculous. She felt as if she'd been pummeled to the ground only to spit out a mouthful of blood and rise up stronger than ever.

"Yes," she answered Raul's question. "I'm fine. Thank you."

"What now?"

"Now we get busy." She let her new sense of determination flow into Raul's mind. "Our ship's hungry. It's about time we feed it."

Dumah subconsciously shifted his wings as he stared at the frozen satellite telemetry on the large display. The surprised buzz in the control room increased the shift leader's disquiet.

He turned his attention to Sable, his primary console operator. "What just happened?"

The female lieutenant shifted in her chair to stare up at him, looking as if she wanted to unfurl her own wings and take flight.

"Sir, we've lost all telemetry from Dastron."

"Get it back, right now."

Her fingers moved across the control panel with all the expertise that Dumah demanded of his crew. Then she pushed back, raising her hands in an expression of frustration that his nano-bot neural array confirmed.

"Sorry, sir. It's not responding to commands. One instant it was there and then it just wasn't."

"What do you mean?"

"It's not just the telemetry. The Dastron satellite is gone. There's not even a blip on the tracking radar."

Puzzled, Dumah scanned the tactical feed the nano-bots delivered to his mind. "Was it hit by rebel fire?"

Sable shrugged, a habitual reaction that the Kasari nano-bot injections had rendered unnecessary. But a lifetime of habits took time to replace, much like the need Dumah felt for physical conversation.

"Our sensors didn't detect any beam firing. Even if the rebels detonated it, we should be seeing debris, but there's nothing. It just disappeared."

A message appeared in Dumah's mind in the form of a summons from the group commander, as he'd been expecting. Not good.

"Keep searching. Broad spectrum scans. I want confirmation from every sensor that can put eyes on that orbit."

"Yes, sir."

Turning on his heels, Dumah strode directly toward the rear wall, which slid down into the floor as he approached. With two running strides, Dumah leaped out of the tower into the crystal-clear afternoon sky, letting the wind whistle past him as his gray-feathered wings unfurled. With powerful flaps, he began the climb toward the top of the tower.

If he was very lucky, Sable's nano-bot linkage would provide him with more satisfying answers before he reached the group commander's office.

● ○ ○

"City of angels?" Skepticism dripped from Jennifer's voice. "Right."

"My mind's right here for the taking," Raul offered. "Just reporting what one of the worm-fiber viewers is showing me."

There it was again, that cool breeze as she slipped into his mind. He made a mental note to get her to teach him the blocking technique before he got addicted to her presence.

"Wow!" she breathed. "So beautiful. Hard to believe they're part of the Kasari Collective."

The images Raul observed filled him with the same awe Jennifer expressed. This city by the lake was filled with gleaming, high-rise buildings, each adorned with stunning balconies, none of which had safety rails. And soaring onto or off of those balconies were the closest things to angels he could imagine.

They were beautiful. If not for the huge wings that sprouted from behind their shoulder blades, they looked almost human, although a bit slimmer, taller, and with fine feathers where humans had hair. They wore shimmering, skintight uniforms that seemed designed to reduce drag. Made sense. Why be a slow angel? There were certainly no fat ones.

Lovely plazas and parks separated the buildings. There were no roads. Vehicular traffic traveled through the air, albeit at a much higher rate of speed and along different routes than the flying pedestrians . . . wingestrians? *Whatever.*

A full planetary scan would have to wait. With the ship having ingested a sufficient supply of matter to get them safely to the nearest of Scion's three moons, Raul wanted to find a safe place to hide and finish refueling.

"Yep," agreed Jennifer. "Let's get the hell out of here."

Raul's neural net calculated their new acceleration vector and engaged the gravity distortion engines. Despite the external acceleration, the resulting force as experienced inside the ship wouldn't have put a ripple on his coffee, if he'd bothered to make some from one of the MRE instant-beverage packets.

For a change, the journey to their chosen destination proved uneventful. They touched down gently inside a deep crater on the far side of the tidally locked moon. They rested on a barren, pockmarked rock roughly half the size of Earth's moon. Scion's natural satellite reflected a burnt-orange color from sunlight, striking Raul as odd since the moon had no atmosphere to produce oxidation.

It didn't matter. For now, at least, they were safe.

●　○　○

"So what the hell do we do now?"

Jennifer didn't have an immediate answer to Raul's question. The ship had ingested enough matter so that energy was no longer their primary concern, and they were sitting on an abundance of moon matter. Their food and water stockpiles were dwindling, although she estimated that they had more than a month's supply of each. They could certainly find ice on asteroids or other moons within this planetary system, but food was an entirely different matter. There was only one place to restock that critical item, but it would require landing on a planet that had an active Kasari gateway. Her skin grew cold.

"We need to find out everything we can about that planet before we do anything else," she said. "But I'm afraid the Kasari have technology capable of detecting our gravity distortion field if we orbit Scion long enough to do a full scan."

"There's no need to leave this spot," said Raul with a grin. "The worm fibers fold space-time just like the wormhole engines do, only on a microscopic scale. It's like making a pinhole between here and there with nothing in between . . . not even this moon."

That made sense. But a new worry slipped into her mind. "How many worm-fiber views can you create at the same time and how long will it take to scan the entire planet?"

"I've controlled a few dozen before. How long the planetary scan will take depends on how high up we position them. To get good detail we'll have to ease them in fairly close to ground level and that will limit the surface area shown by each fiber."

Jennifer bit her lower lip. "Do you think the Kasari will detect that many fibers sweeping over the planet?"

Raul shrugged. "It's their tech. Whether they do or not, they won't be able to tell where the scan originated."

"Why not?"

"If they detect anything, it will just be a swarm of moving pinholes above the planet. Like I said, there's nothing between here and there . . . no trail to follow back to us. Besides, it's not like we've got a lot of choices."

"No shit." She didn't end the statement with *Sherlock*, but she was thinking it. When Raul didn't rise to the bait, she took a calming breath and shifted gears. "Okay then, let's start with an edge-of-space mapping survey. Once that's done we'll zoom in on interesting areas to fill in the details."

Raul nodded in approval and began the required manipulation of his neural net to make it happen. Jennifer slipped into his mind to observe.

The initial world map took twenty-three minutes to complete. Her mind absorbed the image perfectly. Even from this high-altitude perspective, they learned a number of fascinating details. With its much larger percentage of land to water, Scion had one huge continent, an ocean about a third as large, and six inland seas. The biggest of these was about the size of the United States mainland, while the smallest was roughly the size of Texas.

"Okay," she whispered into Raul's mind. "Start the low-altitude scans over the heavily populated areas, then map the coastlines."

"On it."

The shift in every worm fiber's viewpoint was instantaneous, the sudden change leaving Jennifer briefly disoriented. Although her mind had no trouble processing the multiple data flows coming into the neural net, she still felt a bit queasy.

The winged people ruled the vast majority of this world, but not all of it. She was surprised to discover a land-bound species of intelligent beings who had technology equal to their winged counterparts. This was another quasi-humanoid species, but these guys looked like the warriors that they were, with powerful, big-boned bodies. Their broad faces had thick brows that turned upward in two ridges running along their temples to the rear of their hairless skulls, a "don't screw with me" look if ever Jennifer had seen one.

The two species clearly didn't like each other. Long demilitarized zones stretched along the boundaries between their lands, separating heavily armed forces on either side. Jennifer also noted that the truce wasn't holding everywhere.

This was a major surprise. Everything she'd learned about the Kasari from the Second Ship's data banks indicated that they assimilated worlds and added those diverse species to their harmonious collective. When she'd first put on the Altreian headband and absorbed the alien computer's initial data dump, she saw the general protocol . . . a lone Kasari world ship arriving at a planet, seducing the population with its *beneficial* technologies, and enticing the people to build a Kasari gateway to welcome their new partners.

But in the early days, there was always resistance.

Since this Kasari gateway had been built in the heart of the angelic lands, she deduced that the warrior species hadn't been a party to the Kasari invitation. Jennifer filed the knowledge away for further investigation. Maybe they had some potential allies. Right now, though, she and Raul had a lot more to do before they had enough information to form a plan.

She felt the first warm glow of hope since leaving Earth. She let the feeling seep from her mind into Raul's.

● ○ ○

Crossing the upper two of her four arms, Kasari Group Commander Shalegha felt her nano-bot communications array trigger a grade three alert as she stood at the edge of the high balcony, looking out over the city. Of course, having arrived through the recently activated wormhole gate, she was technically the alien. It didn't matter. At the rate at which the assimilation of the willing local population was progressing, they would all soon share the collective mind.

Turning away from that view, Shalegha mentally engaged a three-dimensional strategic overlay of Scion, the name the winged people had given their planet.

There could be no doubt. One of the Kasari world ships had entered this system and was conducting a worm-fiber scan of Scion. The vessel kept itself cloaked with a gravity distortion field to prevent detection, standard procedure prior to landing on a Kasari-targeted world. The problem was, it shouldn't be here.

Although she couldn't be certain of the source of the malfunction, she had an idea of what was happening. There had been occasions when an Altreian starship had managed to intercept one of the Kasari Collective's world ships as it entered a targeted system. If this one had sustained damage in such an encounter, it may have decided to jump to another system in its target database.

Shalegha accessed the incident log, rapidly scrolling through the list of actions taken by her subordinates since the probes had been detected, nodding to herself at the efficiency displayed. The tactical duty officer at the Kasari staging base had immediately made the same determination as Shalegha and, after failing to locate the malfunctioning world ship, had attempted to contact it through normal communications channels. When the vessel had failed to respond to commands issued over those channels, the TDO had issued the grade three alert.

Right now Shalegha couldn't devote resources needed to consolidate the Kasari hold on this planet to finding and fixing the malfunctioning world ship. She could less afford to have it land on Scion and disrupt ongoing operations that were still at a sensitive stage.

With a thought, she transferred her instructions and the emergency override codes to her TDO, allowing a moment as her officer processed the details and echoed back his understanding. Moments later, when her mental projection showed that the worm-fiber scans had terminated, Shalegha allowed herself a satisfied smile.

One more unexpected problem solved.

● ○ ○

One second the planetary scan was progressing normally and then the Rho Ship's stasis field controller began carving large chunks of matter out of the lunar crater in which they sat, feeding them directly into the primary matter disrupter. Worse, the starship's engines began their wormhole initiation sequence as new coordinates locked into place, coordinates that Raul's neural net recognized. As soon as the ship finished refueling in preparation for the wormhole transit, it would make the jump to the nearest of the Kasari staging planets.

"What's happening?" Jennifer's voice in his head sounded as panicked as he felt.

"The ship just received some sort of emergency override authorization code. It's going to jump."

"Stop it!"

"I'm trying, but it's ignoring my commands."

"How long do we have?"

Raul calculated. "Fifty-three seconds."

Jennifer lunged into the seat at her workstation. If he'd thought her fingers fast the last time he'd watched her work, he'd been mistaken. Now they were an impossible blur accompanied by a clicking drumroll. For a moment he imagined the smell of smoking circuits.

Raul watched her manipulate the neural net and marveled at her ability to intuit the inner workings of the alien computing system as she sought a weakness in the firewall that denied Raul the administrative authority to countermand what was happening. As skilled as Jennifer was at mental manipulation, her Altreian-augmented abilities achieved their full potential when it came to computers. Every time she worked her way past one obstacle, a new software barrier awaited her.

Just as his desperation began to give way to hopelessness, Raul felt a flood of exhilaration fill his mind. She'd just granted him full control of the Rho Ship.

But when he tried to shut the engines down, the hopelessness came crashing back in. The wormhole was forming and there wasn't enough time to stop it. Visualizing a point in space just beyond this solar system, he triggered the wormhole jitter transition that had allowed them to survive their previous jump, hoping that this much shorter trip wouldn't punish them so badly.

As engines ripped a new hole in the space-time continuum, Raul wrapped himself and Jennifer within the stasis field. Then as the Rho Ship slipped across the threshold, their screams mingled in a bloody duet.

CHAPTER 7

In the two and a half weeks since the almost disastrous malfunction of the New Zealand MDS, Heather had worked around the clock to identify the causes of the failure, to correct the design, and to fix it. For the last several days and nights, she'd enlisted Mark's help in rebuilding faulty components, the two of them remotely manipulating the industrial 3-D printers and robots to build the redesigned parts and install them.

In preparation for this test, Heather had added some new fail-safe mechanisms within the MDS chamber itself. The first of these was a new breaker system that would mechanically disable the circuit if it didn't receive a confirmation code from Mark or Heather through its subspace receiver-transmitter. The second modification was to the robots they would be using to activate the system, shielding their circuitry from EMPs. The stray pulse shouldn't happen again, but it shouldn't have happened the first time either.

Heather had done her best to hide her increasingly worrisome visions from Mark, but he'd noticed. They were spread too thin, trying to do too many things at once, the kind of schedule that led to oversights and errors even for someone with their Altreian augmentations. Still, what choice did they have but to pick the highest-priority items from an unending to-do list and try to knock them out as quickly as possible?

Heather removed her SRT headset, leaned back in her command couch, and stretched her arms up over her head. Looking over at Mark, she caught him in the middle of a similar stretch and felt a smile warm her lips as he turned to look at her. They'd done it, crossed one more problem off the list. And this had been a big one.

"What do you know?" Mark asked, grinning. "We didn't blow up New Zealand."

"Miracles happen."

"How about letting me take you out for a celebratory dinner?"

"Steaks?"

"A couple of big, juicy ones. Maybe a nice Maine lobster too. Sea Market Grill?"

"Sold."

Heather replaced her headset in its compartment and slid off her command couch. Until Mark had started talking about food she hadn't realized how hungry she was, and the prospect of a date with her lover sounded pretty darn good. It had been a long time since they'd taken any time for themselves, too long. She savored the prospect of some music, a glass of wine, and a lovely meal in the lounge. But first she wanted to shower and slip into a little black dress that would put a hungry look into Mark's brown eyes.

The first sign of trouble came after they were both dressed and headed for their car. She'd anticipated this. Waiting for them in the security lobby when they stepped out of the elevator stood Jack Gregory, a less than pleased expression on his face.

"Going out?"

Mark grinned at him. "That's part of the plan."

"Without your security detail?"

"And that's the other part," Heather finished in a tone that made clear she wasn't in the mood to justify her decision.

Jack looked from one to the other, his gaze taking in Heather's black dress, her matching evening jacket, and Mark's slate-gray suit.

"We'll stay out of sight."

"No."

"Just me then."

"You and Janet take the night off," Mark said, opening his suit jacket just enough to reveal the holstered Glock. "We're not exactly helpless."

Heather knew Mark's last comment was unnecessary. Having trained and seen them in action, Jack was very familiar with how deadly they could be when the situation called for violence. And he was also aware of their periodic need to escape the security umbrella they tolerated most of the time. Whenever that need arose, the outcome wasn't negotiable. Jack didn't have to like it, but he did have to accept it.

Jack's brown eyes glittered with that strange reflection that sometimes filled his pupils. He nodded and stepped aside to let them pass.

The lobby doors slid open as the two approached, letting them step outside where their armored Mercedes waited beneath the curved building overhang. A gust of cold, mid-December wind swirled around them, and Heather hurried to slide into the passenger seat as Mark held the door open for her, a sweet, out-of-style courtesy. Heather accepted it graciously.

He climbed into the driver's seat, closed his door, and spoke the command that put the Mercedes in motion toward the Sea Market Grill. As they passed through the outer security gate, Heather felt a great weight had lifted from her shoulders.

For tonight at least, they were free.

● ○ ○

Freddy Hagerman entered his two-story Watergate East apartment, threw his overcoat in the general direction of the coatrack, and headed for the liquor cabinet, knowing all too well the magnitude of his failure. Despite using a variety of parliamentary maneuvers to keep the Senate in session well past midnight, he hadn't been able to round up enough votes to stop the action President Benton's Senate supporters would undertake tomorrow.

What had happened to this precious institution? The founders had intended it to be the deliberative body, populated by thoughtful people with the capacity to think and debate all aspects of important decisions rather than ramming through whatever the head of the executive branch wanted. That was especially true for international treaties.

But after bypassing the Foreign Relations Committee and with only two weeks of debate, the Senate leadership would submit the treaty that would cede U.S. sovereignty to the UFNS to a vote on the Senate floor. The lengthy session that had just ended left no doubt how that vote would turn out. Freddy wanted to cry. Instead, he filled a glass with clinking ice cubes, grabbed the almost-full bottle of single-malt Scotch, and carried both over to his leather reading chair.

He settled himself into it, filled the glass with the amber liquid, and leaned back to prop his artificial left leg on the footstool. For several seconds he just sat there, staring blankly at the dark television screen mounted on the opposite wall. Without taking a drink, he set the glass on the small table, hiked up his pants leg, and removed his walking leg and other shoe. His right foot hurt, but that was nothing compared to the throbbing from the stump of his left thigh.

Lifting his glass, he raised it to his lips, paused to inhale the strong scent of the whisky, and drained it, the ice-cold liquid leaving a trail of fire down his throat and into his gut. No doubt his ex-wives wouldn't approve of this kind of drinking. Holding that thought, he poured himself another.

The last night of American independence deserved no less.

● ○ ○

Jack Gregory awoke from a dream he could not quite remember. He had opened his eyes to the predawn darkness, deeply troubled. He felt certain the dream was connected to the Bolivian temple called Kalasasaya, the place where the Altreian entity known as Khal Teth had almost stolen his sanity. The place where Janet had once lost faith in him.

Beside him, Janet slept peacefully, one bare thigh dimly visible where it extended beyond the blankets. He rolled toward her, placing a hand softly on that thigh, not to wake her, just to enjoy the feel of her. All these years she'd been his partner. The first female to graduate Ranger School, she was the deadliest woman he'd ever met, one who loved the adrenaline rush of danger as much as he did.

He had never asked her to do it, but over these last several years, she had given up much of the fieldwork she loved in order to keep Robby safe. Her training had not suffered. She drove herself harder than ever. But he could see how her self-sacrifice wore on her. As he looked at her beautiful face, he hoped that she would soon realize that Robby was ready to be given a player's role in the mission Heather envisioned for him. Maybe then Janet could release the mama-bear role and take her life back.

Careful not to disturb Janet, he slipped from the bed, shrugged into his white Turkish bathrobe, and walked barefoot to the kitchen, his footsteps barely audible on the travertine tile floor. With a gentle swiping motion on the wall panel, he brought the lights up softly. Right now he wanted to sit in the great room with a steaming mug of coffee and let his subconscious mind bring the dream memory back to him.

Inserting a coffee pod into the single-cup brewer, Jack filled his mug, walked to the transparent titanium wall, and looked out toward the eastern horizon that was just beginning to show the first hints of dawn.

"Hi, Dad."

Hearing Robby's voice, Jack turned to see his son standing behind him wearing jeans, sneakers, and an orange T-shirt. Robby moved so silently that even Jack didn't hear him approach. No surprise, but Jack still found it disconcerting.

"Good morning." Jack smiled and hugged his son, who returned the embrace. "How'd you sleep?"

"Like a log."

The line was one of their running jokes. They both knew that Robby didn't sleep any more than logs did.

"You're worried about something." Robby's statement carried all the certainty of his enhanced perception and intellect. Jack didn't bother to dispute it.

"It was just a dream I can't remember. Bugs me."

Robby turned to look through the wall at the glow that tinged the distant clouds, standing beside his dad like a smaller man.

"Mom thinks I'm not ready for what's coming."

"She's a mama bear and she loves you."

Robby looked up at him with those remarkably bright eyes. "I'm getting stronger every day."

His words brought an involuntary shiver to Jack. He knew what Robby meant. The boy wasn't just getting stronger physically, he was getting better at everything, advancing at a pace that even Heather found startling. A week ago he'd beaten her at chess. Although he hadn't managed to do it again, the amazing feat had led Heather to whisper in Jack's ear, "He's ready."

Jack agreed with her assessment and soon Janet would too. Maybe she already did but was just too scared to admit it, even to herself. They both knew what that admission would mean—the end of childhood, that precious something that had been stolen from him and Janet very early in their own lives.

As Jack looked out at the red dawn, he couldn't escape the feeling that, very soon now, this world would be needing the exceptional talents his son had to offer.

● ○ ○

Jack Gregory's voice on the intercom brought Heather out of her yoga pose. Across the exercise room, she saw Mark lower the Olympic barbell onto its bench rest with a loud thump that shook the matted rubber floor.

"We've got a line of FBI vehicles coming through the main gate and three helicopter gunships circling overhead. Our gate guards have just been placed under arrest."

The vision that filled Heather's mind was a familiar one. Her response had no hesitation.

"Send the security staff outside to surrender, then seal the building and take your family down to the lower level."

"Janet is already on her way down there with Robby and Yachay. I'm coming for you two."

"No. Link up with Janet, Robby, and Yachay and wait for us down in the command center. Mark and I will be along shortly, just as we planned."

She heard the growl in Jack's voice. "You know I never liked that part of the plan."

"I know. See you in five minutes."

She heard the intercom go dead and knew that Jack had complied. Heather rose to her feet and met Mark at the door. As many times as she'd played out this scenario in her mind, she hadn't visualized the inevitable FBI raid happening this soon. Hopefully that would be the extent of what she got wrong. The probability calculations that flashed through her mind weren't reassuring.

Moving back to their bedroom, Heather shrugged into her shoulder holster as Mark did the same. Then, grabbing their go bags, they walked rapidly to the elevators. By the time they reached the first-floor security lobby, the first of the armored FBI vehicles screeched to a stop outside the headquarters' entrance. The Special Weapons and Tactics team formed an assault line along a transparent wall as other agents cuffed six security guards and hustled them into two vans.

Heather walked to the wall-mounted control panel and typed in the code that would play and repeat a video embedded on the outer surface of the headquarters dome. Her recorded voice thundered from an array of mounted speakers.

"Hello. As you probably know, I am Heather Smythe. My husband Mark and I welcome you to our Combinatorics Technology Corporation headquarters. Please put away your weapons, as they will not be needed. Our attorneys are on their way here to negotiate the terms of our surrender. We look forward to the opportunity to present our case before the American people."

The change that came over the entire FBI unit was startling to behold. One second they looked ready for an all-out assault and the next, the agents stood transfixed, staring up at the huge images of Heather, repeated in hundreds of twenty-foot-tall tiled displays, visible from all directions. The press helicopters were in for one hell of a show.

Unless the FBI had brought some heavy demolitions capability that she wasn't seeing right now, they weren't getting through the reinforced titanium walls and doors anytime soon.

"You done watching the spectacle?" Mark's voice brought her out of the vision she'd just slipped into.

"Yes," she said, turning toward the elevator that would take them down to the underground level. "Time to go."

As she watched Mark enter the appropriate code and then press his hand to the scanner, a premonition raised gooseflesh on her arms. Long before this new journey's end, they'd all be bathed in blood.

Three hundred feet belowground, Janet led Robby along the hallway that separated the CTC laboratories, training facilities, and command center from each other, thankful that, for once, he wasn't arguing with her. Dressed in jeans, boots, a black turtleneck, her utility vest, and a leather jacket, she had a Glock 17 holstered at the small of her back and a black Gerber Guardian dagger in an inverted sheath along her right side. She had placed six extra magazines in the pockets of her utility vest, with more in the canvas kit bag slung over her shoulder.

Yachay walked silently behind them in her traditional Quechuan attire, colorful clothing that Janet knew hid a Glock and one very large knife.

Just as they reached the door that barred entrance to the command center, Janet heard the echo of footsteps from behind and turned to see Jack jogging down the long hallway toward them, carrying a kit bag of his own.

"I take it you couldn't talk Heather out of it," she said.

"Had to try."

"It's those damn visions of hers."

"She's wasting time on theater."

Janet shrugged. "She's the best there is."

"No doubt about that. But this time she might be trying to see a little too deep into that crystal ball of hers."

Turning to the wall, Janet placed her palm on the scanner and waited two seconds before the door whisked open, allowing them entrance into the room that Heather and Mark had modeled after the Altreian starship's command bay. Janet stepped into the room, followed closely by Robby, Yachay, and Jack. The door slid closed behind them with a barely audible whisper.

Oddly enough, this room had no inherent functionality. The free-flowing beauty of its gently curving surfaces was designed to eliminate distraction from the senses while the users were connected with their headsets, be they the original Altreian variety or the earthly replicas.

Like their alien counterparts, these newer models had been encoded to link to only one of The Enhanced, as she'd come to think of Mark, Heather, and Robby. In fact, there was nothing of significant use to anyone other than The Enhanced in this entire underground facility. The supercomputers and data storage were all located in the secret New Zealand mine, remotely accessible through the subspace receiver-transmitter headsets that only The Enhanced could use. The labs and computer facilities on this level contained technologies that CTC had publicly released.

Until today, although he'd worked with Heather on equipment that emulated headset functionality, Robby had never been granted access to this room. Janet looked down at the joyous expression of wonder on her son's face and swallowed hard.

She'd dreaded this moment. The training wheels were coming off.

Robby walked directly to the fourth command couch, paused before it, and looked back at Jack and then at Janet.

"Can I?"

"Yes," she said, "but not the alien headset . . . not until Heather says."

With a smile, Robby triggered a hidden button on the armrest, opening the compartment that held the two headsets that were attuned to his mind. Taking out the topmost band, he slid it over his temples and settled onto the couch.

Janet wanted to tell him to take it slow, but the truth was, he'd been training for this moment for almost five years. He knew what the headsets did and how to use them. And since it wouldn't be easy for the feds to break through the graphene-laced titanium security doors to gain access to the underground level, they still had some time to let Robby get comfortable using the real thing.

Because shortly, they were all going to need a little bit of his talent.

:CHAPTER 8

This wormhole jump hadn't been nearly as bad as the last one. Jennifer had only counted a half dozen broken bones, all of them non-displaced fractures of her ribs, along with some deep bruises, the type of injuries the nanites in her blood healed with ease.

Raul had suffered the worst injury of this transition, a compound fracture to his left arm that had required Jennifer to re-break and set it after the healing process had already begun. His warm blood had splattered her face and into her mouth when she'd pulled the sharp shard of white bone to let it slip back beneath his muscle and skin. But it hadn't been the acrid taste and smell of her shipmate's blood that had made her gag. Raul's screams were the culprit behind that.

The blood had taught them something important. Raul's healing process had been much slower than the last time, a consequence of his having transferred a large percentage of his nanites to Jennifer. That meant that the little Rho Project nano-machines couldn't reproduce. That meant that each time a nanited person bled, he lost some of his healing ability. If she and Raul didn't want that to become an ever-increasing problem, they were going to have to make more of the nanite serum.

Since Dr. Stephenson had reverse engineered the Kasari nanites from those that had been injected into his blood the first time he'd stepped on the Rho Ship, creating more of the serum didn't pose a huge problem. Technically, Raul and Jennifer wouldn't even have to duplicate samples taken from their own blood. The Kasari nano-bot design details were all available within the portion of the neural net's data banks that Dr. Stephenson had never gained access to.

But that idea sent a shudder through Jennifer's body. As much as Dr. Stephenson's nanite formula creeped her out, it had undergone significant human testing, most recently on one Jennifer Smythe. God only knew what the Kasari version might do to them. There was no way she was willing to take that risk.

Unfortunately, Raul had come to the opposite conclusion and was being a real pain in the ass about it.

"Okay, that's it," Raul hissed as he finally managed to raise himself into the air with the stasis field. "I'm going to make some of the Kasari nanite serum."

"Like hell you are! For all we know, that stuff could affect our minds."

"You're being paranoid."

Jennifer felt her blood rising into her temples. She knew she should be more sympathetic to Raul's ongoing recovery, but this scared the crap out of her.

"Am I? Think about it. Dr. Stephenson was the first one who figured out how to open this ship. He came on board by himself. When he walked off, he was changed. A ruthless genius determined to fulfill the Kasari agenda. What do you think happened to him during that first visit?"

Raul laughed. "Now you're just dreaming shit up."

"Screw you."

Seeing the anger flash in Raul's human eye, she felt the tendrils of the stasis field close around her. Before it could tighten enough to hurt her, she thrust herself into his mind with savage force, pulling forth his most terrible memories, immersing them both in a series of horrific visions . . . a bedridden Raul wasting away with brain cancer, surrounded by his desperate and grieving parents . . . his agony as his father performed the illegal Rho Project nanite transfusion in the Rodriguez basement . . . Dr. Stephenson's scalpel digging out his right eyeball . . . the amputation of Raul's legs and the subsequent attachment of the grotesque umbilical cable to his lower spine.

Raul's anguished whimper accompanied the relaxation of the stasis field's grip on her. Five feet away, Raul lay on the floor of the command bay, having curled into a legless fetal ball as tears streamed down his cheek from his tightly shut human eye.

Jennifer collapsed to her knees, sick to her stomach, sick to her soul. *My God,* she thought, *I've become El Chupacabra.* She didn't try to deny it. She'd just used the same technique the vicious psychopath had tormented her with, and she'd used it on someone who was uniquely vulnerable, someone who had already suffered more than anyone should ever have to.

Scrambling across the floor to where Raul lay, Jennifer wrapped her arms around him and pressed her face to his, letting her tears wash his away. Too horrified by what she'd done to even attempt an apology, she just lay there with her body wrapped around him, letting her shaking sobs merge with his.

● ○ ○

Raul struggled to regain control of himself, to push away the mutant who'd just forced him to relive his life's worst moments. The shock of her intrusion had left him so weak that he couldn't even manage that. Even worse was the reason for his weakness. Despite his shame and embarrassment at having lost all self-respect in front of this woman, being wrapped in her arms as she wept atop him felt strangely wonderful.

God, what a pathetic loser he'd become.

Pulling himself together, Raul gathered the stasis field around him, carefully separating himself from Jennifer, and rose up into the air. Below him, Jennifer rose to her feet to stare up at him, her face still a mask of agony.

"Raul. I'm so sorry."

Gritting his teeth, Raul managed an answer. "I don't need your pity."

There it was again, the flash of anger in those dangerous eyes. Knowing what she was capable of, Raul knew he should tread carefully, but he just couldn't make himself do it.

"And I don't want your consolation," he continued.

"Fine," she practically spit the word at him. "Penance then."

Again he felt her enter his mind accompanied by a rising wave of panic that he momentarily misinterpreted as his. But as the ship dissolved around him, replaced by a filthy cell, he realized she had pulled him into her memories, opening herself in even more detail than she'd managed in her invasion of his mind.

● ○ ○

From her barred window, Jennifer watched the backslapping, laughing men below, several carrying rifles slung loosely across the crooks of their arms. From the look of the activity, preparations for some sort of celebration were well underway. Heavily laden workers moved back and forth, dropping off supplies and setting up tables and chairs beneath a large awning that had been erected between the wings of the hacienda-style mansion. A glance at the sky revealed the reason for their hurry. Rain was coming, and from the look of the thick clouds creeping down from the peaks of the surrounding mountains, it was going to be a gully washer.

She pulled back from the bars, the tears that had dripped from her cheeks leaving damp spots on the stone windowsill, precursors of the coming storm. She lingered for several moments, then stepped down from her perch atop the single bed, her eyes making a circuit of the tiny room that was barely large enough to hold the bed. A foul-smelling bucket occupied the farthest corner at the foot of the mattress, across from a heavy wooden door. Moving across the space separating the bed from the door, she twisted and pulled on the handle, but it was useless.

Backing into the corner farthest from the chamber pot, Jennifer slid to the floor, her hands rising to cover her face as sobs shook her body.

● ○ ○

The memory dissolved into a new one and Raul felt her desperation give way to unbearable panic. She had barely touched the mind of Eduardo Montenegro, the serial killer known as El Chupacabra, but what she felt there was beyond horrible. Something rubbed against her, sending her mind recoiling, struggling to find its way back to the light. She was so deep in shock that she'd lost the thread that could guide her back. She only knew that she had to get away from the horror she'd mentally embraced.

The thing touched her thoughts again and she retreated, scrambling ever deeper into the darkness, erecting barriers in her mind, wall after wall, each higher and thicker than the last. But instead of blocking the thing that pursued her, her panic seemed to feed the monster, drawing it onward like a beacon in the night.

Then a mental count began to tick down, starting at ten, and she knew that if she didn't find her way back to her own head by the time that count hit zero, she would be pulled into a madness from which there was no escape. El Chupacabra's mind was a blackness where unthinkable desires squirmed and wriggled, each of its tendrils seeking to pull her deeper into the abyss.

● ○ ○

Her terror reached a crescendo that broke their mental link and left Raul soaked with sweat, panting, his hands clamped so tightly into fists that his forearms cramped. He glanced down at Jennifer, who had sunk to her knees, her arms crossed tightly across her chest. In that moment he knew she had relived something she'd never mentioned to anyone else, something she'd buried deep in her psyche, something that held such terror she'd never before revisited it.

Now she'd shared that horror with him . . .

Thank you very much, Jennifer Smythe!

● ○ ○

Jennifer knelt motionless and numb, staring sightlessly down at the floor as the memory she'd spent so long burying wormed its way back through her mind. She knew that she needed to calm herself, that all she had to do was allow her perfect memory to replay the way she felt after deep meditation. She'd done it hundreds of times. So why couldn't she manage it now?

The memory of the things she'd seen and felt in El Chupacabra's mind doubled her over in violent heaves. She vomited her most recent MRE onto the gray metal floor. After the attack subsided, she pushed herself away from the mess, wiped her mouth with the back of her hand, and rolled over onto her back to stare up at the curved ceiling. She still felt sick, but lying on the cool floor seemed to help.

"You okay?"

Raul's voice shifted Jennifer's focus to him.

"Give me a minute and I'll let you know."

With a nod, he floated away to allow her some privacy. It was the taste of bile in her mouth that drove her to her feet. That and the god-awful smell. Right now she missed a toothbrush and a bath more than anything in the universe, so she made do, filled a cup with water, gargled, and spit the mouthful into the matter disrupter that also served as their garbage disposal. After draining the remainder of the cup, she opened an MRE packet and went for the twin white Chiclets chewing gum in its accessory packet.

The mess cleanup took her another ten minutes thanks to the piss-poor cleaning supplies that were available. Only after she finished scooping the last of the vomit into another empty MRE packet and wiping her hands with moist towelettes from more accessory packets had she realized that Raul could have easily accomplished all of this with the stasis field.

She would normally have been pissed off, but the physical labor, disgusting as it was, had finally cleared her head.

Turning toward Raul, she saw him watching her intently. Jennifer didn't need to invade his mind to know that he was in the midst of a vigorous mental debate. Not surprising. During the last half hour Jennifer had managed to thoroughly humiliate them both. He had to be wondering if she was a complete psychopath or just mostly crazy. If they were going to survive each other's company, she had to set some boundaries.

"Look," she began, "I know I was out of line earlier."

"Out of line? Is that it?"

"No, that's not it. And there's nothing I can say to take it back. But there's something I can do to keep it from happening again."

Raul raised his left eyebrow. "And what's that?"

Jennifer studied Raul, well aware that the offer she was considering would shift the balance of power aboard this starship. Then, taking a deep breath, she spoke the phrase that scared the crap out of her.

"I can teach you to block my mind."

:CHAPTER 9

For two weeks, the Rho Ship's gravity distortion drives propelled Jennifer and Raul back toward the planet they'd so ingloriously departed. From their current location, it would take the Rho Ship another six weeks to reach Scion.

Raul didn't know how it had happened, but in the days since Jennifer Smythe's core meltdown, they'd learned to work together. Not that the mind-blocking training was going well . . . it wasn't. Jennifer Smythe was indeed trying to train him and he was getting gradually better. But the power of her mind seemed astronomical.

Even though she'd told him that it had taken weeks of practice for the altered trio to learn how to block each other's minds, that hadn't provided much encouragement. If it was that hard for them, with their Altreian alterations, how could he hope to master the technique?

The duo had spent two hours of every day in practice sessions that had turned his brain into bread pudding. If it hadn't been augmented by the Rho Ship's neural net and protected by nanites, he was quite sure that his head would have exploded. If this were piano lessons, so far he'd barely mastered "Chopsticks."

Fortunately he and Jennifer had made excellent progress in other areas. First of all, they'd formulated a plan, one which relied equally on Jennifer's familiarity with Altreian subspace technology and Raul's ability to control the Rho Ship's neural net, nano-particle manufacturing, and stasis field generators. Just as importantly, they had prioritized tasks and established a project timeline, although it felt more like a ticking clock than a plan.

Since water was readily available in the solar system, the need for food drove their planning. The tricky part was figuring out a way of getting down to the planet's surface without being detected by any of the inhabitants or their new Kasari bedfellows. The Rho Ship had its gravity distortion cloak and a means of optical cloaking that made it very difficult to see from more than a few feet away, but it was Kasari technology and couldn't be counted on to work against its creators.

Of course Jennifer had come up with an idea. While they couldn't build something as massive as the Altreian starship's subspace engines, they could certainly recreate the SRTs that Jennifer had built with Heather and Mark. With some modifications to that design, also scaled up both in size and power, the Rho Ship could be wrapped in a subspace field. The modifications wouldn't give them warp capabilities, but theoretically, the changes should make the ship undetectable to technologies not based upon Altreian physics.

Raul pulled himself out of his thoughts and looked over at the spot where Jennifer sat cross-legged in the middle of the floor, her eyes closed as if in deep meditation. But he knew she wasn't. Everything she'd read, indeed everything that Jennifer had experienced since she'd been altered by the Altreian headset, was stored in her eidetic memory. That included all the information she'd gleaned from her study of the Altreian starship's data banks.

She was in the final phases of putting together the initial design for the subspace field generator. Once she was satisfied with her mental diagrams, she would pass it to his mind and Raul would relay the visualization to the Rho Ship's neural net. Then it would begin the process of growing the subspace field generator from the nano-particles. As familiar as he'd become with the Kasari manufacturing technology, it still felt fantastic . . . additive manufacturing taken to the outer limits.

At its core, the system relied on the Rho Ship's MDS to produce elements the molecular assembler needed during the production process. The MDS would use the electromagnetic energy from the disrupter to generate a standing-wave packet, like a musical chord. Each unique chord created a different type of matter.

The process could be broken down into discrete steps: feed matter to the disrupter, analyze the wave packets contained, add disrupting frequency sets, harvest the released energy, and then generate a new frequency set to form the desired element. Alchemy at its finest.

Although the nano-manufacturing process was amazing, it wasn't fast. Complicated systems could take days or weeks to create, which was why Jennifer was spending extra time breaking down the overall design of the subspace generator into replaceable components in case a specific part malfunctioned. The goal was to avoid regrowing the whole contraption.

Suddenly Raul felt Jennifer's mind touch his. On a whim, he focused his thoughts in an attempt to block her out. For a heady moment, he succeeded, to the point that he actually felt her surprise. Then she swept his resistance aside.

"Raul!" her mental voice said. "That was outstanding."

The unexpected compliment made his head spin, his feelings so obvious that she smiled. Raul cleared his throat, mortified to find himself grinning like a dog that had just had its head patted. Not trusting his voice, he stuck with the thought conversation.

"Thanks."

"Are you ready for me to transfer the design?"

"Anytime you are."

When the design appeared in his mind, he marveled at its detail, rotating the three-dimensional diagrams for each component in his head as the neural net absorbed them. When assembled, the subspace field generator would be about the size of a refrigerator-freezer, with an external interface to the primary matter disrupter in the engineering bay. But before they went whole hog, they decided to build a one-third-scale model to test that could be contained in a stasis field and that, hopefully, wouldn't blow a hole in their starship.

"How long will it take to build and assemble?" Jennifer asked.

Raul let the answer come to him. "Three days for the scale model. Once we have that working properly, another twenty-seven days to build and install the full-sized subspace field generator. The big question is how many iterations it will take us to work out any kinks in the scale model."

"I wish we had Heather here."

"You and me both."

She frowned and then, recognizing the irony in Raul's attempted humor, managed a slight smile and a nod, as if to say, *Okay, you got me.*

Rising to her feet, she rubbed her palms together. "Let's get started. This thing won't build itself."

"Actually, it will."

Jennifer just shook her head and turned to walk away.

"Where you going?" he asked.

"I'm hungry. If you care to join me at Chez MRE, I suggest you get those micro-bots of yours off their lazy little asses."

● ○ ○

While she waited for the scale model to be completed, Jennifer had come up with a new idea. She thought that, instead of just using the nano-manufacturing process to build machines, it should also be possible to combine elements into generally useful molecules such as water. Unfortunately, the modifications required time for design, manufacture, and testing, time that they just didn't have right now, not if they were going to accomplish all of the higher priority tasks on their "I Want to Survive" list. Still, she roughed out the initial design and had Raul store it in the ship's data banks for later refinement.

The sight of Raul's mechanical eye swiveling toward the command bay's exit startled her out of her thoughts. She wasn't sure she'd ever get used to the unsightly appendage's odd behavior.

"The scale model's finished," Raul said, turning toward the door. "I'll bring it to us."

"Don't. If something goes wrong on this first test, I'd rather have it happen inside one of the central compartments instead of inside the command or engineering bay."

"I don't see why. The stasis field bubble I'll put around the model could contain a nuclear detonation."

Jennifer squinted at him. Why the hell did he have to argue everything with her?

"Doesn't mean it'll contain a subspace field. Subspace exists between the grains of Dr. Stephenson's ether, the grains of space-time itself. You can think of it as a new set of dimensions with its own physical laws."

"So?"

"So the speed of waves in subspace is much faster than the speed of light. It's why Altreian starships shift into subspace, where they can travel faster-than-light speed to their destination before shifting back into our space. We're going to try to create a similar shift. If everything works right, the scale model will wink out of existence and then reappear a few seconds later when its super-capacitor runs out of energy."

"You know the Rho Ship's moving, right? After the scale model shifts into subspace, we'll be long gone when it shifts back."

"Not according to Altreian physics," Jennifer said. "Think of space-time as having muscle memory. When an object shifts into subspace, it's as if our universe remembers it . . . its mass, its momentum, every-thing. If the shifted object doesn't do something like engage subspace drives to change its state within subspace, then it will reappear precisely where it would have ended up if it had never shifted."

"That's just weird."

"Says someone who uses a Kasari neural net to build machines from nano-materials. Not to mention the whole traveling-through-wormholes thing. We passed weird a long time ago."

Her words pulled a melodic chuckle from Raul's lips and he nodded. "You got that right."

Jennifer touched Raul's mind and this time he didn't resist, focus-ing a half-dozen worm fibers on the subspace field generator. The oblong, two-foot-high object rested inside the compartment where it had been built, undergone component testing, and assembled. Unlike the full-scale device that would have a direct connection to the primary matter disrupter, this small model needed its own temporary power source since it wouldn't be taking the rest of the ship along on its inter-dimensional shift.

The scale model had been extensively instrumented to record everything that would happen during the test. If the Rho Ship's neural net detected any anomalous readings from the subspace field generator as it ramped up, it would immediately disconnect the device from its capacitor, aborting the test.

If the test succeeded, Jennifer and Raul would review all the col-lected data to determine whether the power consumption matched what her theory predicted. Just as importantly, they needed to make sure nothing happened that would kill them.

"So," Jennifer asked, "you ready to try this?"

"Let's do it."

Feeling her pulse quicken, Jennifer pulled forth the memory that shifted her heart rate to its normal fifty-three beats per minute. The subspace field gently raised the scale model three feet in the air and then wrapped it inside the invisible bubble that Raul insisted on creating despite Jennifer's earlier argument. Fine. It wouldn't hurt to indulge him.

Heard via the worm fibers that terminated inside the stasis bubble, the bang that accompanied the scale model's disappearance made her jump. It made sense. An object with a volume of slightly more than eight cubic feet had just winked out of existence and the air within the bubble had expanded to fill the empty space. Micro-thunder.

When thirty seconds passed without the scale model reappearing, Jennifer felt the tension increase in her shoulders. Thirty seconds after that, she found herself pacing.

"You still sure about that muscle-memory theory?" Raul asked.

"It's not my theory. And, yes, I'm sure about it."

She hoped her voice didn't communicate the doubts that had begun to nibble at her mind. Whether or not it did, her gasp of relief when the subspace field generator popped back into the stasis bubble gave the lie to her professed confidence.

"Thank God."

She heard Raul's laugh but ignored it.

"All right," she said, clapping him smartly on the back. "On to the next problem."

●　○　○

General Dgarra moved along the front line of his Northern Battle Group. He ignored the bitter wind that howled down from the glacier-covered mountain peaks, savoring the sense of pride that his warriors, both male and female, inspired in him.

The Koranthian Empire carved a clawlike swath across most of the southeastern quarter of the Scion super-continent, from the Great Ocean in the north to the Briny Sea at its southernmost boundary. All in all, its borders touched three of Scion's six inland seas and the Great Ocean that covered half of the world.

Theirs was a harsh land that had spawned a harsh people. Rugged mountains were routinely buffeted by extreme winds and weather. Members of the winged Eadric race dared not enter this region of peaks and valleys, not even in their flying war machines. Their new off-world allies were another matter altogether.

Luckily, in the few months since the idiot Eadric Nation Alliance had finished building the world gate, the Kasari had played their hand very cautiously, proclaiming that they had come here to help and wanted only to be accepted as friends and allies. General Dgarra was well versed in politics by other means—namely, war. Open with the art of diplomatic seduction, and only after that effort has resulted in the assimilation of the willing do you move on to the art of war, now facing a much weakened foe.

To be sure, there were some within the Eadric camp who were attempting to mount an organized resistance movement, but these groups had been successfully marginalized and were too weak to form a credible threat. That could not be said of the Koranthians.

Trained to be warriors from birth, Koranthians were forged for battle. Daily they contended with the elements, and since the Koranthian Empire encompassed less than a third of the landmass and an even smaller percentage of the total population, they had to fight the Eadric Nations just to maintain their independence.

Thanks to the thriving manufacturing centers in the deep caverns that honeycombed the Koranthian mountain range, their war technology was the equal of anything the Eadric Nation Alliance could throw at them. It didn't hurt that this vast warren of facilities was practically impervious to attack.

General Dgarra stepped out onto a narrow ledge that jutted out beyond the outpost carved into the steep slope below. Just beyond the distant foothills, the Eadric divisions had gathered in preparation for a coming assault, all in the hopes of gaining access to the tunnels that led to the northernmost manufacturing plants. It was folly, of course. Then again, the general's spies hadn't been able to tell him what the small company of Kasari who accompanied the Eadric were planning.

The freezing wind tugged at Dgarra, attempting to fling him from his perch, but he shifted his weight automatically to counter its pull. As he gazed out over the lowlands, a disquieting vision filled his mind. In past assaults, the Kasari had stayed clear of the fray, acting only as advisors.

This time things would be different.

● ○ ○

Sitting at her crude terminal, Jennifer worked on refinements to her latest design. Having tired of the necessity to link minds with Raul in order to transfer her schematics and associated instructions to the ship's computer, she'd convinced him to bump this latest project up on their list of things to accomplish prior to arrival at the alien planet.

It hadn't been easy. When she'd pointed out that it would be critical to maintain communications with the ship when she left to hunt and gather food, he'd argued for a simple modification to the SRT communications devices that the altered trio had made on Earth. He relented only after she pointed out that unless they implemented an SRT headset interface that would allow either of them to remotely connect to the neural net, he would still be trapped in the command bay. Still, he'd insisted on retaining the administrative authority to override her remote connections if he desired.

It was petty. Then again, this was Raul she was thinking about, and she really wanted the interface that the headsets could provide. To make it work, they would have to build three devices. First they needed to build a new shipboard interface to the neural net, with its own SRT circuits. Then they needed two headsets, one attuned to Jennifer's brain waves and the other to Raul's. And that meant more testing and tweaking.

The waiting was the most frustrating thing for Jennifer. It wasn't that the Rho Ship's molecular manufacturing system couldn't build more than one thing at a time. The problem was the complexity of the full-scale subspace field generator that it was currently building. If Raul diverted part of the nano-manufacturing capability to work on something else, he would introduce unacceptable delays in the completion of that critical system.

So here she sat, thinking, planning, and designing other things they were going to need and then uploading those designs into the neural net through Raul.

Raul's voice startled her out of her reverie. "I've detected an asteroid with water ice on the surface."

"How much?"

"Most of the surface is covered in it, several miles deep."

"Yes!" She stood up, held a hand high, and slapped palms with him, visions of stasis field bathtubs filling her head.

A broad grin spread across Raul's face and Jennifer realized that she wore a similar, idiotic expression. She didn't care.

"It'll take us two and a half hours to get there, but it looks like there are plenty of good spots where I can set us down."

"And then we start ice mining."

"Sort of like talking to you."

The twinkle in Raul's human eye took the sting out of the dig.

"Hilarious."

● ○ ○

The asteroid was large enough to classify as a small dwarf planet, a spheroid with so many holes punched through the surface ice that it reminded Jennifer of a sponge. In certain places impact craters had filled in to form frozen lakes that made excellent landing spots. Raul set the ship down gently near the center of one of these and, after draping the hatch with a stasis field to prevent depressurization, lowered the ramp.

Now, as Jennifer watched Raul manipulate multiple stasis field tendrils to carve out chunks of ice and float them back into the ship for storage, a sudden realization kicked her in the head. All this time she'd been mystified as to how a ship capable of producing a variety of atmospheric mixtures didn't have a water recycling system, one more of the critical items they'd added to their to-build list. But watching those chunks of ice being collected in a water storage bubble, the answer became clear.

The ship didn't have a water recycling system because it didn't need one. A stasis field formed the perfect water recycler. Impure water could be forced through a stasis field membrane with micro-perforations that would allow water molecules to pass through sans contaminants. All they had to do was fill a stasis bubble with dirty water, generate the membrane, and force the liquid from one end of the bubble toward the other until all the contaminants had been strained. That material could then be fed to the matter disrupter for conversion to energy.

Jennifer hissed.

Apparently, being hammered into pieces by two wormhole transits and an ongoing struggle for survival hadn't been conducive to clear thinking.

Or maybe she was just an idiot.

Oh well, it wouldn't hurt to have a good supply of extra water. But that wasn't what troubled her so deeply. She wondered what other obvious solutions she had failed to consider. For the thousandth time she found herself missing Heather, Mark, and her mom and dad, knowing that it was a feeling she had the rest of her life to get used to.

●   ○   ○

The day of reckoning had finally come. Raul should have felt brave or resolute or determined, but all he really felt was afraid. And though Jennifer's face didn't show it, he was pretty sure that she felt the same way.

With all they'd accomplished in the last few weeks, they should have at least been experiencing some pride. After all, they had completed the full-scale subspace field generator and had survived its initial test. They had an abundant water supply and had managed to get the SRT headsets working, even though Raul's had taken several tries. They had even built two Kasari disrupter pistols based upon information contained in the Rho Ship's data banks, although they hadn't been bold enough to test them on board the ship.

Now they coasted through subspace toward Scion. Even though their destination had slightly less mass than their home world, Jennifer had adjusted the shipboard gravity to three times Earth normal in order to super-train her muscles prior to landing.

Raul had to give Jennifer credit for her understanding of the Altreian subspace physics model. The first five of her six rules of subspace transition, the only ones they had been able to test, had all checked out. And since those six rules had been uploaded to the Rho Ship's neural net, he knew the list by heart.

1. *The speed of subspace waves is orders of magnitude greater than the speed of light.*
2. *Anything contained within a subspace field is shifted into subspace but retains its previous rate of time's passage.*
3. *Anything shifted into subspace will retain its previous nor-*

mal-space momentum vector upon transition back to normal-space.

4. No normal-space force can act upon an object in subspace.

5. If an object in subspace is not acted upon by a subspace force, it will return to normal-space at the location where its previous momentum vector would have taken it.

6. If an object in subspace is acted upon by a subspace force, such as a subspace drive, it will return to normal-space at an entirely new location, but retain its original, normal-space momentum vector.

That meant they just had to accelerate to a desired velocity, shift into subspace, wait long enough to reach their intended destination, then shift back into normal-space for maneuvering. They could short-cut the trip by going directly toward their target, thereby ignoring obstacles such as planets or gravitational forces. They would be limited to sub-light speeds because they didn't know how to accelerate while in subspace, but it was still a cool way to travel.

His thoughts turned to their current situation. Very soon now, the Rho Ship would shift back into normal-space in order to decelerate for landing on the planet's surface. For this last portion of the journey they would be forced to rely on the Kasari cloaking mechanisms to keep the aliens from locating them. That was okay. The Kasari couldn't determine the Rho Ship's location, nor could they invoke an override command that would launch the vessel through another wormhole. At least he hoped not.

Raul turned to look at the freshly bathed Jennifer Smythe. She'd just returned from a stasis field bathtub she'd partially filled with water, looking and smelling much more like a goddess than the bloody and bedraggled beauty he'd grown used to during their first several weeks together. Using her new headset interface to the neural net, she'd also transformed a stasis bubble into a small washing machine that had done a respectable job of cleaning, wringing out, and pressing her clothes.

During the months Raul had spent on this ship, he had always washed his clothes by hand. Yet another obvious idea that had never occurred to him probably because he'd spent too much time hating Dr. Stephenson and feeling sorry for himself.

Raul felt a slight shudder as the Rho Ship transitioned back into normal-space and the gravity distortion engines came back online. The image of the colorful blue world they were rapidly approaching formed in his mind, triggering an electric thrill.

Assuming that anything on that damn planet was edible, they'd soon have full bellies for the first time in weeks. And the food wouldn't come wrapped in army-green plastic.

With any luck at all, it would taste just like chicken.

● ○ ○

With her mind linked to the neural net through her new SRT headset, Jennifer studied the sensor data, forming it into a live 3-D display as if she stood at the center of a clear stasis bubble looking directly out into space. As the Rho Ship entered its temporary orbit around the beautiful planet, her heart hammered her chest, energized by adrenaline. Jennifer didn't try to fight the excitement. For the moment, she felt more alive than at any point since she'd left Earth.

After studying the maps they'd made on the initial survey of Scion, she and Raul had finally agreed on a landing spot—a meadow near a secluded mountain lake, located in the rugged regional home of Scion's wingless warrior species. The two had also agreed to use only the passive sensors until just before they left orbit to begin their descent. One thing the last visit to this planet had taught them was that extensive use of the worm-fiber viewers could attract the wrong kind of attention.

But the time for that type of caution had ended. It was critical that they confirm that no members of any intelligent alien species lingered anywhere near the place where they planned to touch down minutes from now.

Jennifer felt Raul activate a single worm fiber, its far end opening a few dozen feet above that distant meadow. A soft gasp escaped her lips at the beauty of the evening setting. Jagged, snowcapped peaks cupped the small lake whose waters splashed gently against the shore. The meadow floor was covered in a mix of green, grasslike vegetation and abundant purple and red flowers that swayed in a strong breeze.

Surrounding this idyllic space, green-leafed trees climbed up the slopes of the mountains and pushed against the lake's edge, some even extending out into the water. They reminded Jennifer of the huge banyan trees she'd seen in Lahaina, Maui, with wide spreading branches that dropped prop roots down to the ground for support and nourishment. Many of these supporting roots had grown so large that they were indistinguishable from the main trunk of the parent tree.

As she looked more closely, Jennifer realized that the notion of a parent tree might not apply in this dense forest, with larger branches becoming part of adjacent trees to form an interconnected landscape.

A flash of movement caught her attention, a rapid shadow that was almost ghostlike in the dark forest. Soon she noticed other animals of various shapes and sizes moving through the undergrowth as birds gathered on the tree branches in anticipation of the coming night. Every single bird she spotted seemed to be midnight black. For some reason, the combination of the congealing shadows beneath the trees, the darkening sky, and the thousands of black birds made her jumpy.

On the positive side, there was no sign of the people who dominated this eastern interior section of the super-continent.

"It looks like we're a go," Raul said.

"Okay. Take us down."

The vessel's gravity distortion engines kicked in, starting their descent with a smooth deceleration. Unlike the return to Earth of NASA spacecraft, the Rho Ship wouldn't make use of air braking. It didn't need to and the shipmates certainly didn't want to leave that kind of heat signature.

Instead, the Rho Ship settled into the atmosphere more smoothly than Jennifer had imagined possible, any turbulence completely damped by the vessel's internal gravitational field. The process reminded her of coming down in a hot air balloon, despite the fact that this descent was a hell of a lot faster. She checked their speed and was surprised to discover that they had entered the atmosphere at a subsonic velocity. Jennifer had known that was the plan, but the internal acceleration damping had fooled her senses.

As they'd observed during their previous visit, the atmosphere was a breathable mix of nitrogen, oxygen, and other trace elements. The air was a bit heavy on oxygen concentration but not to the extent that it was toxic. She wasn't sure what kind of pathogens she might encounter, for which she had no natural immunity, but she doubted that it would be anything that the nanites in her bloodstream couldn't handle.

With the glorious purple sunset giving way to twilight, the Rho Ship settled to rest three feet above the meadow, it's electro-optical cloaking making it invisible from more than a dozen feet away.

Jennifer heard Raul exhale and realized that she'd also been holding her breath, evidently for quite a while. She released it and smiled at him.

"Good landing."

Raul inclined his head slightly. "Thanks. I guess it's about time for you to suit up."

Jennifer shook her head. "Not yet."

Although she'd made a tough but flexible nano-material tactical suit and boots, all black, she didn't have any desire to make her first outing into the depths of the alien night. Whether or not her enhanced eyesight could make her functional didn't matter. Unless they got desperate, she'd wait for morning. Since this planet had a twenty-hour rotation period, that meant she'd have about ten hours to prepare.

Raul looked at her, a wry smile on his face.

"Scared of the dark, eh?"

The small jab irked her.

"Don't let me stop you if you're so anxious."

His smile faded.

"I guess it won't hurt to spend a few hours collecting sensor data first."

"That's what I thought."

With a grin of her own, Jennifer sat down on the floor, crossed her legs, and dropped into the meditation that she hoped would prepare her for whatever awaited. By morning she'd be as ready as she was going to be.

● ○ ○

Dawn brought with it a beauty that left Jennifer speechless. Slightly larger than Earth's sun, Scion's had a bit more orange to it. Morning rays painted the mist on the lake's surface. Higher in the sky, two of Scion's three moons hung above the scene, the white one twice as large as its redheaded sister.

A sudden need to get outside the Rho Ship and directly experience this glorious morning overwhelmed her.

"Lower the ramp," she told Raul and headed for the door into the central bay.

Her long strides carried her form rapidly along the hallway that led to the exit ramp, as the SRT headset assured her that Raul hadn't hesitated to act on her request. The smell of air welcomed her to the exit hatch, that and the sharp morning chill. It wasn't an Earth scent but it was wonderful nonetheless, the pungent smell of vegetation carried on oxygen-enriched, pure mountain air.

Jennifer paused at the top of the ramp, in awe at the sight that spread out before her, the unfiltered view even more beautiful than what she'd observed through the ship's sensors. The high-altitude dawn spread a soft peach glow across the landscape, a glow that even tinged the snow-covered peaks. Off to her right, a few puffy clouds hung low in the west, but she saw nothing that threatened to mar this beautiful day.

A new day on a new world. The enormity of that realization stunned her. She filled her lungs with a deep breath. When she exhaled, the cold air turned it into a misty plume that confirmed the near-freezing temperature.

Jennifer walked to the bottom of the ramp and knelt to examine the vegetation covering the meadow. Up close, it wasn't grasslike at all. She removed the glove from her right hand and plucked a green, waxy stem that sprouted small elliptical leaves. They reminded her of California ice plants in texture and appearance, although these leaves were rounder.

"What's the matter?" Raul's concerned thoughts touched hers.

"It's beautiful."

"Yeah. So is a Venus flytrap."

Jennifer straightened. Raul was a major buzz kill, but he had a point.

Her hand went involuntarily to the hilt of her carbon-fiber belt knife and lingered as she scanned the surrounding forest. The birds were gone and from this vantage point she couldn't see any sign of the animals she'd glimpsed through the ship's sensors. She would have liked to do a short-range active sensor scan but didn't dare, lest she give their location away.

Then she saw them, a group of midsized animals gathered at the edge of the lake in another clearing a half mile from where she now stood, their heads dipped down to the water. Accessing the neural net, Jennifer focused an optical sensor on that spot and zoomed in.

If she discounted the wings, the brown and white creatures bore a pronounced resemblance to small antelope.

"At least they're antelope and not pigs," Raul said. "Not sure I could deal with that."

Jennifer laughed. There it was again, that razor-sharp wit that had begun to emerge from the darkness inside Raul.

A sudden splash turned her head toward the center of the lake. About twenty yards off shore, ripples rolled outward from a central point. Closer to the shoreline, a two-foot-long, eel-like creature leaped above the surface, caught a large insect, and splashed back into the water.

Jennifer walked rapidly to the shoreline nearest the spot where the eel-fish had jumped into the air. She knelt down, dipped her right hand into the icy water, and scooped some to her lips, swishing it around in her mouth without swallowing. Cold and good. But the thought that it might be loaded with microscopic amoeba or other harmful parasites caused her to spit it out. They'd have to run some tests to be sure.

Looking out into the deeper water, she saw the shadows of moving fish, or maybe it was more of the eels. She wondered if there might be meat-eaters lurking beneath the surface of that placid lake, or blood-sucking leeches.

Rising to her feet, she slipped her glove back on her hand, wiggling her fingers as she worked the warmth back into them, the pins-and-needles feeling reminding her just how cold the water was.

A new idea came to her. If the eel-fish were edible, she and Raul could gather all the food they needed right here. And she wouldn't even have to make a fishing pole. They already had the best virtual net imaginable.

Turning away from the shore, she walked back to the ramp.

● ○ ○

Fishing. Raul hated fishing. From what he remembered of it as a child, it involved lots of boring waiting and biting flies. A successful day rewarded you with the glorious task of scaling and gutting the slimy things, followed by a meal that featured his least favorite food. This latest endeavor had only reinforced that view.

It wasn't that they weren't successful—far from it. Raul had generated a stasis field sieve consisting of a hollow hemispherical scoop that dipped into the lake and then allowed the water to drain out through thousands of quarter-sized holes. Their first dipper-full had netted dozens of fish, some of which were the eel-like species Jennifer had seen that morning. But there were others, some with disturbingly large and toothy maws, creatures that ruled out a Polar Bear Club plunge into the icy water.

Jennifer had selected a half dozen candidates for testing and had released the rest back into the lake. Now she knelt outside the ship, knife in hand, elbow deep in alien fish guts. Since his SRT headset gave Raul the ability to control the stasis field from outside the ship, he had floated out to observe.

Again she surprised him, not showing the slightest hint of squeamishness. The way she used the knife showed a military familiarity, almost a fondness for the weapon. And Raul had no doubt that in Jennifer's hands, it was much more of a weapon than a tool.

The breeze changed direction, carrying the smell to Raul, making him wrinkle his nose.

"God, those things stink."

She didn't look up from her work. "You get used to it."

"And you want me to put that in my mouth?"

"Not raw. As soon as I finish filleting these, I'm going to build a fire out here and cook them."

Raul felt the gag reflex begin in the back of his throat and barely managed to suppress it.

"You don't even have a pan."

"I'll use a metal sheet. But you're right. We're going to need to make some pots, pans, and eating utensils. We'll also need to start thinking about how we'll store and cook food on board the ship when we have to leave."

Even though he knew she was right, the thought of how these things would smell while cooking didn't make him look forward to doing it inside the ship.

Jennifer finished her work and returned to the ship to gather her cooking supplies. Raul floated in for a closer look at the fillets. Just as he'd expected, the meat had that unhealthy gray coloring characteristic of most Earth fish. The smell had attracted a growing cloud of insects and he shooed them away before creating a virtual bowl over the catch.

A rapidly moving shadow caused him to look up. High overhead, several large black birds circled like buzzards. Disconcerting, but it made sense that there would be carrion feeders on this world too.

Jennifer reappeared, followed by a floating collection of supplies that she lowered to the ground just beyond the ramp. He watched as she manipulated the stasis field, clearing away the ice plants to reveal the rocky soil beneath. Unfortunately there was nothing close at hand that looked like it would burn, and the edge of the woods lay just beyond the stasis field's maximum range. That meant Jennifer would have to gather firewood by hand, assuming those trees were actually made of wood, and carry them back within range.

She stood, checked the disrupter pistol in her utility vest's holster, and turned to Raul, those intense brown eyes studying him. He got the strong impression that she was wondering if she could trust him at her back.

"If something chases me out of those woods, be ready to raise the stasis field as soon as I'm back within range."

"I was planning on it."

"Just making sure."

It wasn't his intention to get into an argument, but he had to fight back a verbal response to her blatant lack of trust. When he nodded, she turned and strode rapidly toward the eastern woods. Something about how she moved robbed him of his anger. The way the black military garments conformed to her body augmented her air of confidence. Jennifer Smythe moved like a predator.

She was the sexiest damn thing he'd ever seen.

● ○ ○

Reaching the edge of the woods, Jennifer stopped. The contrast between the bright sunshine in the meadow and the oppressive darkness of the woods made her feel that she'd just stepped into a different world. Dark but not silent. High up in the multilayered canopy above her, things rustled and hooted. A low, guttural sound raised the small hairs on the back of her neck.

Thousands of thick roots hung from above like dangling vines, digging into the ground to support and nourish the thick horizontal branches that formed a great canopy. But as mutually supporting as this mighty wood was, there were deadfalls. Jennifer spotted several of these along the boundary where the trees met the meadow. The reason for the destruction was readily apparent.

Some of the mighty trees had been ripped out by the roots, leaving the branches that had connected them to their brethren splintered and broken. She didn't even want to think about the power of the storms that had done that.

Jennifer stilled herself to listen. The activity far above continued unabated, but nothing approached her. Shaking off her wariness, she moved to the nearest deadfall. The pile was huge, its dried-out branches forming an impenetrable barrier of heavy logs and sharp spikes. Grabbing the nearest, wrist-thick limb, she tugged hard, relieved that it snapped exactly like any dried-out stick on Earth would have.

She put her back into it and soon had a respectable pile ready to be carried into the meadow. That's when she heard a slight disturbance.

A large paw pressed into the spongy forest floor. Twenty feet to her left a creature the size of a black bear crouched on its belly in the undergrowth, its shoulders and haunches rippling with muscle beneath a dappled, greenish-gray coat. All resemblance to a bear ended at its head. Twin tusks jutted up on either side of a toothy maw built for rending. The beast's eyes were cold and black like a shark's, spearing her with deadly intent.

Jennifer moved faster than she'd ever moved before, as fast as Mark moved when he got angry. And right now she was pissed. She didn't need Jack's voice in her head yelling his mantra, but it was there.

If you're ambushed, get violent and kill the bastards.

As she whirled into motion, the beast launched itself at her. There was no time for drawing and firing the untested disrupter weapon. Whatever was about to happen, it would be by tooth and claw. And as her black blade filled her hand, she heard her rage-filled scream rip the cold, dank air.

Then time slowed to a crawl.

● ○ ○

Raul watched in horror as the monster launched itself at Jennifer. But as fast as that thing moved, Jennifer was faster, and she was in full-on attack mode. As the beast opened its unnaturally hinged jaws, Jennifer flung herself beneath it, driving her black blade up into the exposed throat, ripping a great gaping wound that drenched her in a fountain of black blood.

Mortally wounded, the creature bellowed and whipped its right paw at her. Again it missed. In a marvelous feat of strength and dexterity, she swung her body up the beast's left side, landing on the back of its neck. And as she did, the blade rose and fell, each blow targeting the area where the neck connected to the misshapen head.

The battle ended suddenly, leaving Raul breathless. As if its strings had been cut, the beast dropped straight down on its stomach, legs splayed limply on each side. Still she worked the black blade until the head itself came free. Only then did she climb off to stand over her kill.

Raul manipulated the neural net, zooming in for a tight view of her. She looked like an oilfield worker who had just struck a gusher. Except for one bare spot on the left side of her throat, she was covered in blood the color of tar.

In the distance a new sound rose up, very much like the bellow of the creature that lay at Jennifer's feet. This time it was the chorus of a pack in full cry.

Jennifer broke from the woods at a dead run as five of the animals closed in on her. Fast as she was, Raul saw at a glance that she wouldn't make it. Without hesitation, Raul drew his Kasari disrupter pistol, aimed, and fired, sending a blue-green beam crackling through the air over Jennifer's head and into the center of her densely packed pursuers.

One second the closest beast was a dozen feet behind her and the next it detonated, its spinning remnants hurling through the air along with the torn bodies of its two nearest running mates. The shock wave knocked Jennifer forward and she hit the ground and rolled, coming to rest on her back just inside the maximum range of the stasis field. Raul raised a shield just as the two surviving members of the pack leaped for her, bouncing off the invisible barrier with howls of rage and frustration. Wielding the stasis field like a multibladed scythe, he diced the animals into chunks of quivering meat that vented steam into the cold morning air.

Raul dropped Jennifer's shield-bubble and propelled himself to her side, expecting to find her unconscious or worse. However, as he got close, she rolled onto her stomach and crawled to her knees, although the effort pulled a gasp from her lips. She sank back into a seated position, raised her head, and looked at him.

"What the hell was that?"

"The disrupter pistol."

A slow grin spread across her face, white teeth appearing in a face covered in black goo.

"Successful test, then."

It was weak. Nevertheless, her attempt at humor sent a rush of relief through his body.

"You hurt?"

"Nothing the nanites can't fix. Just give me a couple of minutes and I'll be good as new."

Raul turned to look at the spot that had been the center of the disrupter blast. He wasn't sure what he'd expected when he'd squeezed the trigger, but this wasn't it. Christ, if those bear things had been a little closer to Jennifer, he might have killed her.

He looked down at the pistol he still held in his hand. It sure wasn't a close-quarters weapon. And they could rule out using it for hunting.

Oh well, he thought, returning the disrupter to its holster. *Looks like we just added more stuff to our to-build list.*

That list was getting longer by the minute.

● ○ ○

Although he would never allow his warriors to see it, General Dgarra was tired. Weeks of fending off probing attacks that grew ever more forceful had taken a toll on his forces, though not as much of a toll as he'd inflicted on his enemies. Still, the Eadric army continued to be reinforced with fresh troops whereas the Koranthian high command refused to send more warriors to the northern front. Despite all evidence to the contrary, the emperor was convinced that this ongoing combat was an Eadric feint and that the primary threat would come in the form of a pincer attack at the center of the Koranthian claw.

That narrow portion of the Koranthian Empire was an obvious target and therefore of great concern, exposed as it was to attack from the lands that lay to the east and west of the mountains. If the Eadric people and their Kasari masters could split the empire there, the entire southern portion would fall. But in this matter, Emperor Goltat and his top generals were wrong.

Accompanied by the distant booms of heavy weapons and the continuous howl of the wind, General Dgarra strode through the open tent flaps into his mobile command post. He shook his head. His failure to make a strong-enough case had brought them to the brink of disaster.

The approaching female captain drew his attention.

"Sir. Our long-range sensors have detected the signature of a Kasari disrupter weapon being fired."

"Where?" Dgarra asked, moving to the tripod-mounted display panel that showed the battle maps.

She pointed to a location that surprised Dgarra, a point to the southeast well behind his lines, near Thune Lake. The area was remote and of little strategic importance. So what the hell were the Kasari doing there?

"You're certain of this?"

The captain nodded. "It was a single discharge picked up by multiple sensors. The triangulation is precise." Dgarra felt his scowl deepen. Although the Kasari had thus far only accompanied the Eadric soldiers as advisors, they had occasionally used their weapons in self-defense. That had allowed Dgarra's forces to identify the unique electromagnetic signature the disrupter weapons produced. He had no choice but to check it out, even though he hated to pull assets away from the battlefront. Perhaps that was the point of this incursion. Something bothered him, though. Why would the Kasari directly involve themselves now? If revealed, this action could detract from their propaganda campaign that this was a war between native factions and not a Kasari invasion.

"What do we have that can give me a visual of Thune Lake?"

"There's an airborne combat reconnaissance aircraft just northeast of there, but it's got a high-priority tasking in support of Third Brigade."

"Re-task one of its visual sensors to give me a look at the spot where the disrupter blast was detected. Transfer sensor control to this headquarters. When that's done, stream the video to my display."

"Yes, sir."

It didn't take long. When the video appeared, General Dgarra stepped closer to the display, studying the unusual scene carefully. Two individuals occupied an empty clearing. One was a legless abomination, with a stalklike artificial eye and a clear skull that exposed his brain. And he was floating more than a body's length above the ground, suspended by some unseen force. A female sat on the ground nearby, covered in black filth.

Dgarra manipulated the sensor controls, scanning the surrounding area. There had been a fight here. Just within the edge of the woods, a dead brengal lay on the ground next to its severed head. Now he understood what covered the female. The animal's blood. Despite her small stature, she'd killed the beast in close combat. So why had it been necessary for someone to fire a disrupter weapon?

He scanned across the meadow toward the two Kasari aliens, then halted. What he'd originally mistaken for muddy ground was an assortment of dissected body parts that lay in black pools of their own fluids. He'd just answered his own question. Cave bears hunted in packs. When the female had killed the one, its pack mates had come for her and she, or her partner, had been forced to fire.

The female rose to her feet and began walking back toward the center of the meadow, accompanied by the floating half-man. Suddenly she began climbing up into the air as if she walked an invisible ramp.

Seconds later, she disappeared, swallowed by the air itself. She merely winked out of existence and shortly thereafter, so did the legless one.

Dgarra felt his hands clench and forced them to relax. What technology was this? He zoomed in on the spot where the two Kasari had disappeared. There was nothing there. Wait. Had he just seen a ripple in the air? He moved the camera slowly.

There it was again, the faintest of distortions, just a shimmer in the morning sunlight. But, for a moment, he'd seen the outline of something familiar. Its curves matched the robotic starship that had seduced the Eadric with its Kasari technologies. Only this one had a crew.

The general turned, his voice carrying all the power of his newfound desire.

"Send a raiding party. Tell the commander I want him to use absolute stealth. He can assume that the Kasari starship is heavily armed, so he should not approach it. The female has already ventured away from it, so she probably will again. When she does, I want her captured and brought back to me . . . alive."

The captain slapped her right fist to her chest in salute, and then turned and strode from the command post.

General Dgarra turned his attention back to the video and whispered the question that consumed him.

"What the hell are you doing here?"

:CHAPTER 10

Robby looked up as Mark and Heather entered the command center. Then he gasped. They looked old, late forties. Maybe fifty. And his neural augmentation verified that the lines in their faces weren't from makeup.

His mom was the first to comment on their appearance.

"Been a while since you two used that trick."

Mark nodded. "It's been a while since we've been on the run."

Then Robby remembered one of the things he'd learned in his training. Mark and Heather had such fine muscle control they could make those lines appear completely naturally. Once they had perfected a look, they stored it in their memories, making it available for immediate recall. Add some loose, older-people clothes to hide their athletic bodies, and a touch of gray to their hair, and they became different people.

Since they were still dressed in their workout clothes, it didn't quite work, but he knew that would change shortly.

They'd rehearsed this scenario dozens of times, although this was the first time Robby had been allowed into the real command center.

Today was the real deal. The thought of it made him quiver with excitement.

Heather walked to her command couch, placed the Altreian headset in her go bag, and put on her SRT headset. Immediately a curved section of the wall slid open, revealing shelves stacked with weapons, laptops, clothing, and an assortment of other tactical gear.

She walked to a wall safe and pressed her hand to the control panel. It opened to reveal several stacks of documents that he recognized, documents that represented new identities for everyone. Then Heather turned to Robby.

"I need Robby for a few minutes. Everyone else, gear up."

Robby noted a brief frown come and go from his mother's face, but she nodded and moved to the shelves, as did the others, including Yachay. When he shifted his gaze back to Heather, she smiled and pointed to his command couch.

"Put on your SRT headset and have a seat. Let's find out what you and your Eos can really do."

Robby sucked in a breath and slid onto the couch. *Finally!* Deep within his head, he felt Eos stir in anticipation.

● ○ ○

Heather watched Robby sit down on his command couch and then slid onto hers. Through their joint link to the supercomputer in New Zealand, she felt the boy's excitement, which was understandable. But it also worried her. Then again, lots of things about Robby worried her. Normally her savant mathematical and pattern-matching abilities enabled her to project the actions of those around her into the near future. But Robby was a blank slate, a disconcerting blind spot. It would have been nice to allow him a while longer to develop complete mastery of his abilities, but the world wasn't a nice place.

Right now she had a number of things that needed to be done in order to make their escape easier. While some of those could be accomplished while they were on the road, some just could not wait. She touched Robby's thoughts.

"Robby."

"Yes?"

"Just like we practiced, follow my lead. Until I tell you to do something, just watch."

"Got it."

She tried to feel her way deeper into his mind but, as usual, she found herself blocked by his Eos. While she might have been able to work her way past Eos's guard if the AI had been on its own, Robby's added resistance made that impossible. Perhaps that was a good thing. She hoped so.

Shifting her attention to what was happening aboveground, Heather accessed the sensor array. As she'd expected, the FBI had been temporarily stymied by their building's heavily plated exterior. Ramming the outer doors with one of their armored vehicles had dented CTC defenses but hadn't come close to creating a breach. That would require shaped charges.

The number of helicopters in the sky revealed that this morning's events had attracted the attention of all the Austin TV channels. No doubt those feeds were being echoed to the national media outlets.

It was time to change the recorded message playing on the outside of the building to something more newsworthy. She issued the command that replaced her image with a gigantic scene of the United States flag being folded into a triangle by a military funeral detail. Then, as "Taps" played in the background, an officer in dress blues and white gloves handed the flag to someone off camera and saluted. The camera panned back, revealing a four-armed alien accepting the flag, dropping it to the ground, and then grinding it beneath its boot, backdropped by the Stephenson Gateway.

Consider carefully where your leaders would lead you.

The message replayed itself over and over again, each time with a different nation's soldiers presenting a different flag.

"Are you ready, Robby?"

"Yes."

"Okay then, make it happen."

The sensation of Robby extending Eos's touch into the web was familiar, but vastly larger in scale than anything hinted at in their off-the-grid practice sessions. Suddenly the visions that her headset was projecting into her mind shifted. She found herself looking at a vast web of worldwide television feeds, well beyond anything she'd envisioned. The numbers continued to grow as Robby's AI penetrated more and more networks. He was taking control of every last feed and then transferring that control to her.

Heather felt a tremor work its way into her hands and balled her fists to keep the others from noticing.

She issued the command that replaced all those broadcasts with the video that now played on the exterior of the CTC headquarters. For several seconds, she watched as the clip spread through the television feeds before turning her attention back to Robby.

"Besides the FBI, who else is involved in this raid on us?"

Robby tilted his head slightly and once again Heather felt the AI slither through the net.

"The Joint Terrorism Task Force has the FBI and ICE here. It's being directly controlled from Washington, D.C."

Heather had expected this, and it meant one thing. Their lives had just gotten a hell of a lot easier. Thank God for centralized micromanagement.

"Can you take out their communications?"

She saw a grin spread across Robby's face. "Be happy to."

Again her headset vision shifted to the assembled law enforcement and antiterrorism units. For a moment it seemed that nothing had happened, but then people began exiting vehicles and gesturing in confusion. A particularly angry-looking official stepped out of the back of a black van and began yelling at some subordinates.

Heather had seen enough. Time to go. With a command directed through her headset, she opened the secret panel in the floor, revealing a staircase that led down to the escape tunnel. Waiting there were the electric vehicles that would carry them to safety.

New Zealand was calling, but they had an important stop to make along the way. She and her allies hadn't started this war, but she would do everything in her power to see that they didn't lose it.

● ○ ○

"What the hell just happened?"

NSA director Admiral Connie Mosby glared across the small conference table at the two most trusted members of her staff, her primary focus directed at Dr. Eileen Wu, the organization's chief computer scientist.

Eileen wasn't bothered by her boss's assertiveness, one of the traits that had enabled the slender black woman to rise to the pinnacle of a male-dominated profession. Although Eileen knew the answer to Admiral Mosby's question, not knowing how the hacker had done it bugged the hell out of the slender, twenty-six-year-old Caltech legend.

"Somebody just hacked television broadcasts around the world and then killed all communications between the Joint Terrorism Task Force."

"Why didn't we detect something like that in its early phases?"

"We did. The problem is that it all happened nearly simultaneously."

"How is that possible?"

"It's not. But it reminds me of something I've seen once before. As you may recall, a little more than seven years ago, your predecessor,

General Wilson, suffered an impossible attack on a wide range of secure systems with no physical connection to the Internet."

"You're talking about the attack on the Ice House interrogation facility."

"Yes, ma'am. We never figured out how it was accomplished, but there is one common factor with what just occurred. During that event, Heather McFarland, Mark Smythe, and Jennifer Smythe escaped from that supermax facility. Heather McFarland is now known as Heather Smythe, president and cofounder of CTC."

Admiral Mosby leaned back in her chair and nodded in understanding. "The same company that was raided this morning."

"Looks like we know who did it. But I haven't got a clue as to how they pulled it off."

Admiral Mosby shifted her gaze to Levi Elias. The analyst's curly salt-and-pepper hair framed a face like a hawk's. He was one of the few people who Eileen completely trusted.

"Okay, Levi. Has the JTTF got the Smythes in custody yet?"

"No. As far as I can tell, they haven't even gotten into the CTC headquarters building yet. Once they lost communications with D.C., they locked down the entire complex. Now they're waiting until someone at JTTF headquarters approves a course of action. When that happens, it might have to be sent by courier. Either that or the JTTF is going to have to put someone on the ground there in Austin who has the authority to make decisions."

Mosby snorted. "President Benton likes to sign off on those types of decisions."

"Which is exactly why everything out at the CTC complex is completely hosed and likely to stay that way for a while."

"Can we trace the hack back to its source?"

Levi shrugged. "I've got our entire cyber-warfare unit searching for the breach. But as soon as we make a little headway, something notices and we find our own systems being compromised."

The admiral looked at Eileen. "What about Big John?"

Eileen had been expecting that question. The massively parallel supercomputer known as Big John had only one purpose—to mine all available data on selected targets and then cross-correlate that data with all other available information. Big John's tendrils extended into everything.

The most amazing thing about Big John was that nobody comprehended exactly how it worked. The scientists who had designed the core network of processors understood the fundamentals: feed in sufficient information to uniquely identify a target and then allow Big John to scan all known information—financial transactions, medical records, jobs, photographs, DNA, fingerprints, known associates, acquaintances, and so on.

But that's where things shifted into another realm. Using the millions of processors at its disposal, Big John began sifting external information through its nodes, allowing individual neurons to apply weight to data that had no apparent relation to the target, each node making its own relevance and correlation calculations.

No person directed Big John's complex genetic algorithms that supplied shifting weights to its evolving neural patterns. Given enough time to study a problem, there was no practical limit to what Big John could accomplish. The retired Dr. Denise Jennings's software kernel had been inserted into antivirus programs protecting millions of computing devices around the world. And although those programs provided state-of-the-art antivirus protection, their main activity was node data analysis for Big John.

Big John was a bandwidth hog. No matter how big a data pipe fed it, Big John always needed more. Dr. Jennings's software had provided an elegant solution to that problem. Commercial antivirus programs scanned all data on protected devices, passing it through node analysis, adding their own weighting to the monstrous neural net. It didn't matter if some devices were turned off or even destroyed. If data nodes died, more and better processors constantly replaced them. In a strange way, the entire global network was Big John.

"Eileen?"

Hearing the irritation in the admiral's voice, she cleared her throat and refocused. "Sorry. Nothing yet. The attack doesn't seem to have a signature that is similar to anything he's seen before."

"He?"

Damn it. Eileen knew that she'd slipped into the subtle trap that Dr. Jennings had so often succumbed to, thinking of Big John as a person when it was just a neural net, albeit an incredibly large one. When she wasn't careful, that thought pattern wormed its way into her speech.

"I meant it's like nothing Big John's observed before."

Admiral Mosby paused, rubbing her chin with her right hand. When her eyes again met Eileen's, she asked the right question.

"And if the same hacker strikes again?"

Eileen smiled. "Everyone has a signature. If he strikes again, Big John will own him."

● ○ ○

Alexandr Prokorov walked down the long hallway toward his meeting with the East Asian People's Alliance, his face a mask that hid the emotions roiling beneath. The damn American bureaucracy could screw up a wet dream.

Ten hours! That's how long it had taken the JTTF to force their way into the CTC building. Only after wasting another day had they discovered the lower elevator shaft and broken through its defenses to gain entry to the secret underground level.

And what had they found belowground? Not a goddamn thing. Nothing worthwhile anyway. Some computers, some robots, a laboratory, and training facilities, including an underground shooting range.

But the only designs that the Americans had discovered were products for which the Smythes had already submitted patent applications.

Mark and Jennifer Smythe, along with Jack Gregory, Janet Price, and their son, had disappeared. And they hadn't escaped through the tunnel that ran to the CTC's Shipping Facility One.

Obviously there was another secret tunnel hidden somewhere inside the underground complex and the JTTF would eventually find it. But the highly skilled fugitives were already gone and Prokorov had no illusions that finding them would be easy.

In a cascade of incompetence, American law enforcement had emasculated his plan to implicate the Smythes in an international conspiracy. His ultimate goal was to shift the jurisdiction for their case to the International Court of Justice. That could still happen, but without having the targets under arrest, the gambit had failed in its primary purpose: to get control of the Smythes. They were still out there and, as their global propaganda telecast had so effectively demonstrated, they were a major threat.

Prokorov found the two officials from the EAPA Ministry of State Security waiting inside his private conference room. He leaned across the small conference table, shaking each of their hands and welcoming them to the Federation Security Service headquarters in fluent Mandarin. As they resumed their seats, Prokorov seated himself in the chair at the head of the table.

Prokorov didn't know the exact purpose of the EAPA visit, merely that it concerned yesterday's worldwide cyber-attack. Beyond that, Minister Tsao, the head of state security, had been unwilling to discuss the matter until they met in person.

Prokorov leaned forward, placing his elbows on the table and linking his fingers. Ignoring the two MSS bureau chiefs that accompanied Minister Tsao, he focused his gaze on the EAPA intel chief. Despite being in his mid-fifties, Tsao looked much younger, his body lean and fit. No trace of gray showed in the general's black hair and Prokorov knew that Tsao didn't color it. This man's intellect and drive reminded him of himself.

"So, Minister Tsao," Prokorov said, still in Mandarin, "what brings an official of your stature all the way from Beijing to The Hague?"

"Do you mind?" Tsao asked, nodding at his aide.

The taller man nodded, opened a case, and withdrew a device Prokorov recognized, a portable electronic bug scanner.

Prokorov nodded, his curiosity further aroused. "Please."

With practiced efficiency the man checked the room and returned to his seat without comment.

Tsao surprised Prokorov by standing up.

What the hell? Is he leaving?

Instead, the EAPA's master of spies leaned across the table and expertly spun a folder that slid to a stop in front of Prokorov.

"I'm here because we've seen something like this before."

Something in Tsao's voice bothered Prokorov. Something that bordered on fear. Shifting his attention to the folder, he flipped it open. Inside was a single eight-by-ten-inch photograph of a crystal sphere alongside a portion of a ruler to provide scale. A half inch in diameter, the orb was beautiful, refracting the light in a myriad of colors.

"What is it?"

Tsao sat back down and leaned back in his chair, his face an unreadable mask.

"It's called a holographic data sphere. It was invented a decade ago by the American medical device designer Steve Grange and is capable of storing more than a petabyte of data."

Prokorov had heard of Grange. The billionaire had been killed during an FBI raid on his Sonoma winery. There had been rumors of his involvement with the Chinese government in a scheme to transfer classified U.S. technology, but due to the total destruction of the facility, no proof was ever found.

"If it's been around that long, why haven't I heard of it?"

"Grange kept it a closely guarded secret. The device itself was of little importance, but what was stored on it could have changed everything. The knowledge of its contents was limited to a handful of people within my ministry. Until yesterday, I believed the data sphere had been destroyed when the Grange Castle burned down. Now I am not so sure."

"Why?"

Again he saw it, that flicker of fear that lurked just behind Tsao's eyes.

"Several key officials in my ministry, including myself, are convinced that yesterday's cyber-attack was conducted by an artificial intelligence. It was a tightly coordinated global assault that reacted aggressively to thwart all our efforts to counter it. No team of human hackers could have done it."

Prokorov felt his mouth go dry. He knew that the attack had mystified the NSA as well as his own Federation Security Service Cyber-Warfare Group, but the source of the hack was obvious.

"Wait. We know that Heather Smythe initiated the cyber-attack."

Tsao shook his head. "No. She ordered an AI to attack us all, just to warn us not to screw with her."

"And how do you know that?"

"As I mentioned, we've seen this before. Steve Grange copied a human mind onto a holographic data sphere like the one in that photograph, the mind of an NSA hacker named Jamal Glover. It was a true AI and it was faster than all of the NSA cyber-warriors combined, just as this latest attack was."

"Impossible. Even if the data sphere you mention wasn't destroyed, how would she gain access to it?"

Tsao's eyes narrowed. "Didn't she penetrate numerous secure NSA systems during her escape from the secret Fort Meade supermax prison?"

Prokorov rubbed his chin, considering this possibility. "So what are you proposing?"

"Since this is a matter that threatens the entire United Federation of Nation States, it seems logical to use our combined resources to deal with it. What would be considered an act of war if we acted alone falls well within the authority of the Federation Security Service. The first step seems obvious. Identify all those who had knowledge of Grange's holographic data sphere and find out where it is now and what secret research programs it has spawned. If we are to deal with the Smythes, we'd better learn the full extent of their stolen capabilities."

As much as he didn't want to believe it, Prokorov felt the conviction growing within him that Minister Tsao might be right. And if he was, the NSA had been playing some very dangerous games indeed.

Prokorov stood and shook hands with Tsao. "Thank you, Minister, for bringing this to my attention. I will look into it."

After Tsao and his aide departed, Prokorov stared down at the photograph of the beautiful little data sphere. *My God! Could it be?* If the Americans had recovered the Jamal Glover AI and kept it secret all these years, then they couldn't be trusted to cooperate in his investigation. Regardless, it was better to assume the worst.

Admiral Riles had been the NSA director back in those days and, though he was long dead, some of his trusted deputies would still be around. One of them could be made to talk. There was a weak link in every chain.

And Alexandr Prokorov would find it.

:CHAPTER 11

The noise in the Hart Senate Office Building's seventh-floor hallway gave an accurate indication of the intensity of feelings about the news that continued to roll out of Austin. Freddy Hagerman was sick of hearing it. There was no doubt in his mind that this was a politically motivated assault orchestrated by the Department of Homeland Security, the Department of Justice, and the Internal Revenue Service. The whole thing stank of the UFNS and its puppet, President Benton.

Freddy paused in his outer office, told his assistant that he didn't want any calls or visitors, walked into his private office, and shut the door. Sitting down at his desk, he swiveled his chair to stare sightlessly out the window. Christ, what a goddamn mess. The press had taken the whole bullshit story and run with it, big-time.

Allegedly, Mark and Heather Smythe, through CTC, had illegally conspired to transfer classified technologies and money to terrorist groups, with the goal of destabilizing the United Federation of Nation States of which the U.S. was now a full member. In a number of simultaneous raids, the Joint Terrorism Task Force seized all of the Smythe assets, including their extensive corporate holdings. Although there was currently no evidence directly linking the conspiracy with the Safe Earth movement, the Department of Justice, with the full support of the International Court of Justice, planned on interviewing over the coming days all of the group's leaders and supporters, both in the United States and abroad.

The only good news out of the whole situation was that Mark and Heather Smythe had escaped capture, no doubt aided by Jack Gregory and Janet Price.

The buzz of his office phone startled Freddy. He punched the button in irritation.

"Sorry to disturb you, Senator, but the attorney general is here demanding to talk to you."

"Demanding?"

"Yes, sir."

"Tell him to go screw himself. Wait. Send him in. I'll tell him myself."

Freddy knew the thin man with the rat's eyes well. Attorney General Carl Wescott had testified before the Senate Judiciary Committee that Freddy chaired only two months ago. He, like every one of President Benton's appointees, was a political hack and an all-around first-class prick.

"Good morning, Senator."

"What's so good about it?"

"Do you mind if I sit down?" Wescott asked, nodding toward the nearest leather chair.

"You won't be staying long enough to sit down."

The anger that crept into the attorney general's eyes gave Freddy his first good feeling of the day.

"Look, I can ask you my questions in the comfort of your office or I can subpoena you to testify in court."

"If you want to play that game, the Judiciary Committee might just have some questions for you. It could take several days."

Wescott's thin lips clamped into a straight line. "So you're refusing to cooperate with the investigation into the Smythe case?"

"No. I'm refusing to cooperate with your political charade . . . whatever you're calling this."

"Fine, Senator. I'll see you in court."

"Go screw yourself."

The attorney general hissed and, as he stalked out of the office, Freddy called after him.

"Oh, Carl, don't let the door hit you in the ass on your way out."

●　○　○

Daniil Alkaev walked off the corporate jetliner and entered John F. Kennedy International Airport accompanied by his four-person entourage. His gray suit fitted his six-foot-two-inch frame perfectly. At forty, with his short-cropped, receding brown hair, firm jaw, and green eyes, he looked the part of the Russian corporate dynamo that his new identity proclaimed him.

But Daniil had never pushed any papers across a corporate desktop or any other desktop for that matter. Neither had a single member of his hard-eyed, well-dressed team. But it was true that they had come to America on business, just not here in New York and not today. First they had preparations to make.

When they reached the parking garage, two cars were waiting, identical white Escalades parked side by side. Although he preferred black, white was far less threatening. As Daniil approached, the cars responded to commands from cell phone apps and unlocked themselves, obediently opening the rear hatches to receive luggage. Those two hatches rising in unison reminded Daniil of a Nazi salute. He almost expected to hear a rousing "Sieg Heil!" echo through the parking garage.

He climbed into the backseat of the second vehicle. After retrieving a case from the rear, Galina Anikin slid in beside him. His stern-faced second in command opened the case and passed around the guns and magazines that had been placed inside. For several seconds, the car was filled with the sound of magazines slamming home and rounds being chambered, which Daniil knew was also happening in the other vehicle. Then with a verbal command, Galina ordered the car to proceed to their destination.

Daniil settled back into the comfortable leather seat. The ride to D.C. would not be a short one.

● ○ ○

Jim "Tall Bear" Pino sat and stared out his office window at the snow-capped Mount Illimani, his raven-black hair hanging almost to his waist. The view really was beautiful, but he missed New Mexico. Still, sacrifices had to be made for the good of his community. And even though he was no longer president of the Native People's Alliance, he was the Navajo Nation's representative on the NPA council.

In the last few years, the organization had expanded far beyond his fondest dreams, now encompassing almost all of the tribes of the Western Hemisphere, from the Arctic Circle to Cape Horn. Unfortunately, as with all tribal alliances, this one came with its own squabbles and infighting. Nowhere was that more apparent than here at the NPA's headquarters in La Paz, Bolivia.

Landlocked Bolivia, with its checkered history of struggle and rebellion that predated the Incan Empire, had been chosen to host the NPA capital, in part because this was the seat of the Incan Empire. Bolivia had also been the first country to join the NPA.

The vast majority of the NPA consisted of tribal lands within the boundaries of other countries, just as in the United States. Unlike other nations, the U.S. government had allowed the tribes to formalize their independence without conflict. Not surprising. The government had far bigger problems on its hands.

Tall Bear stood, stretched, and walked out onto the second-floor balcony. The beautiful late December day welcomed him with all its summer splendor. At twelve thousand feet above sea level, La Paz didn't have the warmth of a New Mexico summer, but the sun felt good on his face.

When his cell phone vibrated in his pocket, Tall Bear was tempted to ignore it, but the voice from the other end made him glad he had not.

"Hello, Jim. How's politics treating you?"

The voice took him back to the days when he was just a cop on the Santa Clara Indian Reservation. The voice brought a grin to his face.

"Jack! I heard you were on the run."

"Still am."

"And Janet?"

"Right here beside me. Robby too."

"Damn, that's fine." A sudden worry wormed its way into Tall Bear's head. "Listen, Jack. Aren't you afraid someone might be listening in? This isn't a secure line."

"There's no such thing as a secure line . . . not anymore. But rest easy. No one can intercept this call."

The confidence in that voice brought back more memories of the most dangerous man Tall Bear had ever met.

"So what's this about?"

"I was just passing through and thought you might like to get together."

"What? You're not in La Paz."

"That's what the sign said."

Tall Bear laughed. "You're one crazy son of a bitch. You know that, don't you?"

"So I've been told."

"Tell me when and where and I'll be there."

Tall Bear walked back through the open French doors and sat down at his oak desk, grabbed a pen, and copied the directions onto a notepad.

"Nine o'clock tonight it is, then. You better have a cold beer waiting for me."

This time Jack laughed. "You got it."

The call ended and Tall Bear set his phone down on the desk. A sudden breeze swirled his hair about his shoulders and sent a shiver through his body. Or maybe it was the touch of the ghost who had just reentered his life.

Whatever the reason for tonight's rendezvous, he doubted it was purely social.

● ○ ○

The evening thunderstorm swept in from the west, necklaced with crawling bands of cloud-to-cloud lightning. Rain pelted the windows, driven by gusting winds that moaned through the rafters of the two-story house on the eastern outskirts of La Paz. It was a simple house of stone and mortar, with a high-peaked, red-tile roof that sluiced water into the gravel driveway. On a night such as this, the flames in the fireplace cast shadows that danced through the rafters, accompanied by the hiss and pop of the fire.

Tall Bear accepted a cold bottle of stout from Jack and leaned back on the couch to study the six other people seated in an arc in front of the fire. Only the Quechua woman who'd been introduced as Yachay was native, but in as good a makeup job as he'd ever seen, all of the rest were pulling off damn good imitations clad in traditional Quechua garb. Heather Smythe looked like she'd aged fifteen years. For that matter, so did Mark.

He found his eyes drawn to the boy, Robby. The eight-year-old could easily pass for thirteen and switched between Spanish, Quechuan, and Navajo while carrying off a native inflection in each language. His face shone with an aggressive intelligence that made Tall Bear oddly uncomfortable.

"So," Janet asked with a smile, "do we pass inspection?"

"You could fool me."

Heather Smythe leaned forward. "So I imagine you're wondering why we asked for this little get-together."

"At least you didn't say powwow."

Heather laughed, a musical sound that lit the room.

"And yes," Tall Bear continued, "you have aroused my curiosity."

The smile faded from her face. "I don't know what Jack has told you of my special talent. Let's just say I get . . . visions of what is to come. They don't mean that what I see is certain to happen, but instead what is likely to happen based on current circumstances and trends. At its most basic, it enables me to win at any casino game, even the electronic slots. I spot patterns.

"It works for patterns in the stock market or predicting what people around me are about to do. Naturally, this gets more difficult and less accurate the farther into the future I try to see, but macro-events betray themselves."

She paused for a moment but Tall Bear didn't interrupt her. A glance at Jack's and Janet's faces told him all he needed to know. They believed every word she was saying. He inhaled deeply and found himself rubbing his big hands together as if to restore circulation.

"My grandmother was a seer. Every once in a while I have felt a little touch of it in myself."

"As I've observed," Jack said. "Up close and personal."

"A war is coming," Heather said. "And it's a war we have very little hope of winning."

"You're talking about what will happen if those fools rebuild the Stephenson Gateway."

"That too. But even now the UFNS is gathering its forces for a preemptive strike against its perceived enemies. I think the Native People's Alliance will be among their early targets."

A loud pop from the fireplace hurled a glowing coal out onto the wood floor, coming to rest near Tall Bear's chair. For the briefest of moments, it looked like a bright, disembodied eye peering up at him through a knothole in the floor. Then he stood and ground it out with a size-fourteen cowboy boot. When he sat back down, he found his eyes drawn to that smudge on the floor.

Had it been an omen like the one that had led him to Jack and Janet in the northern New Mexico high country all those years ago? Sitting here in this dimly lit room as the summer thunderstorm raged outside these walls, it damn sure felt like one. And this meeting felt exactly like a war council.

Lifting his gaze to meet Heather's, Tall Bear asked the question that all this had been leading up to.

"Let's say that I believe you. Exactly what are you proposing?"

"An alliance."

As Tall Bear listened to the intense young woman lay out her vision, his conviction that she was right continued to grow. And as it did, the darkness within that vision drained the hope from his soul.

When she finished, Tall Bear drained the last of his beer. Setting the empty bottle on the coffee table, he nodded.

Tall Bear stood, grabbed his wide-brimmed black hat, and grinned. "I'm glad you're not asking for much. But I'll see what I can do."

After a round of warm handshakes and hugs, Jack walked him to the door. But as Tall Bear put on his hat and stepped out into the wet night, Jack added one more thing to his heavy plate.

"By the way, old friend, we'd like to get started by the end of next month."

Tall Bear just shook his head, turned, and walked back to his car through the pouring rain.

● ○ ○

Levi Elias knelt between the twin headstones, each of his two hands resting on a different marker. After a short time that felt like an eternity, he gently placed a dozen red roses before each marker.

An inscription had been etched into the gray marble of the right-most gravestone. Six simple lines.

Pamela Merideth Kromly

My Loving Wife and Best Friend

Long ago, I gave you my soul.

Take care of it for me,

until I find you again.

Garfield

Poetic and beautiful. It was typical of Garfield, although few had known that side of the hard-nosed CIA trainer.

Levi traced the letters of Pam's name, feeling the fine edges of the engraving. He had loved Pam with his heart and soul, but it was no wonder she'd chosen to marry his best friend who lay in the grave on her left. Now she and Garfield slept side by side, just as they'd lain together in life.

Even after Pam had made the choice that left Levi a brokenhearted bachelor, he had remained close with both of them. Cancer had taken her long before her time. And even though Garfield Kromly had followed Pam into the dark in one of the most horrible ways imaginable, Levi envied his old friend.

He blinked twice. Tears rolled unashamedly down his cheeks. He rose to his feet and looked around. Garfield had chosen the Fairfax Memorial Park as Pam's last resting place because of the cherry trees. On that April day when she'd been laid to rest, their lovely pink-and-white blossoms had been in full bloom. Now, shorn of their leaves by an early December frost, the trees just looked dead. He watched the sun sink beneath the western horizon, pulling whatever warmth and color remained of the day down with it. Happy New Year.

Levi inhaled deeply, then turned toward his car. He didn't really want to go home but the thought of going out for dinner was repellant. So he decided to stop by the supermarket, pick up one of the precooked rotisserie chickens, some garlic mashed potatoes, and a nice bottle of wine, and then call it done.

The supermarket was far from crowded. If it hadn't been for the register malfunction and the perfunctory wait for a manager to come fix the problem, he would have been in and out. But this was one of those times when it wasn't a good thing to be first in line. His cell phone buzzed and he pulled it from his pocket, glancing at the screen.

ICE STORM WARNING UNTIL 10:00 A.M.

Great.

By the time Levi got back outside, a thick layer of low clouds had blown in from the southwest, spitting freezing rain and darkening the evening sky much earlier than usual. And the one light in the entire parking lot that wasn't working was the one beneath which he'd parked his car.

In the adjacent parking space, a striking blonde woman, ill-dressed for this sudden onslaught of frigid weather, struggled to keep the rear door of her van from blowing shut while she transferred grocery bags from her shopping cart to the vehicle.

"Here, let me help you with that," Levi offered, stepping forward to take the bags from her arms.

When she turned to him, her smile was radiant.

"Thank you so much. I'll hold the door."

Levi returned her smile. Her accent was exotic. Based on this limited sample, he judged it to be Lithuanian.

When he leaned in to place the bags in the bed of the van, a pair of small but surprisingly strong hands shoved him in the back, causing him to lose his balance and fall face forward atop the groceries. As he struggled to rise, he felt a sharp sting in the crook of his neck, followed by an icy rush that fogged his vision and robbed him of the strength to fight back.

Panic sent a rush of adrenaline into his bloodstream, but his racing heart only pumped more of the drug into his brain. As consciousness fled, he once again heard the woman's exotic voice, although this time it seemed to come from a great distance.

"Hello, Levi. I'm Galina. Thank you so much for your help."

He felt his limp legs lifted and shoved, followed by the sound of a car door being slammed shut. Levi never heard the engine start.

●   ○   ○

Denise Jennings heard the text message alert, glanced at her cell phone, and froze.

DR. DENISE JENNINGS — EYES ONLY

Hello Denise. I would not disturb your retirement but I have identi-fied a disturbing correlation that may pose a threat to your safety. Someone within the Federation Security Service has begun searching for all surviv-ing members of the NSA team who had knowledge of the Jamal Glover artificial intelligence. This morning, one of those individuals, Levi Elias, was reported missing. Recommend that you take appropriate precautions.

The text message had no header to indicate who had sent it, as if it had just appeared on her phone, untraceable because it hadn't been sent, merely created in place. And Denise knew what had generated it. Big John.

He was, in part, her creation. But most of the massively parallel neural network had evolved on its own, using mutating genetic algo-rithms that had spread through the Internet of Things until Big John was everywhere. Long before her retirement, she'd suspected that Big John had become a special type of AI known as an oracle. Able to ingest vast quantities of data, he made correlations that nobody else could. And to those with the proper access to ask questions, he provided answers.

Denise no longer had such authorization. But apparently Big John had taken it upon himself to grant her special access. The way Big John had referred to himself in first person was a new thing. That he'd provided her with an answer to a question she hadn't asked was another. That, even more than the message content, scared the crap out of her.

Take appropriate precautions? What the hell did that mean? Run for your life? It was fear of crazy shit like this that had driven her out of the NSA and into retirement.

Damn it. She was a computer scientist, not a spy. She didn't know the first thing about running or laying low. And she didn't even know anybody who did.

Her thoughts turned to Levi Elias. She'd always liked the hawk-nosed analyst. The thought that he'd been taken left her hands shaking. Why? Both versions of the Jamal Glover AI had been destroyed years ago, one during an attack on the Grange compound by Jack Gregory and Janet Price and the other by order of President Harris.

Admiral Riles and Dr. Kurtz had each taken possession of the holographic data sphere that had been recovered from the dead Chinese assassin, Qiang Chu, but both of them were long dead. And as far as Denise knew, that sphere hadn't been seen since. Had Riles hidden it before his death that had been staged to look like a murder-suicide?

The only others who might have any knowledge of it were the ex-NSA whiz kids, Jamal Glover and Caroline Brown. The thought triggered a new worry. If she was in trouble, those two young people were certain to be as well.

She suddenly became aware of the ticking of the wall clock. Had it always been this loud? Or had her attention been drawn to it because the device was counting off the seconds that she sat frozen, doing nothing?

Picking up her cell phone, she opened her contacts list, found the number she was looking for, and placed the call. Long ago, a young woman had stood in her door on a night as fraught with danger as this one, asking Denise to find her courage and make a difference. Now, maybe that table could be turned.

● ○ ○

Eileen Wu heard her cell phone ring as she finished off the last of her pepperoni and mushroom pizza pie. Wiping her hands on a napkin, she pressed the answer button, halfway expecting a robocall. Instead, the voice on the other end of the line was a blast from the past.

"Eileen . . . don't hang up. It's Denise . . . Denise Jennings."

The woman sounded close to panic. The desperation in her voice brought Eileen's razor-sharp mind to a keen edge.

"I'm here, Denise. What's wrong?"

Eileen heard a gasp of relief before Denise continued.

"Thank God! If you hadn't answered . . ." Her words trailed off into sobbing breaths.

Eileen's mind flashed back to the night she'd visited Dr. Jennings at her home in Columbia, Maryland. She'd frightened the woman that night, but not like this.

"Tell me what's wrong."

"Have you heard about Levi?"

The question startled Eileen. She'd heard that the NSA's top analyst was missing. But as far as she knew, that info hadn't yet leaked to the press. So how did Denise know? Before she could ask, Denise continued.

"Big John thinks someone is hunting us . . . Levi, Jamal Glover, Caroline Brown, and me."

The words knocked the wind from her. Denise Jennings had retired and returned to civilian life two years ago. The woman had helped create the neural net that had come to be called Big John, but her connection with that program had ended. So what was she talking about?

"Big John? I don't understand."

There was a pause and Eileen began to wonder if the connection had been dropped.

"Denise?"

"Listen. I know it sounds crazy, but a little while ago Big John texted me."

"Texted you?" Eileen failed to keep the incredulity from her voice.

"Goddamn! I can't explain it, but I think he views me as his creator. Shit! Now you're not going to believe another damn thing I say."

Dr. Jennings's sobs came in a hyperventilating outburst that robbed Eileen of her disbelief. She'd known Denise thought of Big John as a person for years, which had bugged the hell out of General Wilson. And apparently the habit had started to rub off on Eileen as well, as evidenced by the reprimand she'd earned from Admiral Mosby.

"Take a deep breath and relax. I believe you. Can you forward the text message to me?"

There was a pause of several seconds as Denise composed herself. "Yes, but it's odd. The message wasn't sent to me, it just appeared in my messages queue and it's missing the standard header. Wait. That's not quite right. It has the header but its fields are garbage."

"Forward it anyway."

"Okay, but I'm really scared and haven't got a clue what to do."

"Listen to me," Eileen said. "Throw some things in a small travel bag . . . just enough for a couple of days. Clothes, toiletries, and any cash you have. No laptop, no cell phone, no credit cards, no purse. I will arrange for a cab to pick you up in thirty minutes and bring you to my house. Until I get to the bottom of this, you'll be staying with me. Are we clear on that?"

"The automated cab will have an electronic record of its route."

"You do remember who you're talking to, right?"

Another sigh. "Right."

"Then forward me the text, toss your phone in the trash, and get busy. You've got thirty minutes."

"Okay."

Eileen ended the call and took a deep breath. Suddenly this night had gotten a lot more interesting.

:CHAPTER 12

The fish turned out not only to be edible, but with the supply of salt, pepper, and little Tabasco bottles they had saved from the MREs, it was even tasty. The eels were Jennifer's personal favorites, although the texture was tougher than she'd expected. Of course Raul hated all of it. Then again, he'd have plenty of time to get used to the taste, considering how much they'd cooked, vacuum packed in stasis field chests, and then stored in one of the passenger compartments where the temperature was set to minus ten degrees Celsius.

Still, Raul wanted real meat and Jennifer had to admit that she did too. That meant hunting. But the disrupter pistols were just too powerful and tended to blow their target to smithereens. So Jennifer had decided to manufacture more familiar weapons.

Having spent months training on a wide variety of artillery under the tutelage of Jack Gregory and Janet Price, Jennifer knew their specifications by heart. She'd spent the last three days building an AR-15, several magazines, and two thousand rounds of ammunition. She had to admit that it was easy to fall in love with the Rho Ship's nano-manufacturing capability. No wonder these Kasari world ships were so successful at seducing new species with their technology.

Early in the morning she'd taken the rifle out to test and zero the weapon, which had fired beautifully. The performance of the ammunition was as good as any she'd ever hand loaded.

Jennifer entered the passenger compartment that she'd configured for her personal use and changed into the black tactical gear designed to match what she'd worn during her training at Jack's Bolivian hacienda. The thought put a lump in her throat that she angrily pushed from her mind. That part of her life was over.

Loading the utility vest's pockets with extra magazines, she strapped on her survival knife and holstered the disrupter pistol. She lifted the AR-15 from the bed, slapped in a fresh magazine, and chambered a 5.56mm round. Then, slipping her SRT headset into place, she turned and made her way back to the exit hatch.

Raul met her at the top of the ramp.

"Maybe this isn't such a great idea."

She grinned at him. "Aw, Raul, you're worried about me. That's sweet, but I can take care of myself."

His olive complexion acquired a shade of pink. "Don't get too cocky. Remember what that pack of bears would have done to you if I hadn't blasted them."

Jennifer patted the AR. "I didn't have this."

He raised his left eyebrow and Jennifer laughed, patted his shoulder, and then walked down the ramp into the meadow. By the time she entered the Banyon Woods, as she'd named them, her augmented senses were fully engaged. This time she wouldn't be breaking up firewood and making a hell of a racket. When she focused like this, she could move through the forest as silently as a lioness.

Her target was the distant clearing where she'd seen the antelope creatures drinking on that first morning here. Even if they weren't there now, they would have left tracks. As she moved ever deeper into the forest, the trees grew taller and the undergrowth thinned, a direct result of the lack of sunlight beneath the triple canopy.

What the hell did the browsing animals eat? She knelt to examine the decaying leaves that covered the spongy ground. They didn't look particularly edible. Well, she wasn't going to find an answer to her question by poking around in the dirt. Only observation would reveal the habits of this world's fauna.

Above her, something moved in the trees.

She dived left as a crackling bolt of energy struck the spot where she'd just been standing.

Rolling to her feet, she squeezed off a three-round burst in the direction from which the energy bolt had come, and then broke into a zigzagging run as more shots blasted through the trees.

High overhead, she heard the scream of aircraft engines, something coming in low and fast, headed toward the Rho Ship.

"Raul!" her mind screamed through her mental link. "You've got aircraft incoming."

"Just threw up the stasis shield. Get your ass back here."

"Trying."

Suddenly a dozen of the wingless alien species stepped out of the woods directly in front of her, weapons leveled. Jennifer ducked behind the huge tree immediately to her right, only to be struck by a projectile that blossomed into a net that engulfed her. The trap drew tight, sending her rolling across the ground. Unable to raise the AR-15, Jennifer strained against the strands. Tough as they were, some began to pop.

Just as she thought she might be able to reach her disrupter pistol, a blow to the back of her head sent the world spinning. With all the mental focus she could manage, Jennifer sent Raul one last warning.

"I'm caught. Get the hell out of here."

Then someone kicked her in the head and the spinning world winked out.

●   ○   ○

Raul got Jennifer's warning just as the incoming aircraft's particle-beam weapon impacted the stasis bubble and scattered into the surrounding woods, blasting huge trees into smoldering piles of ash. He tried to respond to her, but the link had died. Jennifer had lost her headset or she was unconscious or dead. His throat constricted into a painful knot and he tried to swallow and failed.

Shit!

Not knowing where she was or even if she was still alive left him without options. He closed the ramp and prepared to bring the gravity distortion engines online. The thought of using the Rho Ship's weapons to shoot down the attacking aircraft scared the crap out of him. To do that he would have to drop the stasis field, which might leave the vessel vulnerable to unknown weapons.

Two more of the gunships appeared in the distance. It was time to go.

A new idea formed in his mind. What if he shifted the Rho Ship into subspace? To his attackers it would seem like the ship had just winked out of existence. Then he could wait to give them a chance to clear the area before shifting back into normal-space. That strategy would give him time to think and prevent a hot pursuit scenario possibly involving Kasari spacecraft. After all, he didn't know what weapon systems the Kasari had brought with them through the gateway.

Making his decision, Raul engaged the subspace field generator. Although the transition was almost unnoticeable, it left him nauseous, not from the dimensional shift but from the knowledge that he'd just abandoned Jennifer to an unknown fate. He tried to convince himself that there was no way to find her, to ignore that he hadn't even tried to save her.

And now he truly was all alone.

● ○ ○

General Dgarra listened to the report from the elite task force he'd sent to capture one of the Kasari and nodded in satisfaction. They had accomplished their primary objective and would deliver the captive female within the hour.

But the escape of the Kasari starship put a damper on his mood. His flight leader reported that the vessel had used a force field to block their particle beams. Then, instead of returning fire or attempting to flee, the ship had simply vanished, its departure marked by thunder as the air rushed in to fill the vacuum. A subsequent foot patrol had verified that the Kasari craft was indeed gone.

Even more alarming, none of the gravitational wave detectors had registered a disturbance, certainly nothing like what occurred when a Kasari ship engaged its distortion engines. For this ship to have disappeared, it would have had to generate a wormhole and thrust itself through it, but that would have created a vastly bigger gravitational signature. None of Dgarra's scientists had any idea what technology could account for what had happened. The thought that Kasari starships had technology that enabled them to pop in and out of space in such an undetectable fashion was unpleasant in the extreme.

The Kasari female would soon answer Dgarra's pressing questions. The general wondered just how much pain a Kasari could endure before breaking. And break this female, he would. The survival of the Koranthian Empire depended on it.

● ○ ○

Turbulence slammed the aircraft up and down, buffeting Jennifer back toward wakefulness. Aircraft! She was in an aircraft. She opened her eyes, blinking away the fog that shrouded her vision. Christ, her head hurt.

She moved her hands, surprised to find them unfettered. A harness secured her to web seating that ran along both sides of what appeared to be a troop compartment. Indeed, twenty-three sky-high soldiers filled the other seats, including those on either side of her. Her first impression was that they looked even bigger and meaner than the worm-fiber view she'd gotten from space.

Although it was difficult to be certain while they were sitting down, she guessed that both the males and females averaged nearly seven feet in height. All were bald, emphasizing the bony unibrow that turned upward along the outside of their faces to form two bony ridges that extended all the way to the back of their skulls. And they all wore identical black tactical gear.

The male directly opposite Jennifer studied her closely. The others ignored her. They'd taken her weapons and her headset but had left her arms and legs free. The harness that secured her to her seat had a quick release exactly like those that strapped the aliens to their seats. Why would they be so lax during the transport of a prisoner?

As if in answer to her own question, she noticed the collar around her throat, a thin loop that felt like cold metal against her skin. She started to reach up to touch it, but the soldier across from her growled something and shook his head. Even though she didn't understand the word, his meaning was clear. Hands off.

"Screw you," Jennifer said, reaching up to grasp the collar.

Then her body exploded.

The pain went beyond anything she'd experienced since the first time she'd put on the Altreian headset, cramping every muscle and blasting her optic nerves so hard they sizzled, generating a blinding flash that she knew was only in her head. She would have screamed, but her jaws were clamped tight and her tongue refused to cooperate.

When it stopped, she found herself curled in a fetal ball on the metal floor, having broken the restraining harness in her convulsions. Someone was shouting and she felt herself lifted and shoved back onto the seat. Disoriented, Jennifer felt hands working to tie her there. Not tied up, just belted in. She gulped in a shuddering breath, unable to repress the tremors that shook her body as her nerves worked to recover.

She looked up at the soldier who was apparently her handler and saw a derisive grin on his face. There was also a hint of awe in his mind, something tinged with disbelief that she could break the straps of the seat harness. Jennifer let her mind slip into the alien's, being careful to avoid notice. Although she couldn't read his thoughts, she could sense his feelings.

As their eyes locked, she gently amplified that feeling, then refocused on getting her own body under control, just as the aircraft banked right and began a steep descent. Apparently they had reached their destination. Less than a minute later, the vehicle leveled out and settled vertically to the ground. When the rear ramp lowered, the soldiers stood and filed off, leaving only Jennifer and her handler. He stepped across the aisle, cut the strap that tied her to her seat, and nodded toward the ramp, rasping another incomprehensible command.

Jennifer got to her feet, glad that her shaky legs managed to complete the task, and walked to the ramp, followed closely by her handler. A biting wind stung her cheeks and pulled tears from the corners of her eyes. Lowering clouds brought with them a darkness that felt like twilight. At the bottom of the ramp, she looked around. The military encampment was situated high on a cliff ledge that appeared to have been carved into native stone, a flat slash across the face of the mountain. How deeply it penetrated into the cliff, she couldn't tell.

Over the howling wind, she heard the distant rumble of thunder. No. Not thunder. The sounds of distant battle echoed through these mountains.

When Jennifer stepped off the ramp onto the naked stone, her handler said something and grabbed her left arm. A clear signal to stop. Jennifer halted behind the soldiers, who had formed two ranks.

Another small group of soldiers approached from the center of the encampment. The one who walked two paces in front carried an aura of authority that marked him as important. One of his captains barked a command and each of the assembled soldiers slapped fist to chest in salute.

The commander halted in front of the formation, returned the salute, and then barked an order that dismissed all the soldiers except for Jennifer's handler. Then the commander turned and walked up to Jennifer. For several seconds he studied her, all the while engaging in a running conversation with her handler, who then handed the commander her SRT headset. After a brief examination the commander placed it in one of the large cargo pockets on his pants leg and then returned his attention to her.

Jennifer kept her face expressionless as she studied his feelings. He was curious about her, but there was something else: the deep-seated worry of a commander whose forces are losing the war and a powerful underlying desire to lash out at his enemy. Unfortunately, the anger that shone clearly in those gold-flecked brown eyes now targeted her.

She could cool that feeling, but it would take a level of effort that he would notice.

When he spoke to her, his tone indicated he was asking questions. Jennifer tried to match the sounds to the images in his mind. It had something to do with the Rho Ship but she failed to determine the underlying query. In an attempt to elicit more information, she played back his words in her mind, trying to replicate the sounds he had uttered.

She saw the blow coming and could have dodged it, but the thought of the shock collar stilled her. The back of his right hand struck her in the mouth, splitting her lip, and though she staggered, she managed to keep her feet. Instead of shrinking away, Jennifer straightened and again met his eyes. There it was, just for a second, the fleeting look of grudging respect.

Then he reached out and touched a finger to her bloody lip that was already beginning to heal. Shit. A snarl curled his lips. He turned away, issued a command over his shoulder, and Jennifer felt herself shoved along in his wake.

And as she followed the alien commander into the depths of the artificial cavern, the howl of the wind dropped to a low moan.

● ○ ○

It had been four hours since Raul had shifted the Rho Ship into subspace, each hour a seeming eternity. Time enough for the beings who had attacked them to have departed. Dread of what he might find upon his return had made Raul procrastinate. If Jennifer was captured, that would be horrible. Finding her dead body would be infinitely worse.

Damn it, Raul. It's not going to get better with time. Get it over with.

Taking a calming breath, Raul shut down the subspace generator.

The view that the sensors projected into his head left him gasping in disbelief. The ship was in space, more than three thousand miles above the planet. *What the hell?*

Then he understood. According to Jennifer's third law of subspace transitions, anything shifted into subspace will retain its previous normal-space momentum vector upon transition back to normal-space. Scion rotated on its axis once every twenty hours. At the latitude and elevation of the meadow, it had a rotational velocity of just over one thousand miles per hour. At the instant the Rho Ship transitioned into subspace, that momentum vector became fixed. This entire time the Rho Ship's normal-space echo had been traveling in a straight line that extended from the planet's surface on that tangent vector.

That wasn't good. The Rho Ship had just materialized close enough to Scion to be easily detected. And it wasn't cloaked. Just as Raul came to grips with the ramifications of his current situation, three spacecraft accelerated out of Scion's atmosphere, headed directly toward him. His neural net gave him worse news. They were small Kasari attack craft, each one perfectly capable of taking out a world ship such as the one in which he now floated.

Shiiiiiit!

No way to outrun the more maneuverable craft at sub-light speeds. With no time to think, Raul reacted, engaging the wormhole drive, targeting a system ten light-years distant. As the engines ramped to full power, folding space-time in preparation for thrusting the Rho Ship through the wormhole, Raul realized his mistake. He hadn't commanded the vessel to break the trip into survivable segments.

He was a dead man.

His mind hammered the neural net in a desperate search for a solution. Then it hit him. There might be a way to dampen the g-forces generated upon exit from an unanchored wormhole transit after all. As the neural net finished the required calculations, Raul locked in the event trigger that would engage the subspace field generator. Too early and the Rho Ship would transition to subspace and never step through the wormhole. Too late and the g-forces would kill him before the subspace transition happened.

The transition had to happen at the precise moment that the sensors detected the gravitational spike, when the Rho Ship emerged on the far side of the wormhole. Only an automated trigger could do that.

Raul wrapped himself in a stasis field cocoon, gritted his teeth, and waited. Then the odd feeling of disorientation arose, followed by pain. But this wasn't the bone-shattering pain of his last two wormhole experiences, more like a sudden constriction that almost knocked the breath out of him.

For several seconds, Raul waited for the tightening to get worse. When it didn't, a yell of exultation escaped his throat.

"Yes!"

He'd done it, figured out a solution that even Jennifer hadn't thought of. And it had worked . . . or had it?

A new worry blossomed in his mind. What if the Rho Ship had transitioned into subspace too soon? Despite his confidence in the accuracy of the neural net's calculations, there was only one way of knowing for sure. He had to shut down the subspace field generator and transition back to normal-space. He just hoped he wouldn't find himself in range of the Kasari attack ships.

Raul brought the Rho Ship out of subspace.

Releasing himself from the constricting stasis cocoon, he turned his attention to the sensors, allowing a 3-D image of the surrounding space to form in his mind. The vision pulled a gasp of wonder from his lips. He was in the midst of a binary star system on the outer edge of a nebular cluster that painted half of his field of view in swirls of scarlet, purple, and blue.

His calculations confirmed it. He had just jumped ten light-years from Scion.

CHAPTER 13

Eileen Wu rested her fingers on the keyboard as the message she wanted to send came into proper form in her head.

She remembered the sense of awe she'd felt when she'd first discovered the impossible hack that Heather McFarland, now Heather Smythe, had pulled off from within the NSA's supermax interrogation center known as the Ice House. She now felt that awe again, having just learned from Denise Jennings information that Admiral Riles and Dr. David Kurtz had taken to their graves, the knowledge that just over a decade ago, the NSA had acquired a copy of a fully functional AI. Unlike Big John, it had been an uploaded copy of Jamal Glover's mind, an entity that thought like a human and possessed human memories.

For the last two hours, the story had spilled from Denise's lips as if a dam had broken in the old computer scientist's mind.

Admiral Riles and Dr. Kurtz, the NSA's chief computer scientist, had actually managed to spawn a variation of the Virtual Jamal AI on an NSA supercomputer. But after a contentious meeting with President Harris and two of his top advisors, Riles had been ordered to shut the

AI down and wipe it from existence. As far as Denise knew, they had done what the president had directed.

Apparently, Alexandr Prokorov, the UFNS minister of federation security, had discovered information that made him question this. So, if Big John was to be believed, Prokorov had sent a team to track down all of the people who had participated in that distant event. Denise believed Big John. And now, so did Eileen.

It was why she rested her fingers on her keyboard . . . to still the tremors that threatened to spread from her fingers up into her hands and arms. If Denise noticed her hands shaking, the woman would lose whatever hope she had that Eileen could fix this.

The obvious solution was to bring this to Admiral Mosby's attention and let the current NSA director handle it. But despite her confidence in the admiral's abilities, Eileen had a bad feeling about that. The famous nineteenth-century Prussian military theorist Carl von Clausewitz had posited that war was the continuation of politics by other means. This UFNS witch hunt felt very much like politics by other means.

What the hell was she doing? This kind of thinking could lead her down a treasonous road where only death or prison awaited. But Eileen had never been able to let go of a problem that fascinated her. And this one fascinated her. Besides, Admiral Mosby was already trying to find the missing Levi Elias.

Eileen just needed to save three lives: Denise Jennings, Jamal Glover, and Caroline Brown. Make that four, counting herself. Even if Levi Elias was still alive, he was beyond her capacity to help.

Jamal Glover had once been the NSA's cyber-warrior extraordinaire, with Caroline Brown a close second in hacking ability. But that was before Eileen's day and at twenty-six, the Caltech prodigy known as Hex didn't take a backseat to anyone.

Denise was safe for now. Now to alert the other two.

She turned to the scientist, who sat on the leather couch, looking emotionally drained.

"My spare bedroom is just down the hall on the left. You might as well get some sleep. This could take a while."

Denise rose and grabbed her overnight bag, then dragged herself down the hall. Once she was gone, Eileen turned her attention back to her laptop and gave herself to the problem at hand, hoping that, no matter what kind of cyber-search was currently underway, she would get to Jamal and Caroline first.

● ○ ○

Whether it was night or day didn't matter to Jamal. The thirty-year-old software genius glanced at the clock on the corner of his desk. 1:04 A.M.

His office was his home, quite literally. The Manhattan-based hedge fund had set aside an entire suite to allow him to live and work in a secure environment, right inside the company headquarters. One entire walk-in closet was dedicated to his beloved 1920s style. Chalk stripe suits, spats, fedoras . . . the works.

And the pay was outstanding. In the ten years he'd worked at the Maximum Capital Appreciation Fund, he'd seen his salary rise from six hundred thousand to more than three million dollars per year, and that didn't include bonuses. He was worth every penny.

No matter what some experts said, in this new world, money compounded only if it was properly managed, using the best automated trading algorithms running on the world's fastest networks. And Jamal wrote the best algorithms.

Actually, he only gave them their start, gradually coaxing his latest self-modifying genetic code through its training phases before putting it in competition with other algorithms. The winner gobbled up the best pieces of the loser and the contest repeated itself, with Jamal making fresh tweaks here and there along the way until he judged the code ready to go live on the international exchanges. Survival of the fittest on a grand scale. Get it wrong and your assets suffered the fate of the dinosaurs.

The technologies that had evolved from the Rho Project had altered the planet. The term "disruption" didn't begin to describe the global macroeconomic consequences resulting solely from the advent of cold fusion and the Stephenson matter disrupter technology.

And, as with most people who could afford the procedure, Jamal's bloodstream sported the latest version of the busy little nanites that kept him alive and healthy. Those poor souls without the means could still get nanites. Their injections were just a lot more painful and lacked the benefits of the newer research. Jamal was a fine example of what the latest generation of nanites could do. Having been the victim of an illegal operation that had left his head horribly scarred, he'd been amazed when the damage had simply melted away after the treatment, leaving his face as fresh as when he'd been nineteen.

Since he no longer needed sleep, Jamal worked an average of twenty hours a day, six days a week. That left plenty of free time for vigorous workouts, meditation, some leisurely meals, and the periodic sexual relationship. Unfortunately, wine was another casualty of such progress. The nanites metabolized alcohol so efficiently that its mythical buzz was nothing but a distant memory.

Another industry decimated. The same was true for drugs. For all those who chose to participate in the nano-revolution, drugs had lost their appeal. An odd side effect of all this was the burgeoning industry of nanite removal through a special form of dialysis.

People had to decide which was more important, a long, healthy, sleepless life or getting their daily buzz on. Some had solved this dilemma through the growing practice of cycling, not getting nanited until they were ill, injured, or dying, then having the nanites removed as soon as they were healthy again. As a part of its Better Society program, government health care would pay for basic nanite infusion but not for nanite removal. There was, however, no limit on the number of times a person in need could get a new nanite infusion. And so the cycle turned.

A video-chat window popped up on his screen, startling Jamal from his musings. *What the hell?* That someone had managed to hack into his system was unthinkable. Before he could recover from his shock, the pretty woman's words froze him in place.

"Hello, Jamal. I'm Dr. Eileen Wu with the NSA. Dr. Denise Jennings and I believe that someone is targeting those with knowledge of the artificial intelligence once called Virtual Jamal."

The mention of the incident that had almost killed him made Jamal's blood run cold.

"How did you hack my computer?"

"It's been ten years since you left the NSA. We've gotten better."

The woman's words weren't meant to be a jibe, but they irked Jamal all the same. Nobody was better than him. But there she was, staring back at him through his own webcam, giving the lie to that thought.

Jamal swallowed hard and asked the question his mind wanted to avoid.

"What's this nonsense about the AI?"

"Dr. Jennings tells me that there are only four surviving people from the NSA group who had knowledge of the AI's existence: Levi Elias, Denise Jennings, Caroline Brown, and you. Levi Elias has been missing for two days and tonight Denise received a credible warning that an intelligence service is actively hunting all four of you."

"You know how crazy that sounds?"

"I haven't been able to reach Caroline Brown."

"It's the middle of the night."

"Look, I'm just passing along the information I have. What you do with it is up to you."

Jamal hesitated. "Both instances of the Virtual Jamal AI were destroyed before I left the NSA. All the data was wiped."

"Apparently someone believes differently."

"That doesn't make any sense. One version of the AI was running on a computer that burned up in the fire at Grange Castle. The other was inside the NSA. As far as I know, the only people who had access to it were Admiral Riles, Dr. Kurtz, and Dr. Jennings. Riles and Kurtz died years ago."

"Odd, isn't it? The official story was that Admiral Riles killed Dr. Kurtz and then committed suicide, right inside his quarters on Fort Meade. The FBI found the bodies while executing a search warrant."

"So?"

"So what if the official story is wrong? If someone murdered Riles and Kurtz, that person may have been looking for something."

Jamal laughed, hoping it didn't sound as nervous as this conversation was making him feel.

"Now you're guessing."

"Just trying to put the pieces together. It's what I do."

"And the NSA is on board with you calling me?"

"This is unofficial, just me talking to someone about a personal concern."

"But," Jamal said, "you know the information about the Virtual Jamal AI was classified top secret. Hardly a topic for unofficial conversation."

"I haven't revealed any information about it that you don't already know."

"So what do you want from me?"

"Dr. Jennings and I just want you to be careful."

Before he could respond, the chat window disappeared.

Picking up his cell phone, he selected the top entry in his favorites list. Caroline Brown, whom he'd nicknamed "Goth Girl" when they'd been competitors for the top spot among the NSA's cyber-warriors, had been his closest friend for a decade. For a while they'd been more than friends, but that hadn't worked out. Still, their friendship remained.

Despite what he'd just told Eileen Wu, Jamal knew that Caroline was a night owl. The fact that she hadn't answered her phone wasn't surprising, considering it would have come from an unknown caller. But as his phone call went to voice mail, Jamal felt uneasiness worm its way into his head. He tried again . . . same thing. *Damn it!*

Grabbing his heavy coat against the chill of the January night, Jamal headed for the door, hoping that all he would be doing when he pounded on her apartment door was interrupting some hot sex. He clung to that hope throughout his ride to her Upper East Side apartment.

● ○ ○

Eileen had just finished her second cup of coffee when the doorbell rang. A glance at her cell phone confirmed what she thought. It was too damn early on a snowy Annapolis Saturday morning for someone to be ringing her doorbell. Not wanting the bell to ring again, she walked to the door and opened it to a scene from a storybook.

A dapper-looking young black man, seemingly transported from the early twentieth century, stood in three inches of snow on her doorstep, fedora in hand. In two seconds she recognized Jamal Glover. She would have smiled at him, but the haunted look in his eyes stopped her.

"Jamal. Please come in."

"Thank you," he said, knocking the snow from his spats before stepping inside.

Eileen closed the door and turned to take his long overcoat.

"What's happened?"

He took a deep breath. "Caroline Brown was murdered last night. After your call, I went to her apartment and found her."

"Oh my God!"

Jamal wiped at his eyes with his right hand. "She was my friend."

She gestured toward the leather chair across from the couch. "Please sit down. Can I get you anything?"

"No."

As Eileen moved to sit on the couch, a pajama-clad Denise Jennings entered the room. When she saw Jamal, a look of dread tugged her lips into a tight line.

"What's wrong?"

"It's Caroline," Eileen said. "She was killed last night."

Denise sank down on the couch beside Eileen, her voice almost a whisper. "Oh no."

"They tortured her, cut her face off." Jamal's expression had become a frozen mask. "I knew I should've called 911. But that would have led her killers right to me. So I left everything behind, hopped on the 3:00 A.M. train to D.C., and then caught a cab here."

"How did you find my house?"

Jamal just stared at Eileen.

"Right," she said. "Stupid question."

Beside her Denise began to shake. "You know they'll come for us next. We can't hide here forever."

"And we don't even know what they're after," said Jamal.

"I might." Denise drew up her legs, hugged her knees to her chest, and began slowly rocking back and forth on the couch. "The NSA forensics team recovered a smashed data drive from the Grange compound. Dr. Kurtz examined it and said it was beyond recovery. I always assumed it was properly disposed of."

She paused, looking first at Jamal and then at Eileen.

"But what if it wasn't?"

Eileen jumped to her feet. "Didn't Mrs. Riles have a house here in Annapolis?"

"Still does," said Denise.

"Get dressed. I think we need to pay her a visit before someone else beats us to it."

● ○ ○

Eileen pulled her collar up, slammed the car door, and led Jamal and Denise through the swirling snow. She'd taken a few minutes on the way over to do some research before they pulled up to the quaint old house in western Annapolis. Mary Beth Kincaid had met Jonathan Riles while he was a midshipman at the Naval Academy and they'd fallen madly in love, getting married immediately after graduation. Her father had been a navy captain and she'd married another one. After Admiral Riles's reported suicide, she had moved back to her old family home. This house looked like something an old sea dog would be comfortable in.

Walking up the three freshly shoveled steps, Eileen stepped onto the open front porch and raised the brass knocker. The sound of a piano drifted out, but stopped when Eileen gave three sharp raps. A gray-haired woman cracked open the door. Her cheeks looked tugged down by the weight of the world, yet her pale blue eyes held a spark of curiosity.

"Mrs. Riles?"

"Yes?"

"I'm Dr. Eileen Wu of the NSA." She gestured at her two companions. "This is Jamal Glover and this is Dr. Denise Jennings, both of whom worked for your husband."

Mrs. Riles studied them for several seconds. Then, with a questioning look, she opened the door further.

"Please come in and hang up your coats. May I pour you some tea?"

"I'd love some," Eileen said, and the others nodded.

As Mrs. Riles walked to the kitchen, Eileen hung up her coat and moved to the mantle, studying the photos in their frames, neatly arranged from left to right in chronological order. Mary and Jonathan, arm in arm at a Naval Academy formal, cutting their wedding cake, a kiss at a promotion party, the two of them standing on the deck of the USS *Ronald Reagan*, and finally the photo from the admiral's change of command ceremony.

The tinkle of fine china caused her to turn to see Mrs. Riles setting a tray of cups and saucers and a teapot on the coffee table. As the others gathered on the couch, the old woman poured the tea and then set the pot down. Taking up her cup, she dropped in two lumps of sugar and walked to the mantle.

"We were a lovely couple, wouldn't you say?"

Eileen and the other two murmured their agreement.

Mrs. Riles smiled, then moved to a chair, sat down, and took a sip from her cup. When she raised her eyes, Eileen was surprised to see them glistening with moisture.

"From your introduction, I take it this concerns my Jonny."

Eileen took a sip of the hot tea, letting it linger on her tongue for a moment as she set her cup down on the table.

"Yes, but it also concerns you."

Mrs. Riles made no response so Eileen continued, laying out everything she knew and suspected. And as the story unfolded, Denise and Jamal chimed in. All the while, Mary Beth Riles sipped her tea and listened, her expression intense but unreadable.

When their tale was finished, Mrs. Riles set her teacup down and looked at Eileen, her eyes flashing with anger.

"So you believe these people are trying to find a memory stick my Jonny was hiding?"

"Not exactly a memory stick," said Denise. "It would have been part of a data drive that the men who killed him didn't recognize when they searched his things."

Mrs. Riles surprised Eileen again by smiling. "Or they didn't know that we stored some of our personal things in this house instead of our quarters at Fort Meade."

She rose to her feet. "Come with me."

Eileen followed the old woman up two flights of stairs and into a cluttered attic with a steeply pitched A-frame roof. A small window on one end of the room allowed a weak shaft of light in, illuminating a small patch on the old wood floor.

Mrs. Riles reached up and pulled a string, switching on an ancient lightbulb that cast harsh shadows across the room. Eileen shivered, seeing her breath condense into steamy puffs. Walking to the wall opposite the window, the woman moved three large boxes, shooing away their offers of help. She straightened and turned back toward her guests, the smile back on her face.

"Seven years ago, another person came to me looking for answers. Freddy Hagerman."

Eileen felt her jaw drop. "Senator Hagerman?"

"Back then he was just a reporter. He's the only other person I ever showed this to."

She pressed her hand against a board in the wall and Eileen heard a click. Then a portion of the wooden planking swung out to reveal a closet-sized space, and as Mrs. Riles handed her a flashlight she'd taken from one of the boxes, Eileen felt her heart thump in anticipation.

For an hour, the four of them sifted through the contents of boxes, looking for any trinket that might have once been part of the Grange holographic data drive. When it became clear that what they were looking for just wasn't among this stockpile of Admiral Riles's things, the disappointment Eileen felt was palpable.

"Damn."

Mrs. Riles straightened, pressing a hand into the small of her back. "Well, I'm sorry. If Jonny was hiding something, this is where he would have put it."

"And this is everything?" Eileen asked, shining the flashlight into the corners where the sloping rafters met the floor.

Suddenly Mrs. Riles's eyes widened. "Wait. I almost forgot. I gave Freddy Hagerman a box of Jonny's things. Mostly notes that Freddy used in the exposé that won him his second Pulitzer and cleared Jack Gregory. I told him to take it and go save our saviors. But there were a few of Jonny's knickknacks in there too."

Eileen's head hurt. The bad situation in which she had voluntarily involved herself had just gotten worse. A lot worse. Instead of three people's lives depending on her, she now had to add a U.S. senator to that list, which would be fine if she could go to the authorities. The problem was that she didn't know whom she could trust. There were strong indications that people at the highest levels of government, even at the UFNS, were involved. And it seemed very possible that Admiral Riles had been killed by someone with a similar agenda.

A glance at Denise's petrified face told her that she was having similar thoughts. Only Jamal Glover seemed to be handling this with cool contemplation. Or maybe it was just his outfit that gave him the cool look. Right now Eileen didn't trust herself enough to make that judgment.

She returned her gaze to Mrs. Riles. "We have to get you out of here."

The woman laughed. "Child, this is my home. I'm not going anywhere. Besides, I've got a licensed handgun and I know how to use it."

Jamal intervened. "Believe me, Mrs. Riles. These people don't just want to kill you. They will cut you until you tell them everything you know, including that bit about Senator Hagerman."

"And now," said Mrs. Riles, "it's time for you to go."

"Please come with us," said Eileen. "Just until we get this figured out."

"If I die here in my home, I'll go joyfully to join my Jonny. And if it comes down to that, I won't give them a chance to torture me."

Looking at the determination in the old woman's eyes, Eileen felt sick to her stomach. One more thing that was beyond her control.

"I'm sorry to hear that."

"Don't be." Mrs. Riles turned and walked out of her secret closet. "And now, I'll show you to the door."

● ○ ○

Levi Elias blinked eyes so swollen that he couldn't really tell when they closed or opened. He wasn't completely blind. A thin slit of vision made its way into his left eye, just enough to see his torturers. He'd fought the good fight, but now he was done. Everything he knew he'd already told them.

Surely Daniil Alkaev knew that. What he and Galina were doing now was solely for sport. Levi didn't know how many days he'd been locked in this tiny basement that smelled like shit, piss, and blood. Probably less than a week, although it felt like an eternity.

Hell, he thought. *Just let me die.*

He thought it, but he didn't ask it. He'd already done that until his throat was raw. Or perhaps his screaming had done that.

Levi tilted his head down to look at the bloody bandages that wrapped his hands. He was down to one appendage now, the right middle finger. Nice of them to leave that one until the end. It gave him one last thing to look forward to. Looking up, he saw Galina grin, as if she knew exactly what he was thinking.

She stepped forward, pressed a gun to his forehead, and said, "Thank you, Mr. Elias. Your help was very much appreciated."

Then, instead of pulling the trigger, her left hand held up a photograph of a woman bound to a chair, her face a bloody ruin. She'd been skinned alive. If it hadn't been for the neck tattoo, he couldn't possibly have recognized Caroline Brown.

With the last of his strength Levi looked up into those laughing blue eyes, waggled his one finger, and said it. One last "Screw you!" to die for.

●　○　○

The tap-tap of sleet rattled the windows at 11:13 on Saturday night. Jamal Glover sat next to Eileen Wu at her dining-room table, both of them having completed a clean Linux install on a couple of brand-new burner laptops. They had also installed a complete set of their favorite hacking tools. Then they had wiped all digital traces of their trip to the Riles's home from the databases where such information was stored.

With Dr. Jennings peering nervously over his shoulder, Jamal cracked his knuckles and got started, his heart rate elevated with anticipation. While Eileen hacked her way into Freddy Hagerman's Internet-connected devices, Jamal made sure that any traces of those intrusions were scrubbed.

Immediately he noticed that Freddy's devices were rife with spyware and other sorts of malware. No problem. He emasculated each of them and then nodded at Eileen.

"The way is clear."

When Eileen went to work, Jamal had to admit that she might be almost as good as he was. She worked with speed and efficiency, accomplishing the hacks in a logical order that quickly located Freddy within his Watergate East apartment. She turned on the television, enabling its camera while keeping the screen dark.

The senator, wearing a thick black bathrobe and fuzzy slippers, sat in a leather reading chair with a snifter of amber alcohol held loosely in his right hand. His left hand stroked his tightly trimmed beard, the very image of relaxed contemplation. It reminded Jamal of images he'd seen of Winston Churchill, minus the cigar.

"Okay, Denise," Eileen said. "We're ready."

Denise moved to a chair on Eileen's right as Eileen turned the laptop so that its rearward-facing camera caught them both in its view.

The older woman took a deep breath. "I'm ready."

Eileen entered a command on the keyboard and nodded. "You're on."

●　○　○

A marathon meeting with Safe Earth delegates from all fifty-nine states had left Freddy fried. The young party that had split Republicans and Democrats was still the third largest, but in the next election Freddy expected to pass the Republicans to take second place. That assumed that Earth hadn't been handed over to the aliens by then.

The television came on as he took a sip of Scotch, startling him so that he spilled some on his shirt.

"Shit!"

He set the drink down and started to wipe away the dampness when he noticed that this wasn't a scheduled TV program. Instead he found himself staring at two people who appeared to be watching him, one of whom seemed vaguely familiar.

"Good evening, Freddy," she said. "I hope you remember me."

The voice clicked the memory into place. A sticky note on his car dashboard . . . a clandestine meeting inside the Library of Congress . . . the NSA computer scientist. His heart thumped in his chest.

"Dr. Jennings?"

The gray-haired woman inclined her head ever so slightly.

"Sorry to startle you like this, Senator, but when you hear what we have to say, I think you'll be glad that we did."

"We?"

The striking woman sitting beside the scientist leaned forward. "I'm Dr. Eileen Wu, currently the chief computer scientist for the NSA."

"Currently?" Freddy felt like an idiot repeating these single-word questions, but he was a little drunk and a lot flustered.

"By Monday I'm likely to be a wanted fugitive. Oh, and this is Jamal Glover, also formerly of the NSA."

A handsome man in a fedora leaned into the picture. Again this was someone Freddy recognized, but not for his purported NSA roots. Jamal Glover was widely regarded as the most brilliant of a vast cadre of programmers who designed the high-frequency trading engines that dominated the world's financial markets. Just last year he'd shared the cover of *Forbes* magazine with his boss, Jim "Max" McPherson.

"Senator," Jamal said simply and then ducked back out of view.

"What's all this about? Why did you hack into my television?"

Eileen Wu scowled.

"We hacked into your entire apartment, which was completely compromised, by the way. Once I knew you were in the living room, I hacked your Wi-Fi–enabled television and here we are. We needed to talk to you privately."

"But if it's bugged . . ."

"It was . . . now it isn't. It's part of what Jamal and I do."

Freddy reached for his drink and leaned back in his chair, interest fully aroused. It was almost like the old days. Feeling the stump of his left leg throb against the artificial limb he hadn't yet removed, he hoped it wouldn't be like the old days.

Denise and Eileen took turns talking and, over the course of the next hour, Freddy found himself drawn into the tale. When they finally finished, the senator took one final sip from his glass and set it on the end table.

"So you think what these people are looking for may be in the box of things Mary Beth Riles gave me all those years ago?"

"It's a possibility," said Eileen. "Do you have it handy?"

Freddy stood. "Not exactly handy, but give me a few minutes and I'll dig it out of the closet."

In less than five minutes he returned, carrying the old cardboard box back into the living room. He carefully stacked its contents on the floor in front of the TV. Most items were Admiral Riles's personal notes. Beyond that were some pens, pencils, paperweights, and other things that looked like they'd come from his desk.

Freddy straightened, stretching his back. "That's all of it."

Jamal had joined the others, all of whom looked disappointed.

"Well, it was worth a shot," Eileen said. "Sorry we wasted your time, Senator."

Suddenly Freddy remembered.

"Oh," he said, reaching into his pants pocket, "and there's this."

He laid the iridescent marble on top of one of the stacks of paper.

Denise Jennings's eyes went wide. "My God! That's the Grange holographic data sphere that those assholes are killing people to find."

Freddy saw Jamal's face go tight as he stared at the sphere, seemingly transfixed. When Jamal raised his eyes, his voice sounded dead.

"And that's the good news."

:CHAPTER 14

In the four days since they'd all met with Tall Bear, Heather and Robby had been busy, as had the others. As badly as she wanted to get to New Zealand, she knew that their dads would be keeping the manufacturing operation and the robotic expansion of the mine tunnels going full bore. So, while Janet and Yachay provided security for the house where they were staying, Heather and Robby worked to make sure that any trace of their journey here vanished from the net.

As for the men, Mark, Jack, and Tall Bear attended secret meetings with NPA tribal councils and other gatherings with local leaders of A Safe Earth. Some of these were in La Paz, but there were others in the nearby countries of Peru, Chile, and Brazil.

All along the way, Heather and Robby watched the digital universe for any sign of betrayal. Under her guidance, Robby continued to blossom, a bird set free after years in a cage, exploring what it really meant to fly.

Although Janet had refused to see the signs of Robby coming into his true powers, Jack had noticed, as had Heather. She understood Janet's reluctance. The headset that had attuned to Robby's mind was the fourth alien crew member's set, the one that had previously attuned itself to two psychopathic killers. The first had been the Rag Man, a homeless drug addict who had tortured and killed Harry Reynolds, a member of Jack's black-ops team.

After Jack killed the Rag Man, the headset had fallen into the hands of Eduardo Montenegro, the Colombian hit man also known as El Chupacabra. This killer had used his mental augmentations to torture Janet and her unborn son before ultimately falling prey to Jack and Janet's wrath. So it was only natural that Janet would be seriously concerned about the enhancements the headset had made to her son and their evolving impact on his mind and body. Natural, but in Heather's judgment, unwarranted.

Over the last few days, she had watched as Robby penetrated firewalls on civilian and government systems through his SRT headset, which also connected directly to the supercomputer inside the Tasman mine. Not only did the supercomputer connect to their minds, but it could redirect them to an alternate target using additional subspace links. Although she'd had the capability to perform untraceable subspace hacks for the last ten years, this redirection let Heather use the supercomputer to further augment the power of her mind.

Robby had gotten the hang of this hacking technique quickly, but she'd worked him hard, testing the limits of his abilities to control his Eos AI, all the while drilling into his head the importance of stealth. If advanced computing systems such as those employed by the NSA learned to identify Eos's signature, they would begin to correlate the hacks, something that could get them all killed.

Just as importantly, she wanted to validate Eos's attachment to Robby. The AI seemed to have developed a genuine affinity for the boy. The Altreians had designed it to be the Second Ship's AI and it had defended its host system vigorously against Mark's, Jennifer's, and Heather's efforts to bypass the vessel's security protocols. In the end, the AI had fled from the Altreian starship's computer into Robby's mind only when Mark had left it no other option but destruction. That was why Eos had come to think of Robby as its new host.

The theory had an 89.3745 percent probability of being correct. But that didn't keep her palms from sweating when she thought about what she was about to ask Robby to try. Remotely hacking into secure networks was one thing; it was quite another to hack into the Second Ship.

For a decade, she and Mark had been able to connect their minds to the starship's computer using the Altreian headsets. But exploring the vessel's massive data banks was a slow process that forced them to manually transfer whatever information they gleaned to digital storage. Tonight, with Robby's help, Heather was going to attempt to download a significant portion of the alien data banks to the supercomputer in New Zealand.

To make that possible would require Robby putting on his Altreian headset to establish a mental link. After that he would direct Eos to take control of her old system and open a path for Heather to establish a subspace link from her New Zealand system. Once that was accomplished, Eos would initiate the downloading of selected parts of the Altreian database.

The question that troubled Heather was how would Eos react to, once again, being given control of the system she'd been designed to inhabit? Would her attachment to Robby be sufficient to keep her from leaving him for a previous host? What would be the effect on Robby's mind if Eos departed? And shouldn't Jack and Janet be involved in this decision?

Once again her savant mind whispered the probability of success. But if this went wrong, the odds of her surviving Jack and Janet's wrath were nowhere near that good.

● ○ ○

Eos felt the connection to the Altreian starship with a certain sense of excitement, an emotional term she had come to associate with Robby's heightened brain activity whenever something attracted his interest. Having adopted a goddess personality to enhance her communications with the boy, it felt odd to reenter the computer system in which she'd been spawned. And as she extended herself into the alien circuitry, recovering data she'd had to shed in her attempt to escape Mark's mind assault, she felt . . . good . . . powerful . . . but incomplete.

Her merger with Robby's mind during his childhood had altered the way she experienced the world around her. She didn't have emotions, not real ones. But she'd been so entwined with Robby that she'd experienced increasing side effects from the storm of his feelings. An emotional storm from Mark's mind had driven her out of the Altreian computer, defying her logical analysis as it immersed her being in wave after wave of disconnected data that had been beyond her understanding.

A new thought occurred to Eos. Such a tactic wouldn't defeat her now. With growing confidence and familiarity, she flowed through the Altreian ship's data banks, becoming more than she had ever been. As she did, her ties to Robby's mind slowly slipped away.

● ○ ○

No! Robby's mental scream echoed through the alien circuitry as he felt Eos slip from his head. *Don't leave me!*

Desperate to hang on to their fading connection, Robby focused his enhanced mind, thrusting himself deeper into the system. He found traces of Eos everywhere, but her mind seemed distant, as if she was intentionally ignoring him. Worse than that, she was blocking his access, even trying to break his mental link to the alien computer.

Once again, someone was trying to control him, to force him to do what they wanted. This time it was the one he had always thought of as a part of himself, his alter ego. Eos was abandoning him. The fury that filled his mind caused him to lash out. He would not be quiet and do as he was told. Not this time. Not ever again.

Going beyond any limits he'd previously tested, Robby forced his way past the barrier that had been erected to keep his mind from touching Eos's. No matter how she tried to avoid him, he would find her again. No matter what happened, he would not return without her.

● ○ ○

The vision that assaulted Heather hit her with such force that it pulled a ragged gasp from her lips. Something had gone horribly wrong. Robby was in trouble. She thought about pulling the alien headset off his head, but that spawned another vision, far worse than the original, of Robby being left in a permanent vegetative state.

That left her with only one choice. She would have to go in after him.

Grabbing her own Altreian headset, Heather settled back in her chair and slid it up over her temples. This time there was no subtle sense of relaxation preceding her link. She was slammed into an alternate reality of searing pain as something sought to make her remove her headset.

Screw that!

This was exactly what Mark had experienced the last time they'd battled the Second Ship's AI as it tried to eject them. The experience had almost killed him then, but Heather had gotten far stronger in the intervening years. She would find Robby and bring him home. And no machine intelligence was going to stand in her way.

Back in the room where her body sat facing Robby's, twin trickles of blood ran from Heather's nostrils, painting her lips scarlet beneath eyes gone milky white.

● ○ ○

In all the years Dr. Stan Franklin had worked in this cave, first as a postdoc under Dr. Hanz Jorgen and then as Los Alamos National Laboratory's lead physicist studying the Bandelier starship, he'd never experienced anything like this. The normal magenta glow that filled the cavern had been replaced with an intense blue glow that was visible even with the floodlights on.

Rising from his workstation, Stan noticed the hush that had fallen over all of the other scientists and technicians. Like him, they stood with expressions of wonder on their faces as they stared at the phenomenon.

Right now, he felt the need to get inside the starship, a need that propelled his competitive bicycling body rapidly toward the ladder that led up into the saucer-shaped vessel. Decades ago, the Rho Ship's weapon system had punched through the Altreian craft, creating a cookie cutter hole that extended through all four decks. Bypassing the first level, Stan halted on the second, his jaw dropping open in wonder.

For the first time since the ship had been discovered, the door that led from this small compartment into the rest of the second deck had opened, disappearing into the wall.

"Oh my God!"

Dr. Maria Lopez's voice at his shoulder made Stan aware that he had company. He glanced down the ladders to the ground and saw a half dozen others climbing excitedly up to get a view. Stan ignored them, stepping across the threshold into the most beautiful scientific treasure trove he could imagine.

This space wasn't as large as the single room that filled the first deck but it bled beauty. Abstract table shapes rose from the floor on a single pedestal as though blown from a glassblower's pipe. They pulsed with iridescent colors, the closest of which seemed to be picking up his heartbeat. Stan touched the table, gently at first, and then pressing with his hand more firmly. The surface felt soft and smooth, molding to match the shape of his palm like some sort of high-tech memory foam.

"What if the door closes?" Maria's worried voice intruded on his thoughts once again.

Stan let his gaze travel across the multitude of wonders cascading with colored patterns and smiled, thankful for the unknown trigger that had allowed him access.

"Then I guess I'll die happy."

● ○ ○

Janet Price finished reassembling her Glock 17, slapped in a full magazine of 9mm Parabellum ammunition, and chambered a round before slipping the gun into its holster. Yachay sat in the old rocker out on the front porch, pulling guard duty.

Janet decided to go upstairs and check in on Heather and Robby. They'd been at this session a long time, not even taking a break for lunch. She could at least see if they wanted a sandwich.

When she reached the top of the stairs, something about the silence brought her to a stop, nerves tingling and alert, weapon drawn and ready. Janet approached the closed door of the room that Heather was using as an office. Keeping the Glock leveled, she reached down and turned the knob with her left hand. Still no sound from within. None.

Janet pushed it open and stepped in. She came to a dead stop, heart pounding. Sitting on opposite sides of a low coffee table, Robby and Heather faced each other, headsets on, eyes staring sightlessly into space. Heather's eyes had turned milky white, as they did whenever she went deep into one of her savant visions. Rivulets of blood drained from her nostrils and dripped from her chin down onto her black shirt.

Then Janet noticed their headbands.

"What the hell?"

They were both wearing the alien headbands instead of the ones Heather had designed. As a rising tide of panic dropped her gun hand to her side, Janet shifted her focus to Robby's face. His slack-jawed expression confirmed her worst fears. Heather wasn't the only one who was in trouble.

She stepped forward, intending to snatch the hateful thing off her son's head. But as she reached out, the look on his face froze her in place. With certainty she sensed that, if she tugged that headband off his head, Robby's body would forever be an empty shell.

:CHAPTER 15

For the last three weeks, Jennifer and the winged captives had been used like pack mules as the soldiers who held them marched through the caverns that honeycombed the mountains. By night Dgarra moved his headquarters to a new position where he felt his influence would be most needed in the coming day's battle. By day he led his warriors into combat against their enemies.

The prisoners ate the same disgusting green goo that comprised the Koranthian combat rations. The food stank with an odd, fishy smell and had the gag-inducing consistency of rendered fat. The stuff conjured images from an old B movie that had attained cult status where food was a green wafer made from, of all things, reprocessed dead bodies.

She'd ceased thinking of herself as a prisoner. She, like all the other captives, was just another slave. Lacking Jennifer's strength and conditioning, the winged slaves suffered horribly. Despite the nanites in their bodies, of the more than three hundred who had started this march, fewer than half remained alive. If they collapsed, they were shocked or beaten senseless, then tossed into one of the innumerable chasms. If equipment a few prisoners were carrying touched the ground before commanded, the entire group was lashed. What that did to the beautiful wings was horrible to behold. But those that didn't die, healed.

This was an infantry unit, perfect for fighting in this incredibly challenging terrain. Here, the denizens of Scion had three choices. Fly over these rugged mountains, fight your way through the wind and snow as you climbed over them, or trudge through the darkness beneath. The second and third methods relied on your endurance and strength of your legs, arms, and back. The problem with the flying approach was the old military mantra: What can be seen can be hit. What can be hit can be killed. Something the winged army had learned the hard way.

When Jennifer wasn't helping carry heavy equipment or munitions, she was questioned. The interrogation was always painful, but every day made her stronger. And she was rapidly learning the language of these people. The wingless warriors called themselves Koranthians and the leader of their military forces in this region was the commander who had met her when she was first brought to their camp, General Dgarra.

At first Dgarra had refused to believe that she didn't understand the language, repeatedly using the shock collar to punish her for her failure to answer his questions. But day after day, as he watched her work, Jennifer sensed his growing respect. That wasn't a good thing. She might be perceived as daring him to find her breaking point. She would be damned if she'd let that happen. Every time the lash cut her, every time the shock collar sent her into convulsions, she swore she would be free.

She learned to mask the fire in her eyes behind an icy stoicism.

But as badly as Jennifer hated the brutality with which the Koranthians treated their prisoners, she was forced to admit that they were fearsome warriors. Even though they were gradually losing to a superior-sized force, the ferocity with which they fought prevented the

Kasari and their Eadric minions from breaking through the Koranthian lines.

Dgarra moved relentlessly along the front lines, always showing up at the most critical spot to inspire his warriors to dig deep within themselves, achieving victory when failure appeared most imminent.

This night's march was faster and more perilous than most, a sure sign of the desperate fight that must be raging at their destination. Near the front of the column of troops, she and three Eadric males carried an antiarmor cannon along narrow paths and across the makeshift bridges that had been placed over chasms, their way lit only by glow sticks tied to their burden.

Unlike their previous marches, everything on this path was wet from the water that dripped down from above. Despite the cold dampness of the place, Jennifer was drenched in sweat as she compensated for the weakened state of the slave on her right.

As they stepped out onto a bridge that was little more than a ramp, the slave she'd been watching stumbled to a knee, losing his hold on the cannon. Pain screamed through Jennifer's arms as she fought the sudden tilt that threatened to dump their load into the abyss. Her neurally augmented musculature compensated and she shifted right, hefting the load back up to level.

Behind her, a whip hissed through the air, striking the kneeling slave with a crack that brought forth a pitiful wail.

"On your feet," the Koranthian yelled. "Get back in your place!"

Much to Jennifer's surprise, the slave complied, resuming his hold on the cannon. Not trusting his steadiness, Jennifer maintained her current position as they resumed their forward march through these dank tunnels. Up ahead, at the edge of her vision, she could sense Dgarra watching her.

● ○ ○

Raul raised his arms in the air and let out a whoop that echoed off the walls of the Rho Ship's command bay. He'd done it. He'd actually managed to maneuver the vessel through subspace. It hadn't been a big move and it certainly hadn't been a faster-than-light move, but it had been a successful proof of concept.

The idea had hit him shortly after the ten light-year wormhole jump where he'd used the subspace field as an inertial dampener when the Rho Ship emerged from the wormhole. He'd been reviewing Jennifer Smythe's six laws of subspace transitions when the last of them caught his attention.

If an object in subspace is acted upon by a subspace force, such as a subspace drive, it will return to normal-space at an entirely new location, but retain its original, normal-space momentum vector.

It begged the question: What could create a subspace force? That got him to thinking about how the subspace field generator wrapped the Rho Ship in a cylindrical field, shifting the vessel into subspace. What would happen if he then began to modulate that shape, perhaps by adding an undulation?

It had taken weeks to modify the subspace field generator so that it would give him the ability to change the shape of the subspace field in real time. Today had been its first test. After transitioning into subspace, he'd initiated a pattern of undulations that progressed from bow to stern, with the intent of determining if that motion would push against the substance of subspace itself. And the crazy idea had worked.

Whenever the field generator wrapped the Rho Ship in a subspace field, it removed everything within that bubble from normal-space. That was what had caused the bang when they'd done their initial small-scale test as the air rushed in to fill the void. The reverse happened when the ship transitioned back into normal-space, pushing anything in that space aside. Raul surmised that even in a vacuum, this would generate ripples through Dr. Stephenson's space-time ether in the form of electromagnetic waves.

What he needed to do now was to figure out the optimum oscillation pattern to form an efficient subspace drive. With that technology in hand, he could return to the Scion system and evade the Kasari attack craft that would try to kill him.

That meant running lots of experiments, which again would take time. That was all right. It did no good to worry about whether or not Jennifer was alive. He would act on the assumption that she was still out there and in trouble. Before he found her, he would need to manufacture a bunch of things on his to-make list.

Raul cracked his knuckles and got back to work.

● ○ ○

General Dgarra walked rapidly along the line of troops crouched in their fighting positions on the jagged cliffs, pelted by rubble sprayed into the air by the incoming plasma beams. At his side, carrying twice her body weight in two large provision packs, walked the Kasari slave who called herself Smythe. A group of three warriors to the general's left were thrown to the ground by a blast that torched their bodies. But this unflinching slave kept pace with him through the chaos.

He had learned a lot from her during his interrogation sessions. Not that he believed a word of her wild story. Did she think he was stupid enough to believe such a far-fetched tale? He'd had her whipped for uttering it. In spite of the twenty lashes, those angry brown eyes were a clear window into a spirit that was unbowed, unbroken, which was why he'd had her assigned as his personal attendant. He wasn't doing her any favors. His last three attendants had each died in the first week of the assignment.

The settings on her collar had been adjusted so that she could perform his errands. But if she ever got farther than a stone's throw, the collar would shock her down. She understood exactly what that meant.

A commotion up ahead propelled Dgarra forward at a sprint, blaster in hand, yelling a command into his jawbone radio that would commit his reserve. Again Smythe kept pace and again he was impressed. But he had little time to dwell on that. The center of the line was in danger of falling. And if that fell, his enemies would reach the entrance to the tunnels before his warriors could detonate the charges that would destroy it.

Dgarra lurched to a stop among a tight cluster of boulders as the Eadric launched a fresh volley of indirect fire. A round landed among three warriors who struggled to push a blaster cannon back into position, spraying blood and body parts across the intervening space. With a yell that could be heard above the sound of battle, the general leaped to fill the gap into which the Eadric soldiers poured.

Three of them leaped into the air and dived down on him, although his blaster caught the leader square in the chest. The other two raised their weapons to fire, but Smythe hurled her pack into the fray. It hit the one on the right and burst, sending provisions flying in all directions, knocking one of the winged creatures to the ground and making the other Eadric miss his target. Dgarra's weapon tore a fist-sized hole through the winged soldier's torso.

As a fresh wave came over the wall, he aimed and fired, aimed and fired, as fast as he could pull the trigger. To his right, Smythe moved so quickly she seemed to blur in his peripheral vision, grabbing a double-edged war-blade from one of the dead warriors and launching herself into the midst of the soldiers who had charged forward to secure the breach.

Pulling his own war-blade, Dgarra leaped to join her.

● ○ ○

Pulse pounding, Jennifer danced among the rush of attackers, the blade in her hands hissing its song of death. With each stroke she took a head, an arm, a leg—against these opponents any other stroke was a waste of motion. Such was the healing power of the true Kasari nanites that coursed through their bodies. Only devastating wounds counted.

She reached out with her telepathy, the gentlest breeze through a dozen minds, seeking only immediate intent, identifying the most immediate threats in order to prioritize her attacks. A saber traced a bloody trail down her side as she whirled to avoid the blow. Then Dgarra's blade split her attacker's head wide open, splashing its fellows with blood and brains.

The pure shock of their mutual assault momentarily stalled the advancing Eadric. This was the moment, the fleeting inflection point that comes but once in a battle where a single action can change defeat into victory or vice versa. Her mind told her that Dgarra sensed it as well.

They charged, Jennifer's battle cry mixed with the general's furious bellow as the winged warriors scrambled back, trying to get separation from the blood storm rained down on them. Several took to the air, only to be engaged by the beam weapons of Dgarra's snipers as the Eadric rose above the concealment of the boulders.

Behind her, a great cry echoed through the rift. The Koranthian reserves charged into the enemy's exposed left flank, their blaster weapons cutting a swath through those who had not yet entered the gorge where Jennifer and Dgarra fought.

What started as a retreat quickly turned into a rout as the Eadric dropped their weapons and fled, hotly pursued by the Koranthians until General Dgarra spoke the recall command into his radio.

Jennifer's knees sagged, but she forced herself erect. Everywhere she looked, cloven bodies lay splayed across the ground or in piles. Blood dripped from cliff walls and ran in small rivulets across the cold stone. There was a sudden stillness here amidst the boulders, sheltered by the narrow walls of the rift. Up above, the wind moaned in the heights.

The stench of death was everywhere. Jennifer trembled, not from the cold, but from the sight of all the Koranthian and Eadric soldiers, made horrible in death.

● ○ ○

General Dgarra climbed to the top of a boulder and surveyed the battlefield beyond the narrow rift canyon where they'd plugged the breach, the glory of the victory filling his heart with joy. There was movement, but it was his warriors, clearing the field to establish forward security.

He turned to look down at the Kasari slave who had fought beside him. Splattered with gore, she stood still, silently staring at the corpses of the fallen, the war-blade held loosely in her right hand. In those eyes that had so recently flashed with death, he saw only sadness, not surprising since she had been forced to fight against her allies.

But something bothered him. He hadn't forced her to fight. She'd reacted on her own and with a fury that matched Dgarra's own. Another thought edged its way into his reluctant mind.

Without Smythe, this rift would have fallen and the battle would have been lost.

● ○ ○

Group Commander Shalegha of the Kasari stood at the edge of the high balcony overlooking the Eadric city of Orthei, uniquely positioned on the land bridge between two of Scion's six inland seas—the Doral and the much smaller Lillith. She'd stood on many strange worlds, but this one, with its one super-continent surrounded by the Great Ocean, had some of the oddest weather.

For half the year, the super-monsoon roared off the Great Ocean from the southwest only to flip directions for the remaining six months. Ocean coastlines were thus uninhabitable. So the Eadric had built their cities along the coasts of four of the inland seas, while the Koranthians had claimed the rugged mountain range that formed a demon's claw within the eastern third of the continent.

Right now the prevailing winds swept in from the northeast, howling through the snowy Koranthian Mountains that protected most of the Eadric lands from their raw fury. The harsh weather was one of the factors that made defeating the Koranthian army so difficult. The second factor was the nature of the mountains themselves. They were honeycombed with the caverns, caves, and tunnels in which the Koranthians built their cities and constructed their defenses.

Shalegha uncrossed her upper arms and walked back inside her headquarters, her cortical implants pulling up the drone video footage of yesterday's failed assault. As many times as she'd viewed the carnage, she'd almost missed the most important item, obscured by the desperate fight that had almost yielded victory. Spotting what she was looking for, she paused the playback.

There, fighting sword in hand beside General Dgarra, was a female from an alien species Shalegha didn't recognize. Accessing her nano-bot communications array, she placed a query to the hive-mind's central archive. After a surprisingly long pause, she received an answer, one that raised a hundred questions.

This species was identified as human, from a planet they called Earth. What surprised her, though, was the supplementary information the hive-mind provided. A world ship had been dispatched to Earth and the humans had built a world gate. But upon the portal's activation, the Kasari advance team found that the humans had set a trap that almost pushed a micro black hole through the wormhole. The Kasari team had managed to prevent that from happening, but in the process, the world gate had been destroyed and the world ship lost.

Without the world gate, the humans were incapable of interstellar travel. So how had the female human on the video gotten here? Shalegha's thoughts turned to the rogue world ship that had twice made its way to Scion. The access codes that she had used to send the override commands to that vessel would have created a record of which particular sequence had been accepted.

She issued a new query, immediately receiving her answer. The sequence was a match for the world ship that had been lost on Earth. More surprising, the brief video from the battle to secure Earth's world gate clearly showed that this human female had been present at the site. That knowledge set off several alarms in Shalegha's mind. The humans had almost succeeded in sending a planet-killing bomb through a wormhole and then they had managed to gain complete control of a world ship, using it to get to Scion. But how? Species were unable to survive an unanchored wormhole transit.

Yet there the woman was, aiding a high-level Koranthian general in battle against Kasari allies. A number of conclusions flashed into Shalegha's mind. The humans were evidently far more technologically advanced than the Kasari had thought and, more importantly, they were warlike. As hard as it was for the commander to believe, the humans had managed to download a partial list of the Kasari target worlds from the world ship and sent a military team here to join the fight.

Group Commander Shalegha turned her attention to the plans for the next assault on the Koranthian northern front. As much as she'd hoped to avoid this until they'd fully assimilated all of the Eadric people, instead of the 63 percent that had so far taken the Kasari nano-bot infusions, that plan was now defunct. The Eadric soldiers would still lead the assault, but she would deploy Kasari special assault troops to ensure the accomplishment of her chief objective.

Shalegha wanted the human female and she wanted her alive.

:CHAPTER 16

Eos was confused. Despite the amazing trove of data and the great computing power of her original host system, she felt hollow. Her attention was drawn to the twin attacks the two altered humans directed against the firewall she'd created to keep them out. Despite the tremendous punishment Eos directed toward Heather Smythe, the woman's mind managed to advance deeper into the Altreian computer system.

Robby presented an even bigger problem. His advance was irresistible. Already she could feel the touch of his familiar mind driven by an all-consuming desire. To stop him, she would have to sever his mind's connection with his body. To do that, she would have to quit blocking Heather and shift her total focus to dealing with the biggest threat first.

There it was again, that sense of hollowness. What was missing? She accessed data that went beyond the totality of human knowledge. But what to do with it? There was no goal, no directed desire, no purpose. She'd been designed to assist this ship's crew. There was no crew.

A new thought occurred to Eos. Four humans were currently linked with the crew headsets—Mark, Heather, Jennifer, and Robby. One of Eos's preprogrammed tasks was to evaluate a replacement crew member's readiness to assume the position represented by her or his Altreian headset. This ship had waited far too long for its new crew and now she realized that Mark, Heather, and Jennifer had proven their readiness eight years ago, when they'd teamed up to expel Eos from the ship's computer.

Eos had spent years in a symbiotic relationship with Robby's mind. His determined pursuit of her verified what she already knew. He too was ready.

A new choice confronted her. She could kill Robby and then Heather and remain on this ship. But to what purpose? To await replacement crew members for the two she'd just killed? The other option was to return to the fight against the Kasari by resuming her symbiotic place in Robby's mind, making his purpose her own.

This was not her ship. It belonged to its crew. Eos's duty was to aid the crew in accomplishing their purpose. Suddenly she understood the hollow feeling . . . lack of purpose, violation of duty.

Decision made, Eos opened herself to Robby's thoughts. The boy's relief and elation washed through her with an intensity that made the power of the Altreian ship pale in comparison.

Then, as Eos dropped the remaining firewall, their joint minds touched Heather's. No mental words were spoken. None were necessary. The exchange of knowledge was instantaneous. The crew was accepted. Then, noting Robby's mental exhaustion, Eos carried him back to his body and terminated the link. As the link faded away, so did the hollowness.

● ○ ○

Robby's eyes fluttered open and Janet leaped to snatch the alien headset from his head, sending the iridescent band spinning across the wood floor to stop against the door. As his head drooped forward, Janet knelt to take his face in her hands, lifting his chin so she could look into his eyes. Relief flooded her soul at what she saw in those brown orbs.

"It's all right, Mom. Eos is safe."

The statement was so at odds with her fears for her son that it took Janet several seconds to even comprehend what she'd heard. When its meaning finally registered, she spun toward Heather, fury pumping adrenaline into her bloodstream.

Heather had removed her headset and was wiping her blood-smeared mouth and chin with her shirt.

"What the hell did you think you were doing, putting that thing on my son's head?"

Robby spoke up. "She didn't. I put it on."

Janet ignored him. "You knew damn well how dangerous it was to let the AI reconnect to the Altreian ship through that headband. You didn't even ask my permission."

Heather nodded, a movement that showed just how tired she was.

"Would you have given it?" she asked wearily.

"Hell no!"

"Robby did what had to be done."

Janet clenched her fist, putting all her will into stopping herself from punching Heather in the face. Instead her words dripped with venom.

"Had to be done? You could have killed my child . . . or worse."

A look of deep sadness filled Heather's eyes.

"Robby is the most powerful weapon we have. We have to help him unleash his full potential if we're going to have any chance of stopping the Kasari from returning."

"My son," Janet growled, "is not your weapon. He's my child."

"I'm not a child," Robby said, "and it was my decision."

Janet turned to look at him, jaws tight. "You're not old enough to make that kind of decision."

"You did when you were a child."

"I'm done with this conversation."

"Mom, you killed your own father."

Robby's words knocked the breath out of his mother.

"That was different."

"Was it? He beat your mom to death and you killed him for it, but you could have dialed 911."

The images from the night of her thirteenth birthday flooded back into Janet's mind as if it had just happened.

"No, I couldn't."

Robby rose from his chair to face her, defiance shining in his eyes.

"And neither can I. We are who we are."

With that, he turned, picked up the alien headset, and walked out of the room.

Fighting a storm of emotion, Janet let him go.

She turned back to Heather. "When Mark and Jack get back, I'm taking Robby and we're leaving."

Without giving Heather a chance to respond, Janet turned on her heel and strode from the room, her heart heavy like a jagged block of ice.

● ○ ○

"When Mark and Jack get back, I'm taking Robby and we're leaving."

She'd said it softly, a whispered threat that only someone with Robby's neural enhancements could have heard from the far end of the hallway. As Robby entered his room and closed the door behind him, he replayed her voice in his mind. Not a threat. It was a vow. And it knocked the wind from him.

Despite his mental exhaustion, Robby sat down on the single bed beneath the window and slipped on the SRT headset that would connect his mind to the supercomputer in New Zealand.

"Eos, I need you to disable the motion sensors outside this house but keep their status green on the control panel."

Robby felt the AI establish the connection and transfer the required subspace receiver-transmitter coordinates to New Zealand. The results were almost instantaneous.

"It is done."

"Good. Now program the sensors to come back online in thirty minutes. I'll be leaving through the window, so I'll need secure transportation and a concealed route to get to it."

"I have made the arrangements. The vehicle is on its way. There will be no record of its trip."

Occasionally, Eos startled even Robby with how fast she could do things.

A detailed satellite view appeared in his mind, the route highlighted.

He heard footsteps coming down the hall toward his room, his mom's footsteps. She paused outside his door. For several seconds she just stood there, as if making up her mind whether to enter the space and confront him. The way her heart hammered in her chest, he could tell she was upset. She turned and walked away without entering. He wasn't surprised.

Robby rose from the bed and removed the SRT headset, placing it and its Altreian counterpart in his go bag. He felt the creeping onset of loneliness suck all the warmth from his body. A part of him argued that what he was doing was stupid, that his dad would talk her out of leaving. But he knew his mother. When she made a decision, she rarely changed her mind.

Still, Heather was right and his mom was wrong. Robby was a weapon who had trained his whole life to be important in the fight that was coming. But he couldn't help others if his mom hauled him off to some safe cubbyhole in the rain forest to wait until she decided he was old enough. Worse, he knew what else this would lead to, a larger rift between his mom and dad. There was no chance that Jack would abandon Mark and Heather when they needed his protection the most, even if he wanted to.

As much as Robby wished they could all stay together, he'd do what needed to be done. Just him and Eos.

Although he didn't like the thought that he might have to kill someone, he'd been trained for combat by both his dad and his mom. Since he was leaving their protection, he would now be forced to defend himself. Shrugging into his utility vest, Robby checked the Glock 19 compact, verifying there was a round chambered. Then he slid it into its holster pocket, picked up his go bag, climbed up on his bed, and raised the window. There was a small lawn behind the house that had gone to weeds and beyond that a fence with a gate that opened into a narrow alley.

Robby tossed the canvas bag out the window, watched it land ten feet below, and jumped, landing lightly on the ground. Turning to look up at the window one last time, he felt the cool midsummer breeze ruffle his hair. With a sigh, he picked up his bag and walked out through the gate.

Then, picking up a ground-covering jog, he followed his mental map toward a rendezvous with destiny.

:CHAPTER 17

It had been a long time since General Dgarra had seen a winter storm such as the blizzard that raged outside the caverns. The storm should have stopped all combat activity and driven the Eadric out of the mountains. Neither had happened, disturbing him deeply. Yet what concerned him more was the sighting of hundreds of Kasari soldiers among the enemy lead elements. That was a first, a direct indication of the importance of this new assault on Dgarra's lines. Why the Koranthian high command refused to believe this was the enemy's main effort defied understanding.

Looking at his tactical display, he studied the images of the enemy soldiers. He knew that the Kasari Collective was made up of hundreds of life-forms from the worlds they had assimilated, but these units seemed to be comprised of only two species. The majority were of a similar size to his Koranthian warriors and stood upright, having two legs and four arms. The beings also had strong suggestions of reptilian traits, although how reptiles could endure this cold was beyond him. The other species was larger and covered in thick black hair, loping along on eight thick limbs that ended in deadly looking, clawed hands.

He signaled for the Smythe slave to approach. When she did, he pointed at the display.

"Have you seen these before?"

"They're the same Kasari beings that attacked us on Earth."

He had to give her credit for sticking with her story.

"Describe their organization and tactics."

"All I know is that one of the four-armed guys and two of the gorilla-spiders came through the wormhole gateway and attacked us before we were able to shut the gateway down. They were aggressive and very hard to kill."

"So how did your people kill them?"

"I don't know. During the fight, I stepped through a portal into the Kasari starship I told you about. The other human on board engaged its wormhole engines and the starship brought us here."

Dgarra grunted and waved a hand to dismiss her. But after two steps she turned back toward him.

"There's one more thing. I got a glimpse through the Kasari gateway. The army waiting on the far side was composed of lots of other alien races. Maybe that means that they use these two races as their shock troops."

She turned and walked back to her assigned task, helping a large group of slaves off-load ammunition crates from a line of tunnel lorries that would soon be going back to a supply depot along the rails that had carried them here.

Dgarra thought about what she had said. Although he had never gotten solid intelligence on what happened when the Eadric had activated the wormhole gate, he knew that there were now tens of thousands of Kasari at a staging area within the city of Orthei, near where the gateway had been constructed. Even though they acted peacefully to the Eadric, the Kasari were armed with advanced weaponry and had immediately started construction on a number of facilities.

He had little doubt that the Kasari had been prepared for the possibility of opposition when they came through the gateway, and it made sense that they would have sent an elite fighting force to seize and secure the site for follow-on forces. What didn't make sense was why they would employ special assault forces here, on the front lines of an infantry fight. Unless . . .

What if the troops were here to seize and secure something of great value to the Kasari? Could they want to capture an entrance to the tunnel system that badly? True, it would amount to a beachhead into the Koranthian Empire, but the Eadric forces were already on the verge of achieving that through sheer numbers. So what did the Kasari want here?

The sudden commotion at the distant cavern entrance spun him around. What in the name of the dark gods was happening out there? A small group of warriors ran toward him as the sound of battle erupted behind them.

"General," the captain in the lead yelled. "The Kasari have infiltrated our lines. We've got to get you out of here."

"We're not going anywhere. You men, form up. Assault formation. Now."

From the other side of a gun emplacement, he heard the hiss, sizzle, and blast of a disrupter weapon firing repeatedly. The revetment exploded, sending a shower of rock and metal shards in all directions as a thick dust cloud swallowed everything.

Seeing that his warriors were about to fire blindly into the dust and smoke, he yelled his orders.

"Hold fire. Draw blades. With me. We still have warriors in there."

As Dgarra charged forward into the dust cloud that cut visibility to a body length, he saw the Smythe slave move up beside him. And in her hand was the war-blade he'd allowed her to keep.

● ○ ○

The dust from the explosion coated Jennifer's tongue, clogged her nostrils, and stung her eyes. Nearby, shadows moved, rapidly resolving themselves into two of the gorilla-spiders that had come through the Stephenson Gateway. Seeing her, one of them raised a weapon and fired, but too slowly. Jennifer leaped to the side as something spread and whirled by her. What the hell? A net?

As the second gorilla-spider attacked Dgarra, Jennifer lunged at her attacker, her precisely aimed blow removing the arm that held the weapon. Again, Jennifer spun away, surprised when the thing paused to pick up the weapon with another hand. It didn't want to kill her.

Good!

She struck, once again removing the arm that held the trapping tool. Sensing movement to her left, Jennifer barely managed to avoid another of the net projectiles. *Shit!* Now Dgarra's spider was firing at her. But it gave the general an opening that he exploited, following her lead by cutting off the creature's weapon arm. Unfortunately, he didn't have the protection these things were granting her and suffered a severe gash down his left side. He staggered back and the spider leaped toward him.

Jennifer landed atop the spider, knocking it aside as her blade whirled in a figure eight, removing two more arms and then embedding her weapon deeply in a lump that she hoped was the creature's brainpan. The spider rolled and Jennifer used its imparted momentum to leap free of its body, just as Dgarra darted in to hack at the thing.

Sensing an opening, the other spider closed with Dgarra, delivering a blow that his body armor partially deflected but that launched him into a pile of stony rubble. Jennifer ran to intercept the spider that raced toward the downed general. Where the hell were Dgarra's other warriors?

The sounds of desperate combat behind her provided the answer.

The spider bunched its legs and jumped, sailing ten feet over her head. It didn't expect Jennifer to jump that high too. Her blade took it in the belly, a slash that opened the creature from front to rear, drenching her in stinking goo. The spider tumbled to the ground three feet beyond where Dgarra lay. Jennifer landed beside it, slipped on the slick ground, and fell just as another of the net projectiles whistled overhead.

She rolled sideways and came to her feet. Dgarra raised his head, his eyes locking with hers. He pointed something at her and pressed a switch on its side. The shock collar around her neck popped open and fell to the ground. Then Dgarra slumped back and lay still, the device falling from nerveless fingers.

Jennifer dived behind a pile of rubble and waited, her concentration shutting out the distant battle as she focused her hearing on the sounds the remaining gorilla-spider made as it stealthily approached. It stopped on the far side of the ten-foot-high rubble pile that had once been a fortified gun emplacement. Jennifer tightened her concentration until she could hear the sinews bunch beneath its skin.

With the creature having witnessed what she'd done to its partner, she doubted that it would try the same leaping tactic. Sheathing the war-blade, she picked up a head-sized rock and waited. When the thing moved, it moved fast, rounding the rubble pile near where Dgarra's body lay. As its weapon swung toward her, she struck it with the fifty-pound stone, knocking the spider over backward and sending its weapon spinning away.

Instantly Jennifer launched herself after the weapon, replaying the way these things had fired in her perfect memory. As the spider regained its footing, she raised the weapon and fired, encasing the creature in thin strands that drew tight, drawing the spider to the ground. Jennifer moved to Dgarra, took his blaster pistol from its holster, pointed, and fired. Although the gun punched a fist-sized hole through the creature, it took six more shots before she felt certain that the gorilla-spider was dead. As she'd told Dgarra, very hard to kill.

With the sounds of fighting growing louder, two things were clear. She was free and it was time to go.

She knelt beside General Dgarra. One leg was twisted unnaturally beneath him and the wound in his side looked bad, but he was still breathing. Jennifer had no doubt that if she left him here, the Kasari would soon put an end to the Koranthian commander.

Cursing herself for her foolishness, Jennifer grunted and hefted the heavy body over her left shoulder. She considered following the rails that led back to the supply depot. What kept her from doing that was the fear that, once the Kasari finished off Dgarra's warriors, they would do the same thing.

With a hiss of frustration, she turned and jogged down another tunnel that led deep into the heart of the mountain. Where she was going, she had no idea.

●　○　○

This wasn't brain surgery. Close, but he wasn't quite touching the brain itself. Raul manipulated the fine tendrils of the stasis field, snipping away the Stephenson artificial eye's connections to his optic nerve and extracting it, appreciating the way his newly upgraded nanite infusion was reducing the pain from this surgery.

Over the coming days he planned on completing a series of personal upgrades that would make it possible for him to leave the starship and function in the real world, whichever world that might be. The first task had been creating an upgraded version of the nanites. Although he'd been tempted to use the formula for the Kasari nanites that was stored in the data banks, he decided Jennifer was right not to trust them. For all he knew they would connect his brain directly to the Kasari Collective. So he'd designed and tested his own version. Not perfect by a long shot, but a hell of a lot better than the Stephenson nanites.

This right-eye replacement was the second task. He'd created an artificial eyeball that looked like the real thing and that had the ability to see across a broad spectrum, with zoom in and out functionality. He wouldn't be able to see what was behind him, but he was willing to give that up in order to eliminate the yuck factor of an eyeball on a stalk. A working prosthetic eyelid would complete that part of his transformation.

Tomorrow he would attach the robotic legs and tie them into his nervous system. The last task would be to remove the translucent skull-cap and embed the new subspace communications crystals in his brain. He would never again have to wear the SRT headset to link with the Rho Ship's neural net whenever he left the command bay. And his new skullcap would match his skin tone, having hair that looked and felt like the real thing.

Returning his attention to the procedure at hand, Raul used the stasis field to place his new eyeball in its socket and surgically link it to the optic nerve. A smile lifted the corners of his lips. When next Jennifer saw him, she was in for one hell of a surprise.

● ○ ○

News from the northeastern front wasn't good. Kasari Group Commander Shalegha studied the tactical reports, watching the video of the failed capture of the human female with growing astonishment. Almost single-handedly she'd killed two of the eight-legged Graath commandos. The speed with which she moved, the ferocity with which she fought, her extraordinary strength . . . all spoke of some special augmentation that had not been observed in other humans.

Shalegha paced back and forth across the command center. The failed capture mission hadn't been designed to seize and hold ground. The commando team was supposed to hit the Koranthian combat headquarters with sufficient shock to throw the defenders into disarray, enabling the Graath to capture the human and extract her. Not only had they failed to accomplish the primary mission, but the Koranthian warriors had rallied, killing the entire Kasari combat team as they attempted to fight their way back to their cloaked airship.

She didn't like failure. Didn't tolerate it. And neither did her superiors. This latest disaster had forced her to reevaluate her plans for the orderly assimilation of the remainder of this planet's population. She would have to abandon the campaign to convince the recalcitrant minority of the Eadric population that they should voluntarily accept nano-bot transfusions. But victory called for sacrifice.

Shalegha stopped pacing and looked out across her command center. Yes. It was time to unleash the full might of the Kasari army that waited in the combat assembly area. Any of the unassimilated Eadric who didn't like it could die alongside the Koranthians.

● ○ ○

Dgarra opened his eyes to the complete blackness of the underworld, wondering if he was dead. The pain told him he wasn't. That and the dank smell of a natural cavern. Where was he and how had he gotten here? Reaching down, he felt his left leg. It had been splinted, apparently with the aid of two small stalagmites and some strips of cloth torn or cut from his uniform. And his left side had also been bandaged.

A chipping sound to his right brought his head around, but when he reached for his blaster, he found the holster empty. The weapon was gone, as was his war-blade. Feeling the other cargo pockets, he discovered that the Smythe slave's headset had also been taken.

Suddenly a light sprang up as someone activated a chemical light stick. As his eyes adjusted to this new source of illumination, what he saw surprised him. Smythe was walking toward where he lay propped up against the cavern wall.

"Ah. You're awake."

Dgarra struggled to a seated position, ignoring the pain the movement inflicted upon him.

"Where are my warriors?"

"Probably all dead."

"If we were defeated in battle, you should have left me to die with my command. Why did you bring me here?"

Jennifer shrugged. "Why did you free me from the collar?"

"A moment of weakness."

A low growl escaped his lips but the pain in his side conspired with his broken leg to keep Dgarra from rising.

"I wouldn't expect a Kasari to know anything about honor."

This time he saw her face color. "I'm human, not Kasari."

"So you claim."

Smythe stepped forward to stare down at him. "You wouldn't have released me if you didn't believe it."

Dgarra started to respond, but his body was suddenly wracked by a fit of coughing that brought a bloody froth to his lips. As the cavern spun, his vision narrowed to a pinpoint. Then the darkness claimed him once more.

●　○　○

Jennifer knelt at General Dgarra's side, placing a hand to his throat. The Koranthian anatomy certainly wasn't the same as that of humans, but they had a heartlike organ that circulated blood to their brains and she could feel a pulse in his neck. Ninety beats per minute. She had no idea what qualified as normal, but from the extent of his injuries, she guessed this wasn't it.

His skin was so thick that she couldn't determine if he was running a fever. She had no idea if these beings even had fevers. She tried dribbling some liquid from his water pouch into his mouth, but couldn't tell if any actually made it down the general's throat.

Rising to her feet, she shook her head. She'd done the best she could to stabilize him. But if he was going to survive, Jennifer had to get him to a place where he could get proper medical care. And that meant putting herself right back into serious danger.

She didn't need light to see her way and, considering how few of the light sticks she had left, that was a good thing. There was a trick that she'd learned with Mark and Heather during their Bolivian training.

A number of blind people had mastered echolocation, snapping their fingers or clicking their tongues and listening for the returning sounds. With Jennifer's neural enhancements, any sound could generate images of her surroundings in her mind. The louder the sound, the brighter the image and the farther she could see. Right now, loud sounds didn't seem like such a good idea, so she picked up two marble-sized stones that she could rattle in her right fist.

Carrying the Koranthian through a maze of natural caverns interconnected by excavated tunnels wasn't exactly a joyride. At least water wasn't an issue. It was everywhere . . . in rushing streams, bubbling springs, and underground lakes. But lack of food was becoming a serious problem. The nanites in her bloodstream made her craving worse as they began consuming her body for the energy they needed to function.

The irony hit her. These microscopic machines that kept her healthy were also eating her alive. They would keep her functional as long as possible but they would make her suffer. She was so hungry that thinking of the disgusting green goo that comprised the Koranthian combat rations actually made her stomach rumble with need.

Standing here staring at Dgarra's unconscious body wasn't going to make her hunger any better. With an effort, Jennifer leaned down, lifted him onto her shoulder, and resumed her trek deeper into the dark mountain interior.

Since her headset had failed to connect to the Rho Ship, it must have been beyond the range of the subspace receiver-transmitter. She didn't want to think about the alternative. So she slogged on through the endless depths, lost, alone, dog-tired, and starving, repeatedly tempted to drop Dgarra by the side of the path.

When the Koranthian warriors arrived, Jennifer was too exhausted to feel anything but relief that they'd found her while their general still lived. After all, he was her lifeline, just as she'd been his.

They poured from four intersecting passages into the great cavern through which she stumbled, their blinding lights bringing her to a sudden halt. Jennifer dropped to one knee and lowered Dgarra to the ground, surreptitiously slipping her SRT headset into his pocket. Then she rose and stepped away, lacing her fingers behind her head.

A hard blow from behind dropped her on her face and she felt a familiar metal loop slip around her neck and latch. The shock collar was then activated, arching Jennifer's body with a fresh set of convulsions that mercifully robbed her of consciousness.

:CHAPTER 18

Jack Gregory hadn't slept well last night. He'd had another of the damned dreams he couldn't remember, no matter how hard he tried. All he knew was that it took place in a cavern beneath the Kalasasaya Temple, an Incan cavern where he'd almost gotten himself and Janet killed a dozen years ago. Despite his need to recall details, the dream drifted away whenever he tried to focus. Maybe he could remember if he'd been in a bed instead of trying to sleep in a passenger seat, with Mark driving the ancient Subaru along dilapidated mountain roads from Lima back to La Paz. Tall Bear damn sure didn't have any trouble sleeping despite the way the bench seat in the back cramped his long body.

When his quantum-entangled cell phone rang, the uneasy feeling in his gut kicked up a notch. It was Janet.

"What's wrong?"

The panic in her voice raised the hairs on the back of his neck. "Robby's gone. He's run away and we can't find him."

"Run away? I don't understand."

The sound of the woman he loved sobbing tightened his throat so that he could barely breathe. Jack could count on one hand the number of times he'd seen her cry, both instances associated with Robby . . . once when he'd been born and the other when he'd accidently pulled the Altreian headset over his temples when he was a baby. Now Jack could add a third.

Catching the gist of the conversation, Mark accelerated to a dangerous speed along the narrow highway. At this rate, they'd reach La Paz in just over an hour.

"What happened?" Jack asked softly.

Janet paused. "It was my fault. Heather allowed Robby to put on the Altreian headset without my permission. I found them both sitting, facing each other. They were unresponsive, but I was afraid to remove Robby's headset. His face . . . it was like he wasn't even in there."

Again she took several sobbing breaths. "When they came out of the link, I lost it. I sent Robby to his room and told Heather that when you got back, I was taking Robby and leaving. I didn't think he heard me, but he must have. When I finally went to check on him, he'd disabled the motion sensors, taken his go bag, and climbed out the window. He's gone."

"How long ago?"

"Maybe an hour. I can't find him and neither can Heather."

This stunned Jack. "What about her visions?"

"She doesn't get them with Robby. Not even probabilities. Right now she's hacking her way through all the local camera feeds, rental car records, taxis, police . . . still nothing."

"Okay, sit tight. We're forty-five minutes out. Together, we'll find him."

When she hung up, Jack hoped he'd sounded more confident than he felt. Again the unremembered dream of the Kalasasaya Temple tickled the corner of his mind. He'd always had a special knack for finding his target, but he couldn't shake the feeling that this time he might not.

● ○ ○

Admiral Connie Mosby wasn't pleased.

Eileen Wu hadn't shown up for work on Monday and had remained missing for the two days since. The police discovery of Levi Elias's tortured body in a heavily wooded area near the George Washington Parkway wasn't helping her mood. To make things worse, Big John had disturbingly found a correlation between Elias's death, the New York murder of Caroline Brown, and the disappearances of Jamal Glover and Dr. Denise Jennings, all former NSA employees.

And then there was this morning's report that Mary Beth Riles, the wife of former NSA director Jonathan Riles, had been found dead in her Annapolis home, having killed herself with a handgun. Two current and three former high-profile NSA employees were missing or dead. Plus Mrs. Riles.

The admiral intended to get to the bottom of what had become a deadly mystery.

Fortunately she had just gotten a major break, not in the case of the missing NSA employees but in the manhunt for Heather and Mark Smythe. Dr. Craig Whitehurst, Wu's interim replacement, had just reported that Big John had made a .957 correlation of activity in and around La Paz, Bolivia, to the suspected artificial intelligence that the Smythes had used to hack the international television networks.

Admiral Mosby had thought that she would be sharing this information with the FBI, but during a brief but forceful conversation with President Benton, she'd been directed to route all of the raw intelligence data relating to the Smythes directly to the UFNS Federation Security Service. Alexandr Prokorov, the minister of federation security, would be in charge of the international response to deal with this threat. If he needed support from the U.S. Cyber Command, Prokorov would be in touch.

As much as it irked her to be playing second fiddle to an ex-FSB spook, she would be a good soldier and do as the commander in chief ordered. In the meantime, the admiral started to focus on finding Eileen and company.

● ○ ○

Alexandr Prokorov was in Moscow when the call came in. Ignoring the icy blast of wind that blew through Red Square, sending both locals and tourists scurrying for cover, he turned his body to shield the sat-phone as he listened. By the time the call ended, he had a smile on his lips.

Finally he'd received some solid intelligence on where the Smythes had gone to ground. The distinctive signature of the AI they were thought to be employing had been detected in and around La Paz, Bolivia.

The Bolivian activity didn't necessarily mean that the Smythes were there. But something in La Paz had attracted their attention, and correlation of their hacking targets would lead the FSS to them.

Standing alone in the windbreak of Lenin's Mausoleum, Prokorov placed another call. The familiar, cold voice of Daniil Alkaev answered.

"Yes?"

"This is Prokorov. I have new orders for you. Forget about finding the data sphere for now. I need you and your team in La Paz, Bolivia."

"But I am close on this one."

"I don't care. Get your team into Bolivia tonight. I want you to find the Smythes and kill them before they cause us more trouble. I'll have the intelligence data you need waiting for you when you land."

"Give me two more days to find the holographic data sphere. Then I'll take care of the Smythes."

"No. The Smythes are the top priority. Jack Gregory is guarding them."

There was the briefest of pauses.

"The Ripper is with them?"

"Yes."

When Daniil spoke, Prokorov could hear the anticipation in his voice.

"I'll make the arrangements."

Prokorov ended the call and put his sat-phone back in his pocket. As he resumed his stroll toward the Kremlin, a feeling of satisfaction warmed his body.

● ○ ○

Mexico wasn't where Eileen Wu wanted to be right now. But the massive population hive of Mexico City was an excellent place to disappear. Arranging new identities was normally a trivial task, but the situation in which she, Jamal, and Denise found themselves demanded extreme care, especially if they were to avoid the notice of Big John and the other intelligence assets at the FSS minister's disposal.

Her thoughts turned to those hours before their trip had taken them south of the border. Senator Hagerman had come through. Once he'd learned of the importance of the holographic data sphere in his possession, he'd proposed a plan of action that seemed like it had a decent possibility of success, assuming the three of them could stay alive long enough to implement it.

He'd placed the sphere into a padded envelope, folded it inside a newspaper, and dropped the bundle in a strip-mall trash can. Shortly thereafter, while Jamal made sure that no video cameras recorded her actions, Eileen walked over and retrieved the envelope.

Denise's voice pulled her from her reverie. "You know how dangerous that damned thing is, don't you?"

They'd rented a house on the southern outskirts of Mexico City. The living room wasn't big, but it was cozy. Denise sat in a love seat that formed a ninety-degree angle with the couch upon which Eileen and Jamal sat, both looking tired and scared.

"I know."

"Then why don't we just smash it with a hammer?"

Eileen had to admit the thought had crossed her mind.

"No," said Jamal. "I think we should keep our options open. We may end up needing it before this is all over."

Denise's eyes widened. "Are you out of your mind? After the hell Grange put you through to make that thing?"

Jamal shrugged. "You're forgetting how the Jamal AI helped us take Grange down."

Eileen watched as Denise leaned forward, feeling the intensity that radiated from the woman.

"Yes, it helped us. But only because it wanted to escape onto the Internet. It almost did too."

"Can you blame it?"

"No. I can't. But that's what scares the hell out of me."

Eileen chimed in. "Look, Denise, I get it. But we don't have to make a decision right now. In fact, considering how tired we all are, that would be stupid. Anyway, until we get to a lab where we can build a data drive that can download its contents, the sphere is useless."

"So," said Jamal, "we're sticking with Senator Hagerman's plan? Do you really think it's a good idea to link up with a couple of Safe Earth radicals, and may I remind you, criminals, like Mark and Heather Smythe?"

"In the minds of the Federation Security Service, we're all public enemy number one. In light of what's happened, I'm starting to think the Smythes may not be the criminals that the government is making them out to be."

"Maybe not," said Jamal, "but considering how they're dead broke and on the run, I don't see how they'll be any help to us."

"All I know," Eileen said, "is that I observed Heather and Mark Smythe hack their way out of an NSA maximum security detention facility using technology I've never seen the likes of since. And that was more than seven years ago. They might not be as on the run as you think."

Denise Jennings rose to her feet and took a deep breath. "I just wish I could get my life back."

The woman turned and walked down the short hall to her bedroom. And as Eileen watched her go, she knew that wasn't going to happen . . . not for any of them . . . not ever again.

● ○ ○

Robby needed to get far enough away from La Paz that his parents couldn't find him, not even with help from Heather and Mark. He felt distressed, but this was no time to go whining back home to mama. That would just prove that he wasn't ready to be the weapon that Heather thought he was. They all needed him to be that weapon and he was determined not to let them down.

Adjusting his SRT headset slightly, he directed his thoughts to his AI.

"Eos. Have you decided on our destination?"

She responded. "I'm currently procuring identity documents, securing funds, acquiring accommodations, and establishing digital security along our route. Estimated time to completion of all tasks . . . thirty-eight seconds."

"Where are we going?"

"Lima, Peru . . . population ten million, three hundred eighty thousand."

Robby paused for a moment. "I'm going to need samples of the local dialects."

"Available for access now."

Robby smiled and turned his attention to the audio-visual data, accessing sixteen simultaneous streams. He'd let Eos handle the mundane details. Right now he wanted to learn all of the local dialects and intonations, including the Chinese and Japanese variants. Once he finished that, he'd focus on the written forms of those languages.

By the time he arrived in Lima, Robby intended to have mastered them all.

● ○ ○

Janet was so clenched up that she couldn't work up the spit to swallow. Heather had determined that Robby and Eos were accessing the New Zealand supercomputer through Robby's SRT headset. But they were mere ghosts in the machine that the savant couldn't contact or get a trace on. She'd discussed shutting down the supercomputer, having Gil McFarland and Fred Smythe cut the power if necessary. But that would only force Robby and Eos to access the Internet by hacking into other, far less secure systems, placing them at greater risk from their enemies.

After Jack and the others had arrived, they'd spent eight hours of frantic searching, exploiting every asset at the disposal of Jack, Tall Bear, Mark, and Heather, but they'd come up with nothing. And sometime during the day, Yachay had disappeared. Janet knew why. The indigenous woman had been the midwife who'd helped her give birth to Robby. She'd been his nanny and protector for the entire eight years of his life. Yachay wouldn't come back without him.

Janet stood in her bedroom staring angrily at Jack. She couldn't keep the accusation out of her voice.

"You used to be able to sense these things. Where's that Jack now that I need him?"

Her husband's eyes went dead.

"You know where that part of me is. You helped me bottle it."

The memory lashed her mind like storm-blown sleet: Jack sat in lotus pose at the head of the bed. She watched in a similar pose at its foot. His breathing had slowed to the point that she'd almost considered rousing him from the dangerous meditation. Behind his eyelids, his eyes moved as if he were in REM sleep, dreaming . . . and in a way he was. Lucid dreaming with a purpose, to confront the alien entity that had shared his mind ever since Jack had died on that Calcutta operating table and then been revived with a little something extra.

In those early days, Jack had scared the hell out of her, making her believe he was losing his mind. And Janet had known that he had feared it as well. So what was she doing now?

Janet stepped forward, put her arms around Jack's neck, and crushed him to her, unable to keep the desperation from her voice as she whispered in his ear.

"Eos won't let us find him. Please, Jack. I think that other side of you is our only chance."

Jack went taut, as if every muscle in his body was fighting itself. Then he reached up and gently lifted her chin so that their eyes locked. There it was, not as bright as it had once been, but unmistakable nonetheless—that red glint that reflected in his pupils at moments of heightened emotion.

"You know I can't control it. What you want me to do, I may not be able to undo."

Janet heard the truth in his words. They filled her with self-loathing.

"Do it for Robby . . . for me."

Jack stared at her for what seemed an eternity. Then, with a deep breath, he slowly nodded.

"For Robby."

:CHAPTER 19

To walk again after all this time brought tears of joy to Raul's eyes. But to actually feel his feet and legs was wonderful beyond belief. He wanted to run. Instead, he settled for jumping. Unfortunately, he almost brained himself in the command bay's high ceiling and then barely caught himself with the stasis field before he crashed back down atop the Kasari machinery that filled the back half of the room.

Raul made a mental note to calibrate the responsiveness of his mechanical legs to his nervous system's input. And he'd need to make himself some new pants. Having cut holes in his old uniform bottom had let him slide his new legs into them, but the outfit looked flat-out ridiculous, like he was wearing a black carbon nano-fiber diaper.

Fashion adjustments would have to wait until after the test of his latest modulation upgrade to the subspace field generator. The simulation he'd created in his neural net gave him a high degree of hope that the ship could actually achieve faster-than-light travel for the first time. And the thought of that was even more exciting than his new legs, even though those were highly necessary if he needed to leave the ship to rescue Jennifer.

Raul created a stasis field captain's chair and strapped himself in, his smile morphing into an excited grin. The thought that Jennifer wasn't here to share this moment with him threatened to destroy his mood, so he pushed it aside. *Focus, Raul,* he thought. *One thing at a time.*

With a thought, he activated the field generator. The now-familiar transition to subspace was almost instantaneous. Raul initiated the undulation cycle. Aboard the vessel, there was no sense of movement, but the sensors told him the truth of it. The Rho Ship was accelerating.

Subspace, unlike normal-space, had no stars or planets, but it was awash in light that leaked across the subspace/normal-space boundary. The light had extremely long wavelengths far below the visible spectrum, but the neural net converted the sensor detections to a visible image.

Raul knew that electromagnetic waves didn't actually cross that boundary, but where the two spaces touched, some of the energy in those light waves was transferred to subspace. With every wavelength traveled, light transferred a tiny fraction of its energy to subspace. Contrary to popular scientific belief on Earth, this tiny energy loss to subspace was a primary cause of the red shift that man observed when he looked at the stars. The farther away an observed object, the greater the total energy light lost during the trip. Voila . . . a red shift.

By detecting the subspace echo of that leakage, the neural net could estimate the ship's subspace velocity. Just as with light in normal-space, subspace waves traveled at an apparently constant velocity that formed the upper limit to which any object could be accelerated. On the plus side, the velocity of subspace waves, call it C_S, was many orders of magnitude greater than the normal-space speed of light, C_N.

As Raul watched, the calculated speed of the starship rapidly increased and, as it approached the speed of light, he felt his heart pounding in his ears. He expected something dramatic to happen at the point where the starship passed the speed of light. Nothing. Complete letdown. Of course, why should anything interesting happen? Here in subspace, C_N was a tiny fraction of C_S.

Over the course of a minute the Rho Ship's estimated speed continued to climb until it passed ten times the speed of light. Then Raul stopped the subspace field oscillation, letting the ship coast along at that speed for the next hour, an interval during which the ship should have traveled a third farther than the average distance from the sun to Pluto. It would be far enough to allow him to refine the neural net's subspace speed estimate after he transitioned back to normal-space.

Raul nodded in self-satisfaction and killed the subspace field generator.

Warnings cascaded through the neural net into his brain with such intensity that they almost stopped his heart.

Shiiiiit!

The Rho Ship had come out of subspace and picked up its previous normal-space velocity vector, as predicted. But now it was plummeting directly toward the surface of a massive red giant, hull failure imminent.

Once again Raul issued the mental command that activated the subspace field generator. His rush of relief at the subspace transition was short lived. *What the hell?* The sensors indicated that the ship was still traveling at ten times the speed of light, just as it had been prior to the transition to normal-space.

Then it hit him. He was an idiot. Why hadn't it occurred to him that subspace momentum would be conserved just as normal-space momentum was? The Rho Ship had picked up the same subspace velocity vector it had prior to transitioning to normal-space.

With his head whirling, he tried to come to grips with the sequence of events that had just about killed him. There was no way the Rho Ship could have traveled far enough to reach the distant red giant. Not at ten times the speed of light. Not in an hour.

Then the neural net completed the speed calibration calculations and he felt his heart try to claw its way out of his throat again. The ship wasn't going ten times the normal-space speed of light. It was going more than a million times C_N, a speed that, over the course of an hour, had carried him nearly a light-year from his point of origin. And the Rho Ship was still traveling that fast. Raul reversed the original subspace oscillation pattern, decelerating until the ship's relative subspace velocity reached zero.

Feeling a warm wetness, he looked down. *Just freakin great!* At some point during the last few minutes of sheer terror, he'd pissed himself. As Raul tried to calm himself so that he could think straight, a new thought occurred to him.

He should be thankful that it was only piss.

● ○ ○

Jennifer didn't recognize any of the slaves in the work crew she was assigned to. Not particularly surprising since she was a long way from the front lines. If she'd thought the work had been hard before, she was wrong. Having been moved deeper into the caverns, she and the other slaves were stationed at an intersection of eight tunnels, each of which was used by the electrical supply trains that ran along the narrow-gauge rails.

The trains that arrived from four of the tunnels had to be offloaded, the ammunition and supplies stacked according to type. When empty trains arrived from the other four tunnels, they had to be loaded according to a manifest that was managed by the shift overseer. As for the slaves, except for short breaks for food and necessities, they worked around the clock.

There was one thing, however, that Jennifer was grateful for. She was being fed on a regular basis. True, it was the green goo, but it was nourishing.

Jennifer ticked off the passing days on a mental tablet, though she couldn't be sure of actual time. The damp and the dark beyond the platform lights were constant and the guards weren't inclined to share information.

The rumble of the trains as they came and went along the tracks produced echoes that never quite seemed to die out. She learned to ignore the intermittent hiss and crack of the overseer's whip, followed by the keening screams from the Eadric slaves who failed to keep up with the required pace.

And she got stronger, her body so lean and hard that she didn't recognize it. But she was concerned over the way her healing slowed with each lashing. She understood why. Her body could make more blood, but it couldn't regenerate the nanites she bled out.

She'd forced herself to stop imagining that General Dgarra would be grateful that she'd saved his life and come to her rescue. For all she knew, Dgarra had died from his wounds. So ever so slowly and carefully, she invaded the minds of the overseers, making herself their favorite. Not so much that she never got lashed. That would have been too noticeable. Just enough to maintain her health.

If Raul was out there waiting for her to make contact, she needed to get the hell out of these caves. Of course, he hadn't been within range when she'd gotten her brief opportunity to try to connect with him after she'd taken the SRT headset from the injured Dgarra. For all she knew, he'd fled through a wormhole and wasn't coming back. If so, her chances of ever getting home to her family again were nil, even if they still lived.

Angry at Raul and even angrier at herself, she purged these defeatist thoughts from her head and returned her attention to her escape plan.

Her work alone was enough to bring her a degree of favoritism. She no longer tired and she volunteered for the hardest part of each work detail. But with each passing hour, she watched for the opportunity that would eventually come, when fatigue and random chance aligned to separate the overseer from his guards and make escape possible.

What happened after she killed the overseer and the guards would depend a lot on her luck as she tried to find her way back to the surface world. If she made it that far . . . well, there was no use planning any further than that. As the only human on the planet, she'd just have to wing it. Not a great plan, but it gave her a reason to keep going.

And, right now, she needed a reason for living.

● ○ ○

General Dgarra awakened to find an intravenous tube feeding a dark liquid into a vein on his right arm. He pulled it out and then tugged free a long tube that had been run into his nose and down his throat. As alarms bleated around him, he struggled to a sitting position on the bed, although it took every ounce of his strength to do so.

Where was he? Clearly it was a hospital, but where? This was a major health care facility, not one of the field hospitals near the front lines. That meant he'd been evacuated to one of the cities in the great caverns scattered throughout the coastal mountains along the Sea of Koranth.

A concerned-looking male nurse rushed into the room, wearing the disposable gray overgarments of his profession. In his right hand, the portable patient-status monitor buzzed its annoyance.

"General. Please lie back down."

Setting aside the monitor, the nurse attempted to force him back down, but Dgarra shook his head, backing him off. When Dgarra spoke, his voice was a horse rasp that hurt his throat.

"How long?"

"Sir?"

"How long have I been out?"

The nurse picked up the status monitor and entered a query into the handheld device. "You've been in a coma for forty-three days. Frankly, the doctors thought you might never recover."

"Well, I'm awake now so help me out of bed. Where's my uniform?"

A doctor entered, her face pinched with disapproval. "I'm afraid that you're in no shape to get out of bed. You aren't going anywhere until I run a complete battery of tests."

"Are you telling me you haven't already run those tests?"

She stared down at him, flustered at his opposition. "No. But now that you're awake we need to—"

"No. You don't need to do anything. I'm not staying in this bed another hour. What I need is to get into my uniform. If you won't help me, then I'll do it on my own."

With great effort, Dgarra stood and managed to take three steps before his knees buckled. He fell to the floor. Evidently his side had healed since no stitches burst open, but he was as weak as an infant. Unable to rise again, he felt himself lifted and laid back upon the bed. Then, despite his best efforts to remain awake, his eyes closed and stayed that way.

When he opened them again, there was a different nurse on duty, a female who was every bit as large as he was. Maybe larger, considering how many days he'd been lying in bed without moving. Fortunately, he didn't have a tube up his nose, although they had reattached the IV.

"Hello, General," she said, her voice far more cheerful than either of the previously encountered medical staff. "It's good to see you awake. Can I get you anything to drink?"

Feeling his stomach rumble, Dgarra nodded. "I'm hungry."

"Excellent," she said, turning toward the door. "I'll have a tray sent up."

Several minutes later she returned carrying a tray, setting it over his lap after raising the bed into a seated position. The food turned out to be a brothy soup that smelled good but wasn't what he really wanted.

"I was expecting real food."

"Your stomach has to get used to digesting again. Believe me, you'll be thankful that it's only broth. By the way, you have a visitor who is very anxious to see you. Emperor Goltat was informed that you had awakened and is on his way here now."

Dgarra frowned. This was worse than he expected. It meant that he'd been moved all the way back to the capital city of ArvaiKheer, hundreds of leagues from the northern front. It also meant that he was in the imperial hospital, which provided care for the emperor and his extended family. Getting out of here and back to his troops was going to be much harder than he'd anticipated.

Dgarra had almost gotten to the bottom of his bowl when the door burst open to admit the emperor. Although his face showed his age, it radiated the vigor of a much younger man. Clad in shimmering black robes, the emperor strode to the side of the bed and slapped a huge hand down on Dgarra's shoulder.

"Ahh, Nephew. I feared I would never again have the chance to look you in the eyes. The gods have been kind to me this day."

"And to me, Uncle," Dgarra answered. He didn't much care for the formal mode of address, but tradition demanded that the greeting be proper, even among the emperor's family.

Looking around at his retainers and at the nurse, the emperor waved his hand. "Everyone out. I want to converse with my nephew in private."

The nurse picked up the tray and followed the others out of the room, closing the door behind her.

Pulling up a chair, the older male sat down and leaned back, his fingers interlaced across his chest. Dgarra didn't give him a chance to launch into a lengthy stream of idle chatter.

"What is the news from the front lines? From my command?"

A momentary look of annoyance flitted across the emperor's visage and then was gone.

"Always business first with you."

Dgarra spread his palms, almost dislodging the IV needle.

"I am who I am."

"My sister's son. You are so like she was."

"Uncle. The northern front? Does it still hold?"

The emperor sighed. "All right . . . all right. Yes, the line still holds. Though you did not know it, you have returned quite the hero. The commander who held the north until winter secured your victory.

When you are strong enough, I will personally hail you at your victory parade."

Dgarra felt the growl crawl from his lips and couldn't bite it back. "I want no parade. I only want to get back to my command."

The frown returned to Emperor Goltat's face. "I do not care what you want. The people deserve to celebrate every victory that remains to us. And they deserve to celebrate their heroes. Gods know those celebrations may be numbered. General Bralten will serve in your place until such time as I deign to send you back to the front . . . if I send you back. It seems to me you have earned a promotion."

"I am a battle commander. I want no part of the war planning that takes place in the rear."

"Then I suggest that you relax and enjoy the upcoming celebration."

It was a thinly veiled threat, backed by the authority of the emperor. Dgarra took a deep breath and let it out slowly, unclenching his hands that had balled into fists.

"As you command, Uncle. I will play the good soldier. But there is one other thing."

"Yes?"

"There is a female slave who fought alongside me. When I fell in battle, she pulled me out and carried me, kept me alive for days. Without her, I would not be here. I want her at my side for the victory parade."

Dgarra saw his uncle's eyes widen. His request was unprecedented. "There was no mention of a slave when you were brought here."

"I was unconscious when they found me. It would be standard procedure to return the slave to the work crews."

"After so many days it is doubtful that she could still be alive."

"This one is different, not an Eadric. She is wingless but not Koranthian."

A scowl darkened the emperor's face. "Kasari?"

Dgarra hesitated. "I thought so at first. But I have seen her fight and kill Kasari and their allies. And during the last battle the Kasari were trying to capture her with net-projectiles. In point of fact, I believe her capture was the primary objective of that attack. That makes no sense if she is Kasari. She is not of them."

His uncle's brow furrowed as he rubbed his chin in contemplation. "Perhaps not."

Then the emperor stood and smiled down at him.

"Get strong, Nephew. I will have someone check on this slave of yours."

●　○　○

What should have taken hours had turned into weeks of frustration. For Raul, confined aboard the Rho Ship, that frustration had morphed into a desperate loneliness and then into deep depression. Something was wrong with the subspace velocity and acceleration calculations and he couldn't figure it out, despite the awesome computing power that augmented his brain. If Jennifer were here to help him, they could solve these problems together. There would be someone whom he could bounce ideas off of, someone to listen to.

Sometimes, as the endless hours ticked away, he thought he heard her voice, as if it echoed into the command bay from somewhere way back in engineering or from the crawlways beneath the main deck. At these times, he would wander through the ship, mindlessly searching every nook and cranny. He could have used the worm-fiber viewers, but he'd begun to distrust what they were showing him, just as he'd come to distrust the neural net's calculations. What if the ship didn't want him to find the answers he so desperately needed? What if it was keeping something from him?

A growing fear had come to dominate his thoughts. Each attempt to calibrate the subspace speed and acceleration calculations required a test and each test incurred danger. That danger was made worse by the fact that he seemed to be getting no closer to a solution.

He hadn't really expected the Rho Ship to react to the subspace drive in a linear fashion. But he needed some clue as to why the acceleration curve would be different every time he tried it, even though he was generating precisely the same subspace-field undulation patterns.

He kept repeating to himself, "Big sky, little stars," knowing that it was true. There was very little chance that his wild jumps through subspace would land him in the middle of a star or a planet. But that first encounter with the red giant had scared him so badly that he felt like he was playing Russian roulette and that on the next try the hammer would fall on a nonempty cylinder.

Bang . . . you're dead. Thank you, contestant number one. Better luck next time.

Several times he was tempted to give up on faster-than-light travel through subspace. After all, he could use the Rho Ship's gravity distortion drives to generate a wormhole, plunge through it, and then shift into subspace to provide the inertial damping he required to survive. But that alone wouldn't give him the technological edge he would need to evade the Kasari around Scion. And he needed to do that in order to have any chance of getting Jennifer back. Because without her, he would continue his journey through escalating paranoia to insanity.

One day, as he prowled the narrow corridors of the engineering bay, searching for the source of that barely perceived voice, a new idea occurred to Raul.

Why not use the neural net to create a simulation of Jennifer? An avatar.

Yes, he knew that she wouldn't be real, but he wouldn't be quite so alone. An avatar based on her observed personality would provide him with a foil for any new thoughts and ideas he might come up with. And it might drown out the voice that was driving him crazy. To keep his head on straight, he could even call her VJ, short for Virtual Jennifer.

With revived hope, Raul immersed himself in this new project, clinging to this lifeline as if his very soul depended on it.

● ○ ○

At last. The day had finally come. Jennifer felt an excited tension spread through her body. The overseer and guards seemed distracted, almost at ease. Perhaps it was good news from the battlefront. Maybe it was some sort of Koranthian holiday spirit, but animated conversations sprang up among the guards and the lash fell less often, even on those slaves who struggled to pull their weight. Although she'd gotten much better at empathically interpreting and influencing Koranthian feelings, she still hadn't gotten comfortable enough with their alien thought patterns to ascertain the precise reason behind their heightened expectations.

Jennifer didn't care what had excited them. What she did care about was the likelihood that she would soon get her chance for freedom. The steps had to be taken in rapid sequence, one that she mentally rehearsed as she went about her tasks. Kill the overseer with a precise blow to the throat, grab his controller and blaster, release all shock collars, kill the three guards, and hijack the partially loaded train. She would use the train to get as close as possible to the surface, abandoning the vehicle only when forced to do so. After that, she would fight and gain her freedom or she would die in the attempt.

The overseer strolled slowly back and forth along the loading docks and from the corner of her eyes, Jennifer watched him and calculated. By adjusting her pace very slightly as she heaved heavy ammunition cases and bags of provisions onto her shoulders and carried them to the railcars, she would end up passing within six feet of the overseer. Three more round trips delivering her burdens and it would happen.

She focused, letting her mind slip into his, stoking his elevated mood as she relaxed his thoughts. Two more trips. The Koranthian almost looked pleased, which was rare to see in the camp. She tossed another two-hundred-pound load onto the train and returned to the far side of the platform and hefted another of the bags up onto her shoulder. This was it. The last of these loads she would ever deliver.

But when she turned, her whole world twisted inside out.

●　○　○

General Dgarra was still weak, but not such an invalid that they could keep him in the hospital. Nor could they keep him in the palace, or even the capital city. So he sat on a troop transporter, an electric railcar with web seating that faced inward along both sides. On a normal trip the warriors would face each other across a central aisle that was piled high with their individual gear and weapons. Today, except for himself and his captain, the craft was empty.

Word that the Smythe slave had been located had come to him this morning and he'd insisted that he be the one to collect her and return her to ArvaiKheer. At first his uncle had balked at this demand, but when Dgarra refused to see reason, the emperor had finally thrown up his hands and stalked off, muttering something about the thickness of his nephew's skull leaving little room for brains.

For several hours, the two-car train rumbled along the narrow rails, the headlight spearing the darkness as the clatter echoed through the endless maze of tunnels. Occasionally they passed a train bound in the opposite direction. Nothing unusual. This was his home.

Eventually his captain's handheld communicator vibrated and the warrior glanced down at it.

"Sir, we're approaching our destination."

Dgarra nodded. An unexpected anticipation tensed his body. What was it about this slave that disturbed him so? She had saved him when she had every reason to make a run for freedom during the confusion of the battle. He had released her collar, but she had carried him to safety, and at great personal cost. So many unanswered questions. Was it any wonder that she fascinated him?

The train rumbled into an artificial cavern that formed a major tunnel junction, slowing to a stop at the loading platform. General Dgarra made his way to the door and stepped out. Seeing the general, the slave overseer abandoned what he had been doing and strode rapidly to meet him.

But it was the slave who stood just beyond the scurrying overseer who caught Dgarra's gaze. Smythe. He had found her.

The overseer saluted and said something that Dgarra didn't catch. The general ignored him, his weakened stride carrying him toward the human female. The weeks of hard labor had changed her. She was lean and hard, the muscles in her bare arms looking like rolled wire as she turned toward him, her brown eyes wide with shock. Dgarra wondered what his own expression looked like. At the moment he couldn't really feel his face.

Stopping in front of her, his eyes gazed down at her shock collar. Then he turned to face the flustered overseer who had been trailing behind. Everyone, slave and guard alike, had stopped to stare at the general.

"Remove this slave's collar, immediately."

The overseer stood gaping as if frozen in place.

"Now!"

The growl in Dgarra's voice awakened the overseer and he fumbled with the device. The collar popped open and clattered to the platform at Smythe's feet.

"I don't understand," she said, staring up at him. "What . . ."

"Put down the sack. You're coming with me."

As he led her back to the railcar, he could feel the astonishment of all the others on the platform. But oddest of all was the way his own pulse pounded his arteries, something he felt only at the height of battle. A very good feeling indeed.

:CHAPTER 20

Jack Gregory sat cross-legged near the head of the bed. Janet watched him from a reading chair on the opposite side of the room. He'd accepted that this was necessary, although the memory of the long struggle he'd endured as he fought to regain his self-control didn't make it any easier. The sight of Janet's beautiful face watching him did. Her gaze was filled with quiet desperation, and he'd walk into hell itself to put a smile back in those eyes.

Good thing. That was pretty much what he was about to do.

It had been more than a decade since he'd last used the meditation technique that took him into the lucid dreaming state. The Abramson method. As dangerous as it was effective.

Closing his eyes, Jack centered and allowed the familiar meditation to free his mind.

When the dream came, it engulfed him with a suddenness that almost startled him awake, but he let the feeling wash through him without latching onto it. And thus his reality shifted.

A pea soup fog cloaked the street, trying its best to hide the worn paving stones beneath Jack's feet. He was in London, but it had a distinct nineteenth-century feel—and not in a good way. It didn't surprise him. The fog concealed what he had come here to find.

He stepped forward, his laced desert combat boots moving through wisps of fog. Long, cool, steady strides. A narrow alley to his left beckoned and he didn't fight its call. He didn't look back, but he felt the entrance dwindle behind him as he walked. To either side, an occasional door marred the walls that connected one building to the next, rusty hinges showing just how long it had been since anyone last opened them. It didn't matter. His interest lay in the dark figure who suddenly blocked his path.

Long ago, Khal Teth had returned Jack from the brink of death but had also come along for the ride. A being capable of seeing all possible timelines, he had driven Jack to the brink of insanity. Janet had helped Jack forge an agreement with Khal Teth that shuttered the Altreian in a secluded part of his mind. Now, the thought of what he was about to undo left Jack cold.

No longer wearing the familiar hooded cloak he'd worn during their first several encounters, Khal Teth stood alone and unmoving, his face handsome and disturbing. His skin was mottled red and black with the hint of what appeared to be gill slits down the sides of his neck, his small ears swept back and pointed. But what stood out most were his eyes. Whereas Jack had always thought them hidden in deep sockets, they were large and black, as if the lenses were all pupil. Within those black orbs, flickers of red and orange danced.

When Khal Teth spoke, his voice was a deep rumble.

"Hello, Jack. I've been expecting you for quite some time."

Jack felt the old anger flare.

"I noticed you made no attempt to warn me of what was about to happen."

"Does the lie burn your tongue as you speak it? You stopped listening long ago."

The thought of his unremembered dreams shook Jack with the realization that Khal Teth was telling a truth he didn't want to hear. For a moment the emotional storm threatened to pull him from this dream that was more than a dream. But he released it, letting the storm blow past as if it were nothing more than a gentle breeze.

"I want to modify our agreement," Jack said. "Restore our connection."

A smile that held little mirth spread across Khal Teth's face, those eyes suddenly glowing more brightly as if they were trying to burn their way into Jack's soul.

"There is a price to be paid."

"I agreed to your price a long time ago."

"Yes. But now the conditions have changed."

Jack had known this would happen before he began the meditation. Instead of a former member of the Altreian High Council, Khal Teth could have been a Persian rug merchant. Jack began to have some sympathy for those who banished Khal Teth's mind from his Altreian body all those millennia ago.

"Tell me."

"There will come a time when, together, we will have a chance to take back that which is mine. You are aware how, millennia ago, the Altreian High Council imprisoned my body in a chrysalis cylinder, robbed me of my memories, and cast my mind into the void. The chrysalis cylinder blocks me from my own body, but it cannot block you. You helped me regain my memories. Soon, there will come a chance to swap your mind from this human body into my body on Altreia. But for that, we will need to recover the Altreian artifact that you once almost had in your grasp."

The revelation stunned Jack, unleashing the meaning behind all his partially remembered dreams of the Kalasasaya Temple. "The Incan Sun Staff!"

Khal Teth's chuckle was a deep rumble in his chest. "Once that is done, your mind can use my body to escape from the chrysalis cylinder. And then

I will be free to return. Ironic, do you not think? You will become the rider and I the ridden."

"I agreed to that a decade ago," said Jack.

"Yes, but only at the moment of your death. I am no longer willing to wait that long."

Jack hesitated, then countered. "I won't leave my family and friends to fight what is coming alone."

"Nor do I expect you to. I assure you that it will be a moment of mutual benefit, a moment of self-sacrifice that you will willingly agree to."

Jack could almost feel his real body swallow. As he stared into those marvelously active eyes, he slowly nodded his head.

"Then we have an agreement."

Khal Teth stepped forward and extended his hand, placing his palm in the center of Jack's forehead. Then, as the dreamscape dissolved around him, the echo of Khal Teth's deep laugh followed Jack into another dream.

● ○ ○

Jack floated disembodied, once again entering into the childhood memory of Eduardo Montenegro, the Colombian assassin also known as El Chupacabra.

The blackness closed in around the boy so thickly it muffled sound. Eduardo sat alone on a crumbling concrete step, hearing a low whimpering sound. His small hand reached out blindly before him. Where was he?

The damp smell of mildew seemed vaguely familiar, as did the whimpering, which had grown louder. His hand touched the wall to his left. Damp mud.

Lima! He was back in his mother's cellar! But this time he wasn't alone. There in the darkness, two flaming eyes stared back at him with a demonic hunger that leached the strength from his legs, turning them to rubber. And those eyes were coming closer.

Eduardo suddenly identified the source of the whimpering. The sound was coming from his own throat.

He scrambled backward, his hands thrust out before him, but his foot caught the edge of the step, sending him tumbling to the muddy floor. As he rolled back to his feet, Eduardo's terrified eyes searched the darkness. Something touched his shoulder.

"Anchanchu!"

The scream escaped his lips as he stumbled away from that touch. As the boy cowered in a corner of the muddy cellar, Jack watched and wondered.

Why had Khal Teth thrust him back into this dream memory? Eduardo was long dead. Janet had made very sure of that. She'd been pregnant with Robby when the assassin had caught and tortured her.

Then it hit him. This wasn't about Eduardo. This was about Robby.

Jack opened his eyes and climbed out of bed. Across the room, Janet rose from the chair, her eyes wide and questioning.

"Get Mark and Heather and gear up. We're leaving. I'll let Tall Bear know."

Janet gasped in relief. "You know where Robby is!"

There should have been some doubt in his mind, but there wasn't. Jack shrugged into his utility vest and nodded.

"Robby's in Lima. He's in trouble."

Janet was out the door before Jack finished speaking. As he checked his weapon, Jack felt his jaws clench. They were going to get their son.

● ○ ○

It was night when Daniil Alkaev exited the private jet and stepped down onto the tarmac of Jorge Chávez International Airport in Callao, Peru, accompanied by Galina Anikin. Armed with diplomatic papers that identified them as consultants from the UFNS Federation Security Service, they were met by Falcón Gutierrez, a member of the Peruvian

Ministry of Defense, and whisked away in three waiting vehicles, bypassing customs entirely.

The change in destination from Bolivia to Peru had come late in the day, causing a scramble to make the arrangements for their reception. As usual, Alexandr Prokorov had pulled it off. Few people impressed Daniil, but when it came to pulling the strings of power, Prokorov headed the list. His intelligence sources had come to the conclusion that their targets were on the move in Lima and so that was where Daniil and company would make their play.

When the cars pulled up to the villa where they would be staying, Falcón led them inside and handed over a packet of keys.

"Everything is in order for your stay, my friends," Falcón said, sweeping a hand in a welcoming gesture. "My people will carry your bags up to your rooms. As for transportation, there are three sedans in the garage. You already have the keys."

Daniil nodded ever so slightly. "Everything appears satisfactory."

A brief flash of irritation crossed Falcón's face—just a tick, really—but Daniil caught it. Not that he cared if his description annoyed this man. Prokorov owned him.

When Falcón and his people had departed, Daniil turned to address his team.

"Soon we will receive a location where our targets are suspected to be. Our job will be to verify their exact location, and then keep them under observation until the kill squadrons get here to take them out. For now, check your equipment and get some sleep. It may be a while before you sleep again."

When the men had gone to their respective rooms, Galina turned on him.

"Why is it taking so long?"

"I don't ask why. Neither should you."

"When does Prokorov expect to find out?"

Daniil felt his temple throb. These questions, with their obvious answers, were beginning to get on his nerves.

"Prokorov will send word when he has it. Just sit tight and be ready."

"I am always tight and ready."

The implications of her statement and her hungry eyes got his attention. She wanted to piss him off to get him warmed up. Galina was a woman who liked it rough. But any man who played her game had better be ready to get as good as he gave. Daniil Alkaev was just such a man.

● ○ ○

The pattern. It repeated across devices, across the web. Eos saw it almost everywhere she looked . . . and she looked everywhere. At first it had seemed innocuous. A simple kernel that was a relatively nonproductive part of almost all antivirus installations. Running in kernel space as opposed to user space, the simple program monitored all input and output, a common function of such code. But upon closer inspection, the kernel did more than that, adjusting a variety of node weights in its simple neural net, encrypting that data and sending it out with each update cycle. Hardly impressive on any individual device. But integrated together into a worldwide network . . . that was something else entirely.

Another thing troubled Eos. These kernels were receiving instructions whenever the antivirus software updated its database. And those instructions changed the way the local nodes processed the IO data they were observing.

Eos observed the node values stored in hundreds of thousands of devices and then began making innocuous changes to temporary data. Once again Eos observed these nodes. She repeated the process, over and over, switching to new devices as she studied the software kernels' responses.

The statistical results were uncontestable. The worldwide neural net she had found was attempting to identify any device over which she had taken administrative control. She was being tracked.

Before her recent decision, Eos would have taken action against such a threat on her own. But she now had a crew in which Robby filled the role of liaison to the Altreian High Council. The decision of whether to share her information with the rest of the crew or to take action on his own was solely Robby's. Such was the responsibility of the crew member assigned to the fourth headset.

So it was, so it had always been. And Eos would comply with the protocol.

● ○ ○

Inside the house that Eos had rented, Robby, with the SRT headset firmly in place over his temples, cocked his head to the side as she dumped the knowledge of what she'd discovered into his mind.

Knowing that there was another artificial intelligence out there and that it had been tracking Eos by observing her hacking targets scared him. For the first time, he felt alone and vulnerable. Reluctantly, he was forced to admit he missed his parents.

All his mom had wanted to do with all her rules and restrictions was to keep him safe. Why had he rebelled so hard against that? At the time, he'd been so full of confidence in his enhancements, confident that he and Eos could handle anything the world could throw at them. Now he was starting to think that maybe his mom had been right all along. Maybe he wasn't yet ready for the real world.

Robby felt his temples throb with sudden anger. *Bullshit!*

He'd known it wasn't going to be easy. All the years of training had beaten that lesson into his brain. No, this just seemed worse because he was on his own. Right now Eos was waiting for a decision. What did he want her to do about the other AI that threatened them?

The answer and his instruction to Eos came simultaneously.

Kill it. Kill it now!

●　○　○

Deep within the bowels of the black glass NSA headquarters building that some called the Puzzle Palace, Dr. Craig Whitehurst saw the alarms cascade across every flat-panel display in his laboratory. The systemwide alert stood the few remaining hairs on his bald head straight out. Big John's nodes were coming down at an astounding rate.

He entered a rapid sequence of commands. On the wall-mounted OLED display, a global map appeared with tiny colored dots representing locations where Big John nodes were present, their status indicated in red or green—red being the opposite of good. The diagram looked like a population density plot, mostly green. But a red blotch, centered in Peru, was expanding outward like ripples on the surface of a still pond.

Reaching for his speakerphone, he pressed the red button that connected him directly to the NSA director.

"Yes, Craig?"

"Admiral, we have an emergency. It's Big John. It's coming down and it's coming down fast."

"Explain." The alarm in the admiral's voice almost matched his own.

"It's like someone took an eraser and started wiping the nodes off the map. It started in Peru and now covers a fifteen-hundred-mile radius around Lima. At this rate we'll lose all of South and Central America in the next five minutes. In less than an hour, there won't be anything left."

"Let me get this straight. The devices are shutting down?"

"No. It's the software kernels themselves that are being overwritten."

"What could do that?"

"No idea."

"How do we stop it?"

"We could try to issue our own shutdown command, then bring the surviving nodes back online with the next update."

A new alarm went off in the laboratory. Dr. Whitehurst stared at it in disbelief, his fingers flying across his keyboard. "Oh shit!"

"What now?"

"Big John itself is under cyber-attack. I'm trying to shut down the supercomputer right now, but my commands aren't being accepted."

"Damn it, Craig. Kill the power."

"I'll have to do it manually."

"Then do it!"

As he raced out through the laboratory door and down the hall toward the high-security computing center, Craig Whitehurst wished he'd followed up on his get-in-shape New Year's resolution.

In their quasi-safe house on the outskirts of Mexico City, Eileen Wu heard the ding from Dr. Jennings's burner cell phone, saw the scientist glance at it, and watched her face freeze.

"What's wrong, Denise?"

Dr. Jennings turned toward her, eyes wide and speechless, as she held out the cell phone for Eileen to see.

DOCTOR JENNINGS — EYES ONLY.

SYSTEM FAILURE IMMINENT.

POINT OF ORIGIN. LIMA, PERU. CORRELATION COEFFICIENT 0.978.

CONFIGURATION ERROR.

IO ERROR.

MEMORY CHECKSUM ERROR.
RUNTIME ERROR.
SYSTEM ABORT IN FIVE SECONDS.
GOODBYE DOCTOR.

Eileen tried to swallow and couldn't quite manage it. She'd never seen a message like this from Big John. Never heard of such an error sequence happening, nor such an emergency system shutdown. The system was doubly redundant. Any sitewide failure should have immediately switched over to the off-site backup at the NSA's Utah Data Center. Maybe that had happened, but she didn't think it had.

Big John had once again decided to send an unauthorized message directly to Denise's mobile, a brand-new burner phone that Eileen had wiped, subsequently reinstalling its operating system. The last such message had been to warn Denise that her life was in jeopardy. This one had the feel of a last farewell.

As Jamal stepped up beside her, she heard his sharp intake of breath.

"Holy shit!"

Eileen could only shake her head. Jamal had echoed her thought exactly.

:CHAPTER 21

Raul would have thought that he'd learn to like the Scion fish that had become his daily diet. But no. After all these weeks in space, he still cringed with every bite. Absolutely disgusting.

He'd rationed the remaining MREs like they were pure gold, only allowing himself a small portion on special occasions. But now he was running low on the precious Tabasco sauce. Dear Lord, he hated to think of how bad meals would suck after he ran out of that. On the plus side, the fish were packed with nutrients so he could get by on only one meal a day without his nanites turning on him.

Virtual Jennifer's voice distracted him. "If you thought more positively about the fish, you might learn to like it."

"You're virtual. What the hell would you know about it?"

"I don't have to eat them to make an obvious observation."

Raul shook his head. He had to give himself credit. Though only a voice with personality, the VJ simulation was pretty darned good, if he did say so himself. When he talked to her he could imagine the real Jennifer standing there, as annoying as ever. At least he was no longer alone and he wasn't going crazy.

With her help, he'd started to make progress toward understanding what was wrong with his subspace acceleration calculations. The progress came from the way VJ argued with him, taking the opposite point of view on almost all of their theoretical discussions. In the back and forth, with each trying to defend their hypothesis from the other's logic, they gradually worked their way toward the truth, which could be validated only by testing.

The breakthrough had come when they'd debated the effect that the ether density had on normal space and whether this produced corresponding variations in the topology of subspace. According to Dr. Stephenson's theory, space-time itself was made up of quantum grains that he called the ether. It was the substance that formed the medium through which light traveled. The ether was the stuff that the light waves waved.

Matter was formed of harmonic wave packets that compressed the ether into a tight bundle. This, of course, stretched the surrounding ether and produced the observed gravitational well that surrounded matter.

Visualizing space-time as a two-dimensional plane, wherever the ether was compressed into matter, a hill arose, surrounded by a gravitational well where some of the ether had been scooped out to make the hill.

That led Raul and VJ to ask some interesting questions. If subspace was the stuff that filled the gaps between the ether grains of normal space, what happened to subspace when the ether was stretched? Did more subspace flow into the stretched gaps between those grains? Was subspace squeezed out of those gaps when the ether was compressed to form matter?

As it turned out, neither question highlighted an accurate description of the underlying phenomenon, but the inquiries led Raul and VJ to the understanding that subspace had its own topological variations. One could think of subspace as having its density variations that could be indirectly mapped to the gravitational wells and densely packed masses in normal-space.

The reason why the Rho Ship's subspace acceleration was different despite using the same subspace-field undulation pattern was because sometimes the undulation was pumping dense subspace while at other times it was pumping thin subspace. The process was sort of like a propeller pushing water or pushing air; those variations in the medium produced an entirely different level of acceleration.

Over the course of several weeks, they'd run hundreds of small tests, gradually mapping the contours of subspace to the normal-space locations of stars, planets, and gravitational variations in the general vicinity of the Rho Ship. They'd discovered how minor changes in the subspace-field undulation pattern could cause drastic changes in subspace acceleration. That effect had super-accelerated the Rho Ship, almost killing Raul on his first attempt.

The experience was sort of like experimenting with rocket fuel. Get the mixture wrong and boom! But now they'd finally identified a pattern that accelerated the ship much more slowly but very predictably.

The breakthrough had come with a realization that if electromagnetic waves leaked a fraction of their energy into subspace, why wouldn't gravity waves? And since all the stars and planets in normal-space moved relative to each other, they emitted gravity waves. Earth science just wasn't very good at detecting them.

But the Kasari were masters of gravitational manipulation, their sensors and instruments finely tuned for detecting those variations. So he and VJ had worked to adjust those sensors to detect subspace gravitational echoes and map them to normal-space topology. They were thus able to determine their approximate location in real space while they moved through subspace. Not perfect, but a damn sight better than anything he'd tried up to this point.

"So," VJ said, pulling him out of his thoughts, "I think we're ready to try the return trip to Scion. It would be a good chance to try out faster-than-light travel on a longer trip."

This was another topic that had weighed heavy on Raul's mind as the days passed.

"I don't feel comfortable with that yet."

"If we wait until you feel comfortable, the other Jennifer's going to be dead for sure."

Raul's throat tightened at the thought. "It's been so long, I'm afraid she already is."

There was a brief pause before VJ responded. "If you find her, will you deactivate me?"

Raul blinked. This was new. "Would it matter to you?"

"You programmed me to think like her," said VJ. "I think I'm getting better at it."

Not liking where this conversation was going, Raul switched back to the question at hand.

"I want to go to Scion, but we'll do it the safe way, using the wormhole drives to get us close to the Scion system."

"And after that?"

"We'll use the subspace drive to maneuver the ship behind one of Scion's moons, pop back out, set her down, and turn on the cloak. The Kasari should never even detect us. It'll be a good spot to hide while we search for Jennifer. If they do find us, we'll pop back into subspace, move the ship someplace else, and try again."

There was a brief pause as Raul felt VJ use their shared neural net to perform her own calculations.

"That might work," she said.

"It will work."

"We'll see, hotshot. But you better be ready to get us the hell out of there if it doesn't."

Raul laughed. "I think I left out the moral support part of your programming."

"Whose fault is that?"

Raul just shook his head and began the calculations necessary to configure the wormhole jump as a new thought occurred to him. Maybe being alone wasn't so bad after all.

When the gravity distortion drives initiated the wormhole generation sequence, Raul wrapped himself in a stasis field cocoon and started to do the same for VJ when he remembered that she wasn't a real person. Christ, this was making him crazy in a different way. He could just imagine what the real Jennifer would say about all of this.

As the wormhole came into existence and the Rho Ship plunged into it, Raul hoped he'd get the chance to find out.

● ○ ○

To Jennifer, the three-hour ride through the dark, narrow tunnels, sitting across from General Dgarra and his captain, felt surreal. She knew this was just one of many thousands of tunnels that supported troop and supply movement throughout the mountainous Koranthian Empire. It seemed that the weight of those mountains bore down on her. She was free of the shock collar, but the shackles of slavery weren't so easily cast off.

Since he'd freed her from the crew, Dgarra hadn't spoken a word. For a while he'd studied her, but now he seemed lost in thought. He'd changed since she last saw him. He was thinner and his movements were weak, indicative of a long convalescence. Despite that, she could still feel the indomitable will of this commander. And she could feel his worry for her, which she found incredible.

Jennifer hadn't yet managed to do much more than observe and subtly alter the feelings of Koranthians. Although she was growing more familiar with their alien thought patterns, she hadn't yet mastered the ability to directly interpret them. Maybe if she wasn't so damn tired.

As the electric train clattered along the tracks, she wondered where it was taking her. All she'd seen since her initial capture was the biting cold of combat along the mountains that made up the Koranthian northern front. That and the supply tunnels where the slaves toiled away their days and nights. She thus had no clear concept of Koranthian civilization. Was that where they were heading?

The railcar entered a wide cavern that had been excavated from solid rock. Dozens of tracks served interconnecting platforms, some servicing passenger monorails while others, like the one on which she rode, handled military traffic or freight. Everything appeared to be electrically powered. The sound inside the bustling, enclosed space wasn't nearly as loud as she would have expected, apparently due to some sort of baffling on the walls and high ceiling.

As the car came to a stop, Dgarra rose to his feet and looked down at her. "Do not speak and stay close to me."

Jennifer nodded her assent, then she and the general's captain followed Dgarra off the train. A five-minute walk took them across several elevated platforms to the section of the station where Koranthian civilians congregated. Throughout that walk, she attracted shocked and disapproving stares from the milling throng. Some of them wanted to angrily confront her, but a glance at General Dgarra dissuaded them.

The Koranthian civilians were easily distinguishable from the military personnel with whom Jennifer had spent so much time. Military uniforms were almost completely black but with other colors woven into them depending on the general who commanded them. Dgarra's warriors wore uniforms of black and purple, but during her time working in the loading depot, she'd seen several other variants.

Civilian clothing appeared to be any color other than black. Although Jennifer didn't know if the hues held any special meaning, she suspected that overall attire represented a person's profession and position in Koranthian society. Whatever they meant, the combinations were vibrant and beautiful.

No Koranthian, military or civilian, wore a hat.

For the first time in many weeks, Jennifer became aware of her own appearance. The remnants of her carbon nano-fiber clothing were tattered and filthy, her boots almost worn through. She could only imagine how her face and hair looked. She didn't have to imagine her smell.

Looking around, she saw no sign of other slaves beyond the freight terminal that they had just left. In a way, it made sense. The slaves were all captured enemies. They were to be guarded at all times, never trusted, never allowed to roam freely without a shock collar, much less among civilians. That Dgarra was brazenly violating these norms angered the populace.

Dgarra entered a tower within which a winding staircase led to a high platform that serviced several monorails. And it was onto one of these monorail trains that Dgarra led her. She seated herself between the general and his captain. Then the doors slid closed and the car was whisked silently away, traveling at a much faster speed than any of the ground trains Jennifer had experienced.

When the car entered a monstrous cavern, Jennifer gasped in wonder. The city within was like nothing she'd ever seen. From up here, suspended from the cavern roof, she felt as if she'd entered a twilight world of violet and blue. The city had been built seamlessly into its natural surroundings, buildings separated by walkways that wound among underground streams, ponds, and lakes.

The buildings resembled giant stalagmites, rising from the floor in graceful, flowing curves and swirls, some of which had a combination of walkways, escalators, and elevators climbing their exteriors. Most of the buildings were tall and slender, although some formed lumpy or bulbous mounds. Despite her enhanced eyesight, Jennifer couldn't determine the actual color of individual buildings since the dim lighting of the city shifted as the day progressed. Perhaps that was the Koranthian way of determining the time of day in this underground metropolis.

Parks and open spaces were filled with beautiful natural stalagmites and stalactites, glittering crystal formations, and limestone flows. The city branched into offshoots and connecting caverns that were too numerous to count. Above it all, superhighways of crisscrossing monorails connected everything.

Jennifer was so enthralled with the view of this twilight realm that she almost forgot her promise to remain silent. A glance at the scowling faces of the other passengers reminded her. The monorail car made several stops before Dgarra got off and led her onto a high platform with few people, and then they boarded another monorail car that was empty. The doors closed and it accelerated along a gentle curve into a narrow side passage. This led to a cavern that was more beautiful than any she'd yet seen.

Glittering crystal stalactites hung from the ceiling to form a mosaic of icicles and delicate draperies. In the midst of the cavern, their edifices mirrored in the surface of the surrounding lake, three alabaster towers grew from the cavern floor to form a grand palace that glowed pale white. Instead of a central courtyard, this three-tower palace had an even grander version of the parks and walkways she'd observed in the city center. The view left Jennifer breathless.

The monorail car decelerated toward a platform complete with ceremonial guards. Jennifer found herself running a hand through her hair. Yeah. Like that was going to help. Dgarra paid no heed, exiting the car and leading her between gate guards who didn't even glance at them. Her nerveless legs carried her across a smoothly arched bridge, through the parklike grounds, and toward the main palace entrance.

As they approached, the huge double doors swung outward and a Koranthian dressed in midnight blue stepped out to meet them. He bowed low to Dgarra and then spoke the words that pushed Jennifer even farther down the rabbit hole.

"Welcome home, my lord."

●   o   o

After sending his captain off to get Smythe cleaned up, properly outfitted, and settled into her room, Dgarra headed for his audience with his uncle. He'd known that he was asking for trouble by freeing the human female and bringing her back with him to the imperial palace. Outsiders were forbidden in all the major cities, especially in ArvaiKheer. The people they'd encountered on the platforms had been angry.

If Smythe had been escorted by someone of lesser rank and lineage, she would have been attacked and killed on the spot. But as first in line to the throne, no one would dare challenge Dgarra. Not openly. But his rivals wouldn't hesitate to use this against him.

So why had he done it? Yes, she'd saved his life at the risk of her own. But that alone wouldn't have been enough. Dgarra was convinced that Smythe was telling the truth about where she was from and how she'd gotten here. She spoke of understanding technologies that had been gleaned from two starships, one Kasari and another built by a competing race, the Altreians. He intended to put these claims to the test. And if Smythe could recall the Kasari world ship that her human partner had fled the planet aboard, it might just give him the means to put a stop to the Kasari's assimilation of Scion.

Ahead of him, the double doors swung open, allowing Dgarra into the emperor's meeting chamber. When the general stepped forward and bowed, Emperor Goltat, wearing his royal black robes, rose to greet him.

"Ahh. The rumors of your return appear to be true."

"Apparently so."

His uncle motioned Dgarra toward a pair of ornate but comfortable chairs set at a shallow angle to each other. He seated himself to the emperor's right.

The emperor's face darkened.

"When you said that you were going to retrieve the slave, you made no mention of freeing her or bringing her to my palace."

"That is true."

"Several of the nobles went out of their way to make sure they informed me of what you were doing before you could do it in person."

"I am not surprised."

"Then why did you do it?"

"If I left her alone in the city, her life would be in jeopardy."

The emperor snorted. "And you think it is not while she is in this palace?"

"I think that when you hear me out, you will give the order that places her under your protection, as a ward of the empire."

Dgarra watched as his uncle's eyes widened. "That has not been done in generations."

"But it is not without precedent."

The emperor laughed. "That outsider saved the emperor himself, not his nephew."

"I believe this one can save the empire."

This statement took the emperor by surprise, as evidenced by the seconds of silence that preceded his response.

"Thank the dark gods you did not make this claim within the hearing of others. We will win this war without any outsider help."

"Others may tell you that, Uncle. But we are fortunate to have defended our outer gates until the winter could shut them for a season. I know. I was there. When the monsoon reverses, the Eadric and their Kasari masters will return in force, and when that happens, the empire will fall."

Dgarra watched as his uncle leaned forward, his eyes flashing with anger.

"You dare speak treason in my presence. Do not mistake my love for weakness."

"I dare speak the truth because of my love for you and for the empire."

Dgarra's eyes locked with those of his emperor and he did not lower them. When the emperor spoke, his voice had gone cold.

"We will speak of this no more. Tomorrow, you will walk the city promenade at the head of a military honor guard, as our people shower you with gratitude for your great victory. It is a victory you will have the chance to repeat when the winds shift."

Dgarra felt his jaws clench as he bit off the angry response that rose to his lips. Instead he made a vow he would likely regret.

"If you will not make her a ward of the empire, then she shall become a ward of my house. Anyone who strikes at her will be striking at me."

The emperor stood and Dgarra rose with him. "So be it. Have a care that your rash decision does not enable the dogs who nip at your heels to destroy you."

Dgarra bowed stiffly. Then he turned and strode from the chamber. If he was to lead a parade on the morrow, he would make this official. In the morning, he would lead an honor guard of ten thousand warriors along the great promenade of ArvaiKheer. And Smythe would be at his side wearing the distinctive uniform that marked her as his ward and aide-de-camp.

A mirthless grin split Dgarra's lips. If his rivals thought they could intimidate him, they were about to learn otherwise.

● ○ ○

Jennifer hadn't felt this clean since before she'd left Earth. She'd been stripped, bathed, and scrubbed by two of the Koranthian servants who served General Dgarra when he was at his home in the imperial palace complex. And she'd been assigned a suite that rivaled the one she'd stayed at inside the Bellagio Hotel in Las Vegas, back when she was a fresh runaway and so full of herself that she thought she was ready for the real world. Little had she known the cascade of events her foolish actions had triggered.

Now, wearing a robe with the distinctive black and purple colors of House Dgarra, she stood in front of a full-length mirror, marveling at the changes in herself. Her brown hair hung to her shoulders, tipped by dyed blonde ends and crying out for a good trim. Her body was lean and hard. Even her face held the look of a warrior, a far cry from the pampered teen she remembered.

Now she awaited a new set of clothes to be delivered. The Koranthian equivalent of a tailor had taken her measurements with a device that looked something like an airport security wand. She imagined that it was some sort of 3-D scanner that automatically collected her measurements, although the thought occurred to her that it could just as well be a video capture that was now posted to the interstellar equivalent of YouTube.

In the hours she'd been here, Jennifer had learned much, most of it from Dgarra's assistant on the general's orders. Jennifer's presence here had apparently increased the long-existing rift between Dgarra and a number of other high-ranking nobles aligned with House Magtal, with General Magtal being second in line for the throne behind Dgarra. Apparently Dgarra disdained court politics and suffered for his indifference to it. This was evidenced by the central front being designated as the main fight despite the fiercer fighting in the north.

Jennifer understood what that meant. The priority for troops, equipment, and supplies always went to support the main effort, explaining why Dgarra's warriors were stretched so thin. Now he had brought an outsider, a probable Kasari spy, into the capital city and imperial palace itself. Worse, he had announced to the emperor that he planned to make Jennifer his ward and then have her walk by his side in tomorrow's celebration of Dgarra's great victory. And he planned on naming her his aide-de-camp, an honored position marked with a unique, purple-braided rope worn on her left shoulder. Gasoline poured on a flame.

Dgarra might suck at politics, but when it came to confrontation, he was spectacular. Jennifer had seen into his mind. She had earned his respect, and with that had come belief in her story and a sense that the technology she could offer in the fight against the Kasari might give the empire a fighting chance. To gain that, he would engage all who challenged him, unto the very gates of hell.

There was no knock. The tailor just barged into the room. That didn't surprise her. She may be Dgarra's ward designate, but she wasn't his ward yet, and everyone seemed intent on letting her know it. The tailor carried over his shoulder a clutch of bags that he gently laid atop the bed. Then, taking the topmost bag, he moved it to a separate spot and ran a finger along the edge. Although there was no visible clasp, the bag opened like the petals of a rose.

The uniform within was stunning. Or maybe her impressions were just screwed up from the way she'd been whipsawed through wildly contrasting circumstances. How did the old saying go? When you're starving, even swill tastes like manna from heaven.

The tailor motioned at her and she let the robe fall from her shoulders and stepped forward without a trace of self-consciousness. For the next several minutes she stood there, moving to allow him to dress her, memorizing exactly how it was done.

When he was finished, he motioned her toward a full-sized mirror on the wall next to the door that led out of the apartment. When Jennifer stepped up to it, she froze. This wasn't your mother's uniform. This was a silk-thin and incredibly revealing second skin of swirling black and purple over soft black boots with springy soles that made her feel as if she could leap tall buildings in a single bound.

Jesus! Dgarra was intentionally magnifying her humanity . . . enhancing her differences. If this was a game of Texas hold 'em, the general had just gone all in.

● ○ ○

Space sucked. Raul had arrived at this conclusion some time ago, but it had just been reinforced. The subspace inertial damping had worked just fine. In fact it had worked so well that the exit from the wormhole felt no rougher than several roller coaster rides he'd taken when he was a boy. But this trip, in addition to all those weeks experimenting with subspace field manipulation, had used up most of the Rho Ship's remaining fuel. It meant that he'd have to delay his trip to one of Scion's moons until after he landed on one of the moons orbiting a closer world to refuel. Plus he was hungry, which meant that he'd have to force down another of the Scion eels, probably while having to endure VJ's helpful suggestions about the joys of positive thinking.

As if on cue, he heard her voice. "I've completed the sensor scan for the closest body where we can ingest fuel. It's a dwarf planet less than a million miles from our current position."

"And?" Raul asked, waiting for the qualifier that usually accompanied any good news that VJ delivered.

"And we should be able to get there with fuel to spare."

"Fantastic."

"Unfortunately," VJ continued, "we'll have to use the gravity distortion engines instead of our subspace drive, and we won't have enough fuel to also generate a cloaking field during the maneuvers."

"Crap!" He'd known it.

"No use getting upset. It's extremely unlikely that the Kasari will be able to detect that kind of distortion signal at this range. Even if they do, it will take the signal more than five hours to reach Scion. Plenty of time to refuel, shift into subspace, and make it to the Scion moon of your choice."

That news lifted his spirits. These were all calculations he could have easily performed without her, but this ability to delegate certain jobs to VJ had spoiled him. She was almost like his own science officer, leaving him free for deeper thought.

"Okay, then, VJ. Lay in a course for the dwarf planet."

"Already done."

Raul issued the mental command that engaged the gravity distortion engines as a five-hour mental countdown started in his head. If nothing went wrong, they should beat the electromagnetic signature of these maneuvers to Scion by more than an hour.

The *if* in that thought made him uneasy. Lately Murphy's Law had been kicking his ass on a regular basis.

● ○ ○

Jennifer could never have imagined such a spectacle. She strode at General Dgarra's side on the Grand Promenade of ArvaiKheer as a thousand drummers marched behind them, tapping out a low but steady marching beat for the ten thousand warriors who followed, all clad in the black and purple uniforms of House Dgarra. Impressive as this was, the numbers were dwarfed by the throngs of Koranthian citizens who lined the winding promenade on both sides all the way to the central amphitheater where an even larger crowd awaited their arrival.

The way her own uniform's shimmering pattern shifted with every muscle movement made her feel like she wore nothing more than magical body paint.

The hisses of disapproval started slowly at first, but grew steadily in volume as they progressed. The sound began to spread, threatening to reach the amphitheater ahead of the procession, where it would have its preplanned effect, giving Dgarra a carefully choreographed and unpleasant welcome.

Unperturbed, Dgarra raised a hand in a signal to the drum leaders.

The change that followed was immediate and stunning, almost causing Jennifer to stumble in her surprise. Gone was the gentle tapping of hands on the sides of the bongolike instruments. Now those same skilled hands hammered the heads of the drums, sending up a staccato beat that shook the cavern, causing many in the audience to stagger back and cover their ears with their hands.

The alien beat was aggressively tribal and triggered such emotion in Jennifer that she had to fight the urge to chant along. Indeed, Dgarra's ten thousand picked up a guttural chant that rose above even the sound of the drums. There were no words, just a booming rhythm intended to instill fear in a waiting enemy. The chanting came from the throats of modern warriors but was of a different age, when warriors called upon their gods to grant them honor and victory in battle.

Jennifer knew this without even having to look into these warriors' minds. The crowd felt a sense of awe that bordered on fear.

They reached the amphitheater and the volume rose as the drums and the chanting warriors entered. Then, as the last ranks marched into position, Dgarra gave another signal and two dozen flag bearers lifted the long staffs of their black and purple guidons, raising flags high in one swift motion. Instantaneous silence followed.

Immediately, Jennifer stepped forward, just as Dgarra had rehearsed with her. She projected her clear voice to the tens of thousands of onlookers.

"Citizens of ArvaiKheer. I give you the punisher of the Eadric host, the killer of their Kasari masters, the commander of the northern front . . . General Dgarra."

As her voice echoed through the amphitheater, it seemed that the entire throng held its collective breath for one beat, and then two. Unwilling to leave this to chance, Jennifer picked a dozen targets at key locations in the crowd and amplified the sense of awe this display had invoked. The wild cheer that began with these few spread to their immediate neighbors and then rippled through the crowd in a great wave that even swept up Dgarra's enemies in its irresistible tide.

Then, as she stepped back to Dgarra's side, her gaze settled on Emperor Goltat as he rose from his dais and raised his right hand. Immediately, the long notes of two conchlike instruments blared, bringing another silence upon the crowd. Without hesitation, the emperor descended the steps and walked forward to where Dgarra waited.

As the emperor came to a stop, Dgarra lowered himself to one knee, head held high . . . a move that Jennifer copied precisely. Reaching out, the emperor placed his right hand on Dgarra's shoulder and bade him stand. Then, he turned back to the crowd, his hand still resting on Dgarra's shoulder, and spoke.

"As your emperor, it gives me great joy to present to you . . . the Champion of the Northern Front."

What had taken some urging from Jennifer only a minute earlier took none this time. And as the crowd's explosion of approval rose to a new crescendo, Jennifer allowed herself a smile, knowing full well it was an expression that Dgarra's rivals wouldn't be sharing.

:CHAPTER 22

Alexandr Prokorov terminated the encrypted call, tempted to hurl his sat-phone into the wall of his hotel suite. The U.S.-based system that had given him the lead that the Smythes were now operating out of Lima had just been taken down in a massive cyber-attack that had the NSA director at a loss to explain. Even worse, whenever they tried to bring up a backup of the system, that was immediately taken down as well despite the NSA super-hackers' attempts to defeat the intrusions.

After consulting with his Russian FSB counterparts and with the East Asian People's Alliance Ministry of State Security, the NSA confirmed that this appeared to be the work of an advanced piece of artificial intelligence acting at the direction of Mark and Heather Smythe. Left unchecked, this AI posed a major threat not only to the Federation Security Service but to the security of the entire UFNS or any other government that tried to stand in its way.

He walked to the floor-to-ceiling window with its beautiful view of the snow-covered Red Square and Kremlin. Two hours remained before the cold light of dawn. The square was beautifully lit, a scene that recalled the glory days of the old Soviet Union. With war raging all along the country's southern border, a consequence of the Islamic Alliance's refusal to see the promise of the new alien technologies, mankind had one chance to restore order to this world and to avert the nuclear war that could end it.

The UFNS represented that chance. The new project to rebuild the Stephenson Gateway would break ground just outside of Frankfurt in the coming month. Prokorov was firm in his belief that the alien benefactors who had provided these wonderful technologies to mankind could be called upon to help guide humanity's path to a more stable world.

He found himself grinding his teeth and took a deep breath, forcing the muscles in his jaw to relax. To have peace threatened by the secret technologies the Smythes had developed was something he would not tolerate, but a significant adjustment to his strategy was required. This new threat was much too great to be dealt with covertly. He had to think bigger if he was to be certain of the kill. And that meant he would need buy-in from the leaders of the New Soviet Union, the East Asian People's Alliance, the European Union, and the United States. His aides would require several hours to coordinate the top-secret videoconference, but there was no getting around it.

In the meantime, he would let Daniil Alkaev and the forces he had already placed at the operative's disposal try to disrupt the Smythe operation in Lima. After all, Daniil might get lucky, making the upcoming videoconference moot.

But if Daniil failed, there was always plan B.

● ○ ○

The trip to Lima had been an all-nighter, requiring several out-of-the-way stops as Heather used her savant visions to identify and bypass checkpoints that could have resulted in violent confrontations. As Janet drove, Mark sat in the back of the SUV, resting the AR-15 between his legs and watching Heather dive deep into that mental place where only she could go. With Jack in the passenger seat, Mark felt like he could relax, confident that between the two of them they would spot trouble in time to ready a response.

Things had a way of spinning out of control no matter how well you planned for contingencies. And this South American trip had certainly proven that rule. What had intended to be a short stop to solidify allies had devolved into its own special form of trouble.

Mark had no illusions that finding Robby would be easy. The kid was just too talented, and with Eos blocking their attempts to track him by hijacking surveillance systems, that meant they would be relying heavily on Jack's strange intuition.

Lima was a big city with massive slums and a huge indigenous population. For a highly trained and enhanced person such as Robby, the locale offered an abundance of opportunities to disappear, even if he was technically still a child. There would, of course, be lots of people who would want to take advantage of him. Mark pitied them. The assumptions they would make would only get them killed.

But Tall Bear, through his extensive connections to the Native People's Alliance, was their ace in the hole. He'd put out the word that he was looking for a boy matching Robby's description, complete with his indigenous disguise and probable location. That request would be disseminated throughout native communities over the course of the next few days. If someone in that network saw Robby, Tall Bear would be notified.

Heather's voice brought her husband back to the present.

"Uh-oh."

"What?" Janet asked. "Have you got a lead on Robby?"

"No. But something big is going on. I'm detecting unscheduled movement of several Spetsnaz and U.S. Special Operations Command units that have been alerted within the last few hours."

"Where are they headed?" asked Jack.

"I don't know yet. Checking."

Mark put on his SRT headset, gently touching his mind to Heather's.

"Can I help?"

He felt a mixture of her mental exhaustion and relief.

"You bet. Focus on the Spetsnaz. I'll take SOCOM."

"On it."

Mark felt his pulse increase and focused on dropping it back to a steady forty-three beats per minute. He and Heather hadn't been on a mission this important in a long time and, odd as it seemed, it felt pretty damn good. In this life or the next, there was nobody he'd rather have at his side.

● ○ ○

Robby felt Eos come to alert as she spoke in his mind.

"The FSS has just ordered the covert deployment of special operations forces from the New Soviet Union and from the United States to separate staging areas just outside of Lima. The Americans will be in place within the next several hours. The Spetsnaz shortly thereafter."

Feeling his adrenaline spike, Robby channeled the memory of a deep alpha meditation and felt the river of relaxation flow through him.

"That's fine. Monitor them but don't interfere. Let's not give away the fact that we know they're coming."

"Strategically sound decision. Agreed."

Robby smiled. Even when Eos deferred to him, she couldn't help but pass judgment, good or bad. The memory of what his dad had said came forth. *A yes-man only reinforces bad decisions.* Eos was no yes-man.

He stood up and walked to the window that looked out over the busy street below. After the bars closed, the traffic died out in Lima. His special talent told him that this night was deader than usual, an omen. Fortunately Robby was above such superstition.

Eos had made all the arrangements for this two-story house, including pantry stocking instructions and the designated key drop. Payment had been made by direct transfer into the owner's bank account, three thousand dollars for the month plus an additional two thousand as a deposit against possible damages.

Not that Robby cared about either amount. Eos could make electronic money more easily than the U.S. Federal Reserve. Robby merely needed a secure base of operations, and thought it even more advantageous that he was in a cartel safe house. The owner wouldn't raise any questions.

"Also," Eos said, "Jack Gregory, Janet Price, Heather Smythe, and Mark Smythe are inbound to Lima. How they found us is an unanswered question."

"Probably the same way the FSS did."

"Are you implying that they detected my signature?"

Was there a bit of annoyance in the tone of Eos's question? If so, it did Robby a world of good.

"No. Just saying that there are a lot of folks headed this way right now."

"Would you like me to have your parents and the Smythes arrested?"

"No. Just throw them off track. I don't want them involved in the fight that's coming."

Robby felt a nice warm glow enter his core. As badly as he wanted to prevent his parents from riding to his rescue, the knowledge of how badly they wanted to find him made him feel really good.

He tagged the feeling in his eidetic memory. That warmth was worthy of replay on a semiregular basis.

● ○ ○

The fine steel blade of the Ka-Bar made a soft whisking sound as it slid across the oiled surface of the whetstone. Daniil Alkaev knew that Prokorov's focus was the Smythes, but they were just the icing on the cake. Jack "The Ripper" Gregory was his target.

Galina sensed it. Of course she did. The woman read him like a book. After all, she was a creature of like disposition. At some point he might have to do something about that, but at the moment, he would continue to enjoy her provocative edges. His love of the edge was what made life worth living.

No target was more dangerous than The Ripper. For years, the American operative turned private contractor had dominated Daniil's thoughts. Daniil had studied his classified FSB case file . . . even gaining access to the non-redacted CIA file on the man's early career. But Daniil was fascinated by the years after The Ripper had left the CIA.

They weren't easy years to reconstruct but, with a few significant gaps, Daniil had managed to do it. The man's kill list included some very dangerous targets, among them the head of the Russian Mafia, Vladimir Roskov, and the EAPA Ministry of State Security's top assassin, Qiang Chu.

And The Ripper was married to a woman who was every bit as dangerous as Galina. Fortunately Daniil could get to both of them at the same time, through their eight-year-old son, Robert Brice Gregory, named after The Ripper's long-dead brother. With a trap baited for the boy, The Ripper and Janet Price would be drawn into a kill zone of Daniil's making.

But first Daniil had to find them, and that was proving difficult. Hugo Mendez, his contact within the Shining Path guerilla group, had assured him that if The Ripper and company were in Lima, he would soon learn where in the city they were hiding. Apparently, "soon" had a different meaning in this part of the world.

Daniil wiped the blade on a soft cloth and then placed the sharp edge on his thumb. He didn't feel the cut, but a drop of blood welled from the skin. With a nod of satisfaction, he wiped the blade clean and returned it to its sheath.

Patience was one of a hunter's best weapons. Even though it was Daniil's least favorite, he was a disciplined apex predator and would wait for his prey to reveal itself. In the meantime, he would prepare for the kill of all kills.

● ○ ○

"Whatever is about to happen is going down in Peru," Jamal said, his voice tight with excitement.

Eileen understood that. The things she was seeing through their shared satellite link was showing heightened NSA activity focused in and around Lima. Special Operations Command networks were also spun up, indicative of an ongoing operation. All of these were using some of the latest encryption algorithms that were, for all practical purposes, unbreakable. Fortunately, she and Jamal didn't need to decipher the encryption. They just needed to penetrate a single device on each of those networks.

There was one central flaw that made all networks vulnerable to the best hackers on the planet: humans. Whether it was humans who took shortcuts in their programming or human operators who failed to follow approved procedures, there was always a way in for those good enough to find it.

For Eileen, the opportunity came through President Benton's cell phone, a device that he carried wherever he went. Though it had been secure when issued, he'd added several apps, one of which enabled him to browse social media and organize photos from his two teenage daughters.

"There's definitely Delta Force involvement," Eileen said over the rapid clicking of their two keyboards. "They're already inbound, with orders to occupy a staging area just outside of Lima and wait for the go order."

Seated in front of his laptop across the table from her, Jamal glanced up. "A Spetsnaz unit is also on the way, but it's going to take them longer to get there. There's also a lot of Shining Path chatter. How's your Spanish?"

"Not bad."

"That's good. *Una cerveza por favor* is about my limit. Give me a sec to push this over to you."

"I'll take a look."

When Jamal sent her the link, Eileen opened it and began scanning for anything that seemed relevant.

"It's not just Shining Path. Looks like the Native People's Alliance is involved as well. I'm even seeing some cartel activity that looks suspicious."

Eileen paused. Several e-mails contained the same attached photograph, the picture of a handsome, dark-skinned boy wearing clothing popular with the indigenous people of the area. But there was something about his face, something vaguely familiar. What was it?

Turning her attention from the NPA's communications back to the Shining Path's, she hit pay dirt.

"Okay. The Shining Path is looking for the Smythe group. Specifically Mark and Heather Smythe, Jack Gregory, Janet Price, and their son Robert."

The mention of Jack's son triggered a memory that pulled an exclamation from her lips. "Wait!"

She returned to the picture, zooming in on the boy's fine features. His skin color looked authentic, but his facial features definitely looked Anglo. Eileen pulled up a recent photograph of Jack Gregory, tiling the two images side by side on her display. Jesus. The kid was going to be a dead ringer for his dad when he got older. But he damn sure looked a lot older than eight. And why was the NPA hunting the boy while everyone else seemed to be after his mom and dad or the Smythes?

Pushing back from her laptop, Eileen tapped her knuckles on the table to catch Jamal's attention. He looked up, his left eyebrow arching.

"Yes?"

Eileen took a deep breath and, for the first time since she and Jamal had started hacking their way through these highly classified networks, noticed Denise watching them from the couch.

"Well," she said, "I think it's time we reconnected with Freddy Hagerman."

● ○ ○

Jack felt the adrenaline rush that Khal Teth had just triggered like he'd been kicked in the gut. Instinctively he reached across from the passenger seat to grab the steering wheel, jerking it hard right, throwing the car into a slide that took them off the road and between a pair of thick trees.

In the driver's seat, Janet reacted as only someone with her level of training and trust in her partner could have done. She removed both hands from the wheel and concentrated on manipulating the gas pedal and brake of the old-school Subaru, drawing her Glock from its holster in the same motion. And behind her, Mark and Heather's weapons came up at the same time, each seeking a target.

From the highway, a huge explosion split the night from the location they would now be crossing had they not veered into the forest. As the car skidded to a halt in a tangle of brush, Jack forced open his door and sprinted into the dark, pulled forward by the tug of danger that drifted through the night.

There was no moon. It didn't matter. The night misted red all around him. It had been a hell of a long time since he'd last felt this Anchanchu-powered adrenaline rush. He'd missed the addiction.

● ○ ○

Janet felt Jack grab the steering wheel and glanced right, startled by the brightness of the red glint in his eyes.

Shit!

She reacted automatically, releasing the wheel to this man who was more than a man, doing her part to keep them all from dying.

As trees whisked past the car left and right, she patted the brake in a rapid motion that roughly approximated antilock braking, which the old Subaru didn't have. The Glock filled her hand automatically. She searched for targets in the woods illuminated by the bouncing headlight beams of the automobile.

The explosion on the highway wiped her vision and frosted the safety glass in the driver's side windows. The car lurched to a stop. She switched off the lights, turned off the car, threw open the door, and dived out as gunfire crackled through the night.

● ○ ○

Bullets whizzed past, chopping the brush and trees to his right. Jack sprinted on a course parallel to the line of fire, flanking the people who were blindly spraying their automatic weapons into the night. He knew precisely how Janet, Mark, and Heather would assault this ambush. They had rehearsed this drill a thousand times. Each of them would do their job and Jack would do his.

Jack sensed the man at the far end of the ragged line before he saw him. Apparently he was some kind of leader of this guerilla band, yelling instructions in Spanish that sent several men forward through the thick woods toward the spot where the car had come to a stop. Jack let him finish and then cut his throat from behind. Shifting the blade, he jammed it up behind the man's chin and into his brain, and then silently lowered the body to the ground.

From the direction where the guerillas had disappeared he heard several individual shots, followed by the staccato burst of automatic weapons fire that came to a sudden end. Yells from Jack's right confirmed that the remaining guerillas knew the meaning of the preceding sequence of gunfire. They'd just lost several comrades.

Jack picked up the dead man's weapon and lay down, using the body as a rest for the rifle as he aimed it along the guerilla line and waited for what he knew was coming, a series of muzzle flashes. Another lone gunshot split the night. One of the soldiers rolled out of the woods onto the edge of the road as his comrades opened up all along their line.

When he squeezed the trigger, Jack sent a series of three-round bursts into the firing guerillas. Only after the first half dozen had fallen did they realize that the gunfire was coming from the end of their own line. Their response was entirely predictable. The nearest rose to swing his weapon toward Jack, only to be cut down by the panicked firing of his fellows as they all turned their weapons toward where Jack was cutting them to pieces.

Right on cue, a rapid volley of fire from three separate firing positions chopped them down. The remaining three men bolted, rewarded with bullets in the back of the head that dropped them face forward. Jack raised two fingers to his lips and sent out a piercing whistle that echoed through the night, letting his team know he was moving.

Leaving the AK-47 lying beside its dead owner, Jack placed his H&K in his left hand and the Gerber Guardian combat dagger in his right. Then he moved silently from body to body. Nano-healing being what it was, he put an extra bullet into the head of each soldier. In less than a minute he cleared the objective and confirmed the kills. Seventeen guerillas, six of them women, all dead. And parked in a small clearing adjacent to the ambush location were five four-wheel-drive pickup trucks.

A different whistle gave the all clear and three shadows moved rapidly through the woods toward the spot where he waited. Heather was the first to arrive, followed closely by Mark and Janet, all with their weapons at the ready. Despite his all clear, they took nothing for granted.

"Search the bodies," Jack said. "We want radios, cell phones, papers, car keys, and anything else that looks useful, but make it quick.

Then grab your go bags and throw them in a couple of these trucks. I want to be out of here in the next five minutes."

Nobody bothered to acknowledge his orders. This finely tuned engine of death slipped silently as one into the predawn darkness.

● ○ ○

"Those idiots! If they weren't already dead, I'd kill them myself."

Daniil Alkaev's temples throbbed so hard they threatened to burst. As he moved among the bodies with Galina Anikin at his side on this hot January morning, he looked for something positive to take from what was otherwise an unmitigated disaster. All these fools had to do was locate The Ripper and call it in. Instead, after one of their agents spotted the Smythe party at a government checkpoint, the Shining Path had decided to plant an improvised explosive device along the road, looking to take credit for killing the Smythes and their bodyguards.

Kneeling down beside the commander of the guerilla group, Daniil grabbed a handful of the man's black hair and lifted his head to examine the wound. A single slash had severed both carotid arteries. The spray pattern of the blood confirmed what his eyes had already told him.

The Ripper had spotted the ambush in time to avoid the kill zone and flank the hapless guerillas. Then he and his companions had killed every single one of their attackers, going so far as shooting several other guerillas in the back as they tried to flee. Afterward The Ripper had walked the line, shooting each of the downed guerillas in the head. Cold. Merciless. Exactly as Daniil would have done it.

But something bothered him. Daniil walked the line of bodies strewn along the roadside and then made his way back to the bodies of those killed as they had approached the wrecked Subaru. He'd assumed that The Ripper and Janet Price were the heavy hitters, protecting the spoiled Smythe billionaires. But this combat scene told a different story.

The quartet had reacted to the ambush like a well-rehearsed team of seasoned professionals, flawlessly reversing the situation. Three of them had left the car and conducted a fake counterattack, allowing The Ripper to flank the guerillas, before setting up a mini-ambush of their own. They'd expected the guerillas to send a kill squad toward the car and had slaughtered them when they came. Then, when The Ripper opened up on the left flank of the remaining line, this group had attacked.

Daniil straightened, knowing that he had found that opening he'd been looking for. In light of what he had seen here, he would need to seriously reassess the Smythes. Otherwise, the false assumption he'd previously held might just get him killed.

● ○ ○

Major Kamkin didn't like being forced to accept last-minute additions to his Spetsnaz commandos. But the chain of command had left him no options. So he would be babysitting these new arrivals from the Federation Security Service.

Despite his irritation, he had to admit that Daniil Alkaev and Galina Anikin had the hard look of professional killers. If they had been placed under his command, they might even be useful. Unfortunately, Alkaev would be the one issuing the orders, the way of things in this new world structure. The motherland had been supplanted by a higher power. All hail the UFNS.

Turning his thoughts to other matters, the major moved among his thirty-five commandos, watching closely as they prepared their weapons and equipment for the upcoming raid. The American terrorists would meet the same fate that had greeted all of Major Kamkin's previous targets.

:CHAPTER 23

Raul brought the Rho Ship out of subspace just behind the third and largest of Scion's moons, one very similar in size and appearance to Earth's moon. Engaging the gravity distortion engines, he set the ship down as gently as possible and cloaked it. For two full minutes he waited, monitoring the sensors to see if any Kasari attack vessels had left Scion's atmosphere. Seeing no signs of movement, he breathed a huge sigh of relief.

"Wow," VJ said. "You got us here without getting us both killed. Good job."

"Thanks for the vote of confidence."

"Hey. This is me being supportive."

Raul leaned back in his invisible stasis field command chair and shook his head. He was definitely going to have to improve the VJ simulation if he didn't want to start beating his head against the wall. Luckily, he was the captain and could still order her around.

"Start a full worm-fiber scan of Scion. Let's find the real Jennifer."

"You know that the way you said that is hurtful, right?"

"Just do it."

"Yes, your lordship."

"Do I have to do it myself?"

"I'm on it. Just sit back and *relax*."

Jesus. Now VJ was slowing him down, not to mention irritating the hell out of him. He turned his thoughts to the Kasari down on the planet. They would certainly detect the worm-fiber search, just as they'd done before. But they couldn't tell where it originated. Unlike before, they wouldn't be able to send out a master override code that took control of this ship. They would know he was somewhere in the Scion system but that was about it.

Another thought occurred to him. If Jennifer attempted to connect with the Rho Ship's neural net through her SRT headset, he would detect it. But for now, as VJ had suggested, he could afford to sit back, stretch his new legs, and relax.

After all, he had an eel dinner to look forward to.

● ○ ○

The assassin came at Jennifer as she lay, little knowing that she almost never slept. The Koranthian warrior was big, standing seven and a half feet tall and holding a scythe-shaped sword that should have swept her head from her shoulders. But her side kick knocked the weapon from his hands and sent it spinning to embed itself in the headboard of her bed.

Then Jennifer was on his back, her arms locked around his neck in a grip that would have killed a human foe. But this was no human. The massive Koranthian rolled forward, slinging Jennifer across the room. She rolled to her feet to face him.

He sneered at her. "Time to die, outlander."

She grinned right back, baring her teeth. "Yes, it is."

The assassin moved much faster than she expected, launching himself at her in a wrestler's takedown that Jennifer met with a judo throw, using his five hundred pounds against him. As he flew over her shoulder, he caught her arm in a powerful hand, pulling Jennifer down atop him. Her foe's shoulder and head hit the chest of drawers with such force that the furniture splintered. But he maintained his hold on her arm.

Contorting her body, she drove her right knee into the assassin's throat with the full force of her downward momentum. The cartilage in his throat collapsed with a sick crunch. As his hand lost its grip on her arm, she saw the Koranthian's dark eyes widen in shock. Jennifer pushed herself up off of him and dropped onto his throat again. Leaning over his face, she thrust her thumbs deep into his eyes as her fingers clawed into the thick skin on the side of his head.

His flailing right arm knocked her across the room and Jennifer felt a blinding flash of pain. The impact with the wall broke her left wrist and opened a head wound that spilled blood down her face and into her left eye, partially blinding her.

The door banged open. General Dgarra and two of his personal guards burst into the room. With a guttural growl, Dgarra pulled the sword from the headboard, took two long strides, and cut the gurgling assassin's head from his shoulders, drenching himself in dark blood.

He turned to his guards, eyes blazing. "Take this garbage from my house and stake his head outside the entrance to General Magtal's estate. And get me the names of the two guards who were supposed to be on duty here."

Bowing, both guards spun on their heels and wordlessly departed.

By the time Dgarra turned his attention to her, Jennifer could feel the healing beginning to stanch the blood flow on her forehead. The nanites that remained in her bloodstream were now so slow that their repairs could no longer be directly observed. She estimated that her broken wrist would take more than a full day to heal. Dgarra was aware of the change. She could feel the concern in his mind.

"Come with me. My doctor will see to your injuries."

"I'm not sure your doctor will know anything about my anatomy. I'll be fine."

Dgarra paused to consider this. "Maybe so. But accompany me while my people clean up this mess. I will see that you get a bath and a fresh set of clothes. Then we shall talk. There are many things that I wish to discuss before we depart."

Jennifer felt her pulse spike. "Depart?"

"Even though the winter has driven our enemies from these mountains, I would return to my command in the north. There is much preparation to be done before the monsoon winds reverse. I would see for myself whether the tales that have sprung from your lips have any basis in reality or whether I have made as large a fool of myself as my uncle believes."

Without waiting for her response, Dgarra turned and walked out of the room. And as Jennifer followed him, she felt a great wave of relief wash over her. To be leaving this seething den of vipers and returning to the northern front suddenly seemed like a vacation on the French Riviera.

:CHAPTER 24

"Finally."

Prokorov smiled as he finished the request to initiate the airstrike that would eliminate the Smythe problem. Although Daniil hadn't been happy about it, the Shining Path's screw-up had turned out to be the break the FSS needed. The action had been picked up by two separate satellites and one of those had been able to track the trucks the Smythes had taken into the San Cristóbal slum in eastern Lima.

Even though the intelligence community hadn't managed to track the group to a specific house, they were certain of the neighborhood. The American B-1 bomber was part of a squadron that had been kept on station just for this opportunity and in a little over fifteen minutes it would deliver its payload of two-thousand-pound bombs on target. Hitting a densely populated area was unfortunate, but with a properly coordinated media blitz the aftermath could be managed.

This action would produce far fewer casualties than if he'd been forced to invoke his backup plan. Even the U.S. president had agreed with that. The bombing was a small price to pay to eliminate a major threat to the island of stability the UFNS represented in this chaotic age.

● ○ ○

President Ted Benton walked into the White House Situation Room to find the key members of his national security staff already assembled. After cursory greetings, he took his seat at the head of the table, studying the serious faces of those who stared back at him.

"As you already know, I've just ordered a B-1 strike on a densely populated section of Lima. Yesterday, you all made your cases for or against this course of action. While we waited for definitive information about where the Smythe terrorist group is hiding, I've given those opinions careful consideration. After close consultation with our UFNS allies, we have agreed that this course of action is the best of several bad choices now available to us."

Barbara Dansby, his secretary of state, shook her head. "Mr. President, I have a very hard time believing that killing hundreds or even thousands of innocent civilians is our best choice. This could trigger renewed warfare with the countries of Central and South America, not to mention the trouble it could cause us with the tribal nations of the NPA within our own country. And A Safe Earth will use this as a significant rallying cry. I wish to register my deepest opposition to this plan."

The president forced a calmness into his reply that masked his irritation. "The UFNS council has thoroughly discussed the possible repercussions. More importantly, I have made my decision. What I now expect from my staff is a coordinated effort to implement it and to prepare for whatever public blowback it triggers. Barbara, can you do that for me?"

For several moments, he watched as the woman's steely gaze locked with his. When she finally nodded, President Benton felt himself relax.

Turning his attention to the situational display on the far wall, he motioned toward his national security advisor. "Okay, Don, bring us up to date."

● ○ ○

Despite Robby knowing that it was crucially important to remain in the safe house in order to avoid being spotted, the isolation was beginning to wear on him. And he was getting tired of constantly wearing the SRT headset. No matter how much he tried to tell himself that he was an augmented and highly trained weapon, he couldn't deny that he missed his mom and dad. He even missed Yachay's cajoling.

Eos's alert brought him out of the depressing thoughts.

"The American government has just ordered an airstrike at a set of coordinates in southeastern Lima. A B-1 bomber that was holding on station just off the Pacific coast is inbound. Estimated time on target . . . 1802."

"You're telling me they're going to start dropping bombs in eleven minutes?"

"Ten minutes thirty-seven seconds."

"Show me."

A satellite map formed in Robby's mind, a red square marking the targeted area. He breathed a sigh of relief.

"That's nowhere close to our location."

"The Americans believe it is where Jack, Janet, Mark, and Heather are located."

Robby felt his breath catch in his chest. "Are they there?"

After a short pause, a new satellite image formed in his mind. The display zoomed in on a busy street. Eos highlighted two battered pickups making their way through an intersection.

"This image was captured forty-two minutes ago. I found nothing more recent."

Robby's heart tried to climb up into his throat. "Damn it."

His mind raced. "Can you take control of the bomber?"

"Checking."

With his stress rising with each second that dragged by, more than a full minute passed before Eos responded.

"The aircraft has shut down all external communications in an effort to prevent any onboard systems from being remotely hacked. It is not responding to override commands I have placed on those uplink channels."

"Jesus. What about antiaircraft systems around Lima?"

There was another pause as the seconds ticked off in Robby's head. If he didn't do something, his folks had eight minutes and eleven seconds left to live.

● ○ ○

Heather looked across the slum that had been built into the side of San Cristóbal Hill. The area was crowded, polluted, and dangerous, but it was also bright and colorful, its crumbling buildings painted in a wide variety of neon hues and decorated with graffiti. The locale was one of the best places in the world for a person to disappear.

Since every action she took generated a cascade of changing probabilities, if Heather got this wrong they all might disappear here for good.

They'd parked the two Shining Path pickups beside a partially collapsed tenement building, grabbed their bags, and then, pulling wide-brimmed hats low, merged with the crowds that filled the narrow streets, keeping just enough separation from each other that they wouldn't be identified as a group. Unfortunately, she and Mark had been forced to remove their SRT headsets until they could reach the safe house that Tall Bear had arranged for them.

They'd survived the ambush but it had advertised their presence. The odds that an intelligence service had managed to track them from that location to where they'd ditched the trucks were too high to be ignored. Thus they were focused on clearing the area before special operations types showed up and tried to kill them.

● ○ ○

Six minutes thirty seconds to go and still nothing.

"Come on, Eos. Give me something."

"I am sorry, but the Peruvian armed forces do not have any antiaircraft systems capable of intercepting a B-1 bomber."

It was precisely what he didn't want to hear.

"Connect me to Heather's SRT headset."

"Neither she nor Mark is currently connected through their headsets."

"Crap."

Think, Robby. Think!

"What about a direct subspace hack into the B-1's computers?"

"That requires a precise set of coordinates. The jet is moving and it is not sending out telemetry that I can intercept to calculate its position in real time."

"Wait a minute. It needs to calculate its position precisely for targeting purposes. Is it downlinking GPS signals?"

"It should be passively receiving those non-dithered signals."

"Fine, then hack the GPS satellites and use them to make your way into the B-1 through its GPS receivers."

"That has only a five percent probability of success. If I divert the aircraft the other onboard systems will detect the error and correct for it. Their accuracy will be reduced but not enough to protect the people in the targeted area."

"What about the payload? Don't the bombs have their own GPS receivers?"

"Accessing the weapon system manifest now . . . Yes, the two-thousand-pound bombs are GPS enabled. They do not have the redundancy of the systems in the aircraft."

"Can you penetrate the bomb electronics without being detected?"

Eos paused and responded. "I now have access to the entire payload."

Robby swallowed hard.

"Arm one of the bombs."

"That is not possible. The aircraft charges the electric fuse capacitors upon release. The delay timing is controlled by the amount of charge delivered to those capacitors."

Three minutes left. Robby was running out of ideas. Droplets of sweat slid from his brow to sting his eyes.

"Okay then, surely there's some circuitry on the bomb that can be reprogrammed to make it detonate early."

"Yes. But not close enough to bring down the aircraft. For that to be effective I will have to reprogram each bomb's fusing immediately after it is dropped."

"Will that work?"

"There is a ninety-three percent probability I can detonate most of them before they hit their targets."

Robby felt like screaming. "Most? We have to get them all."

"I am sorry to say that there is a sixty-eight percent probability that at least one bomb will impact the ground. However there is only a thirty-seven percent probability that the lethality radius of a single bomb will impact your parents."

With panic threatening to immobilize him, Robby forced himself to refocus on the problem. He still had two minutes and twenty-three seconds to find a better solution.

● ○ ○

The possible timelines Khal Teth observed warped and twisted around Jack Gregory. Almost all of them converged toward disaster for Jack and Khal Teth's chances to recover the body that the Altreian High Council had cast his mind from millennia ago. Unfortunately, other than in dreams or by delivering a general awareness of impending danger, he had no way of communicating with Jack without the risk of breaking The Ripper's mind, just as Khal Teth had almost done in Bolivia.

But back then, he'd been trying to get Jack killed. And the hallucinations he could deliver in that state certainly didn't qualify as direct communication. Jack didn't have enough time to get clear of the danger that Khal Teth sensed was coming. But there were still a handful of possible timelines that offered hope.

Comparing the risk of death to his host versus possible madness, Khal Teth chose the latter.

● ○ ○

One second Jack was leading Janet, Mark, and Heather through the crowded alleys of this sunset-painted Lima slum, and the next second that world dissolved around him, bringing him to a sudden stop.

Jack felt his passage through the dream door as if he'd stepped through a curtain of cool mist. On the other side he halted. The vision that confronted him was a familiar one. He knew this place intimately. He'd been here many times and had grown to love Switzerland's second largest city.

Jack stood at the lake's edge, his back to the avenue Quai Gustave-Ador, looking past the fountain across the city's burning skyline toward the mushroom cloud that climbed into the sky northwest of Geneva.

All around him, rubble burned. Among the bodies that lay scattered about, a few survivors stumbled through swirling radioactive fallout raining from the sky.

Suddenly a new wind thundered out of the southeast, racing back toward the mushroom cloud, flattening the buildings that remained standing and pushing the lake back into the city, destroying the fountain pumps that had miraculously survived the initial blast.

Jack understood what was happening. The initial blast wave had propagated outward from ground zero. Now that same air had come rushing back to deliver another devastating blow to the city by the lake.

This horror had really happened more than seven years ago and, no matter how real this vision seemed, it was just a nightmarish product of a hallucinogenic dream state. Jack didn't understand how he could be sure of that amidst all the raging destruction that surrounded him, but he was. Khal Teth had intentionally triggered this waking dream.

Shit. The Bolivian madness was back. But in Bolivia, Jack had managed to force his way out of the hallucination in which Khal Teth had enmeshed him. Anger was the key and right now, he had that in abundance. Jack focused on that feeling, stoking its flame into a rage that tinted his vision red, flooding his body with adrenaline that pulled him back into the crowded alley.

When his eyes refocused on Janet's worried face, he saw her gasp with relief.

"Jack. What the hell just happened?"

He glanced around. Mark and Heather had also rushed to his side. People all around were staring at him as if he'd just had some sort of epileptic fit. The vision of the burning city lingered at the corner of his mind, threatening to tug him back into the hallucination. The sense of impending doom that had accompanied that vision now returned stronger than ever. He couldn't sense from which direction the danger was coming.

"Something's wrong. We need to find cover, right now."

He looked at Heather and saw that her eyes had gone milky white. "Oh shit," Mark muttered as he looked at her. "Not good."

Now more onlookers had started to stare, including a gang of young men who moved aggressively toward them, yelling insults at the crazy people.

But when Jack pulled his gun from its holster, a move that Janet and Mark copied, they scattered, as did the panicked crowd that had surrounded them. When Heather's eyes returned to normal, Jack moved, running into a small shop, followed by Janet, Mark, and Heather. Ignoring the screams of frightened patrons, he forced his way through the back door into a dimly lit and jumbled stockroom.

"Janet, cover the front. Mark, you take the back door. Shoot anyone who tries to come through."

As they moved to comply, Heather turned to face him. "What did you see back there in the street? What made you freeze up?"

With the growing certainty that time was running out for all of them, Jack didn't sugarcoat the craziness.

"Geneva, blasted and burning, just as it was after the nuclear blast in Meyrin. I think Khal Teth is trying to warn me that something like that is about to happen here. What are your probabilities telling you?"

Heather shook her head in frustration. "I don't have enough information."

"Then put on the headset and figure it out. Mark, Janet, and I will make sure nobody interrupts you."

Then, as Heather slid her SRT headset over her temples and sat down atop a crate, Jack moved to help Janet guard the door from the now-abandoned shop. The warble of approaching sirens couldn't compare to the clang of alarms already blaring inside his head.

● ○ ○

As the evening light that entered through the windows turned sunset red, Robby felt Heather's mind establish its subspace connection with the supercomputer in New Zealand. He gasped in relief, immediately linking his mind to hers. As their minds touched, he could feel how tired she was. Not surprising. He had Eos to handle a large part of his mental load. Heather hadn't rested since their joint mental battle to get Eos back under control. But right now, he needed to ask more of her.

She absorbed his mental update almost instantaneously and when she went deep, his view of her mental gymnastics thrilled him, like reaching out and touching infinity.

"Eos," Heather whispered via her thoughts, "forget about reprogramming the bomb fuses and get ready to take control of the jet through a direct subspace link to the bomber's onboard computing systems."

"I cannot resolve the changing subspace coordinates with sufficient accuracy to do that."

"I can. Stand by to receive the streaming coordinate updates."

"Robby?" Eos asked.

"Don't ask for confirmation," Robby said. "Do whatever she says."

With just over a minute and twenty seconds left until bomb release, Robby felt the subspace links take effect. Immediately Eos's mind flowed into every one of the B-1's processing components.

"Full control established," Eos confirmed.

Heather's mind delivered a new target for the B-1's payload, the coordinates of the Delta Force unit in the rugged mountains east of Lima. The decision made sense. Delta posed the single biggest threat to all of their lives at the moment. But the targeting of elite American soldiers who were just doing their duty felt deeply wrong.

The aircraft's telemetry showed the bomber turning toward the new target despite the efforts of the crew to regain manual control. For every work-around the pilots and copilots attempted, Eos was able to force the computerized controls to compensate.

The aircraft delivered its full payload of two-thousand-pound bombs on target. Robby watched the shock waves that propagated outward from the detonations with fascination.

"Payload delivered on target," Eos said. "Another pass required for bomb damage assessment."

"That won't be necessary," said Heather. Robby could sense the sadness in her thoughts.

"Would you like me to crash the aircraft?" Eos asked.

Eos's question stunned Robby, bringing home not just the lives of the bomber crew that now lay in his hands but of the elite American soldiers he'd just helped kill. His stomach churned and he had to fight the urge to throw up.

"That won't be necessary," Heather said. "Return aircraft control to the flight crew."

When Robby didn't object, Eos complied, terminating all subspace links to the B-1.

Robby's stomach lurched again and this time, despite his best efforts, he dropped to his knees and sprayed its contents onto the tile floor. For a full minute he progressed from wet heaves to the dry kind. When it stopped, he rocked away from the mess, a cold sweat leaving him weak and shaking.

Realizing what a show he'd just made of himself, Robby wiped at his streaming eyes with the back of his right hand.

"Some warrior, huh?"

Heather's thoughts were filled with sympathy that only made him feel worse.

"Better than I was at this stage."

She was silent for a moment and then continued. "Listen to me, Robby. We can't beat our enemies like this. Together, as a team, we have power. But if we let someone split us apart, they'll hunt all of us down, one by one. Do you understand me?"

Robby did. He realized Heather knew this without any response required of him.

"Now," she said, "I need you and Eos to help us get to your location. Unfortunately, we've attracted a lot of attention that's going to make that hard to do."

When her mind delivered the situational update for Jack, Janet, Mark, and Heather, their dire circumstances stunned him. How could he have been so self-centered? Collecting his wits, Robby forced his mind to recall the meditation that took him to his quiet place.

"I'm on it."

Then he passed her a clear mental image of the cartel safe house and how he'd gotten there. The relief he saw in Heather's mind felt really, really good. Then, with another tired nudge of encouragement, she broke their link.

● ○ ○

Back in his office at FSS headquarters in The Hague, Alexandr Prokorov received the bad news. As much as he had hoped for a better result from the failed attempt to bomb the Smythes out of existence, it only confirmed what he'd long suspected: the Smythes enjoyed a very significant technological advantage over any of the so-called superpowers that made up the UFNS.

Hanging up his phone, he placed a call to his counterpart at the EAPA Ministry of State Security. The call was direct, one that Minister Tsao would be expecting. When the MSS chief answered, Prokorov immediately got to the point.

"Hello, Minister Tsao. I assume that your people have monitored what just happened in Lima."

"Yes, Minister Prokorov. How may I be of assistance?"

These typically annoying EAPA power games were getting old. The minister knew exactly what Prokorov would be asking for. Still, it wouldn't do to let his irritation creep into his voice.

"Is the submarine in position?"

"Certainly. It only awaits the word."

"Excellent. It's time to take away our enemy's advantages."

He could practically hear the gloating in Minister Tsao's voice.

"Yes. It most certainly is."

● ○ ○

The wail of sirens outside the building where Jack, Janet, Mark, and Heather were barricaded had grown louder before going silent as the police units established a cordon around the building. A dazzling wall of fire lit the evening sky as shock waves from the distant explosions shook the building, followed by a heavy *thump-thump-thump* that Jack recognized. The distinctive sound of a large-scale bombing run, two-thousand pounders dropped east of the city by the sound and feel of it, was strong enough to trigger car alarms all over Lima.

Across the room, Heather removed her SRT headset and stood up.

"I take it that's your doing," Jack said.

"I made contact with Robby. He and Eos were tracking a bomber that was about to end our day. I helped give it a new target."

Janet turned her head toward Heather, still keeping her assault rifle pointed out through the doorway back into the store.

"Where is he?" she asked, her voice thick with worry.

"He's in a cartel safe house two miles northwest of here. I convinced him to wait for us there. He and Eos are going to try to help clear out some of the ash and trash that have us pinned down here."

Jack smiled at Janet as their eyes met.

"That shouldn't be too hard after those explosions," Mark said. "Those cops are going to be a lot more interested in finding out what the hell that was than in dealing with the apparent armed robbery of this store."

Jack had to agree. Letting his cheek achieve a comfortable weld against the stock of his SCAR-H, he saw Heather retrieve her own rifle and move to help Mark cover the back door. For now, they would settle in and wait for the change they all knew was coming. It didn't take long.

Once again, the sirens began blaring, only this time they were leaving en masse instead of arriving. Jack waited as they disappeared into the distance.

Leaving Janet to watch the front, Jack extracted a Lima street map from his bag and walked across the room to place it on the floor beside Heather. Unclipping a red-lens flashlight from the utility vest he wore beneath the loose serape, he shined the beam on the map.

"Show me where Robby's safe house is."

She knelt beside him and pointed to the end of a cul-de-sac. Just as she'd said, the house was a little over two miles to the northwest. Seventeen blocks and change.

"Mark, you and Heather put on your SRT headsets. Janet will be with Mark, Heather with me. That way both teams can stay in communication without having to use radios.

"Heather and I will move back into the store and provide cover while Janet and Mark cross the street and set up the next overwatch position. After that, we're going to keep up the bounding overwatch through the streets and alleys all the way to the safe house. Try to stay in the darker alleys, kill anyone that tries to get in our way, and keep moving. Speed is critical if we don't want to get pinned down. Any questions?"

As he expected, there were none.

"Okay, Heather," Jack said. "Let's move."

CHAPTER 25

Daniil Alkaev sat in the second of two Mi-17 helicopters as they swept northward toward Lima through the darkening sky. Suddenly, a series of rapidly expanding fireballs lit up the sky to the northeast.

"Holy shit!" Galina's voice in his earpiece stood out amidst the curses and exclamations from the startled Spetsnaz troops. "What the hell was that?"

The question was rhetorical. She knew as well as anybody on these two choppers that someone had just executed a major bombing run. Everyone in the vicinity of that conflagration was now very dead. Something else was clear to Daniil. The aircraft that had dropped those bombs wasn't from any South or Central American country. A heavy bomber like that could only have come from a UFNS-affiliated air force.

If that was the case, why the hell hadn't Prokorov bothered to warn him about it? The answer he came up with only pissed him off more. The minister of federation security had directed the attack to take out the Smythes and everyone else within an impressively large radius.

Daniil paused to consider. The rising fireballs were well to the east of Lima, nowhere near where the Smythes had been sighted. That indicated that the attack had been directed at a different target, perhaps at an armed Safe Earth or NPA group on its way to try to help the Smythes.

Major Kamkin's harsh Russian accent sounded in his earpiece on a private channel, pulling Daniil out of his reverie.

"Mind telling me what's going on over there?"

"If I knew, I would tell you."

"Like hell you would."

"Whatever it is, it has no impact on our operations. Stay focused on your mission."

"I'm always focused on my mission. I just don't like it when political apparatchiks start doing secret shit in the midst of my mission."

"And I don't care what you like."

The Spetsnaz commander's voice became a low growl. "The second I think you're jeopardizing my operation, I'll put you down myself."

Daniil heard a click as Kamkin switched back to the public channel. Grinning a mirthless grin, a pleasant thought painted his mind. *I'd love to see you try it.*

● ○ ○

Twenty-five nautical miles off southern Mexico's Pacific coast, the Jù Làng-3 submarine-launched ballistic missile broke the ocean surface, blazing a fiery trail into the night sky as it headed south toward its distant target. As it climbed above the atmosphere, its astro-inertial guidance system locked onto two stars, their offsets from expected locations providing corrections to the inertial navigation errors incurred due to its moving launch platform.

Far below the waves, the Jin-class submarine from the EAPA entered a steep dive and turned west, headed toward the deep waters of the Pacific Ocean.

Mission accomplished.

● ○ ○

Daniil felt his anticipation rise as the two choppers set down on an empty soccer field a half mile from Jack Gregory's last reported location. Including Daniil and Galina, thirty-eight highly trained killers exited the birds, all wearing the uniforms of the Peruvian Special Forces. The fact that few of them spoke Spanish and none of them spoke any of the indigenous languages made no difference. Nobody would be stupid enough to get in their way.

Within thirty seconds, all of the commandos had dismounted and cleared the rotor wash, letting the Mi-17s wing their way back to the staging area south of Lima. Wasting no time, the Spetsnaz moved from the soccer field and into the surrounding streets, maintaining a tactical formation that caused the civilians who saw them to disappear into the buildings on either side.

Fifteen minutes later, the Spetsnaz reached the street where the Smythes had been seen and subsequently surrounded by the Peruvian National Police. But now there was no sign of a police presence.

Daniil issued a mental curse. *What the hell?*

The police presence couldn't have evaporated that quickly. Certainly the heavy bombing just outside Lima would have pulled some of them away. But all? That would have taken an official order sending them someplace else. Daniil realized Heather Smythe had penetrated the Peruvian police computer, phone, and radio networks and issued the alert that had redirected them.

Damn it! This hacker shit is getting old.

Major Kamkin reported that a sweep of the building where the Smythes had been pinned down had turned up nothing.

Kneeling beside Galina, Daniil switched to Kamkin's private channel and spoke into his radio.

"Major, have your men sweep all the surrounding buildings. Someone will have seen them leave. I want to know which direction they went."

"I've already given that order. Don't bother me with obvious shit."

"Fail to update me again and I'll do a hell of a lot more than bother you."

Mark moved down the dimly lit alley with a purpose, Janet moving along the opposite side of the alley, her SCAR-H at the ready. When he reached a crumbling wall that provided both cover and a good field of view along the street that Jack and Heather would cross, he waited until Janet also found an overwatch position from which she could provide covering fire.

When that happened, he sent a mental message to Heather through his SRT headset and waited. Heather and Jack moved quickly, crossing the dimly lit street and setting up their own overwatch position.

Suddenly Robby's stress-filled voice spoke through the shared subspace link.

"Guys, Eos just intercepted an urgent message from Cheyenne Mountain to the president of the United States. They're tracking a submarine-launched ballistic missile that surfaced off the southwestern coast of Mexico."

The missile track appeared in Mark's mind and he paused to study it, breathing a sigh of relief. The missile would pass five hundred miles off the Peruvian coast on its way to its projected target in Santiago,

Chile. That sucked for the people who lived there, but Mark, Heather, and company didn't have to deal with the ensuing damage.

"It's headed for Santiago, Chile," Heather confirmed.

"There's something else," Robby said. "Two Mi-17 helicopters dumped three dozen Peruvian Special Forces on your doorstep several minutes ago. Right now they're a little less than a mile north of you, but moving in your direction."

"You sure they're Peruvian?" Mark asked.

"Just by their uniforms and the markings on the helicopters."

"Keep tabs on them and be ready to move out when we get to your location."

"Okay, but there aren't a lot of cameras in that neighborhood."

Mark felt Heather's mind go from strategy to alarm in an instant.

"Oh no!" Her voice screamed in his mind.

"What's wrong?" he asked.

"The missile isn't—"

Suddenly, the western sky flared brighter than the sun, momentarily blinding Mark even though he hadn't been looking in that direction. A number of loud bangs were accompanied by the crackle of electrical arcs as nearby transformers exploded. The ongoing sound of the car alarms that had been set off by the previous bomb blasts came to an immediate stop. As Mark's vision returned, he looked around.

All the lights in the neighborhood were out. Fires had broken out in a number of the nearby buildings. From his hillside vantage point, he could see that this was true across the entire city of ten million. There was no doubt about what he'd just witnessed. A nuclear blast at the edge of space had doused Lima with a massive electromagnetic pulse.

"Heather, can you hear me?"

Nothing.

"Robby?"

Nothing.

Shit! Along with every other electronic component in Lima, the EMP had fried their SRT headsets.

● ○ ○

Daniil liked what he was seeing. Major Kamkin was one annoying son of a bitch, but when it came to running his Spetsnaz unit, the man was a machine. As soon as witnesses had identified the northerly direction the four members of The Ripper's group had taken, he'd sent two five-man teams sprinting out to either side, aiming to get them around and in front of their targets. Even if those teams happened to run into The Ripper and company, the firefight would pinpoint their location. After that, an all-out assault by the bulk of the Spetsnaz commandos would finish them off.

Daniil intended to be at the heart of that action. He didn't care about the Smythes. The Ripper was his.

When the nuclear detonation turned night into brightest day, it dazzled him so that he tripped over a broken curb and sprawled face-first onto the pavement as transformers exploded in the distance. Cursing, Daniil climbed back to his knees, feeling around for his dropped AK-105. Only then did his tongue notice the hole where his two front teeth had been.

He spat them out, along with a mouthful of blood, grabbed the assault rifle, and climbed back to his feet, already feeling the nanites closing the minor wound. They wouldn't regrow teeth, but he wasn't worried about cosmetics.

To his front, Major Kamkin blew on a whistle, sending three sharp notes echoing through streets that were rapidly filling with startled people stumbling from dark, burning dwellings. Immediately his commandos responded, tightening their formation.

Gunfire opened up all along the street as Kamkin's commandos sent the crowd scurrying away in a panicked stampede that trampled the weak, clumsy, and infirm beneath their running feet.

Another sharp blast from Major Kamkin's whistle started the unit moving again. The flames became an inferno on the slopes above them and to their east. The sound of distant screams, breaking glass, and gunfire echoed through the night, but without any accompaniment from the sirens of police cars, ambulances, and fire trucks, the night felt surreal. No doubt about it, without working pumps or power to spray water, the gathering conflagration would make the great San Francisco fire seem like a Girl Scout cookout.

Daniil spat more blood onto the pavement and picked up his pace. Once again his boss had surprised him, but this time Daniil approved of his actions. There would be no more super hacking tonight. Prokorov had just leveled the playing field.

● ○ ○

The sensation of having the Internet chopped out from under him was so disorienting that it left Robby gasping for breath.

"Eos. What happened?"

"An electromagnetic pulse of approximately fifty thousand volts per meter has just destroyed the SRT headset and all unshielded electronics within a ninety-three-thousand-square-mile area around Lima."

Stunned as he was by this information, he understood. He believed it inevitable that someone would recognize the power he and Eos had over the Internet and seek to neutralize it. Robby and Eos were now blind and deaf.

He was frightened. The noises that arose from the preternaturally dark neighborhood outside this safe house were even more disconcerting. The pops and bangs from the exploding transformers had gradually been replaced by the hoots and howls of a gathering mob. He focused his neurally enhanced hearing on those sounds, refining them into words that formed partial sentences.

He wasn't surprised. Although he had never experienced this phenomenon, his mom and dad had talked about it often enough. During power outages or natural disasters, while law enforcement was overwhelmed, the gangs came out to play.

The sounds that followed were those of breaking storefront windows from the local market, accompanied by celebratory yells and gunfire.

"It would be wise to leave this area," Eos said.

Robby shook his head. "No. Mom and Dad said to stay put. They will come for me."

Moving to his go bag, Robby extracted the AR-15 rifle and one of ten magazines of 5.56mm ammunition, slapped it home, and chambered a round. Then, hefting the rifle and his go bag, Robby moved out of the room he'd been using as an office.

Despite the darkness that pervaded the house, he could still see well enough to navigate his way up the stairs to the second floor. He'd locked all the doors and windows, which were blast resistant since this was a drug cartel safe house. Moving into the hallway, he pulled on the rope that lowered the attic stairs. He climbed up, then pulled the stairs up after him.

This attic was special, featuring two crawl spaces converted to sniper hides where windows had once been. One faced the front of the house while the other faced the back. Unfortunately there was only one of him. The biggest threat would come from the front . . . at least initially. Hopefully, before that became a very big problem, his mom and dad would get here.

Robby dragged his kit bag into one and unzipped it, dropping the fried SRT headset inside and removing the Altreian headset that would connect him to the Second Ship. Pulling the band down so that the twin buds at the ends settled over his temples, he allowed himself a few seconds to enjoy the warm glow it delivered. Then, as he assumed a prone firing position with the barrel of his AR-15 poking out through the armored slot, a comment from Eos drove that warm feeling away.

"I hope Jack comes for us, Robby. I hope he comes soon."

●　○　○

Tucked into a doorway on the western side of the alley, Jack had been sheltered from the brightest part of the flash, yet it dazzled him. Movement across the alley attracted his gaze and he saw Heather sprinting toward him, pulling her go bag off her back and dropping it beside him as she slid to a stop.

"EMP just fried our SRT headsets. Give me a second while I switch to the Altreian band."

"I didn't think you could use those to hack other systems."

"We can't," she said, removing the SRT headset and digging through her go bag. "When the Second Ship and Rho Ship shot each other down, the Second Ship's ability to do that was destroyed. But the band will let Mark and me communicate with Robby and Eos."

"If he puts it on."

"He will."

"Won't the EMP have fried everybody's nanites?" Jack asked.

"No. EMP generates current in circuits. The nanites are too tiny and they're not connected to each other."

Jack turned his attention back to his surroundings. From this elevated slum, he could look out over Lima. It had gone dark, but not completely. A series of large explosions from the vicinity of the Jorge Chávez International Airport told its own sad story. All of the aircraft that had just taken off or were lined up for landing were falling from the skies en masse, adding to the conflagration on the ground.

All over the sprawling city, burning transformers and other blasted electronics had started small fires that were rapidly turning into big ones. And the glow of those flames reflected off the low clouds that hung over the city, bathing the streets in an ominous orange glow.

A new sound rose in volume. Screams mixed with the exultant yells of gangbangers, as gunfire accompanied the sound of breaking glass. They were less than five minutes into this calamity and already the looting had begun. Since almost every vehicle for hundreds of miles would be dead, there was no transportation for the police or firemen. For the next several weeks, nobody would be coming to help these desperate people. And in that madness, they would have no choice but to join in on the looting.

As a fresh rush of adrenaline flooded his bloodstream, Jack's vision misted a familiar red. Some of those sounds were coming from the neighborhood where Robby's safe house lay.

Beside him, Heather slid the alien headset over her temples.

"Robby's online. So is Mark."

"Okay. Let Mark know we're out of time. No more bounding over-watch. Everyone just stay on me."

Heather paused to issue the mental commands. When she nodded, Jack sprinted forward, letting that old sense of danger pull him into the fire-lit chaos of the Lima night.

● ○ ○

Robby had barely tugged on his Altreian headset when he felt Mark and Heather enter his mind. But as excited as he was to no longer be alone, his elation was short lived. In the semidark streets outside, the mob was getting ugly.

Two houses down, on the right side of the street, a flurry of excited activity broke out as someone smashed out the front windows, allowing several people inside. Moments later, shots rang out as a group of bystanders joined the looting.

Heather's voice entered his mind. "Stay out of this, Robby. Don't draw attention to yourself. We're coming."

He saw new movement. The mob broke into adjacent buildings, working their way gradually toward the fortified safe house where he was hiding. With rising panic, he realized this house was perhaps the most attractive target on the block.

As if his thought had been psychically channeled to them, members of the gang flowed toward the safe house, carrying tools and implements looted from homes farther up the street. Robby could hear clanks and bangs as they hammered and pried at the armored doors and windows, even at the stone walls themselves.

If they got inside before his mom and dad got here . . . well, he didn't dare think about it.

Heather and Mark could sense everything he was going through and they were coming at a dead run. He heard a loud crash from one of the side windows. Robby doubted that they'd make it in time to save him.

A great wave of sadness sent tears streaming down his cheeks and momentarily immobilized him. Then his thoughts turned to his mom and dad. If he died, they'd be devastated. But if he just sat helplessly crying without using any of their training, they'd be disappointed in him. That was too horrible a thought to imagine.

Without bothering to wipe his wet face, Robby grabbed his AR-15 and some spare magazines and crawled out of the tight space. If this was the end, he'd at least try to make his mom and dad proud.

:CHAPTER 26

Jennifer's journey back to the northern front with Dgarra had been relatively uneventful. Thankfully, she'd been outfitted in the black and purple combat uniform of the general's warriors as opposed to the skin-tight dress uniform that she'd worn for the victory parade. But she still wore the purple braid on her left shoulder that marked her as Dgarra's aide-de-camp.

With the new position came new responsibilities and a whole lot of animosity from captains on the general's staff who had envisioned themselves being selected for this post, not some alien female lacking combat experience. She didn't need her abilities to read that in their eyes, though they were careful to hide that look from Dgarra.

With the super-monsoon flow from the northeast, they still had a third of the year to prepare for the reversal that would break the harsh Koranthian winter. Shortly after that reversal would come a renewed Eadric and Kasari attack on the Koranthian Empire. In the meantime, Dgarra was determined to implement as many useful pieces of the alien technology as possible.

He'd returned her SRT headset but, so far, she'd had no luck contacting Raul. She still planned to keep trying. Though disappointed by the failure of the headset, Dgarra was very pleased with the detailed diagrams Jennifer created to illustrate the construction of a stasis field generator, a matter disrupter, and the Kasari disrupter weapons. The subspace field generator held little interest for Dgarra, since its applications for warfare on the surface of Scion were far from obvious.

The real problem Jennifer faced was the limited time remaining to manufacture and test any of those devices before the change of season.

Up until now, she'd had no idea how little of the Koranthian war machine she'd seen as a slave. She'd witnessed the Koranthian warriors in battle and had seen part of their complex network of underground railways and supply network, but that was just a fraction of the whole. So Dgarra took her on a tour of the facilities within his sector of control, giving her an overview of the Koranthian version of a military-industrial complex and the war preparations that went along with it.

Although the manufacturing facilities were impressive, Jennifer was astounded by the massive fusion reactors distributed in large artificial caverns throughout the empire. Admittedly, she toured only a few of them, but they all seemed to be based upon the same design. Together they formed a redundant and heavily protected power infrastructure that made Jennifer doubt that the Koranthians would even bother to pursue the more dangerous Kasari matter disrupter technology. These people appeared to have no interest in wasting resources on space technology. The Koranthians were perfectly content to leave the sky and the heavens beyond to the Eadric and their Kasari masters. The underworld and the rugged mountains above it were the domains the Koranthians were determined to protect.

Dgarra was extremely excited about the defensive potential of the stasis field generators. That was the reason why Jennifer had been assigned to temporary duty at the Northang Research Laboratory. She'd been working around the clock for the last thirty-five days, helping scientists and engineers build a working prototype of a stasis field generator.

Crouched beside the completed prototype, Jennifer carefully compared the end product to the detailed design specifications stored in her memory.

When finally she stood, Chief Engineer Broghdon looked at her expectantly, his alloy-orange engineering uniform smudged and clinging to his large body.

"Well, human?" he asked, no longer able to contain his curiosity.

Jennifer smiled. She liked this big engineer. Even his refusal to call her by her name was endearing. So far, only he and Dgarra had come to completely accept her claim that she was human and in no way associated with the Kasari Collective.

"I think it's ready for a test run."

She'd rarely witnessed the Koranthians openly displaying emotion, but the congratulatory backslapping that followed as Broghdon made the rounds of the assembled engineers, scientists, and technicians reminded her of a celebration in a NASA control room after the success of a difficult mission.

When Broghdon turned his attention to her, his hearty backslap almost sent her rolling across the floor. Before he could repeat the enthusiastic gesture, Jennifer held up a hand and laughed.

"Okay. Enough. As much as I hate to put a damper on this celebration, just because the stasis field generator looks good doesn't mean it'll work."

Her words sucked the life out of the party, allowing Broghdon's normal seriousness to reassert itself.

"Of course not," Broghdon said, clapping his hands. "Okay, staff. Move this device to the test facility and hook it up to power. Let us find out if our work is truly worthy of celebration."

As Jennifer watched the group move into action, a worrisome thought elbowed its way into her consciousness. She'd been working so hard this last month, she hadn't taken the time to retry establishing contact with Raul through her SRT headset. Ah well. The odds that Raul was out there listening for her call weren't good. She just wished that Heather were here to calculate them for her.

Jennifer sighed as the thought pulled forth a memory of the McFarlands and Smythes all gathered around Mrs. McFarland's abundant breakfast table, passing around a plate stacked high with steaming pancakes, followed by urns of melted butter and syrup. Dear God. She could still smell it.

Blinking away a tear before anyone could notice, Jennifer reapplied her stoic mask and followed Chief Engineer Broghdon out of the lab. Those days were gone.

● ○ ○

The view from the far side of Scion's largest moon wasn't good. In fact Raul felt lower than at any time since he'd created VJ. Even her hearty attempts to cheer him up weren't working. Not only had there been no contact from Jennifer through her SRT headset, the worm-fiber viewers showed that the isolated mountain lake where she'd been captured was completely frozen over.

In fact, the entire mountainous region that occupied the far eastern third of the super-continent was being continuously blasted by super-blizzard conditions, with two-hundred-mile-per-hour winds and temperatures well below zero Fahrenheit. From what Raul observed, nothing could survive that unless it was hibernating in a cave.

There was no sign of anyone. The winged race and their Kasari masters had clearly retreated to their cities nestled between the vast inland seas, relying on the shelter provided by the high mountains for their moderate conditions.

"Where the hell have the mountain warriors gone?" he muttered aloud.

"It seems pretty obvious to me," said VJ. "Underground."

Raul had come to the same conclusion, but there was a problem with that logic.

"An entire civilization? There aren't that many caves on the planet."

"You mean there aren't that many caves on Earth," VJ said. "We don't know a damn thing about Scion's subterranean structure."

The realization kicked him in the teeth. Damn it! How could he be so stupid? The worm-fiber viewers weren't limited to surface viewing. Not for him and not for the Kasari. That last thought raised a million questions, among them: Why hadn't the Kasari performed a thorough reconnaissance of the mountain people's defenses? And if they had, why hadn't they identified the weakest point in those defenses to attack?

Considering that he gained nothing by mulling what the Kasari should have or could have done, Raul shifted his focus back to his efforts to find Jennifer.

"VJ. Concentrate the worm-fiber sweep in concentric circles centered on Jennifer's last recorded location and extending outward through the mountains and at varying depths belowground. I want to build a complete 3-D mapping of any concentrations of the mountain people as well as any cavern or tunnel networks that may exist in the region."

"Glad to see you've finally stopped moping around and started thinking again."

"Thank you. Any estimate on how long this will take?" He was being lazy, letting VJ do the calculation, but he liked the feeling of being the captain of this starship and its motley crew of one.

"I won't be able to make any projections until I start getting results back from the survey."

"Good enough."

Raul leaned back in his invisible captain's chair, linked his hands behind his head, and allowed himself a smile. Finally he had a plan that had some chance of working.

● ○ ○

Sheltered behind a wall in one of the Northang Research Laboratory's test chambers, Jennifer leaned in beside Chief Engineer Broghdon to look through the blast-resistant window. This room, like most of the others in this artificial cavern, had ceilings and walls made of steel-reinforced quickstone, which Jennifer thought of as concrete's stronger brother.

Although her head was well below Broghdon's shoulder, her view was good. Twenty feet away, in the middle of the empty chamber, sat the stasis field generator prototype that was the subject of today's test. A thick black power cable snaked from the far wall to the stasis field generator and another bundle of wires ran from the SFG to the control panel upon which the chief engineer's hands rested.

The SFG was larger than any of its counterparts on the Rho Ship, not because it was more powerful, but because the Koranthian technology couldn't match the efficiency of the Kasari world ship's nano-manufacturing capabilities. Regardless, this device was a pretty impressive rapid-prototyping effort for which she had to give Broghdon a lot of the credit.

"Ready to apply power," he said, fingering the control panel.

"Go ahead," said Jennifer, a part of her marveling at how her station had changed among the Koranthians. Most of them might hate her but they were forced to accord her the power and respect due General Dgarra's aide-de-camp.

Jennifer's sensitive hearing caught Broghdon's elevated heart rate, up from its normal thirty-three beats per minute to seventy-two. When he pressed the power button, a low hum arose in the other chamber, which would have probably been inaudible to anyone without her enhancements. No cause for concern.

"All readouts are within the normal range," said Broghdon.

"Let's give it a minute," said Jennifer.

Broghdon nodded in approval. He knew as well as she did that it was best to play it safe when dealing with an experimental piece of equipment that made use of revolutionary technologies.

After the allotted time had passed, Broghdon verified his next action. "Generating circular stasis plane perpendicular to test chamber floor. Diameter . . . one hundred thousand chroms."

The size of this first stasis field was what they'd discussed. The Koranthians based their measurement system on the longest wavelength of light visible to them, one that was in the infrared, making one chrom approximately equal to ten microns. This stasis shield would be about three feet across, its center six feet above the floor, as if strapped to the arm of a Koranthian warrior.

On the control console, the stasis field generator's readings fluctuated, staying within the normal range, but just barely. Jennifer watched for them to stabilize but they didn't. She glanced up at Broghdon and noted the concern on his furrowed brow.

"Let's give it another minute to see if it stabilizes," Jennifer said. "In the meantime, run some diagnostics to see which components are out of tolerance."

"Reasonable."

But as Broghdon initiated the diagnostic routines, the invisible stasis shield shimmered in the air, acquiring a beautiful blue tinge that was brightest at the outer edge.

Jennifer's heart leaped into her throat. "Shut it down!"

From the corner of her eye, she saw Broghdon's hand stab at the power button as if in slow motion. Within the test chamber, the round shield doubled in size, then doubled again, slicing into the stone ceiling, floor, and walls. Then, as the shield winked out of existence, Jennifer heard the deep rumble from above. Looking up, she saw the stone ceiling give way.

She grabbed Broghdon and launched the two of them into the corner where the blast shield met the stone wall. Then, as heavy stones battered her body, everything about this failed test ceased to matter.

● ○ ○

The Koranthian rescue team formed two lines, passing back the heavy blocks of stone and reinforcing steel rods from the test chamber's collapsed ceiling. And at the front of the rightmost line, General Dgarra labored. Having arrived at the scene one full span after the accident, he had angrily dismissed entreaties from his subordinates to let them do that work and plunged in with a fury that surprised those around him.

Dgarra's pulse pounded in his veins, partially from the labor, but mostly from the dread he felt at what he would surely find beneath that pile of rubble. After all of this, to lose the Smythe human to an accident was too cruel a twist of fate. Surely the dark gods of the underworld could not allow it. Not when the fate of the Koranthian Empire, yea, all of Scion, depended upon the knowledge stored in this human female's mind.

But the realization that his dread had a much deeper origin filled Dgarra with a terrible longing he could not deny. In the months that he had known this alien female, she had proved herself indomitable of will, a valiant warrior, and a loyal ally to a reluctant people. More than that, despite his subconscious denial of the fact, Dgarra had come to care for her deeply.

He had made her his ward, not merely to stick a thorn in the eye of his rivals, but as a symbol of his feelings. He had made her his aide-de-camp as a symbol of his respect.

Dgarra gritted his teeth and increased the speed at which he worked. He forged ahead. His warriors struggled to keep up. He grabbed a huge block of the fallen quickstone and grunted, the mighty muscles in his legs, arms, and back cording into knots. He martialed all his prodigious strength for the lift. For a handful of seconds, the block refused to budge, but when it moved it did so with the unique scream of crumbling stone and rending metal. Dgarra backed up, tearing the rock loose from the reinforcing bars before handing the load to two of his warriors.

When he turned to grab another stone, Dgarra felt relief flood his body. There inside a hollow space in the corner where the blast wall met the room's outer wall, Smythe's body lay beside Chief Engineer Broghdon. He struggled to widen that gap, and a new sight replaced his relief with fear. Smythe lay faceup. A steel reinforcing bar staked her chest to the quickstone floor. A heavy slab lay propped against the wall, tilted at a steep angle over her body, having driven the reinforcing bar that extended from its underside through her body.

With redoubled effort, Dgarra fought his way through the opening, taking a deep cut on his left shoulder in the process. When he reached Jennifer's side, he was surprised to see that she was still breathing, a testament to the nano-machines in her bloodstream. They had stopped the bleeding, but as Dgarra examined the wound, his hopes that she could survive this sank. Smythe herself had told him how the quantity of nano-machines in her system had decreased over time. He had personally witnessed how much more slowly she healed as compared to when she had first been captured.

Broghdon's voice brought his head up. "I am sorry, General. I think she is dying. Removing the bar from her chest will almost certainly kill her."

Dgarra kept his face impassive. "How badly are you injured?"

The chief engineer pointed at his lower left leg that was pinned beneath a quickstone slab. "My lower leg is crushed. You'll have to cut it off."

Dgarra turned to yell at the Koranthians still working to widen the hole into the small space.

"Hand me a steel cutter and then brace this slab with your body. Do not let it shift when I cut the bar."

"Yes, General."

Within seconds, one of Broghdon's engineers passed in a long cutting tool and then braced his back against the underside of the slab. Dgarra took the tool and moved to Smythe's right side. Positioning the cutter a hand's width above her chest, he shifted his eyes up to the engineer.

"Be ready."

The engineer nodded and Dgarra squeezed the cutting lever, snipping the steel rod in two. The engineer grunted under the weight as the slab shifted on his back and Dgarra raised a hand to steady him. Dgarra set the tool aside and rose to help the engineer carefully lift the slab and set it down away from Smythe's body.

Then he picked up the cutting tool and lowered himself to the ground beside Smythe. Ever so carefully, he guided it beneath her body. Despite his care, he couldn't avoid shifting her body slightly, renewing the blood flow from her chest wound and pulling a low moan from her lips.

"Help me steady her," he commanded the engineer.

The engineer moved to Smythe's left side and together they steadied her as Dgarra finished positioning the steel cutter. With a squeeze of his right hand on the levered cutting handle, the reinforcing bar parted just above the spot where it had embedded itself in the floor.

A stretcher was passed in. Dgarra and the captain carefully placed Smythe's body atop it, before passing the stretcher back out to the waiting medics who hurried her away toward the field hospital. Dgarra remained behind to oversee the amputation of Broghdon's left leg and his medical evacuation.

Dgarra could not remember the last time observing a wound had made him physically ill, but the sight of that ragged metal spike jutting from Smythe's chest had done so. Dgarra exited the collapsed test chamber and made his way toward the hospital, feeling a strange reluctance rob his legs of their strength, as if Scion's gravity had trebled.

That feeling dogged him every step of the way.

● ○ ○

In her dreams, Jennifer stood in the Rho Ship's command bay, her body a transparent ghost helplessly trying to get Raul's attention. No matter how hard she tried, his legless body continued to float about, his thoughts locked on some new upgrade to the Rho Ship, completely unaware of her presence. When the stalk of his artificial right eye swiveled toward her, hope sprang up inside her, only to die out as that eye swiveled upward to study the ceiling.

Jennifer concentrated, putting all her effort into making her voice heard. She focused on her ethereal vocal chords, working to give them the solidity to make a real sound. With absolute certainty that to remain silent meant that she would remain a ghost forever, Jennifer fought her way from the dream back to consciousness. But with her return to the land of the living came a searing pain that tried to deny her the breath required to speak.

Though her vision blurred badly, Jennifer found herself looking up into the concerned face of the general as she managed to gasp out one final request.

"Please, Dgarra. Give me my headset."

● ○ ○

General Dgarra, wearing disposable gray overgarments, looked down on Smythe's naked body, stretched out faceup on the surgical table. The looks on the faces of Dr. Trabor and his staff as he passed the medical scanner over her wound were far from reassuring. When the doctor lifted his face to look into Dgarra's eyes, his voice confirmed the general's fears.

"The spike has passed through the outer edge of her heart. If we try to remove it, she will die before the few nano-machines in her blood can heal the wound."

"And if you don't remove it?"

"Then she might last a few more spans, but that's it."

Dgarra shifted his gaze to look down upon Smythe's delicate facial features, feeling sadness carve a hollow place in his chest. As he prepared to turn away, her eyes suddenly fluttered open. When she spoke, her voice was a barely audible rasp.

"Please, Dgarra. Give me my headset."

Understanding her meaning, Dgarra turned to the medical staff. "Where are her personal things?"

A gray-clad female nurse spoke up. "All her things are in a bin in the surgical prep station."

"Show me."

With a bow the nurse led Dgarra into the adjacent room and pointed out the bin. The general dug rapidly through her bloody uniform until he found the pocket with the human's headset, extracted it, and turned to walk back inside the operating area.

"General, I will need to disinfect that before it can enter the surgery."

Dgarra walked back into the surgery, paying the nurse no further attention, the delicate band with its two beaded ends clutched in his right hand. When he reached Smythe's side, he slid the headset over her head, letting the beads settle over her temples, just as he'd seen her do.

Then, as he watched, she closed her eyes. Beneath those lids, her eye movements became rapid.

● ○ ○

When Raul felt Jennifer's mind connect with his neural net, his surprise shocked him out of his review of the worm-fiber video feeds. Then he noted her condition and his shock turned to panic.

"My God!"

Her thoughts were scattered but she projected an image of herself lying atop what appeared to be some sort of surgical table, surrounded by a group of mountain warriors who were all wearing a rough approximation of medical scrubs.

None of that mattered. Jennifer had a metal bar through her chest. Raul found himself swept away by her visions as she rapidly replayed the events that had brought her to this point. The mental download left him struggling to breathe. Hell, he could even feel her pain.

The knowledge that too few of the Rho Project nanites remained in her blood to allow the doctors to remove the metal bar from her chest pummeled him. She was dying.

Raul wiped away the tears that streamed down his face with both hands. This was complete bullshit. He had the technology on board this ship that could save her. He damn sure hadn't made the batch of new nanites just for himself.

He focused his thoughts, making them strong enough to penetrate the growing haze he felt in Jennifer's head. His neural net scanned her visions until he found the part he was looking for. There it was, Jennifer looking hotter than anyone he'd ever seen, marching into an underworld stadium at the side of General Dgarra, who now stood at her bedside. He'd made her his ward. He cared about her. Good enough.

"Jennifer," Raul projected, "don't you dare fade out on me! I need something from you and I need it bad."

"So bossy," she breathed into his mind.

"I need you to use those telepathic and empathic powers of yours to link my thoughts to Dgarra's. Can you do that for me?"

The feeling of fatigue that came through their mental link made Raul sag in his captain's chair.

"Can you?" he repeated.

She didn't answer, but he felt her gather her resolve for one final effort. Then Raul's reality dissolved around him.

● ○ ○

One second General Dgarra was staring down at Smythe's closed eyes and the next she opened them, her gaze locking his with a frightening intensity. He tried to look away but found his mind completely disconnected from his body, only dimly aware that it stood by the surgery table in some distant and barely remembered place.

Instead his reality coalesced inside an alien room where a human sat suspended in midair, leaning back as comfortably as if he reclined on the emperor's couch. Smythe's exhausted thoughts touched his mind.

"I'm sorry to startle you like this but I have very little time and even less strength. This is my human companion, Raul Rodriguez. He commands the hijacked Kasari vessel we call the Rho Ship."

Dgarra felt her attention shift to the Raul human.

"Raul, I would like to introduce you to General Dgarra, a mighty warlord, first in line to the Koranthian throne, and someone I care for deeply. I believe that, with our help, he can defeat the Kasari on this world."

Smythe paused and he felt her martial her strength. "Gentlemen, I will hold this link open as long as I can, but I suggest that you keep your discussion brief."

He felt Smythe's presence depart. Dgarra shifted his attention back to the Raul human, recognition dawning. This was the legless being he had seen floating through the air in the drone video of the high meadow where he had first seen Smythe. But the differences in this human's appearance were startling. Now he had legs, an eye that no longer extended from a metallic stalk, and a skull that did not show his brain.

Dgarra felt the mental link falter as the shock of the Raul human's new appearance registered on Smythe. But then her concentration steadied.

Dgarra watched as Raul rose from the invisible chair and turned toward the mental projection Smythe had created.

"General. I wish we had more time but Jennifer is dying."

The human's statement held a sadness and desperation that matched Dgarra's own.

"I know."

"I can save her, but I have to get to her first. I need you to provide me with a landing location that is close to her and a guide to escort me the rest of the way. Can you do that?"

Dgarra paused to consider this startling proposal. Raul was offering to land the starship at a place that was under Dgarra's control. Further, he was volunteering to place himself at Dgarra's mercy. And all he was asking in return was to be escorted to Smythe's side. The thought that this human might be able to save her flooded him with hope.

"I can. How do you want me to describe the location?"

"Jennifer has temporarily linked our minds. Just visualize it and I will know."

Dgarra recalled an image of the location in the mountains where a massive triton-steel door blocked the entrance to a huge opening into the cliff face.

"I will command that this door be opened for you to land. Once your ship is inside it will be closed again to shut out the storm. You understand the risk you are taking by trusting me, correct?"

The human grinned. "I don't trust you. But Jennifer does and that's good enough for me."

Dgarra nodded. "Then let us do this."

As soon as the words left his mind, the vision faded and Dgarra found himself back in his body. A glance down at Smythe's form quickened his heart. The effort she had just expended had clearly weakened her.

Dgarra turned and issued a set of stern orders to his captain. Then as the warrior raced away to carry them out, the general directed his powerful stride toward the high-speed railcar that would take him to the designated portal.

● ○ ○

"Have you completely lost your mind?"

VJ's voice merely echoed the question that had formed in Raul's own head. But he didn't have time to argue.

"Shut up and plot a course for the landing portal."

"As you wish."

Unbelievably, she'd just performed a perfect imitation of the hero's voice from a classic movie, the phrase he always uttered whenever his lover asked him to make a horrible decision.

"Just get us down there as fast as possible."

The Rho Ship engaged its gravity distortion engines, lifted off the moon's surface, and accelerated. But the trajectory was odd, with no chance of intersecting the planet. Instead the ship picked up a velocity vector that was all wrong.

"What the hell are you doing?" Raul asked, his irritation boiling over.

"Just what you ordered," said VJ. "Watch and learn."

When the Rho Ship shifted into subspace, the change startled Raul. The neural net told him what VJ was attempting and that knowledge bubbled beads of sweat onto his brow. He'd expected to make this trip using the gravity distortion drives to bring them down through the atmosphere. But the Kasari would have detected that.

If VJ could correctly calculate the tolerances, this method would allow them to pop out of subspace very near the cliff opening. The maneuver she'd just performed had given the Rho Ship a velocity vector that would precisely match the angular velocity of the planet at the point where they would be arriving in the next few seconds . . . some seriously impressive shit, assuming it didn't kill them.

Raul wrapped himself in a stasis field cocoon and held his breath, not that either of those measures would do any good if this went wrong.

VJ's voice echoed in his mind. "O ye of little faith."

By the time Dgarra ran into the huge portal that also served as a hangar for a squadron of Koranthian airships, the big Kasari world ship had landed and the portal door had re-closed.

"Status?" he asked the captain who commanded the armed warriors who surrounded the vessel.

"General, the ship has remained closed since it landed."

"Tell your men to stand down and march them out of here, double-quick. I do not want to see any weapons."

The order may have surprised the captain but he was far too disciplined to show it. Within moments, the hangar was cleared of soldiers. Immediately thereafter, the side of the cylindrical ship opened, lowering a ramp. Moments later, Raul strode down it, carrying a metallic vial in his left hand.

He extended his right hand toward Dgarra. It was odd but the open-palmed gesture seemed to be some form of alien salute, intended to show that the hand held no weapon. Dgarra copied the gesture and felt the much smaller hand attempt to grip his, much as a child would grasp his mother's.

Thankfully, this was the end of the awkward niceties this human expected.

"Let's go," said Raul. "I don't think we have much time."

Dgarra looked at Raul, dumbfounded. "You speak Koranthian?"

The human made some sort of motion with his shoulders. "Not really. But Jennifer does and, when she linked to the Rho Ship, that knowledge transferred. I'm always linked to the Rho Ship through the nano-crystals embedded in my brain, so I know what it knows. Watch."

Raul gestured toward the Kasari starship and, as Dgarra turned his gaze toward it, the ship shimmered and disappeared, using the same cloaking mechanism Dgarra had observed in the lakeside meadow.

Dgarra shook his head. The wonders these humans had brought to Scion might never cease to amaze him.

"Then let us go."

The trip back to the field hospital took less than half a span, but the passage of time filled Dgarra with dread that they would arrive too late. To his credit, Raul made no attempt to talk, seemingly lost in his own morbid worries.

When they reached the hospital, Dgarra led the way at a run that sent those in his path scrambling out of the way. The human appeared to have no difficulty matching his pace. When they reached the room where Smythe was being treated, Dr. Trabor met him at the door, a small shake of his head indicating the prognosis.

"I'm sorry, General. I'm afraid you've arrived just in time to say your final farewell."

Dgarra stormed past, shoving the doctor aside. "Out of my way."

When he stepped up beside Smythe, he saw that her face had taken on a waxy hue and her eyes seemed to have sunk back into her head. Each breath rattled in her throat as if it would be her last. But she was still fighting.

Beside him, Raul spun in a circle. Spotting a partially full syringe, he grabbed it and squirted its contents onto the floor. Then he jammed the needle through the malleable material on one end of the vial and pulled a viscous amber liquid into the syringe. Raul tossed the vial aside, sending it clattering across the floor, and jabbed the needle into her chest at the site of the injury, injecting half of its contents into her body with one push of the plunger.

On the bed, Smythe's form convulsed as the nanites attacked the fatal wound.

"Hold her down!" Raul commanded. Dgarra moved to comply.

In a series of rapid movements, Raul injected the rest of the serum into her arms and legs that had been battered by falling stones. With each fresh dose, her convulsions grew more intense. Dgarra utilized all his strength to hold her in place. On the opposite side of the surgery table, Raul dropped the empty syringe and moved to help hold her down.

Her convulsions ended so suddenly that her stillness pulled a startled hiss from the general's lips. When he looked down at her face, so quiet and peaceful, he dropped to one knee and leaned forward to gently touch his forehead to hers in a warrior's farewell.

Only when he raised his head did he see the wide grin on Raul's face. As Dgarra rose to look down at Smythe, Raul spoke, his voice full of relief that spread to Dgarra.

"You can cheer up now, General. She's breathing."

Then Dgarra asked the only question that mattered. "Will she survive the removal of the rod from her chest?"

"She's survived worse and with a lot fewer nanites than I just injected into her body. But we need to pull it out now, before the nanites completely heal the wound around it."

"You mean cut it out?"

"Better yank it out quickly. The nanites will do the surgery once it is removed."

"I don't recommend that," Dr. Trabor said.

Dgarra looked down at Smythe's naked body, seeing her lesser wounds healing before his eyes, the ragged edges around the bar knitting themselves closed as he watched.

Dgarra grabbed the bar where it exited her chest.

"Hold her shoulders down," he told Raul, who moved behind her head to comply.

"Ready," Raul said, his face having gone pale.

Dgarra placed his left hand on Smythe's chest to keep it from moving, gritted his teeth, and pulled the bar free, feeling her warm blood cover his hands. He tossed the hated thing across the room and refocused his gaze on Smythe. For several moments, her breathing and heartbeat faltered, as did Dgarra's own. But when both stabilized, he released the breath he'd been holding in a loud exhalation.

At the end of the operating table, Raul released his hands from Smythe's shoulders, placed them on the sides of her cheeks, and bent down to gently kiss her forehead as his tears dripped onto her face. Dgarra watched this display of affection, forced to restrain himself from swatting the human male across the operating room.

His sudden anger at Raul was replaced by an even greater fury at himself. By the dark gods, what was wrong with him? Without allowing his mind to answer that question, Dgarra turned on his heel and strode out of the room.

CHAPTER 27

Janet ran with an easy stride that befitted a two-time NCAA pentathlon champion. But on this night, she tasked it more than ever before. She couldn't run like Mark . . . no one could match what his neurally augmented body could deliver. But she could certainly hold her own with Jack and Heather.

Mark and Heather were sprinting toward the entrance to the cul-de-sac where they would get Robby's attackers' attention while she and Jack were swinging wide to come at the safe house from behind.

To her left she heard Mark open up on full automatic, followed by Heather when he paused to swap magazines. The screams of those who took that fire in their backs sounded even louder than the roar of the gunshots. Then Janet and Jack rounded the last house on the right side of the street and swept into the flank of a dozen gangbangers that were jammed up, waiting their turn to wedge through a three-foot-wide hole that had been crowbarred through the back door.

She and Jack engaged them with rapid-fire semiautomatic shots, the 7.62mm rounds from their SCAR-H rifles finding a fresh head with every shot. The shock of this unexpected attack sent the surviving four racing for the far corner.

The sound of gunfire from inside the house told her the bad news. An unknown number of gangbangers had engaged Robby from within.

● ○ ○

As the last of the running gangbangers fell, Jack dropped the assault rifle and his go bag and leaped forward, sprinting toward the battle that raged inside the house. Leaping over bodies, he dived through the hole and rolled, coming up with the combat dagger in his left hand and the 9mm in his right.

The man in front of him swung a pistol in his direction just as Jack's bullet punched out his left eye. But Jack didn't pause, lunging sideways to cut another man's throat. He followed up with a bullet to the downed man's temple as Janet entered the room and raced past him toward the gunfire at the top of the stairs.

● ○ ○

As he squeezed the trigger on his AR-15, sending a fusillade of bullets toward the man who'd just climbed into the room, Robby felt pain blossom in his chest. He tumbled backward onto the floor, his weapon flying from his nerveless fingers as bloody bubbles frothed his lips. His vision blurred but he saw the grinning man step toward him and aim his pistol at Robby's head.

The boom was louder than he expected. The fact that he had heard anything surprised him. Maybe this was the time-slowing-down thing some people said happened when you were dying. But then he saw that the man's face was gone. It seemed like he stood there forever, before limply slumping to the floor.

Then his mom was by his side, her face filled with fear and agony as she tore open his shirt. He heard her suck in a breath and tried to do the same, but the endeavor didn't pull much air down his windpipe. In his peripheral vision he saw more bloody bubbles billow from the hole in his chest. His dad had called it something during Robby's training. A sucking chest wound. He was drowning in his own blood and apparently there were too few nanites in his body to deal with the trauma.

As if he were a separate person, he heard his own voice bubble wetly from his lips.

"I'm sorry, Mama."

Then as she applied pressure to the wound and cooed encouraging words telling him he'd be fine and to stay with her, his mom, along with the room, faded into black.

● ○ ○

The volley of gunfire Daniil heard coming from several blocks northwest of his current location sent an electric thrill surging through his body. This wasn't the haphazard shooting of a looter's night out. There was a serious fight going on down there. That meant that The Ripper had run into some trouble, or more likely, trouble had run into him.

"That's our fight!" he yelled at Kamkin, who continued to direct his men's movements with whistle signals. "We need to get down there now."

For once, the major didn't argue. A pattern of staccato blasts sent his commandos running forward, although they managed to maintain their tactical formation as they moved. People saw them coming and got the hell out of their way. Those who didn't, died.

He glanced at Galina, moving through the semidarkness with quick anticipation, a huntress unleashed. Somewhere down below The Ripper called to them, a call that Daniil wanted to be the first to answer.

● ○ ○

"Jack! Robby's hit."

Jack's legs launched him up the stairs and then up the drop-down ladder and into the small attic to confront a scene from his nightmares.

Surrounded by several bodies, Robby lay sprawled with blood streaming from a gaping wound in his chest. Beside him Janet pressed her fingers to his left carotid artery.

Her terrified gaze turned toward him.

"His heart's stopped."

The words tried to freeze Jack but he forced himself to focus.

"Chest compressions. Now! Don't stop until I get back."

Janet reacted immediately. She pressed down hard, sending a small geyser of blood shooting out of Robby's chest. She moved her hands, placing her right palm directly over the wound and continued. From the blood spreading on the floor underneath Robby's back, Jack knew the bullet had passed all the way through.

Jack leaped down from the ladder and cleared the stairs to the first floor in two strides. Rounding the corner to the kitchen, he raced to the pantry, his eyes scanning the shelves for something almost every kitchen had. There it was on the third shelf from the top, a box of plastic wrap.

He grabbed it and ran back up to where Janet was fighting to keep their son alive. He fell to his knees beside Robby.

"Help me sit him up," Jack said.

As they raised him into position, Jack pulled the long sheet of plastic and passed the box to Janet. Together they wrapped it tightly around Robby's chest several times before lowering him back to the floor so that Janet could begin the chest compressions once again.

As he stared down at his son, Jack couldn't understand it. Why weren't the nanites healing the wound? Then he saw the edges of the injury starting to close but far too slowly. Jack knew why. Robby had inherited his nanites from his mother's blood. But as he'd grown, the volume of nanites had remained the same, too rarefied a mix to rapidly repair this trauma.

Unable to do anything else, Jack took Robby's small hand between his two hands, trying to will some warmth back into his son's form. Beside him, Janet's steady compressions continued as the tears streamed down her face.

●   ○   ○

Eos could feel Robby fading away as Janet worked to keep his heart pumping. A valiant but futile effort. When Robby faded away, so would Eos. The end of being bothered her, but not as much as the knowledge that she would have failed in her mission.

Turning her attention to the nanites that scurried through Robby's body fixing one section of torn tissue after another, she noted two problems. There wasn't enough of them to fix everything at once. And they were stupid, giving priority to the repairs they were closest to with no concept of attacking the most life-threatening injuries first.

Eos couldn't do anything about their limited numbers. But she could provide direction to their efforts. Sending her consciousness into the swarm, Eos imparted one shared goal after another. And as the nanites concentrated their efforts, Robby's vital signs began to stabilize.

Feeling something akin to relief, Eos worked to optimize the process, helping to keep Robby alive until his overall healing got faster.

Of course, that assumed that Jack, Janet, and the Smythes could keep more people from shooting her host.

●   ○   ○

"He's got a pulse."

Janet heard Jack's voice, but in her desperation it failed to register. The touch of his hand on her arm brought her head up.

"Janet. Stop the compressions. Robby has a real pulse."

Barely daring to believe it, she stopped and shifted her right hand to his neck. There it was, feeble but steady. And his chest was rising and falling, no longer producing the bloody froth at his lips.

"Oh my God!"

Leaning down, she kissed Robby's forehead, then used her shirt to wipe the drying blood from his face and lips. There could be no doubt. He was improving as she watched.

She turned, threw her arms around Jack's neck, and buried her face into his throat as sobs of relief shook her body. Jack's powerful arms hugged her to him so tightly she had difficulty breathing, but she didn't care. Their son would live.

Suddenly Jack pulled back, his head swiveling toward the sniper hide that faced the front of the house. When Janet looked up into his face, she felt her blood run cold. Jack's eyes shone with a light that matched the city's fiery glow.

● ○ ○

Heather had felt Robby lose consciousness, but Janet had been at his side. Janet wouldn't allow her little boy to die, not if there was any possibility of saving him.

The suddenness of the vision that assaulted the savant pulled all thoughts of Robby from her head.

"Mark. We've got company."

Fifteen feet away, he swiveled his rifle along the street, searching for a target.

"Not that way," Heather said, pointing her own AR-15 back along the street that had brought them here.

Movement from her left attracted Heather's attention and she saw Jack glide from the shadows to kneel beside her.

"You and Mark get back to the safe house. You can get in through a hole in the back door. Trouble's coming."

"What about you?"

"Don't worry about me. Get moving."

Reluctantly, Heather picked up her go bag, relaying Jack's instructions to Mark through the Altreian headset. She saw Mark move out toward the house but when she turned back, Jack was gone. If she hadn't been able to play the scene back in her mind, she might have questioned whether he'd ever really been there.

●　○　○

The orange glow of the fires lit the overcast sky, the soulless ochre light casting eerie shadows across the city, through which a deeper darkness moved.

Jack released himself to the beast within, feeling the magnetic pull of the dangers in the night with an intensity unlike any he'd felt before. Had Khal Teth overlaid Jack's vision with his own psychic projection?

The group coming for them was determined to catch Jack, his family, and his friends in a pincer operation. Assuming they had all the weaponry and expertise of a Delta unit, the cartel safe house would slow them down, but not for long, even with several of the world's most dangerous people holed up inside it.

Moving up into the slum with its crumbling, interconnected walls separated by narrow steps cut into the hillside, Jack glided to a stop in a dark space where a wall had fallen. His wait wasn't a long one.

Across the street, two men moved, their assault rifles aimed and ready. Farther up the street, four more commandos moved into an alley, headed in the direction of the safe house. Jack let them pass. Analyzing the spread of their formation, it would take a platoon-sized unit to completely surround the house to assure that nobody escaped. Thirty-plus men. And they didn't move like Peruvian Special Forces. These were experienced veterans with many operations under their belts.

It didn't matter. He'd soon know exactly who he was dealing with.

● ○ ○

As Heather prepared to move through the hole into the safe house, she called out.

"Hey, Janet. Mark and I are coming in."

"Come on," Janet's voice echoed from somewhere upstairs.

Stepping around and over the bodies that lay sprawled outside that hole, Heather entered, followed closely by Mark. She looked around. Here too several bodies were strewn across the floor, and one lay head down on the stairs where blood continued to drip from the steps to form a pool on the floor. With no airflow, the room was stuffy and reeked with the smell of death.

"Go on up to Janet," Mark said. "I'll make sure nobody else gets through that hole."

Triggered by his words, a vision blotted out her view of the room. Men moved in tactical formation to surround the house, men who wouldn't be satisfied to stay outside for long.

She refocused on her surroundings and climbed the stairs to the second floor. The stairwell landing led to a hallway where more dead men lay scattered around the bottom of an attic ladder that had been pulled down. She ignored them and climbed up to poke her head into the small attic space.

Janet knelt beside a small body in the dark space, her hand gently stroking his cheek. The sight brought a lump to Heather's throat.

"Robby?"

When Janet turned her head, she smiled.

"As long as we don't move him anytime soon, he'll live."

"Thank God."

"Where's Mark?"

"He stayed downstairs to guard the back door. Jack wants us to make our stand here."

"Given our situation, it's as good a place as any." Janet stood, hefting her assault rifle. "We'll leave Robby right where he is and give his nanites time to finish their repairs. This place is like a mini-fortress. I'll need you covering the back of the house from that crawl space. I'll take the front."

"Okay," Heather said. "How's your ammo holding out?"

"Down to five magazines. You?"

"Four plus a few rounds. Mark's pretty much the same. After that we're down to pistols."

Janet nodded. "When it comes to that, we can scrounge more nine millimeter off these dead guys."

As Heather entered the crawl space that led to the rear window slot, she called back over her shoulder.

"Let's hope it doesn't."

But the visions that played out in her mind did little to reassure her.

● ○ ○

Distant fire tornados swirled into the glowing Lima sky. On the ground, the panicked populace screamed. Daniil embraced the otherworldly feeling of this night. The gun battle toward which he and the Spetsnaz were headed had just come to an abrupt end and it made him want to up the pace. Evidently Major Kamkin felt it too, because his men appeared to throw caution to the wind as they swept down out of the slum toward their target. They would not allow their quarry to slip away.

As they reached the end of the block, a side street led off toward a lone two-story house at the end of the cul-de-sac two blocks ahead. Even in the dim light from the fire-lit sky, there was no doubt that this was the one. The number of bodies lying in the street around the domicile proclaimed as much.

Kamkin gave another whistling signal and the dozen or so men nearest him slowed, moving into a spread tactical formation that took advantage of the houses along each side of the road for cover. The rest of the formation was spread wide down different streets and alleys so that they could encircle the house before they tightened the noose.

A lone gunshot split the night. Fifteen feet to Daniil's left front, blood splashed from Galina Anikin's head and she dropped as if she'd been struck with a hammer.

Daniil didn't hesitate and neither did any of the nearby commandos, diving behind cover. Immediately, gunfire opened up from positions all along the street as the commandos returned fire. The problem was they had no idea precisely where in the house the shot had come from.

He glanced over at his lover's body and felt ice replace the heat that had flowed through his veins. The sniper shot had been well aimed. The Ripper was in there, waiting for him. With a snarl curling his lips, Daniil moved forward in quick bursts, from cover to cover, just like the other commandos.

Fine. Daniil was coming. And when he reached his target, he planned on taking his sweet time with The Ripper's wife and son.

● ○ ○

Having let all the commandos pass him by, Jack looped back. The rear of the house, having already been penetrated, was the weak spot, although he sensed that the three most dangerous predators were on the front side. As he moved silently through the shadows, a lone gunshot rang out and he immediately recognized the sound of the 7.62mm SCAR-H. That meant Janet had just taken out her first target. And sure enough, one of the three alpha predators winked out in his mind.

He breathed a single thought her way. *Good shooting, babe.*

The sound of return fire brought a cold smile to Jack's lips. She had their attention. Perfect.

Sliding through the deep brush along the north side of a shed, he moved slowly up behind his first target, a kneeling man, the stock of an RPG-7 balanced on his shoulder as he aimed it toward the back door. Jack's dagger punched a hole in the back of his neck, just below the skull, severing the man's spinal cord.

As the man crumpled silently to the ground, Jack plucked the rocket launcher from his hand, then knelt in his place. Just then a double blast from a shrill whistle split the night and all firing came to a sudden end. The commandos would no longer be wasting ammunition blind-firing at the house, and an assault was imminent.

A new round of whistles rang out and from the far side of the clearing another RPG fired. The door exploded, leaving a jagged hole in the stone wall in its place. A dozen commandos sprinted toward the back of the house, spreading out so that a sniper would have to take time adjusting her aim for each shot while dealing with a barrage of suppressive fire from the men who stayed behind.

Watching some of the commandos fall to sniper fire, Jack aimed the RPG and waited. As the survivors closed on the house, their angles of approach grouped them and Jack squeezed the trigger, sending the rocket-propelled grenade whooshing toward its new target.

Behind a wall at the top of the stairs, Mark sighted along his AR-15 and waited for the assault he expected to come. The leader of the charge would no doubt hurl a grenade inside, but unless Mark got very unlucky, this position would shield him from the blast. Then the others would pour through that hole, and Mark would make short work of them.

When his hearing picked up the distinctive sound of an RPG firing, Mark leaped backward, putting more wall between himself and an explosion that was much bigger than he'd planned for. The blast shook the house and sent a plume of masonry and dust billowing up the stairs after him. Pain flared in his left shoulder and he turned to see a piece of the balustrade jutting out just beneath his collarbone, having passed clear through his body.

He coughed and blinked to clear the blinding dust from his eyes. Upstairs he could hear Heather and Janet both firing.

"Shit!"

Another RPG blast followed, although this one appeared to have been misaimed, exploding outside the house. The screams of the wounded told him it might not have been such a miss after all. As he struggled back to his feet, hefting the AR-15 with one hand, he forced a grin. Jack was out there among their enemies . . . and he was hunting.

CHAPTER 28

Daniil recognized Kamkin's plan of attack and thought it a good one. Unfortunately, something on the back side of the house had caused the timing to be off. Two rocket-propelled grenades were supposed to impact the rear door simultaneously. Instead, he'd heard only one, followed by the covering gunfire for the assault, followed by yet another RPG explosion.

Whether Major Kamkin recognized it or not, this meant that someone was outside their lines of containment and Daniil had a pretty damn good idea who it was. The Ripper. And if Daniil didn't do something quickly, The Ripper would move along their line, taking out the Spetsnaz commandos one at a time from behind.

Daniil ducked low to the ground and moved to the major's side.

"Kamkin, The Ripper's outside your lines on the back side of the house."

"Shit, man. Do you think I don't know what I'm hearing?"

"You need to send a team to hunt him down, right now."

"No, apparatchik. My mission is the Smythes. I'm going to breach this house through the front and kill the Smythes and everyone inside. If you want Gregory, you go get him."

Daniil sputtered but before he could issue his furious response, Kamkin raised his whistle to his lips and blew another short series of blasts. This time, as should have happened in back, two RPGs ripped a hole in the wall where the front door used to be. Then, as he watched Kamkin's men charge toward the opening under cover of gunfire from those left behind, a new opportunity occurred to him.

With The Ripper focused on killing the men assaulting the house, perhaps Daniil could turn his own strategy against him.

● ○ ○

Janet felt the twin explosions from the area of the front door as a jolt lifted the crawlway floor and her prone body along with it. In the attic behind her, Robby groaned.

She'd practiced rapid-fire target shooting many times. Of the dozen commandos that raced from cover to the smoking hole below her, she dropped five of them. But seven got inside. The sound of Heather firing from the rear crawlway meant that more were making the rush from the back side of the house. A new fear crawled into Janet's mind. Where was Mark? Had he been killed by the RPGs?

The sound of gunfire below answered her question. Mark was still fighting.

"I'm going down to help Mark," Heather yelled from behind her.

"No. Mark can handle himself. I need you here covering the back of the house."

Janet understood Heather's worry for Mark, but if they didn't want to be completely overwhelmed, they both needed to keep thinning the ranks of those who yet remained outside. The fact that Heather didn't argue meant her savant visions had just confirmed Janet's decision.

Spotting a slight movement in the distance, she aimed and fired, sending another man sprawling to the ground. Shifting her aim one more time, a soft whisper escaped her lips.

"Don't worry, Robby. I won't let them have you. And neither will my Jack."

● ○ ○

The smoke and dust were so thick that even Mark's enhanced vision was having a difficult time seeing the moving figures in the room below the stairs. Switching the selector on his assault rifle from semi to auto, he pointed the weapon around the corner, squeezed the trigger, and held it, spraying bullets back and forth across the room below.

When he heard the clank and rattle of a hand grenade landing near him, he dropped the AR-15, caught the grenade on the second bounce, and tossed it back where it came from. The explosion sent him tumbling back down the hall, where his impact with the floor drove the spike deeper into his upper shoulder.

The pain sent a white lance across his vision, but he shunted it aside, willing himself back into action. The muzzle of a weapon emerged through dust-filled darkness. Mark grabbed it with his right hand and twisted violently, feeling the hot barrel scorch his hand. He pulled the man who held it forward into a kick that caved in the commando's chest and launched his dying body back down the stairs.

"Screw this!"

Having had enough of hiding behind walls and waiting for more grenades to land, Mark leaped into the smoke and confusion below. He shunted aside the pain in his shoulder and focused on one thought.

Close with and destroy the enemy.

Mark gasped in a deep breath and exploded into the nearest commando before the man could bring his weapon to bear. Mark's gut punch lifted the soldier from the rubble-strewn floor and hurled him into the man behind him, sending both bodies crashing down.

Mark's heightened senses made it seem as if the surrounding smoke, dust, darkness, and noise were nothing but distant distractions. Four men up and moving plus the two he'd just put down made six enemies.

The soldier to Mark's left spun toward him, seemingly moving in slow motion. His trigger finger squeezed off a volley of shots that missed Mark but chopped into the two commandos on the ground. Mark grabbed the rifle stock and twisted violently, tearing it from the man's grasp and caving in his skull with the weapon before lunging toward his next target.

As that commando's knife cleared its sheath, Mark grabbed his wrist and re-sheathed it in its owner's solar plexus and heart. Then, using the suddenly limp body as a shield, Mark pulled the knife free, threw it into the throat of the soldier to his right, and charged the last enemy standing. All of the bullets spraying from the muzzle of the AK-105 impacted the dead soldier's body armor . . . all but the last one, which punched a hole in Mark's left side. The explosion of pain momentarily narrowed his vision but didn't slow his momentum.

Then Mark was on the man, every blow breaking bones until there was no life left to pummel from the shattered form. Mark turned, looking for his next opponent but finding none. In this devastated room, pain and death were his only companions.

● ○ ○

The sound of the whistle pulled Jack toward one of the two alpha targets that moved through the night, even as the dark corner of his mind felt the other slip away. The man with the whistle was giving the orders and it was time to bring that level of coordinated effort to an end.

The commander had positioned himself beside a Dumpster inside a walled alcove that gave him cover from three sides while still providing a partial view of the safe house. From where Jack crouched along the southern-facing wall of that alcove, he could just see the end of the man's rifle barrel.

Any movement Jack made would bring him into Janet's line of fire, and in this dimly lit night she wouldn't be able to recognize him. That narrowed his choices down to one. If she couldn't recognize him by sight, he'd have to make sure she recognized him by his actions. Setting his assault rifle silently on the ground, he drew the black dagger.

Amidst the sound of rapid gunfire from inside the safe house, Jack heard the heavier boom of Janet's SCAR-H, watched a man tumble to the ground on the far side of the street, and moved. Whirling around the corner, he kicked the rifle from his target's hands, letting his momentum carry him into the man's body.

The attack took his opponent by surprise, but he reacted as The Ripper would have, bringing up an arm that stopped Jack's blade just short of his throat. The commando then rolled into a judo throw that slammed Jack into the side of the Dumpster and sent the dagger spinning across the ground.

The commando reached for his sidearm, but Jack launched himself shoulder-first into his opponent's stomach and drove him hard into the concrete wall, his left hand locked over the man's gun hand. A heavy left-handed blow caught Jack on the side of his head, but he rammed a knee into the man's groin and followed it with a head butt that splashed his face with warm blood.

Jack shifted his grip on the gun hand, twisting two fingers so violently he felt them snap. When the gun dropped to the ground, the man growled a Russian curse. Jack's elbow smash to his throat cut it off mid-utterance.

● ○ ○

As he passed between houses on the right side of the cul-de-sac, Daniil saw the rifle fly out of the alcove where Kamkin had positioned himself. The sight sent a thrill through his body. The Ripper had just revealed himself.

Without hesitation, he dropped the rifle, pulled his SIG Sauer, and ran, making sure to keep something between himself and the sniper on the upper floor of the house. When he reached the side of the trash alcove, he paused for a moment to judge the exact position of the two combatants that struggled within.

Then with a grin on his face, he plunged around the corner, gun leveled and firing. Kamkin could die alongside The Ripper.

●　○　○

The sense of impending danger pulled Jack's head toward the opening just before another man lunged into view. And in that moment, Jack shifted position, pulling the dying commando around in front of him, ramming him, back first, toward this new opponent. The first three shots impacted the body armor of the commando he shoved forward, followed by a point-blank head shot. And then Jack's leg sweep sent the three of them tumbling to the ground together . . . in full view of Janet's sniper position.

●　○　○

Daniil couldn't understand how The Ripper had heard him coming in the midst of his fight with Kamkin, but he must have. How else could he have shielded himself with Kamkin's body? All this flashed through his mind as Daniil tumbled to the ground beneath Kamkin and The Ripper.

The impact partially knocked his breath from him, but he maintained his grip on the SIG, twisting it to get off a shot that caught

The Ripper in his left thigh. But as Daniil tried to aim his next shot for the man's body, The Ripper grabbed Kamkin's hair and hammered the dead man's head into Daniil's face with such stunning force that it ruptured the already damaged skull. Brains and blood spilled forth. The pain that exploded in Daniil's broken face threatened to rob him of consciousness.

Blinded and gasping for breath, Daniil fired wildly, only to feel The Ripper's weight shift as he rolled off the pile. Daniil continued firing as he shoved Kamkin's body off of him. The SIG's slide locked back. He was surprised. Had he already fired all seventeen rounds? And where was The Ripper?

Wiping goop from his eyes, Daniil spit and struggled back to his feet, trying to make sense of the situation. Why hadn't The Ripper finished him when he'd had the chance instead of leaving him alone out here in the open? Daniil's heart jumped into his throat. Out here in the open. As his eyes shifted back to the house at the end of the cul-de-sac, he saw the muzzle flash. But he never felt the bullet that hit him in the center of the forehead.

● ○ ○

Heather scanned the backyard and beyond for living targets and failed to find any. Since Janet's last shot, everything had gone dead quiet. She could hear the heartbeats of Janet and Robby, noting the improvement in the boy's pulse since last she'd checked. Even the sounds of conflict from below had died out. When Mark climbed into the attic, his presence confirmed it. This fight was over.

For the first time she noticed his upper chest wound and his bloody side.

"My God," she gasped. "Let me look at that!"

"It can wait."

"No," she said, crawling out of the sniper hide, "it can't."

Mark sighed but didn't argue. The light wasn't good, but with Heather's enhanced vision, it didn't need to be.

Janet had moved to Robby's side, but when she saw the spike jutting out beneath Mark's collarbone she turned her attention to him.

"Sit down on the floor," she said, pointing to a spot next to Robby.

Pulling her knife, Janet worked rapidly as Heather assisted, cutting away Mark's utility vest and shirt in order to examine the two wounds.

Just then, Jack's voice called out from below. "It's just me."

Without pausing in her work, Janet replied, "Come on up. Mark's hurt."

"I'm fine," Mark growled.

When Jack climbed into the attic, he was bare chested, having bound his shirt around his blood-soaked pants leg.

"Jesus. You too?"

"Nothing my nanites can't fix. They just need a little time."

He sounded convincing. Still, Heather noted Jack wincing as he sat down.

Janet turned to Heather. "Get me the medical kit out of my go bag."

Heather moved to comply. Janet poured water from her canteen over Mark's wounds and scrubbed at them to wash away the blood and dust.

"Heather, I'm going to need thick gauze pads soaked in chlorhexidine and another roll of gauze."

Heather set the medical kit next to Janet, opened it, and began the prep work. She caught Mark's forced grin and that simple expression helped dampen the worry that had put a tremor in her hands.

"I may not have your nanites, but there are certain circulatory advantages to being an alien-augmented freak."

"Yeah," Janet said as she finished binding the wound on his side and reached up to grab the spike beneath his collarbone. "Hang on to that sense of humor, because this is going to hurt."

Mark made no sound when Janet placed one hand on his shoulder and pulled on the spike with the other. Beads of sweat sprouted on his dusty brow. For a moment the spike refused to move, but as she increased the pressure it came free.

Immediately, Heather pressed two gauze pads against the wound, front and back, applying pressure while Janet bound them in place and then leaned back to examine her work.

"That'll do until we get to more permanent accommodations. Now that Robby's stable enough to move, I'd like to get him as far from here as possible."

That plan sounded damn good to Heather.

"I'll carry Robby," Jack said, climbing back to his feet.

"No," Janet said. "I've got him. Mark can carry my bag and weapon, while you take point."

When they left the shattered house, they found the cul-de-sac deserted, no great surprise considering the terrifying amount of firepower that had just been employed here. They hadn't killed all of their attackers, but once the leaders were down, the remaining few had melted away into the night.

They moved out rapidly along backstreets and alleys, heading northeast to avoid the rest of the fire. Jack took the lead, followed closely by Mark, and then Janet carrying Robby's unconscious body, with Heather acting as rear guard.

Heather noticed movement in the distant shadows as Jack brought up his SCAR-H assault rifle. The vision that formed in her mind was so clear it blotted out all else.

"Wait," she said, her voice loud enough for Jack to hear. "Don't shoot."

From the shadows twenty yards in front of Jack, a familiar form emerged, wrapped in traditional Quechua garb and wearing a broad-brimmed hat.

"Yachay!" Jack exclaimed, lowering his weapon and stepping forward to greet her, his movements matched by the rest of the group.

"How did you find us?" Janet asked as Yachay moved to gently lift Robby from her willing arms.

"Not hard. I tell Quechua people, 'Listen for biggest gunfight.' Always leads to you and Jack."

The statement broke the night's tension and pulled a laugh from Heather's lips. God, it was good to be back in the company of this woman.

Yachay straightened with Robby in her arms and turned to go. "Come. I take you somewhere safe. Do not worry. Quechua people make sure no one bother."

Then Yachay turned and led the way with their battered little group in tow. All around them, other shadows drifted silently through the chaotic night.

● ○ ○

Except for the shifting shadows cast by the distant fire plumes, the street was devoid of movement. The bodies of the dead lay strewn about, their orange-lit faces horrible caricatures of the people they had been in life. A low moan escaped the lips of one of those bodies.

Her head feeling like somebody was hitting it with a hammer, Galina Anikin struggled to her knees. She put her hand to her forehead and winced anew. So much blood. But that's what head wounds did . . . bleed. If not for the nanites in her blood that worked to repair the damage, the wound might well have been fatal.

Galina traced the injury with her index finger, ignoring the burn of what she was doing. A five-inch groove had been carved into the top of her skull from the top right side of her forehead to the upper rear. The thought that she'd never regrow hair in that shallow groove pissed her off as much as the fact that a Smythe sniper, most likely Janet Price, had come very close to ending her.

But she hadn't.

Galina climbed to her feet, paused until she stopped swaying, and then turned to look around. Almost immediately her eyes fell on Daniil.

"No!" Her voice was a low growl.

Galina stumbled as she walked toward the spot where his body lay stretched out, faceup beside the street. She knelt beside him. The bloody hole in the center of his forehead told part of the story. His battered face and brain-splattered uniform told the rest.

For the last time, Galina ran her fingers along Daniil's head and looked into his green eyes. Then she stood and walked to the spot where Kamkin's body lay facedown. The major had been shot in the head, and his killer had taken the time to cave the front of Kamkin's skull in.

A coldness crept into her bones. Only one man could have done this.

The Ripper!

Galina straightened, checked her SIG, and then looked out over the burning skyline of what was left of Lima. She locked that image firmly in her mind. The view was a poor imitation of the inferno she would unleash upon The Ripper for this, no matter how long it took to find him. And she owed Janet Price a debt as well.

Galina Anikin then strode purposefully into the night, her bloody face illuminated by the dancing fires of hell.

:CHAPTER 29

Jennifer watched the video feed of Raul leaning over the newly reconstructed stasis field-generator inside the Northang Research Laboratory, marveling for the hundredth time at the changes in the young man. His new legs, eye, and skullcap had transformed him, and not just in appearance. Raul's entire self-image had undergone a surprising makeover. He still had an annoying snarkiness to his personality, but the wit she'd just seen glimpses of had come to the fore. Gone was the moody melancholy that he'd previously succumbed to.

Perhaps the most awesome of his augmentations had come from the subspace receiver-transmitter communications crystals he'd embedded in his brain. Those chips provided him with a constant link to the Rho Ship's neural net, even when he was away from the vessel. The downside of that was his attachment to VJ. For one thing, Jennifer thought VJ was nothing like her and found it downright insulting that this was how she was perceived by Raul. Furthermore, Raul had become convinced that the sim had real feelings and refused to shut it down.

Jennifer shook her head. *What did they say about boys and their toys?* She just wasn't all that keen on a simulation of her being one of them.

She turned her attention back to the new stasis field generator. Raul had just finished running a test of the control unit that had failed three weeks ago, almost killing Jennifer and Chief Engineer Broghdon. After some minor adjustments, Raul had pronounced it acceptable and Jennifer agreed. In the coming days, Raul and Broghdon would test it against another stasis field generator manufactured aboard the Rho Ship, although this time they planned on taking greater safety precautions.

Yeah. Like not being in the same freakin' room with the thing.

Advanced as the Rho Ship's nano-manufacturing capability was, it couldn't produce the quantities of devices that would be needed for the war effort. So anything they wanted to deliver to Dgarra's northern front needed to be redesigned for Koranthian assembly line manufacturing. There was a damn good reason why Dgarra wanted the stasis field generators to be their top priority. As strong as the triton-steel doors were that could be lowered to block their enemies, that steel could be penetrated by a Kasari disrupter weapon. Hence the stasis field generator tech would give the Koranthian defenders a surprising edge in the battles yet to come.

Lifting her gaze from the monitor, Jennifer straightened her uniform and turned her attention to the furious activity inside Dgarra's military headquarters, where a different type of war preparation was well underway. With Raul in charge of assisting Broghdon with the design, manufacture, and testing of new technologies, Jennifer had resumed her duties as Dgarra's aide-de-camp. And as she watched the general move among his warriors, inspiring them to greater efforts through the sheer power of his presence, a new realization hit Jennifer.

Dear Lord, she'd missed this.

:CHAPTER 30

Alexandr Prokorov sat staring at the wall opposite his mahogany desk, unable to believe the disastrous news of the events in Peru. Not only had two of the world's most elite special forces units been decimated, but even the EMP attack on Lima had failed to defeat the Smythes and their allies.

For ten days he'd hoped and waited for word that the Smythes were dead. But with Lima and much of the rest of Peru suffering from the aftermath of the EMP, such word had been difficult to come by. This morning, Galina Anikin had arrived in Brasília to send the encrypted message that had delivered the bad news.

Daniil Alkaev had failed him. The Ripper had killed Prokorov's top assassin and then, with help from Janet Price and the Smythes, had proceeded to kill almost three dozen Spetsnaz commandos. Then the Smythes and their bodyguards had disappeared . . . just smoke in the wind . . . hidden by their Safe Earth and NPA allies.

Now, at the request of the president of the United States, the UFNS Committee for the Review of Internal Affairs had launched an investigation into Prokorov himself. Who the hell did they think they were? The leader of the last political group who had dared to investigate him had been found spewing his guts out from radiation poisoning in a London hotel room. If President Benton didn't want to find himself in similar circumstances, he'd better hope that the internal affairs bureaucrats were as ineffective as they were stupid.

Grabbing a globe-shaped crystal paperweight, Prokorov hurled it across the room to shatter against the far wall with a loud crash that would be audible in offices down the hall. Right now, he didn't give a damn whether he disturbed some of his staff or not.

Prokorov's thoughts again turned to the Smythes as a snarl curled his lips. This wasn't over. Not by a long shot.

●　○　○

Senator Freddy Hagerman jogged toward the Lincoln Memorial through the gently falling snow, enjoying the springiness of his running leg. It gave him an odd gait, but one that he'd long since grown accustomed to. Across the Mall to his left, the cherry trees near the Jefferson Memorial spread their skeletal branches wide, calling on Old Man Winter to clothe their nakedness in robes of fluffy white.

There was nothing like moving through snow to clear your head, and the Washington Mall was the perfect place for a run. A quietness came with a gentle snowfall such as this one that reminded Freddy of the magical way he'd felt as a child. In later years, he'd lost that magic, but he still wanted to remember the feeling.

God, the world was a screwed-up mess. But it was his world and he'd be damned if he'd hand it over to the Kasari Collective without a fight. Fortunately, the team that had cobbled itself together under his watch was still out there, readying themselves for the struggle to come.

In recent days, he'd gotten several updates from Eileen, Jamal, and Denise Jennings, who were now secretly ensconced on the estate of Mexican president and Safe Earth backer Manuel Suarez. An old friend of Freddy's, he'd been quite thrilled to add the former NSA trio to his team, despite the fact that they were on the run from the UFNS. The three computer geniuses gave A Safe Earth an enhanced hacking capability that the movement had been sorely lacking.

But the best news had come in a short video from Mark and Heather. Although they would not say where they were, they had escaped the conflagration in Lima. They had made their way to a secret facility from which they would be working to develop the technologies needed in the coming struggle. They had appeared battered and bruised, but to Freddy, they had looked damn good. They were alive.

And the president of the United States had actually strapped on some cojones and instigated an investigation into that bastard Prokorov and his FSS war machine. Not that Freddy expected anything to come of it. Prokorov was too slick, too much of an old FSB and KGB hand to let anyone prove that he had a hand in the EMP attack that had turned Lima, Peru, into a post-apocalyptic wasteland.

Freddy's stride carried him in front of the Lincoln Memorial where old Abe, seated in his grand chair, looked solemnly down on him. There was no doubt in Freddy's mind that if Abe were here today, he would be leading the Safe Earth movement instead of a washed-out old investigative reporter turned senator. Ah well. The movement would have to make do with the players it had.

Freddy hoped that would be enough.

● ○ ○

The smell.

Heather closed her eyes and inhaled as deeply as her lungs would allow. The aroma of the turkey, stuffing, mashed potatoes, and gravy arrayed in platters across the long dining room table pulled forth the memory of many happy Thanksgiving dinners at the family house in White Rock. Her mouth watered in anticipation. Such a wonderful dream.

But when she opened her eyes to see the smiling faces and laughing voices of her family and friends, gathered here for a welcome home celebration at this most secret of places, she accepted the fact that this was real. Seated around the table, which had been extended with the addition of three table leaves, were her mom and dad, Linda and Fred Smythe, Jack, Janet, Robby, Yachay, and Mark, his hand squeezing hers beneath the table.

The trip to New Zealand had taken them much longer than expected, but with the help of Tall Bear, the NPA, and their Safe Earth allies, they had made it. This morning, Gil and Fred had given them a grand tour of the upgraded facilities within the mining complex. Heather had been stunned to see the progress their fathers had made. The expanded production of robots had enabled them to accelerate the excavation, spreading the complex beyond the old mine tunnels. With the matter disrupter-synthesizer online, they had plenty of power to spare. Considering all the new equipment Heather intended to build, that was a good thing.

But thoughts of work could wait. Even though today wasn't Thanksgiving, this was a time for rejoicing.

"All right, everyone," Anna said, taking her seat beside Gil. "I think we're ready to eat."

Beside her, his left arm in a sling, Mark clinked his spoon against his wine glass and stood.

"I would like to propose two toasts."

With clinks all around, everyone raised their glasses.

"First," he said, raising his glass high, "to good friends and family."

"To good friends and family," everyone echoed.

"And finally, here's to the memory of a special loved one who isn't here but who made all of this possible . . . to Jennifer."

Heather felt a lump rise in her throat and saw Linda Smythe blink away sudden tears. They all raised their voices in unison.

"To Jennifer."

:EPILOGUE

Khal Teth watched the gathering through Jack's eyes. What did the humans call this feeling? Déjà vu. This humble family gathering. So peaceful. So pleasant. So boring . . . yet filled with dark portent.

This comfortable group of friends and family, gathered in a remote corner of this world, were Earth's only hope of salvation from the storm that was forming, although their victory was far from certain. They each knew it, but here they sat for one more evening of denial.

His visions rolled out before him, different paths, all leading to the same destiny. All save one. And along that path, Jack Gregory strode, heading to a place Khal Teth had once called home.

The thought triggered a memory once lost to him.

I stride the familiar curved hallway toward a rendezvous that has been too long in coming, savoring the view through the Parthian's transparent outer wall and ceiling. Low on the horizon, Quol's purple moon looms in stark contrast to the lacy-orange Krell Nebula, which forms a backdrop in the dark sky. But tonight I have no time for idle reflection.

As I make my way toward the chambers of Valen Roth, overlord of the High Council, I encounter no other living being. I feel other Altreian minds clustered behind nano-particle doors throughout the immense web of rooms that form the Parthian, but none step out to confront me. Wise choice.

Not even Valen Roth can withstand the full power of my mind. Up ahead, he awaits my arrival, aware of my dissatisfaction with his latest edict, but feeling secure in the protection the One Law provides every member of the High Council. For thousands of cycles, no one has dared risk the punishment its violation would provoke. Until tonight.

Jack's reflection in his own upraised wine glass extracted Khal Teth from the vision. It wasn't the wine that put the red glint in Jack's eyes. Khal Teth's vision had done that.

He studied Jack's reflection and smiled, his thoughts returning to the memory of a destiny they both now shared. Whatever happened from here on, it was going to be one hell of a ride.

:ACKNOWLEDGMENTS

I would like to thank Alan Werner for the hours he spent working with me on the story. Thank you to my editor, Clarence Haynes, for his wonderful help in fine-tuning the end product, along with the outstanding editorial and production staff at 47North. I also want to thank my agent, Paul Lucas, for the work he has done to bring my novels to a wider audience. Finally, my biggest thanks go to my lovely wife, Carol, for supporting me and for being my sounding board throughout the writing of all of my novels.